# CONTAINMENT

## Alaskan Undead Apocalypse Book II

"[*Infection* is] a fun, fast-paced tale of zombie mayhem that barely gives you time to breathe, and zombie fans who crave plenty of gore and undead action should enjoy it."
—Patrick D'Orazio, author of *Comes the Dark*

"[*Infection*] will have even the most skeptical, critical zombie fan coming back for more. I can't wait for the next installment…"
—Ursula K. Raphael, The Zombiephiles

"I found *Infection* to be a very entertaining read and look forward to the next book in the series."
—BuyZombie.com

# CONTAINMENT

## Alaskan Undead Apocalypse Book II

### Sean Schubert

Dedicated to the courageous souls who exposed themselves to
*Infection* and came back for more.

A PERMUTED PRESS book
published by arrangement with the author
ISBN: 978-1-61868-048-8 (trade paperback)
ISBN: 978-1-61868-049-5 (eBook)

*Containment* copyright © 2012
by Sean Schubert.
All Rights Reserved.

This book is a work of fiction. People, places, events, and situations are the product of the author's imagination. Any resemblance to actual persons, living or dead, or historical events, is purely coincidental.

No part of this book may be reproduced, stored in a retrieval system, or transmitted by any means without the written permission of the author and publisher.

# PROLOGUE

He was a soldier. It wasn't just his job or even something as distracting as a career. No, he *was* a soldier through and through. In other cultures and in other times he would have been called a warrior...a warlord. He would have been clad in clanging, war-beaten armor and carried a finely honed but often used sword. He would have been riding a stout steed through valleys in search of the good fight, and perhaps the good death.

As it was, his armor had been exchanged for camouflaged Kevlar, his steed was currently an unarmored Humvee, and his sword was a .45 caliber Colt 1911 semiautomatic pistol at his side. No matter. It wasn't clothes, weapons, or transportation that made a warrior what he was.

His earliest memories were of watching Sunday morning war movies with his father and transforming the cornfields and backyard wildernesses of his youth into dangerous battlefields for his friends and him. With wooden, metal, and plastic guns and swords, they would range far and near, fighting sometimes amongst themselves and sometimes against invisible hordes of Germans or Rebels or some other attackers who threatened the realm or its people. It was all about fighting the good fight and usually dying the good death. Trying to outdo one another's death scenes was always an engaging pastime.

His joining the Junior Reserve Officer Training Corps years before most of his peers were even introduced to the organization was no surprise to anyone. Also not surprising was his acceptance to West Point and his subsequent commission in the U.S. Army.

He progressed through the ranks, but by pure chance flavored with very bad luck, he missed his opportunity to command troops in the field of battle time and time again. Grenada, Panama, Kuwait, Kosovo, Iraq, and Afghanistan. He always seemed to arrive after most of the real meat of the event had already been chewed.

## Sean Schubert

And then he was posted to Fort Richardson in Anchorage, Alaska. It was by no means a step down for him; in fact, it was actually a promotion, but it just seemed so far removed to him. It wasn't quite the Arctic Circle posting threat used by many a Commanding Officer to get the attention of subordinate officers, but it was close. He couldn't help but feel benched.

Sure, units from Forts Richardson and Wainwright were regularly deployed to Iraq and Afghanistan, but those deployments would invariably involve others. He would and did visit those units in their temporary foreign homes and review their assignments and successes, but then he would board the big military "commuter" jet and come back to the frozen north. He could feel his destiny slipping further and further away from him every day and all he could do was watch the distance grow.

Weeks and then months and finally years passed with no change...no hope. He was wiling away his time in nearly complete inactivity.

And then early this morning he was roused from his slumber by a phone ringing at his bedside and then a not too distant siren outside his window.

The caller was a flabbergasted first lieutenant. He began to deliver random details about a violent "disturbance" in Anchorage that had all the trappings of a terrorist attack or a full invasion by hostile forces. The junior officer didn't have much in the way of firm facts, only the disjointed reports from field security personnel and the media. The colonel found himself spending more time trying to calm the young man on the other end of the phone than getting information. And then the line went dead.

When his cell phone proved equally as worthless, the colonel went to his garage and got on the wireless radio set in his car. He, of course, was already driving himself to his command post by that point.

He never made it. The security checkpoint across Ship Creek into the Elmendorf side of Joint Base Elmendorf-Richardson had been overwhelmed sometime earlier. By the time the colonel was leaving his house, the chaos was spreading like spilled paint across both sides of the combined military installations. The greatest disturbance seemed to be in the new housing developments just inside the Elmendorf main gate. Several teams of Military Police officers had responded and were engaging the attackers. The colonel listened as the battle unfolded.

There were two sergeants commanding perhaps a dozen troops. They hadn't been ordered to the scene; they'd heard pleas for help and responded. He heard crisp claps of sidearms as the officers stood their ground. The more energetic and desperate voice of an M4 assault rifle soon joined the conversation. There had been screams in the distance through all of this, but then there was a screech of terror and pain that originated from someone wearing one of the radio sets. One of the military police officers was down...and then another and still another fell. They were being forced back on their heels and away from their vehicles. And then the colonel heard one sergeant tell the other that he and his men were out of ammunition. The colonel yelled at the radio to get the men out, but it was already too late. Their voices were gone, replaced by choking, gurgling, dying.

Elsewhere, other security teams were standing up to the onslaught. Some were actual police units and others were merely scratched together battle groups of willing and available soldiers. Each group of soldiers, men and women, boys and girls, stood their ground only to be absorbed by the growing menace.

The colonel ordered any stragglers not actively engaged to evacuate off of base if they were able, or to gather at the Armory. From the airdrome training area, helicopters could ferry his troops to a safer staging area so that they could regroup, reorganize, and then hit back. More to the point, the colonel could get airborne and get a better look at what the hell was happening. All he knew at this point was that everything that stood in the path of the chaos, whatever it was, was destroyed.

As he climbed into the open door of the waiting Blackhawk helicopter, he could hear the staccato chatter of small arms fire down the road.

He'd wanted to be a soldier all his life. He'd wanted to take charge of men in combat. Right now, he was getting his wish and then some. Was this how it always was at the opening stages of a war? Was this how it was during the tense early moments on December 7, 1941 at Pearl Harbor or on June 25, 1950 at the Thirty-Eighth Parallel on the Korean Peninsula?

Anxiety mixed with adrenaline and was then stirred into testosterone to form a very potent elixir. He went to the cockpit and lifted one of the radio headsets, putting it on his bare, greying scalp.

He spoke into the microphone. "You been in the air much today?"

Both pilot and co-pilot nodded without looking back.

"Have you seen what's going on out there?"

Again, his question was met with nods.

"Well, what *is* going on out there? What have you boys seen?"

His question was followed by first static popping over the headsets and then the pilot spoke for both of them. He said soberly, "I'm not quite sure what I've seen today, sir. I'm not so certain that I trust even my own eyes anymore. I can say that I've seen enough now to convince me not to look down anymore. I'm just gonna sit here in this bird and stay in the air as much as I can."

They were in the air by then. The colonel, along with a lieutenant and a squad of combat-ready infantrymen, were all crowded into the rear of the aircraft. The colonel felt a twinge of guilt for commandeering one of the few vehicles that could actually transport people to safety, but he had to get an idea about what was happening. He wasn't quite sure what purpose the young lieutenant or the other soldiers in the aircraft were to serve, but they were with him and could be used if necessary.

In no time at all—in fact the proximity of the uprising surprised him—they were over the expanding edges of the chaos. And almost at once, the colonel could understand the pilot's unease. It wasn't just bad on the ground below; it was horrific. Innocent fleeing people weren't just being attacked or even killed; they were being ripped apart. With flailing arms and desperate shrieks muted by the helicopter's turbine engine, the scurrying, terrified unfortunates below would be wrestled to the ground by packs of clawing, biting attackers. In just seconds, their hands' and arms' defensive gestures melted away, ebbing along with their lives. And then the attackers would move on to their next quarry.

They passed over a group of three Humvees parked bumper to bumper straddling a major thoroughfare. The twelve soldiers climbing out of the vehicles appeared well armed and ready for anything. The colonel instructed the pilot to position himself in such a manner that the helicopter could provide support. It was all for naught though.

When the human surge reached them, the intervention of automatic weapons had virtually no impact. The deluge spilled over and engulfed his soldiers despite their best efforts, and they met with the same grisly end as all of those caught by the flood. The colonel had seen enough.

"Get us outta here pilot. Let's get over to the staging area on the other side of the Knik."

"Yessir."

The pilot nosed the graceful bird away from the burning and chaotic military base. They passed over the vehicle-choked Glenn Highway which was the only northern route out of the city. As if a switch had been thrown and an order given, people began to abandon their idling vehicles en masse. Many looked up at the helicopter overhead, imploring them for help with their outstretched hands and their pleading eyes. They ran and they screamed, but in the end, there was no escaping the murderous wave. Following the roadway north, the pilot ferried the colonel to the makeshift field headquarters near the Knik Bridge.

The Knik Arm was a watery limb originating from the Cook Inlet. Its fingers splayed themselves across the flats that separated Anchorage from the Matanuska-Susitna Valley and the northern two thirds of the state. Across the waterways there was a single concrete bridge for motorized traffic and a single railroad trestle. He couldn't ask for a better position to defend. The attackers would be funneled by the mountains on either side down the single road leading to the bridge. If they wanted to have a fight, he'd be willing to deliver. It seemed almost unfair to him. He would be able to concentrate all of his firepower onto a relatively small patch of land. It had the potential to be a very rich killing ground where his limited heavy weapons could have the biggest impact. Approaching the solution as a simple military problem helped him to remain clinical and unemotional.

Once on the ground, he ordered a contingent of soldiers forward to stall the attackers. He needed to make certain that he had the necessary time to implement his plans. As a precaution, he was having engineers wire the bridge with explosives. If they couldn't stop the torrent with firepower, then they could take away their lone avenue for advance. The blocking force was rushed forward and told to hold at all costs. They needed to have enough time to organize the defense and prepare the bridge for demolition. If the uprising couldn't be stopped at the bridge, then the colonel wasn't quite sure where it would be able to be contained.

He was just getting over to the mobile command vehicle when a young junior officer appeared with a wireless headset. "Sir. It's the governor, sir."

The colonel nodded and took the headset. "Sir, this is Colonel Frost."

The governor's voice was strained and worried. "How bad is it, Colonel?" he asked bluntly.

A pregnant pause followed. The colonel scanned the control center that hopped and buzzed with the intensity of a beehive. The activity to the untrained eye would perhaps seem random and chaotic, but to the colonel it was purposeful and orderly. Multiple radios chirped and hummed as reports came in from all over the adjoining military installations. The details and the locations varied but the consistent message they all delivered was the need for help and evacuation. Most of the reports, the colonel surmised, were not good as control continually slipped further and further out of reach.

"Well sir, I'm not entirely sure yet how bad it is, but I can say that it will take extreme measures to get things back under control. We are organizing a defensive line at Knik. At this point, we're not entirely sure what is happening to be perfectly frank, sir. Richardson is a complete loss. I believe Elmendorf is too."

"Are the dissidents targeting the military installations specifically? Could it be extremists trying to cripple our infrastructure?"

"Sir, the...disturbance moved into Elmendorf and Richardson because civilians from Anchorage ran there for protection. It appears that all of this started in Anchorage and just followed the people. I'm afraid that Anchorage may be in as bad a state as the military bases, sir."

"What are you suggesting, Colonel?"

"I'm not suggesting anything, sir. I'm merely pointing out that I think that this all started in Anchorage and is just spreading."

"Can you stop it, Colonel?"

The colonel...the warrior, wanted to growl to the politician that he and his soldiers were capable of anything. He was on the verge of doing just that when he looked around at the nervous and scared faces that were running about all over the makeshift command post. Men and women, some young and others not so young, were doing their best to get a handle on the events that were unfolding just up the road. There were some sitting quietly being treated for seeping, horrible wounds to their arms, hands, and even faces.

The sedatives to calm their fears and lessen their pain had stolen whatever fire had been in their eyes before.

The colonel took a deep breath and then began, "Sir, I'm not even sure what 'it' is that needs to be stopped. There were things happening over there that I can't even begin to describe to you. Atrocities, really, being committed by what appeared to be normal people driven to some state of insanity. I don't know really what is going on. What I can say, though, is that we are going to stand strong here along the Knik and—"

"Colonel, use whatever means you deem necessary to hold your line. Do you understand?"

"Sir, I would like clarification on what exactly you mean by that if I may."

"Colonel, before we lost contact with the civil authorities in Anchorage, the ranking officers communicating with my staff here in Juneau told us that there were mass atrocities being committed. We can't allow this to spread. You have my full support in whatever decision you make to stop this but I want it stopped. Do you understand?"

"Sir, are you authorizing me to use—"

"You use what you feel you have to use to stop this. We have to regain control and if it requires bringing down the fires of hell, well you do it then."

"I understand sir. I have limited resources at my disposal, but I think what I have will certainly discourage them."

"Good. We've contacted Eielson and authorized them to scramble some support for you as well. Those jets should be arriving soon. Use your discretion as to how to use them. Keep me updated, colonel. I am getting on the phone with the President right now. I only hope that you are successful so that we can focus on sorting this mess out and putting things back to right again."

"Yessir. We will do our best, sir."

"Colonel, I don't want just your best. We *need* you to be successful. This isn't about politics or careers here. This is about survival and you are our last best hope for that. Do you understand? You are all that remains between the people of this state and whatever is happening in Anchorage. We are all counting on you and your men to stop this."

The colonel was nodding and looking back at the soldiers around him. He took a deep breath and said simply, "You can count on us, sir."

"Thank you, Colonel. I hope to be able to sit down with you when this is all over and hear about how you solved this problem for all of us."

The connection was broken and the colonel took off the headset, handing it back to the young man still standing at his side. He looked again at the wounded people being treated. The young officer anticipated the question that was forming and said, "Sir, our medical staff—what's left of it that was able to be evac'd—are treating the walking wounded here, sir, and the more serious cases are further back."

"How many so far?"

"Of the most serious cases, a couple of dozen, sir. The less severe injuries, I'd estimate double that number." The young man wanted to say more but stopped himself short.

"What aren't you telling me, son?"

"Several of the medical staff have pointed out that most of the injuries appear to be...well, bites, sir. And the bites appear to be extremely susceptible to infection."

Bites? *Bites?* Jesus, that's right. Those...people, for whatever reason, attacked on sight, but they did so without the most basic of arms. He became keenly and suddenly aware that he hadn't seen a single weapon in the crowds. There were no guns, no knives, not even any rocks. He shuddered involuntarily at the implications. It was unthinkable.

"Bites? Are you sure?"

"Yes sir."

"Okay son. Why don't you try and raise the governor's office again and pass that along. If they're going to figure this mess out, they'll need all the intel they can get."

"Yes sir. And what are we going to do, sir?"

"We're going to do what soldiers do best."

From off in the distance, the unmistakable chatter of small arms fire suddenly began to filter into the impromptu military camp. "Those boys up there are going to need some help," the colonel said. "Let's get a couple of choppers up there with some firepower and see what we can do."

Almost at once, a pair of Blackhawk gunships roared overhead and made their way toward the fighting. Not able to sit back himself, the colonel found another helicopter and did his best to join his men, who were even then fighting for their lives on the ground.

The battle at the roadblock was virtually no different than those that had been fought all over Anchorage. The two hovering helicopters loosed a barrage of rockets and a shower of machine-gun bullets into the attacking horde, but even those measures had little to no impact. He watched helplessly as his men, disciplined and brave, fought and then, one by one, were overpowered and butchered where they stood by groups of the vile attackers.

A single armored Humvee with a small group of survivors sped away from the disaster before it was too late. Colonel Frost instructed his pilots to lay down whatever cover fire they were able to try and put some distance between his fleeing soldiers and their pursuers. He watched from his hovering perch as high caliber bullets tore into and through flesh to no avail. The people below didn't seem to even register that bullets had just passed through them. This was more than just adrenaline or some external chemical or drug affecting this behavior. What was happening was unreal and unimaginable, and yet he was witnessing it. There was no denying it.

Seeing that these efforts were largely futile, he ordered his pilots to return to the Knik base. It didn't appear that he had any options left other than to allow the incoming jets from Fairbanks to blanket the entire area in fire and death. To him, these people below were still Americans; the same people he had sworn to defend and protect from exactly the thing that he was ordering done to them.

Over the radio, he was connected with the pilots in the squadron of jets that were just beginning to appear on the distant horizon. He issued the order to use any and all ordinance on the crowd advancing through the valley.

And then from a safe distance, the colonel watched as the entire road and all that was on it was engulfed in a sea of seemingly liquid fire that spread out like a searing yellow and black flood. The flash was blinding and the delayed roar of the explosion was deafening even over the clamorous growl of the helicopter's turbines.

The colonel bowed and shook his head. He was a warrior, but never in his career, or even in his lifetime would he have imagined that he would be calling down such horrible death on such a target. He wasn't a praying man, but he found himself asking for forgiveness from above. He knew that there were "bad guys" in that crowd below but he also knew that there were women and children and who knew what else. Was his wife down there? His son? Had they just been incinerated along with everyone else? Maybe this would be enough to end it all so that they could begin sorting out the good from the bad and then figure out who was responsible for this insanity that had cost so much.

He was lingering in those thoughts when his radio headset began to squawk. It was the pilot of his helicopter. "Sir, it doesn't appear to have worked, sir. They're still coming."

"*What?!?*"

He looked out then and saw that, even through the flames that were still melting the paved roads of the Glenn Highway, the rioters, the attackers, the terrorists or whatever they were to be called were still moving forward. It was as if the attack—the deadly fire that had swallowed hundreds of people in a single instant—had not even happened. They were showing no signs of stopping or even slowing. Through his binoculars, he watched as dozens of them appeared through the conflagration with flames still licking at their clothes and hair. They made not the slightest effort to extinguish the blaze that flickered and burned over their bodies. Smoldering and blackened, they continued their trek toward the bridge, swirling black contrails in their wake.

*The bridge.* He had to know if the bridge was ready for demolition. "Connect me with the command post."

"Yessir."

After a pause, with the colonel still watching the horrible parade as it advanced, the pilot was back on. "Sir, I don't seem to be able to raise command."

"What do you mean?"

"Sir, just that. The line is open, but I'm not reaching anyone."

"Get us back over there, son."

"Yessir."

It took only a few brief moments in the fast moving aircraft for them to be over the newly formed command post on the north side of the Knik Arm Bridge. When the colonel looked down, his heart nearly skipped a beat. Below him, the scene resembled what he had left at Fort Richardson. People, soldiers, were running in every direction. Some appeared to be fleeing while others appeared to be pursuing. There were also bodies lying all over the area. There seemed to be a large concentration of them near the critical care unit that had been established to treat the worst cases. And then he saw it. A row of black, zippered bags lying side-by-side behind the unit. Body bags. But not all of them were still. There were several that had something inside that was struggling to get out. They writhed and squirmed like fetuses trying to be born from inside the black, rubbery wombs.

"Oh dear God."

"Sir, what do you want us to do?"

"Get me on the radio with those pilots."

"You're on, sir."

"Pilot, do you have anything left to bring down that bridge?"

"That's an affirmative, sir."

"Then bring it down. We've got to do what we can to stop this."

"Are you asking us to destroy that bridge, sir?"

"That's affirmative."

"Roger that. We are targeting the bridge."

The colonel and the pilots of his helicopter watched as the spans that constituted the Knik Arm Bridge were laid to rubble. There was less fire with this explosion but definitely more smoke than with the napalm bursts on the roadway. One of the jets targeted the more distant railroad trestle for good measure and brought it down in a flash of rising smoke and water. And from the south, getting closer and closer, there seemed to be no stop to the tide of maniacal humanity that pressed ever forward.

When they reached the concrete and steel ruins of the bridge, they merely continued. Those that could find easy footing crossed and those that couldn't fell into spaces and gaps in the span until those spaces and gaps were filled full enough with still twisting and squirming bodies to allow others to cross atop them.

The pilot said flatly, "It didn't seem to work. There's no containment. They're still getting across."

# PART I

# CHAPTER 1

*Several weeks later...*

Neil Jordan, struggling a bit to catch his breath, asked, "What was that, Doc?"

"I said that it didn't work. It doesn't appear as if they contained it," answered Dr. Caldwell.

Now finally on a rise high enough to see the bridge, or more accurately, to see where it had once stood, he saw that while the bridge had been downed, it was obvious by the destruction on the far side that the zombies had made it across. It looked very clearly like military vehicles on the far side in no better shape than those at the attempted roadblock back down the road closer to Anchorage. Curiously, there was a military Humvee beached and abandoned some distance down in the Knik below the bridge.

Looking at the destruction, he didn't know what to do; how to react. He had actually been expecting that this is what they would find. He had assumed that the destruction would have worked in stopping the onslaught of undead, but it appeared that Dr. Caldwell was right. If it had worked, there would likely be several thousand ghouls gathered and milling about in front of the broken masonry.

Neil peered through his binoculars and shook his head. "Damn."

"What?"

"I don't think that the bridge is passable as it is."

"Why not?"

"Take a look for yourself. Pay special attention to the darker spots in the pavement."

The doctor took the binoculars from Neil and looked out. He adjusted the focus slightly and then scanned from one end of the first stretch to the other. He leaned forward, as if getting those few inches closer would help to bring the scene into sharper relief.

"Are those bodies stacked atop one another?"

Neil shook his head in disgust. "No. If those were just bodies, they wouldn't still be moving around."

The doctor looked closer still and could now see a reaching and flexing hand emerging from underneath the top layer of downward-facing bodies. And now he could see the general movement. He was reminded of fish still struggling to breathe and escape from the bottom of a barrel. They were packed so tightly, having been walked on by thousands of their undead brethren, that they were hopelessly tangled and knotted together.

Neil turned to face the rest of the group of survivors, still approaching up the slope. Their weary faces were drawn tight with exertion and deprivation, the only color from the streaks of dirt here and there, as well as the ruddy rose clouds blotching most of their cheeks. They all seemed so gaunt and frail to him. Perhaps it was just a product of his downcast mood, but these people didn't seem to be robust Alaskans ready to face the challenges of the sometimes harsh environs of Alaska. Rather, they appeared to be a lonely group of desperate souls who had somehow managed to stay a single step ahead of the Reaper who had apparently harvested most if not all of the other thousands of souls who had once populated Anchorage, Alaska. When his eyes fell upon the two children, Danny and Jules, still tagging along with them, he managed to control the outburst that was threatening to explode from his mouth. These kids had seen and experienced more than should be asked from any adult, and they certainly didn't need Neil to add to the misery. Instead, he took a deep breath and held it as he turned back to look at the dashed hope that the bridge had once signified.

It was with Jules' brother Martin that the calamity had originally begun. He had been bitten by....*something*, down near Seward. The wound was very superficial, but it had bled well more than it should have and led to a very aggressive infection that within hours had claimed young Martin's life. And for reasons that science could not answer and that religion dared not contemplate, young Martin had risen from his death slumber and began to kill everyone around him, setting off a chain of events that had escalated and multiplied with each victim also rising up to go on a homicidal spree, first at Providence Hospital and then spreading exponentially throughout all of Anchorage.

In a few hours, the city had been overrun with the walking dead. Those survivors fortunate enough were able to flee the city, but the vast majority of the population had fallen prey to the killing hordes. There were others like Neil and his group, still clawing for survival in the city, but he was afraid that all of them, his group included, might be fighting a losing battle against insurmountable odds. He kept his thoughts to himself for the most part, but there were times, like this one, that he felt the weight of that possibility hanging heavily on him. Like Sisyphus' rock, his thoughts just kept rolling down over the top of him.

They had been on the run or in hiding for weeks now. They had seen as much or more destruction, mayhem, and death than even the saltiest of Genghis Khan's Mongol warriors. And neither the running nor the chaos showed any signs of slackening in the slightest.

Fleeing the carnage of Providence Hospital and Midtown Anchorage, Neil and those with him found temporary sanctuary in South Anchorage in a small duplex, abandoned by its escaping owners. With supplies taken from the Fred Meyer where Meghan had been a manager, the group decided that waiting out the storm instead of running was the safer choice. They did their best to quietly entertain one another while avoiding detection by the ghouls that wandered the streets outside. Those were days of quiet, lonely isolation.

After several desolate days in their four-walled life raft, they were joined by another group of three survivors, Dr. Caldwell, Emma, and a police officer named Malachi Ivanoff. It wasn't too long afterward that their refuge was discovered by the terrors outside, and they were forced to run once again.

Since leaving their sanctuary, their numbers had grown and dwindled. The van that had once transported them through the twisted wasteland that Anchorage had become was gone, abandoned by necessity, as it could not navigate the many impassable roads they had encountered. If Anchorage were a person and those roads were its windpipe, the patient would have been asphyxiated long ago. Early on in the catastrophe, the busiest of Anchorage's roads and intersections had become impenetrable barriers that did nothing more than trap the souls whose vehicles created them. Those same people were virtually served up on glass and metal platters bearing the names of Chevrolet, Ford, and GMC.

Neil thought back on the past several days...weeks. How many had it been? He'd lost count. Or, more to the point, he'd stopped counting long ago when the sun rising and setting no longer held the same importance. It didn't matter what day it was anymore because each was going to bring with it the same problems, the same struggles, the same agonizing realizations about their situation without the hope of a weekend to break up the monotony.

# CHAPTER 2

Weeks ago, with the minivan loaded with both people and their dwindling supplies, Neil drove away from their south Anchorage hiding place. The vehicle could outrun the ghouls laying siege to the home that had become their bastion but they were traveling into the unknown, like jumping into a mysterious lake on a dark night. With the exception of young Jules and Danny, everyone in the van had lived in Anchorage for some time. The city, as its former self, was familiar, but as it appeared on that autumn day, they could just as well have been driving on Venus.

Every street, every corner, every building held new mysteries and new dark secrets. The roads, once bustling with cars and pedestrians, were deserted except for the random wandering dog or the occasional plastic shopping bag that fluttered and danced on the gentle breeze. There were abandoned cars here and there, but except for the main intersections, which Neil was careful to avoid, the roads in the city were largely empty. Anchorage had become a ghost town.

The mix of souls in the minivan made for an eclectic stew of ages, backgrounds, and personalities. At the helm both figuratively and literally, was Neil. Before the zombie apocalypse he'd worked in the mortgage industry, though that experience had obviously not hindered his ability to survive the zombie apocalypse. In point of fact, maybe such a ruthless business had prepared him to deal with soulless opportunists.

Next to him sat the more senior Dr. Caldwell who, along with Jerry, who was sitting behind him, had come from Providence Hospital which was the origin of the outbreak. Dr. Caldwell had served in the military and had worked trauma centers, none of which had prepared him to deal with the horrible circumstances that came part and parcel with current events.

Behind Neil was Meghan, who had been a manager at a Fred Meyer store. Neil had wandered in looking for supplies and had found Meghan. She had been at his side ever since.

That's not to say that Neil's trip to Fred Meyer had been otherwise fruitless. Many of the spoils of that visit were still crowding the vehicle. There were piles of canned foods, boxes of crackers and other dry foods, and cases of water and juice all stacked in the back of the vehicle behind the rearmost seats. They had grabbed more than just food that morning as well. The group had a large variety of hunting rifles, shotguns, and sidearms as well as a large stock of ammunition for each. At the very least, the guns provided them all with a sense of comfort, whether it was justified or not.

Beside Meghan on the middle bench sat the most troubled—and troubling—soul in the vehicle. He still wore the uniform of an Anchorage Police Department Officer, but his patrolling days were over. Officer Malachi Ivanoff was as distant from his companions in the van as he was from a firm grasp on reality. Old memories, lurking in the shadows of the past, were punishing him. And in his punishment, all that Malachi could truly feel was fear, but the terror produced only rage. But like a volcano concealing the wrath within its bowels, he contained the anger in silence.

On the floor next to him was Jerry, a young man not even old enough to buy a drink from a tavern but who was far from a clueless kid. He was squeezed into the space between the edge of the middle bench seat and the sliding side door. Jerry had been a Certified Nursing Assistant at Providence Hospital and was finally getting his act together enough to get out on his own. He had a car and was ready to move into his own apartment when.... well, his story from recent weeks wasn't much different than everyone else's in the van. Since that morning, he'd found stores of confidence in himself that, until then, had gone unnoticed and untapped. All of which was rather fortuitous because on that morning, when their world was forever changed, he had been entrusted with the safety of a pair of children, Jules and Danny. The young boy, Danny, had been the best friend and family guest of Jules' brother Martin, who had invited Danny to vacation with them in Alaska.

The pair of youngsters was sitting on the laps of a couple of women situated in the rear bench seat. Emma, sitting behind Malachi, was once an administrative employee at Providence Hospital. She'd had the good fortune of finding Dr. Caldwell early in the emerging catastrophe at the hospital and was saved by his planning and direction. Their harrowing trek through the hospital was followed by a brief trip in a hospital airlift helicopter and a violent crash on the south side of Anchorage. The survivors from Providence were eventually whittled down to just the good doctor, Emma, and the police officer.

Kim, sitting next to Emma on the very back seat asked, "How much gas do we have?"

Neil was relieved to hear her speak. When they made their escape from the safe house, her best friend Tony was attacked and killed by several of the walking dead as he threw open the garage door. The severity of his wounds caused him to die quickly and, therefore, reanimate quickly. With blood still spurting from the gaping wounds on his neck, face, and arms, he chased after the fleeing van. Kim demanded that they stop to help her friend, not willing to accept that it was no longer Tony that was chasing them. Her manic ranting had quickly turned to depressive silence.

Dr. Caldwell asked half-mockingly, "You want to take a road trip somewhere?"

Kim, still looking out the side window, said without much emotion in her voice, "No, I was just wondering how long we had until we would be on foot."

From behind Neil, Meghan asked with a little more urgency, "How much gas *do* we have?"

Neil answered both of them, "Relax. We've got a full tank and this thing gets great gas mileage."

"So, where are we headed?" Meghan continued.

Dr. Caldwell turned to look at the others in the back. "We're going to try and find a way out of the city. I don't think anyone is going to be coming back here anytime soon to give us any help, so it's up to us to save ourselves."

Kim pointedly asked, "You mean the way that we helped Tony?"

"Kim, what is done is done. None of us wanted that to happen to Tony any more than we'd want it to happen to anyone else. We can't do anything about it now and there is no bringing him back. Had we even tried to help him, you know what would have happened to the rest of us. Do you want to be responsible for the same happening to Jules and Danny?"

Kim looked back out the window and didn't answer, tears pooling in the corners of her eyes.

Malachi just shook his head and didn't say a word. In his mind, Tony was destined for such a fate. To Malachi, Tony had chosen his ill begotten path when he decided to lay with other men in sin. It sickened him to even imagine it. The rough groping...the clumsy positioning...the sweating...the struggle... He could feel his heart rate jump; his disgust rising as a sour biting taste in the back of his mouth. He couldn't shake the images though. They just kept running in his mind over and over again. Rather than fight it–fighting it did no good whatsoever–he closed his eyes and relived a past that was never really any further than arm's length away, always hovering on the periphery. The memories were so common that they didn't even bring on the fear or the pain like they once had. They represented no more menace than the memory of his first cavity filling. Through the tangle of grabbing, abrasive older hands and arms, his mind sought out better visions, some token remembrance of happiness however fleeting from a childhood that was as flat in aspect as was the adult Malachi's face.

From deep within his memory trove, he often found his mother with her generous and approving smile. He could see her berry picking with his sisters out on the tundra in the early autumn. She seemed so far away but this memory of her was a thousand fold better than that of the broken woman she became during his adolescent years. But he was able to hold that autumn day from long ago. It may not have even been a memory anymore. He just as likely could be imagining the peace and the supreme tranquility from the vision. It didn't matter to him. It didn't matter that he could still taste the sour and sweet goodness from eating Agutaq, Eskimo "ice cream" made from seal oil and the berries they picked that day.

Looking out the windows to either side of him, he tried to remember and then hold on to the present. It was becoming harder all the time and was made more difficult still by his inability to recognize the present and reality as distinguished from the random images and visitations from the past that threatened to dislodge him permanently.

He could see some storm clouds gathering over the Chugach Mountains sitting to the north and east of Anchorage. The clouds were dark and purple, like a bruise spreading itself over the horizon.

Neil drove them north on Lake Otis Parkway and found a likely path back out to the Seward Highway, which was a primary north-south thoroughfare through town. The van was largely quiet, each of the survivors retreating into his or her thoughts, memories, or torments. Neil didn't have that luxury. By virtue of his being the driver, Neil had to keep his wits about him. There was no pause or moment for him to regroup, though he was punishing himself as much or more than anyone else in the vehicle.

He couldn't shake the guilt that, had he planned better, Tony would still be alive...and so would Rachel. The most unsettling emotion he was feeling, however, was a nagging and punishing sense of relief. It could have just as easily been *him* opening the garage door and overwhelmed by those things. It all had happened so quickly that none of it really hit him until they were well away. He wasn't quite certain if he saw Tony as he was attacked but he was sure that he saw his face after his death and reanimation. Tony wasn't there anymore. Humanity wasn't there anymore. All that dwelled in those dark pupils and gnashing jaws was unbridled rage and unquenchable hunger. And that could have been him.

This stretch of highway, cutting through the heart of Anchorage, was largely empty, free of large pockets of cars and obstructions. There hadn't been any large road construction or repair projects and most of the cars that were scattered here and there were likely already parked or stalled before the tumult had hit. Still, Neil was careful to give any vehicle sitting stalled on the road a wide berth. No point in tempting fate. With the isolation and the quiet all around them, it was hard to remember that they were in the midst of what was once the most populous region in this part of the world.

In the distance where the Seward Highway split and became Ingra and Gamble Streets, Neil could see the glint of sunlight reflecting off of the metal and glass of a large pocket of cars. It was quite obvious that there was a bottleneck in front of them. Looking to either side of them, he determined that this was a good place to sort things out, so he stopped the van and looked back over his shoulder at his passengers, who all looked at him in wonder.

It had been less than an hour since they had made their flight and the tension was still very high for all of them. Neil rolled down his window, just a few inches, and welcomed the refreshing breeze into the vehicle. A lot had just happened…more than any of them could fully digest alone. They were free but now there was a sense of despair as to the choices and the possible consequences in front of them. As Neil had heard it put in the past, sometimes the devil you know is less frightening than the devil you don't. They all knew where they stood while they were still in that house, but now there was no real knowing.

Kim was the first to speak, "So what's up? Why we stoppin'?"

"I think this is as good a place as any for us to figure out what's next. We made plans about getting away, but so far those plans have gone south. What are we doin'? Where are we headin'?" answered Neil.

"We're gettin' the hell away," Kim answered for all of them.

Neil nodded. "Okay. I get that. But to where?"

"Away."

"Okay. Again, where is 'away'? I need to have some idea where we're going or we're just going to drive around until we run out of gas. Do you want to be on foot?"

"So," Emma asked, "can we have this conversation somewhere other than here?"

"Here seems okay for us to talk," Dr. Caldwell said. "It's wide open, so nothing can sneak up on us and I don't see any evidence of those things for as far as my eyes can see. Seems like we're alone out here."

Kim demanded, "Here!?! Here!?! Where the hell is 'here'!?! We're on a fucking highway!"

Her coarse language reminded Jules of Rachel. She already missed her. She was fun. Back at the house, Rachel had tried to help Tony who was in some trouble after he opened the garage door for all of them to get out. In so doing, Rachel fell out of the side door of the van and then ran into the house, with a couple of those scary monsters in tow. That was the last they heard from Rachel.

Jules was starting to understand what happened when people disappeared and never came back. It was also beginning to dawn on her what that meant about her mother, father, and brother Martin. Maybe that was why people acted so strangely around her whenever conversation found its way back to that first day and how all of this had begun. She wondered about her older brother Alec who had stayed behind at their vacation cabin when Martin had been bitten. Was he still at the cabin waiting for all of them to return? Boy was he going to be mad.

Jerry suggested, "If there was anyone that had the means to get through this, it's got to be the military. Maybe Elmendorf or Fort Rich is still holding out. They've got some badass guns and equipment to build earthen-walled fortresses in a matter of minutes. Maybe there're still some people up that way. Maybe they've got the means to get us out."

Again, Jerry could feel all the eyes in the van starting to look his way. Every time he decided that "this" will be the last time that he opened his big mouth, he found himself doing it again. It wasn't a habit that he was trying to cultivate but he was finding it was one that was coming naturally to him more and more.

Dr. Caldwell stepped in with, "I think Jerry is exaggerating a bit in the Army's ability to rapidly construct the defenses, but he may be onto something. There are a lot of trained and battle-tested people on those bases. There might just be a chance that they were able to mount an effective defense. I wonder...."

Neil asked, "Are there any other ideas?"

There was only silence from the others in the van. He was careful to look at each person directly to try and register any sort of response, whether verbalized or not. There was as much silence in their expressions as there was in their voices.

"Military bases win, then. I guess now we just gotta figure the best way to get there."

Without another word, Neil put the van into gear and they were once again under way.

# CHAPTER 3

Always eyeing the north, they seemed to head steadily to the west. Every time an avenue or a street opened up for them heading north, they would invariably run into a roadblock of some sort. They found themselves on International Airport Road heading west. They were approaching an overpass straddling Minnesota Drive, the Seward Highway's little sister. Like the highway, Minnesota's lanes moved largely north and south but its traffic was neither as heavy nor intense as the Seward.

And then, from the other side of the overpass appeared another car speeding in their direction. At first, Neil didn't think anything of it, having settled into the role of driving friends around for an outing. From behind him though, Meghan asked incredulously, "Is that really a car coming at us?"

# CHAPTER 4

The car, a diminutive black Volkswagen Passat, pulled alongside the van and casually its driver side window came down. From within peered out a haggard looking woman with swirling knots of grey smoke for hair and a slightly confused but hopeful expression on her wrinkled face.

Without taking her hands from the steering wheel, she nodded and barked out, "I'm Maggie. Where you headed?"

Neil looked over at the others in the van. He didn't even know quite how to begin. Looking back over at Maggie, he laughed lightly and said simply, "It's really good to see you, Maggie."

"If you're thinkin' about headin' to Anchorage International, don't bother. It's crawlin' with those things...those demons from hell. I think there must've been some survivors holed up in there, but there's no one there now. That place is ugly."

Neil asked, "Is there a safe place we can go and talk? You're the first person any of us has seen alive in weeks." He could feel himself start to choke up a bit, surprising himself, "It's really good to see you, Maggie. I can't stress that enough."

Emma had her hand to her mouth and felt that if she could anymore, she'd be crying as well. She had the tightness in her chest and the burn behind her eyes and nose, but no tears came. There just wasn't anything left; no reserve of tears stashed for such an occasion. She hugged Jules tightly to her chest and let the warmth of hope find a small corner in her soul to set up camp and wait.

They went across the overpass and found their way to De La Vega Park. The sports park was home to a clutch of soccer fields and baseball diamonds. While it sat just south of a major thoroughfare and west of a highway, the entrance was removed and the parking lot open enough to provide a relative sense of comfort.

**Sean Schubert**

They pulled into a pair of parking spots that sat adjacent to one of the baseball fields. At first no one moved. To suggest that anyone should leave the security of their vehicle, regardless of how fleeting and insignificant the illusion of security, was just this side of blasphemy.

Maggie, hopping from her car and strolling around as if casually stretching her legs, encouraged them all to overcome the fear that lurked and threatened outside of their bubble. One by one, the van's doors opened and they climbed out.

# CHAPTER 5

"Where're you folks comin' from?" asked the wild-eyed Maggie.

"We've been in hiding for the past few weeks," Neil explained. "When those things found us, we had to hit the road. That was just today...a little bit ago, in fact. Hell, it seems like days and days ago."

Meghan asked, "Maggie, what about you? Where have you been? Are there any other survivors anywhere?"

"Me? I've just been keeping on the road mostly. Haven't seen anybody in a couple of days but there are still people out there. Every time I start to thinkin' that maybe I'm all that's left, I run into a group like yours."

Dr. Caldwell, his interest piqued, asked hopefully, "What about those other groups? Where are they now?"

Maggie spat into the dust of the baseball diamond on which they were standing. It was the same every time she ran into a new group of survivors. The fools always asked the same questions, hoped for the same answers, but shared in the same disappointments. It was so predictable. She was starting to grow weary of others.

"You folks have any food? It's been a couple of days since I've eaten."

Slightly frustrated that she didn't answer his questions, the doctor took from the back of the open van a couple of granola bars and tossed them to her. He took one of the breakfast cereal bars for himself and started to chew on the honey flavored oats while he waited for the old woman to answer.

Jules and Danny wandered over to the bleachers and started climbing up and down the metal seats. Kim was amazed that, despite all that had happened and threatened to happen again and again and again, kids could still be kids. They could still seek out the simplest of distractions and find entertainment in the most unlikely places in the most unlikely ways. Jules was singing a children's song, one that Kim hadn't heard in what seemed a lifetime, while Danny was just sitting at the top of the bleachers and looking out over the baseball diamond as if he was awaiting the start of a game.

Dr. Caldwell continued, "So? About the others...?"

Maggie sat herself on the hood of her car and chewed one of the granola bars, stuffing the other bar into one of the many pockets on her military-style camouflaged fatigues. Along the side of the car, her sandaled feet dangled freely, banging out a rhythmless beat on the front quarter panel. She leaned her head back between her shoulder blades and breathed deeply.

"When all of this began, I was on the road. I traveled from store to store, mainly the Walmarts and Targets in the area, and merchandised products for vendors. Mostly I dealt with greeting cards and sporting goods, but I really dabbled in just about anything. I liked the freedom of not being tied to one place for too terribly long. It was nice and really ideal for me. I could go into a store, make sure there were plenty of 'get well' or humorous birthday cards in each of the pockets, and then head on my way again. People at the stores knew me...customers, staff, managers. They all knew me.

"You know, it's nice when you can go just about anywhere and people know your name. There's an awful lot of comfort in that. Anyway, I was on my way to the south side Target when emergency broadcasts began to hit the airwaves. So I drove myself out to Kincaid Park and hid out near those old bunkers that look out over the inlet. You know the ones that I'm talking about? I waited for a couple of hours there, and then a few more and then a few more. By that time, the radio had stopped broadcasting. It was just quiet out there. Have any of you ever been around quiet that absolute? I mean, there was nothing. It kind of felt like I was the last living thing left on the planet. Like the good Lord had come down and scooped all of his children up in his great big, welcoming hands but had forgotten about me.

"It must have been about the third day, I was sitting on my car, looking out over the water when it hit me. I wonder if that was how it was with Saint Joan."

Neil asked, "Who?"

Maggie smiled and looked up at the sky, which was by then a solid grey from horizon to horizon. "I heard my true calling. You see, in my previous life, I stocked shelves, hooks, and greeting card pockets by day. At night, I talked to others about the Lord and his message. I saved souls. I went to youth groups at churches and to meetings for drunks and drug addicts who needed to be reminded of His Glory—it's just so easy for the weak and wicked to forget, you know?"

Malachi, sitting on the first bench of the nearest set of bleachers, heard her comment and immediately stood and walked over to the conversation. Finally, someone who knew the word of God was in their midst. Maybe now, people wouldn't look at him like he was crazy every time he brought up salvation.

She continued, "I'd go to any number of meetings around town to hear about suffering and people lost in the wilderness of their lives. I'd go and listen to their lamenting until their hurt filled the room. Then I would tell them all about the hope of salvation for their souls."

She paused and looked at the others, trying to measure any response. Emma, for her part, just walked away shaking her head and mumbling under her breath about "another one of those." Neil and Dr. Caldwell were more patient and willing to listen to her. Neil just wanted to be polite enough to encourage her to talk a little bit about any others she had encountered over the past several weeks. He was especially curious if she was aware of any groups of survivors that were holding out and able to perhaps help their group to do the same.

"Well, on that third day... do you think three is an important number? I mean, Christ rose on the third day, there's the Father, the Son, and the Holy Ghost... I guess that's all I can remember right now, but those two—the third day and the Holy Trinity—seem to be pretty important."

Neil wasn't quite sure what to say. He just wanted her to get on with her story, but he was afraid that if he was rude that she might clam up and drive off and they would be no better off than before she arrived.

"So anyway, it was the third day and I heard God's voice tell me that my days of doing man's work were over and that now I was going to crusade for Him full time. I hopped into my car and I realized that the hunger that had been gnawing at my insides was gone. I was refreshed and invigorated. I never felt so good in my whole life. I felt like a new person. And I guess that I was. My car became my church and His house. We drove out of Kincaid Park together in search of souls to save.

"We hit the road on that first day of my new life but didn't see anyone other than those things. They were everywhere. I drove by Romig Middle School, and the parking lot was full of them. They were pounding on the walls of the school with their hands, arms, and even their heads. I heard some screaming coming from inside the school and just knew that there were people inside that I couldn't save. It made me cry to think that I had already failed the Good Lord. And then I was angry at myself for the fear that I was feeling. I begged for forgiveness for my weakness and drove away. I thought that I was ready and that I could be strong, but I wasn't. Not yet.

"I turned my car around and drove back through town. On my way, I saw the world coming undone. Hell had flung open its doors and let the dead walk the earth again. I was frightened by what was happening all around. I'm not even sure where it was, but I finally came upon a building that was only partially completed in its construction. It was a big office building and most of its paved parking lot was still enclosed by a tall, chain link fence and some of those big dumpsters that you see on work sites. There were people in there and they motioned for me to go to the gate entrance on the fence.

"I whipped my car around and got myself into the enclosure. There were at least a dozen folks that I saw right away trying to hide in there. Of course those things knew that they were in there but the fence was keeping them out for the time. A few of the people had guns and were doing their best to defend the rest of them, but I just knew that... it was just a matter of time before those things got in. I thought about the school and the souls trapped and tortured inside its walls. I was afraid for these people. I wasn't necessarily afraid for myself, mind you. I knew that my time here on this rock was temporary and was waiting for my real life to begin, but I also knew that my work was not yet done. I hadn't been called to return yet.

"So anyway, a fella named Jeffrey led me up some stairs to a floor whose walls were mostly done. It was in here that they were...I guess you'd call it livin'. They'd draped some blue tarps across the still opened, unfinished windows to block out the cool air and the smell and noise from those things. There were a few blankets and pillows here and there but no furniture. It looked like some wooden crates had been broken into pieces to be burned to keep everyone warm, but most of the wood was gone. Whatever food they had was pretty much gone too. There was trash piled up in most of the corners...empty chip bags and cracker boxes and some soup and stew cans.

"And then I saw the children. There were at least ten children with them. They were all huddled together in a small corner in an unfinished office space. Some were crying and some just looked...well, gone. There was barely an ounce of recognition in a couple of their faces. I think they had just seen too much.

"The whole place was filled to overflowing with fear. I started to feel it too. It was just so strong. I could feel the cold grip on my legs and my arms. But then I felt this warmth inside of me. I could feel Him. I could feel His love and His strength like a furnace warm my soul. My arms and my legs may have been useless, but my voice found His Word and I started to speak.

"I began to talk about the Apocalypse and the End of Days and how it was upon us. I talked about the message from His Book about Hell being visited upon the earth. But I also spoke about forgiveness and redemption and the glory of Heaven. I told them that their fear was only so strong because their faith wasn't. I pleaded with them to embrace the Word and that if they did, then all of the horrible things happening around them would begin to make sense. They would be able to see that this was all just a part of His plan for us."

Maggie paused for a moment and looked at Neil, Dr. Caldwell, and Malachi. They were the only ones still listening to her. She looked over them at the children and was disappointed that they weren't close enough to hear her message. They were the ones who really needed to hear. These two, though, weren't looking like the other children with whom she'd had contact over the past couple of weeks. They didn't look as scared as the others. She might have a harder time sharing the message with them, but she also had faith in herself and His power to show them the Truth.

She measured the reactions of the three men listening to her. Other than Officer Ivanoff, she didn't seem to be really connecting with them. She could tell that they were just listening to her because they wanted something else. They weren't truly interested in the Word at all. The police officer however appeared to be very interested in what she was saying. His eyes were not filled with the same fire that she could feel in her own. There was as much confusion as anything else dwelling there. Confusion or not, she could tell that he was a believer and so she welcomed him by her side.

Neil asked, "So what happened at the construction site? Are those people still there?"

Maggie took another bite of the granola bar and chewed it briskly, shaking her head all the while. She looked back up at the sky, as if she were looking for her lost lines from a cue card. Getting down from the hood of her car, she said, "No. They're all dead. I think just about everyone is dead now. I thought I was the last one and then I found you."

Dr. Caldwell, wanting—*needing*—more information, begged, "What happened?" He knew what had happened, he was just curious about the cause, really. He actually suspected that she perhaps had a hand in it, but was looking for anything useful that she might share.

"Later that night, somehow the gate into the parking lot got opened and those things got in. I was in my car and was able to get away, but none of the others made it."

Neil asked, "How?"

Maggie didn't answer at first. She just looked back up at the sky, looking for that celestial teleprompter again. Neil could tell that there was more to the story and was already suspicious of the woman, but he didn't say anything. He was afraid that any confrontation, however slight, might lead this woman to merely leave without telling them if there were others and where they might be. Maybe Maggie knew about the military bases. Maybe....well, maybe she knew *anything* about what was happening, which was a lot more than anyone in their group knew.

Quite simply and direct, she looked at both Dr. Caldwell and Neil. "It was His will. They were called back to their great reward. They all went back home."

With eyes and mouth agape, Neil asked, "What about the children? Didn't anyone make it out?"

Maggie spoke with as much passion and conviction as an automated answering machine, "Their souls are at peace and that's what is important now."

"But how did it happen?"

Maggie wasn't even quite sure how it happened that night. It had been so dark. She remembered going back down to her car to get one of her many Bibles in order to read. The next thing she remembered, she was starting her car and driving out as the gate was pushed inward by the beasts outside.

They rushed into the lot in a frenzy. The fight that followed was chaotic and confusing, the darkness doing its level best to influence the proceedings. The first two unfortunate souls, a man and a woman, to be swept away by the violent tide were standing at a burn barrel trying to warm themselves against the bracing night air. Noticing the rushing surge of rancid, oozing attackers, the woman screamed. Her high-pitched wail was cut short by the crush of grabbing, clawing, tearing hands upon her, transforming her voice into a muted, gurgle drowning in its own spilled blood. The man with her was only able to take two or three quick, desperate steps before he too found himself on the bottom of a pile of ravenous, biting beasts. Their cries sounded the alarm for everyone else, but, with their barrier breached, there was no hope for any of the others.

As she sped away, Maggie was startled by a handful of gunshots and then some screaming. In her rearview mirror, against the backdrop of the moon, she thought she may have seen the fluttering silhouettes desperately throwing themselves off of the highest accessible floors. She was reminded of images she watched of people doing the same from the burning towers on that awful day in September 2001. She felt sorry for their suffering, but was comforted by the fact that at least they were prepared to face their fates with the Word in their hearts.

She drove back out to Kincaid Park that night and found her secluded resting place looking out over the water. She prayed through most of the night, sleep once again eluding her. At first light the next morning, she drove back through town, making sure that she passed the unfinished office building in which she had been sheltered the day previous. The gate was standing wide open and the lot was filled with the fiends milling about waiting for their next meal.

As she passed in her car, a ripple of excitement spread through the crowd and they poured back out onto the road and tried to pursue her. She watched and prayed for them as she drove away. She knew that those lost souls in those rotting, animated corpses were damned for all eternity for their past digressions, but she prayed anyway. What could it possibly hurt?

She, of course, didn't share any of that with the others now. No, they wouldn't understand her, nor would they believe her that she didn't have anything to do with those things getting in there or into any of the other enclaves she encountered. It was just the will of God that he recalled His children to His Kingdom. Who was she to stand in His way? And if she could be an instrument of His Will, then so be it. She was, after all, His lowly servant and a soldier of Christ.

She knew that Neil and the doctor were waiting for an answer, so she merely said, "It was dark. I couldn't see everything as it happened. It was just a matter of time until they came through the gate anyway. There's really no holding them back indefinitely. Eventually, those things find their way into everything. So many walls and so many hiding spots, but so little safety and no security really."

Neil was scratching the scruff that was starting to grow in earnest on his cheeks and chin. "I don't understand, Maggie. How the hell did the gate just get opened?" Neil walked around in circles, kicking at the dusty ground. There was more to this story; he was convinced of it. Maybe in a little bit, she might open up to them with more details. For the time being, his questions may as well have been directed at the tires of her car, so he asked instead, "Where were you headed when we ran into you?"

"I was just moving. You can't stay in one place for too long or those things will find you. You just have to keep moving and you can stay safe."

"But what about gas"? Dr. Caldwell asked. "It's not like you can just pull over at a station and gas up your car. How have you been keeping it filled?"

Maggie smiled, the satisfaction of her own resourcefulness spreading across her face. She reached into her car and emerged with a section of green garden hose in her hand. Neil shook his head as she handed him a second section of garden hose as if to say, "I don't get it."

Dr. Caldwell nodded his head and smiled along with her. He clarified for Neil and anyone else wondering, "You siphoned gas out of parked and abandoned vehicles."

Maggie nodded and took another bite of granola bar. "It's important that you put the right side in the tank and the right side in your mouth or you'll get a mouth full gasoline. Believe me, it's as nasty as it gets. I put marks on the side of the hose that goes in the tank so that I wouldn't make that mistake again. You can't go off of smell, because the whole damned things reeks of gasoline.

"I keep a couple of gas cans in the trunk just in case. So far though, I've been lucky and haven't had to touch them. The Good Lord has provided for me every step of the way."

Dr. Caldwell was smiling as he said, "That's very good. There probably is enough gas to run for a very long time in all of the parked cars around the city."

Maggie nodded. "Yeah, but some of them were left running when the drivers decided to make a go of it on foot. I haven't come across too many of those, but there are a few out there with empty tanks on 'em. The other thing you gotta watch out for is those things in the cars too."

Neil looked back up from the ground. "Huh?"

"Yeah, every now and then, you'll catch one of those things in a locked car."

Dr. Caldwell finished the thought with his own speculation. "Probably, the driver, or someone anyway, got bit and then retreated into the car, locking themselves in. They die and then come back as one of the zombies trapped in the car. We should probably be wary of stalled cars anywhere and approach them with caution. Never know what could be waiting for us in there.

"Well Maggie, I think running into you is the best thing that has happened to any of us for some time. Maybe we can all hang out here for a bit and catch our breath. If you need to get some sleep, we can keep an eye out for a bit."

Maggie nodded and sat heavily into the Passat's driver seat. She took one of the numerous Bibles from her backseat and began to read silently to herself.

# CHAPTER 6

They sat on the top row of bench seats on the metal bleachers, as if they were waiting for a late summer softball game to start. Neil said to all of them, "I don't trust her. There's just something about her that isn't right. I don't think she's tellin' us everything."

"So what do we do?" Meghan asked. "We already have one loony with us..." she added, looking towards Malachi as he stood at the diamond's home plate waiting for an opening pitch that would never come. Danny and Jules were just on the edge of the diamond and using their feet to plow loads of dirt into a pile only to jump up and down on it, causing a dust cloud to form. Jerry was on top of the minivan and scanning all around them with the binoculars hung around his neck.

The sky, though grey, was calm and peaceful. The slight kiss of a breeze causing the merest wisp of a flutter in the kids' dust clouds was moist and still carried the seasonal aroma of the fall rot. The trees surrounding the lot barely took notice, ignoring the air's suggestion to move.

Kim said, to herself as much as to anyone else, "So this is what it was like before we came."

Meghan, who was lifting herself from the uncomfortable metal of the bleachers, asked, "What?"

"It's so peaceful and quiet. No cars. No planes. No nothing. The loudest noise any of us can hear anymore is our own thoughts. Maybe that was why we had so many distractions around us...to silence our thoughts and our insecurities. If you can't hear any doubt, then maybe there isn't any to hear anyway. I guess it takes losing everything to figure out what was really important to you.

"We used to spend so much time entertaining ourselves that we really lost out and maybe forgot what it was to be human. I used to follow a strict TV schedule. I didn't miss my shows and if I did...oh man was I pissed. I lived a tight existence around my TV. And now that I don't have it anymore,

I can't even remember why I watched to begin with. There wasn't any more value to the garbage that I thought was important than the dust cloud that the kids are making over there.

"And now, we drive through the ruins of all that we thought was important, and I can't even fathom why I thought it was in the first place. I have a crap job that got me nothing but more crap from someone else working the same crap job just somewhere else. Really, what was the point? Maybe we've been singled out for extinction with good reason."

Kim was crying by then, but they were silent tears...with not so much as a single sniffle. She looked off at the trees that stood as a buffer between the sports park and the highway. It all seemed so surreal to her that, in the middle of the terrifying storm in which they were traveling, there could be such a peaceful spot as this. She wished that Tony were still with them. With his big arms and bigger heart, he'd know how to hold her and make her feel that everything was going to be alright. He always knew how to make things better for her. She wanted to remember all the good times with him at work and at home, hers or his, on the couch watching whatever they could find on television. She closed her eyes and tried to see his face, but all she saw was the venomous rage and hunger on the face of her friend Tony after he'd been attacked by those things.

All at once, Kim got to her feet and made her way down off of the bleachers and away from the others. She knew that her resentment for the others was unfounded and that they were right in leaving him behind. She also realized that it would have been Tony that would have pointed all of this out to her and helped her to accept it. Knowing, however, did nothing to diminish her pain. If the hot, metaphysical poker that seemed to be jabbing into her chest would stop, that would be a fantastic start.

She walked over to the van and found a large piece of cardboard on the floor behind the last row of seats. Tearing sections out of it as she walked, she came back over to the dusty infield and began to make a pile of her own. Jules and Danny quickly joined her. She said to each of them, "Now this is a pile that we'll make but not jump on, okay?"

Making their feet into bulldozers, Danny and Jules scooped and pushed piles of dirt until they had formed a respectable mound. Danny went so far as to make motor sounds as he pushed the soil forward and beeped whenever he went in "reverse." Kim, meanwhile, went back to tearing and shaping the cardboard. She did so quietly, her back to the others still sitting on the bleachers. She wasn't doing this for them. This was for Tony. And for her.

When she had finished, she paused again. She could feel the heat rising up in her chest. This was how it had been when she attended her father's funeral. Despite not having seen him for years, she couldn't help but be overwhelmed by the loss. She hugged her cardboard creation to her chest and closed her eyes. She lowered to her knees and sank the long end of cardboard into the pile and then stood away from it.

It wasn't as grandiose as Calvary, but on the ground in front of her was a mound with a modest cross rising up. Neil and the others stood and joined her. They gathered round the cross as if it were the single mass grave for all that had been lost in the still unfolding calamity. The solemn silence stood there with them, touching each of them.

And then Maggie was there with them as well. She opened a Bible and began to read. Even the silence paused to listen, perhaps seeking its own sense of solace.

"...though I may walk through the valley of the shadow of death I shall fear no evil..."

Kim produced a Sharpie marker from the pocket of her light jacket and rolled it in her hand for a few moments, decisions just out of reach teasing her. And then she leaned down, took the cross out of the dirt, and wrote Tony's name on it. She held it quietly as Maggie continued to read. With her thumb, she caressed the writing gently, hoping that perhaps touching his name would help mend the deep emotional connection that had once existed between her and her friend. She closed her eyes to see his face one last time, kissed his name, and then handed the cross to Meghan, whose hand was extended to her.

Kim rose back up with a pinch of dusty earth in her palm. She looked up at the sky and then let the dirt sift through her fingers and be caught by the slight flurry of air. Meghan followed suit by writing her fiancé's name on the cardboard and doing the same as Kim. Dr. Caldwell was next in line.

When the cross was handed to Neil, he opened the marker but then stalled when he realized he didn't have a name to write on it. There was no one who immediately came to mind to mourn. His parents, he hoped, were still safe and removed out east in Pennsylvania. His ex-wife had made it abundantly clear that he was less than a memory and a painful mistake for her. He had no children and really no close friends with whom he shared anything. He looked around at the others and was overtaken with embarrassment. He empathized with all of them, but his detachment from all of those around him had the unintended effect of insulating him from the loss that they all felt. He suspected that, perhaps, he was better off than the rest of them when he stopped and considered the isolation that had characterized his life before Armageddon.

Kim, Meghan, and Doc had all walked away and were standing next to the van. Jerry was positioned on top of the vehicle keeping watch, ever vigilant. Maggie and Malachi were still enwrapped in the Bible's words. Emma was staring at the mound and holding Jules and Danny to her legs. Neil was as alone in his moment of self-pity as he was in his miserable life. Not wishing to add irreverence to his misery, he slowly and carefully reburied the long end of the cross into the mound and then walked away as well. Silently, he crept back to the van and took his place behind the wheel without uttering a single word to anyone.

Only a few minutes later, Jerry asked no one in particular, "Can you guys hear that?"

"Hear what?" Dr. Caldwell was the first to answer.

"I can hear...hell, I can basically *feel* a buzzing in the air. It's like the kind of vibration that we all heard back at the house, but it's much lower...not nearly as intense."

The doctor looked at Kim and Meghan, still standing next to him by the van, and both of them shook their heads.

"No. We don't hear anything."

Jerry hopped down from the van, the scoped hunting rifle slung over his shoulder, and said, "I'm not sure, but I think maybe we should get moving again. They may have found us."

Kim asked, "They?"

Jerry nodded and clarified, "Yeah, you know...they. Them. The zombies. I think that's what I'm hearing. But I feel like I'm hearing it in my chest more than anything. It's hard to describe."

Danny, who had come over to the van thinking that they were getting ready to go, added, "It's like holding the lawnmower handle with your stomach."

Jerry wrinkled his brow and pursed his lips, then said approvingly, "That's a great description for it, Danny, my boy. That just about describes it to a tee. It's just kind of a low vibration that buzzes you from front to back but there's a sound element to it too that lurks in the background." He winked at Danny who, once again, beamed with delight at having contributed to the conversation. This was becoming a habit for him and he liked the praise. This wasn't like teachers back home who were paid to give praise. He was earning it because it was merited, and he could tell the difference.

Still looking at Danny, Jerry said to everyone, "Regardless of how it feels or sounds, I still think we should get on the move. It's starting to get stronger, so either they are getting closer or there are more of them."

"Or both!" shouted Emma, running toward the van. She was pointing at the road leading into the sports park. There, coming slowly up the path but gradually gaining steam, was a crowd of maybe ten of the beasts.

Despite the distance, they could still see that the zombies' skin had taken on a slightly grey hue and whatever wounds had originally claimed them were now merely rust colored patches against their skin and clothing. Their movements were stiffer and less organic. They seemed clumsier at first, but as they drew nearer and the scent of their prey became stronger, their shuffle became a slow amble, which transformed into a bit of fast paced walk and then almost a trot.

Jerry stood next to the van as the women and children from the party climbed into the rear. He hoisted the rifle to his shoulder, clicked off the safety, and then sought a target through his scope. He picked out a "man" wearing coveralls that sported the logo of one of the local airfreight outfits.

His dark scraggly facial hair stood out in stark contrast against the practically translucent grey skin of his scarred face. Jerry took in a deep breath, held it, and squeezed the trigger.

Everyone in the van, including Dr. Caldwell and Neil in the front two seats, jumped. Across the parking lot though, there was one fewer attacker coming toward them. Jerry felt that, given the time and opportunity, he could probably take all of them down. He slid the door shut, struck by the ease with which the thought occurred to him. As they exited the park, he sat in his more comfortable spot on the bench seat in complete awe of the change in his temperament and his almost casual acceptance of the way things were now. Maybe that was what was keeping him alive. Maybe. Or maybe deep down, within sight but just out of reach in the well of his soul, there was a sense in him that he was actually thriving and had always sought just such a set of circumstances. This, of course, was absurd. He attributed it to the continual bile of their circumstances. It was ridiculous to think that anyone could possibly be prospering in these difficult days. He was, however, finding himself settling comfortably into the role that he was assuming within their group.

The quiet in the van that followed was not full of hopeless despair as it had been earlier. They weren't the only ones still alive and Maggie was proof of that. Their lot was bad, there was no denying it, but perhaps there was that outside possibility that there were others.

Seizing upon the more open mood of those around her, Emma said, "So, is it just me or does calling those things zombies just seem...I don't know...weird? Maybe a little hokey?"

Jerry asked, "What do you want to call them?"

"I don't know. But, I mean, we don't even know for sure what they are? Do we? Calling them zombies...we might as well be calling them boogie men."

Jerry said sarcastically, "Well calling them mindless, fearless, merciless killing machines is a bit of a mouthful."

Dr. Caldwell suggested, "How about zekes?"

Both Emma and Jerry, incredulous scowls on their faces, asked, "Zekes?"

"Yeah. Zombie. Z. Zeke."

Neil said, "Pretty clever, Doc."

"I can't claim credit for it. Flyers in World War Two in the Pacific called Japanese Zeros 'Zekes'. For a while, Zekes ruled the skies. They killed everything in their paths."

Neil asked, "For a while?"

"Yeah, the American pilots and aviation engineers figured out a way to best them every time. It took some time and some tragedy, but they figured out a way to beat the seemingly invincible. They proved that it could be done."

Dr. Caldwell looked over at Neil, smiled, and said, "They didn't give up. They beat the bastards."

Neil smiled back. "Yeah. I guess anything's possible."

Emma asked, "History Channel?"

Dr. Caldwell replied, "Bingo."

To which she said, "Zeke works for me."

"So, zeke it is," Neil said, ending the discussion. "Thank you Doc. Now where to?"

Dr. Caldwell smiled and to Neil he joked, "Sorry my friend. We're just like Congress. We can only do one thing at a time and it's usually not what really needs attention. We just gave you a name for our foe. Time for our recess."

Neil said, "The park it is."

# CHAPTER 7

Malachi and Maggie were closely following the van in the dusty black Passat. Malachi was finding it easier to stay focused and anchored to the present by staring every now and again at the Jesus statuette on the dashboard. It became his reality beacon and seemed to be working. It was comforting to know where and when he was. It was also much more comfortable to be back on the road again. There was something soothing about the vibrations from the road racing by beneath him. Perhaps, in some preternatural way, he was reminded of gliding around in his mother's womb.

When Maggie began to sing "Jesus Loves Me", he joined in almost immediately, as pleased as a schoolboy at recess. They sang refrain after refrain, each with more gusto than the previous. And when Maggie stopped singing and started to speak, Malachi couldn't stop himself from booming out still more of the song.

"*...this I know. For the Bible tells me so...*"

It took Maggie practically slapping him to get him to stop. Whether she was a God-fearing woman or not, her slapping him sent a sour tone all through his body. She began to speak, but all of his focus was on the dashboard Jesus in front of him and he was unable to follow any of what she was saying. In his mind, he was still singing the song loud and clear. He was hanging on to the present, but his anger was muddying his judgment.

Maggie repeated, irritation surfacing in her voice, "I said are you in or not?"

Having not a clue as to what he was agreeing to, he simply nodded his head.

Maggie smiled at him, the pleasantness returning to her tone, "I knew that I could trust you, Brother Malachi. I could just see the light of the Lord in your eyes. Besides, when it's done, it'll just be better. They'll be happier too. I mean, they'll be home.

"And you and me can go right on down the road spreading His Word and preparing souls for their final journey. Salvation." She winked at him and then launched into *Amazing Grace*.

# CHAPTER 8

They drove west and then south until they got to Raspberry Road. On the corner at the intersection sat a small strip mall which housed several other businesses, including a small traditional ice cream shop called Tastee Freez. In better times, the shop's loyal clientele kept its mostly pubescent workforce hopping, creating delectable frozen treats and better than average greasy spoon food selections.

The treat shop was now dark and deserted, something that Neil couldn't remember having ever seen. He was momentarily reminded of better days and the craving for a chocolate milkshake suddenly hit him.

From behind him, Jerry suggested, "You know, there might be canned food in there. We are running low on supplies. We should probably stock up everywhere we go. There might even be bottled water in there. Probably worth a look."

Dr. Caldwell said half-jokingly and half-accusingly, "You guys are just jonesin' for chocolate milkshakes and are hoping for some still partially frozen ice cream at the bottom of a freezer in there. I can see right through both of you. And I think it sounds like a hell of an idea."

Meghan, who had been looking from Jerry to Neil and now at Dr. Caldwell, asked them all, "Are you guys out of your gourds?"

Dr. Caldwell defended them with, "Actually, Jerry is right. There's a good chance that this place has been free of looters way out here and might just have some goodies inside that we could use. Besides, the toilets might still have water in the reservoir. You could use a flushing toilet again. Remember what that was like?"

*Son of a bitch knows the way to a woman's heart*, Meghan thought to herself. Any of her protests melted away with her innocent and simple observation, "Toilet paper."

They pulled into the parking lot, circling once to look at each of the storefronts in the plaza, all of which still had intact windows. It did appear as if this location was largely untouched by the calamity that had wrecked most of the rest of Anchorage. The two vehicles pulled up alongside one another in front of the ice cream shop.

Maggie rolled down her window and addressed Dr. Caldwell. "What are we doing here? You know, they won't be serving ice cream anymore."

Dr. Caldwell, never taking his eyes off of the darkened windows of the shop in front of him, said, "Yeah. We get that. We're just looking for supplies is all. There might be cans of food and possibly water in there, and we need both." And to no one in particular he asked, "How are we going to get in there?"

# CHAPTER 9

With Jerry back on his roost on top of the van and acting as a lookout, the others assembled in the parking lot and started to discuss their options.

Malachi asked, "Why don't we just smash in a window?"

"We could," Neil said, "but if we could find another way in without making as much noise, I think we would all be better off."

Kim suggested, "Maybe we could just punch a hole through one of the windows big enough to fit one of us through and then that person could open the door."

Dr. Caldwell, peering in the large windows and trying to see any threats lurking inside, said, "That isn't a half bad idea. But who is going to go in?"

Emma said, "It should probably be someone who is smaller so that we can make the smallest hole possible. I guess that means me."

"I'll go."

Everyone turned to the voice of the volunteer. It was Danny. He had been sitting in the van but was now standing in the lot next to Neil. He repeated, "I'll go."

"No," Emma said adamantly. "We don't know what's in there. It's too dangerous. Hell, I don't even want to go in there on my own."

"I'm not afraid. Besides, if I can get in and open those doors fast enough I won't be in there by myself for very long."

Neil was shaking his head but saying nothing.

"C'mon, let me do my part. If I thought I could get hurt in there, do you think I'd want to go? I won't be out of sight one bit. If one of those things is in there, you guys can shoot out the windows and come and get me."

Without thinking or saying a word, Neil walked Danny over to the glass door. He kneeled down with Danny and knocked a small hole in the glass with the butt of his shotgun. The first couple of strikes cracked and shattered the glass, but it stayed in its metal frame. With his third hit, he was able to punch through. The hole was right at ground level, so any falling glass wasn't able to make much of a sound.

Neil looked at Danny. "You crawl through, stand up, and open the door. You don't even take a step away. Do you hear me? You get through and open the door. Nothing else. Okay?"

"Gotcha boss."

Neil smiled, mussed Danny's hair, an action that he had never performed and had never considered doing in his life prior to that moment, and then stood up. He swallowed hard and tried to keep the anxious vertigo at bay and hidden from the others.

Danny was through the small opening in just a few wriggling seconds. Inside, it was dark; darker than it appeared from outside because of the sun-dimming tint on the glass. There was an overwhelming sweetness that filled the air inside the shop. The odor, strong and not entirely pleasant, tickled his nose and throat. He stood slowly, trying not to make a single sound. He was afraid that his thumping heart was reverberating through his chest and drawing unwanted attention to himself from whatever was lurking in the shadows on the other side of the counter.

He leaned into the door handle but nothing happened. He panicked for a moment and was set to crawl back out to the others. Before he was able, he saw what resembled a key on the metal doorframe. He turned it, pressed the handle again, and opened the door, allowing Neil and Dr. Caldwell to enter quickly and for him to start breathing again. The two men stalled immediately, their eyes trying to adjust to the unexpected low light inside. Neil moved Danny behind himself and the doctor. Emma, still outside, then grabbed Danny and pulled him back into the sunshine with the others.

Meghan, with an automatic pistol held in both hands and pointing toward the counter, was the next inside. She looked much more imposing than she felt. The guns afforded a sense of personal security but the reality was that she was anything but competent or even experienced with firearms. Regardless, she stood in the doorway, while Neil and Dr. Caldwell made their way deeper into the seating, which formed an inverted L shape down and around the front counter. Dr. Caldwell stopped just at the angle of the L while Neil continued down and around, disappearing from sight for just a second or two. He reappeared shaking his head and pointed at the counter. Behind it was the unknown.

Emma, now at the front door, was holding it wide open to let in some light. She was brandishing her heavy, shiny revolver in one of her hands as a precaution as well. Holding at bay her frustration with his apparent cowardice, Emma shot a disapproving glance at Malachi, who was standing next to Maggie in the parking lot. He wasn't making even the slightest motion to go into the ice cream shop and help. She only spared a heartbeat for her chagrin and refocused her attention on the task at hand.

Dr. Caldwell, armed with a revolver the size of a cannon, stood at a swinging door leading to the rear of the store behind the counter. It was darker on the other side and much of it was out of view. There was only so much light coming in through the open front door and that was restricted further by the counter and tall kitchen equipment.

Neil raised the shotgun to his shoulder as the doctor went through. They were both holding their breath and walking at a snail's pace. Like two scared deer at a watering hole frequented by predators, their eyes darted back and forth. Soon both of them were through the door. Meghan now entered the shop and stood at the counter, looking as if she was ready to rob the joint.

Danny, largely unattended and free to move about, joined Emma at the door. He looked at the menu board and felt his stomach begin to churn with promises of cheeseburgers, chili cheese dogs, French fries, sodas, and ice cream delights. He looked back at Jules who was still sitting with her legs dangling from the open side door of the minivan. He thought to himself that she looked tired and something else, though he couldn't quite figure out what else it was. Maybe she was just hungry but he found himself getting worried about her. He had promised Mr. Houser that he would look out for her and he took his promises seriously. He stepped away from the teasing menu board and sat next to her.

She said to him quietly so as not to draw attention to them, "I miss my mommy. Do you think she's really in heaven with Grandpa?" She never looked up from her fingers while she spoke.

Danny, looking at her thin fingers with dirty nails, said reassuringly, "Yeah. She was always nice to everyone. She shared with everyone. I think she's up there."

"I still miss her."

"Yeah, Jules. I know."

"What about Alec? What do you think happened to him?"

Danny wasn't sure about that. Alec was Jules' older brother who had stayed behind at the cabin down in Seward when the rest of the family took Martin to the hospital in Anchorage. Danny hadn't really thought about Alec since leaving Seward. As far away as Seward was from Anchorage, there was a good chance that he was still okay. Of course, the "caveman" that the children had disturbed in the melting glacier who was responsible for Martin's injury and the start of all of this was still down there. Maybe Alec had found his way into town when his family didn't return right away. Maybe he was still at the cabin and getting by on the supplies that had been left with him. Danny wasn't entirely sure.

All of that quickly ran through his head, but he said aloud to Jules, "Alec is tough and smart. I'm sure that he is just fine. We'll probably see him soon. As soon as we can find a way out of Anchorage, I'll bet the two of you will get back together."

Jules seemed to roll this around in her head for a second or two before saying, "I'm glad you're here, Danny."

"I'm glad you're here too, Jules. Everything is going to be okay."

"Will it? Really?"

Danny wasn't sure. He wasn't sure of much anymore. In fact, the only certainties that came to him were his hunger, his weariness, and his fear that they would run into more zombies...zekes. For a moment, though, he wasn't forced to answer as the shouting coming from inside the ice cream shop distracted all of them.

# CHAPTER 10

While the others waited outside or in the lobby of the shop, Dr. Caldwell moved slowly through the cooking and preparation stations in the back. He was careful not to disturb anything for fear of making a noise that could compromise their search. Neil was moving just a few feet behind the doctor. He too was moving very gingerly between the stainless steel appliances and hanging kitchen utensils. Nothing seemed to be out of place, but that was no reason for complacency.

At first glance, all seemed to be in order and nothing amiss. Then the two of them spotted an opened box lying on the floor, several empty plastic snack-sized packages of chips scattered here and there on the floor. There were also some empty water bottles kicked under a washbasin.

Neil noticed some muddy footprints coming in through what was more than likely a back freight door. The prints were not new, but they had likely been left after the most recent mopping of the tiled floor. He was fairly certain there hadn't been much mopping going on since that apocalyptic morning a few weeks back. It was apparent to him that someone had come in recently and they were careful to avoid giving away their presence. Toward the back of the kitchen, there was a large stainless steel door to what was quite obviously a walk-in freezer or cooler of some sort.

Dr. Caldwell pointed toward it without saying a word. The shotgun had never left Neil's shoulder, but now he redoubled his grip and found himself holding his breath again. The doctor motioned to Neil to step back and keep his eyes and the shotgun pointed toward the door. He then went to the heavy handle and hesitated. He took in two deep breaths, holding the second, and then pulled the lever opening the door.

There on the floor of the cooler was a man and woman. There were more of the empty chip bags and water bottles as well as other partially eaten foodstuffs. Neither of the people moved and in the darkness, neither Neil nor Dr. Caldwell could tell if either of them were breathing. They were both relatively sure that zombies didn't sleep but both were as frozen in their steps as the banana splits and chocolate sundaes featured in pictures on the walls all around them.

And then the woman on the floor opened her eyes, slowly, blinking them rapidly trying to clear her fuzzy, sleep riddled vision. Her scream startled her companion awake, who leapt to his feet and hoisted a wooden baseball bat onto his shoulders like he was waiting for the next pitch to cross the plate.

Captured in a rigid tableau, they all just held their positions while the woman, still on the floor, continued to utter her single, long syllable shriek. When she had spent all of the air in her lungs and quiet had momentarily returned, Dr. Caldwell emerged from the other side of the open freezer door and lowered Neil's gun with his hand.

There was a pause before anyone moved or said anything. The man and woman, now on her feet, stood their ground, not entirely sure what the gun toting men standing in front of them wanted.

Finally, Neil said, "Do you want to come outside where there's a little more light so we can talk?"

The woman, a thin, hungry looking blonde woman walked around her companion slowly and approached Neil. "Are you part of a rescue team? Is it over? Is everything safe again?"

Dr. Caldwell extended his hand and said, "Maybe we should go outside to talk."

The other man shook his head. "I'm not going anywhere until we know what you guys want."

"Give it a rest, Art. They've got guns. Do you think they wouldn't have already used them if they had anything like that in mind?"

Neil asked, "Like what?"

The woman now turned to Neil. "It's amazing how awful some people can be in times of tragedy. Remember all the ugly things that you heard about people doing to one another during the hurricane and flooding down in New Orleans a few years back? Let's just say that I believe most of that now."

She walked out of the freezer and said, "He's Art. Well, not really, that's just his name. I'm Claire."

# CHAPTER 11

Once outside, questions from every angle abounded, circling the group of people like inquisitive puppies seeking attention. Names, origins, updates, information. Questions flew before answers could be formed. Finally, Dr. Caldwell held up his hands and suggested, "Okay, introductions are important and sharing stories...experiences definitely have value if we have any chance at all of piecing together a plan to live through this, and no Claire, we are not a rescue party. We can get to all of that in a bit, but for right now we should really focus on why we came here."

With a smile Claire asked, "Frosty chocolate milkshakes?"

Neil looked at Jerry and smiled. Dr. Caldwell astonished, asked, "What in the hell is everyone's obsessions with chocolate milkshakes?"

"What's not to love about a good milkshake?" Emma said with a smile. "I personally prefer mine with a little Bailey's. Mmmmm."

With a sense of amused admonition in his voice, the doctor said, "Well stop it all of you. You're making me crave it too and I was never much of one to like ice cream."

Of course the good doctor was right. They found cans of chili, jars of unopened fruit topping in a rainbow of varieties, some bottled water and canned sodas. There were some other odds and ends, like toilet paper, that individuals sought out, but within less than an hour they had more or less cleaned the place out of easily portable foodstuffs. They piled as much as they could into and onto the van. And with the little bit that they couldn't take, they had a very starchy ad hoc roadside feast.

With a mouth full of strawberry topping and bread, Emma asked, "So Claire...where'd you guys come from? How long you been holed up in there?"

Claire wiped a chocolate smear that was just barely more visible on her cheek than the smears of dirt and soot that lined her skin. She was young and probably pretty, though the last several weeks of terror and running and starving had taken toll on her looks. Emma knew that the dark under her eyes wasn't merely dirt. There was a shallowness to her expression that was typically accompanied with dark crescents. She was exhausted. She had scratches, only partially healed and seemingly infected, on her chin and her bottom lip was split. Emma thought to herself that, under more normal circumstances, if she were to run into this girl on the street she would just assume that she was an addict with too much time between fixes.

# CHAPTER 12

The slight satisfaction in Claire's otherwise flat affect faded. The recent past was a blur of terror and loss. No one had asked her what had happened to her on the first morning and she hadn't bothered to ask any of the survivors she had encountered. And at this point, she wasn't quite sure if she would be able to remember most of it. She had been trying so hard to let all of it go, like a nightmare, which it most certainly had become, plaguing her constantly every time she closed her eyes.

"I was going to the UAA Consortium Library to..." She stopped, shook her head, and chuckled for a moment. "It's like I'm still talking to my folks or some of my disapproving friends. I can't believe that I'm still doing it. Even now, after all that has happened, and to complete strangers. Good God. The truth is, I was going over to my boyfriend Michael's house. He lived in APU housing over on the far east side of the campus. I told my mom before I left that the library was opening early and I wanted to get in before it started to get busy. I don't know if she bought it or not but she didn't give me any shit for it. So I left..." She began to cry. "I don't think I even said goodbye to her. Ya know, you leave the house a million times and every one of those could be the last but we take those moments for granted and then it's too late. I didn't even say goodbye." She was shaking her head back and forth, chastising herself.

Emma, hoping to draw her away from that painful place, asked, "So you were headed toward the campus...and that's where it all began. What happened?"

"Christ! What didn't happen? First the radio started talking about some problems at Providence and then the radio just went dead. And then traffic stopped. I've never seen that many cars in Anchorage except for maybe when they shoot the fireworks off on the Fourth and for Fur Rondy. It just felt like every car in the city was right there. There wasn't no going forward or back. We were all just hemmed in nice and tight.

## Sean Schubert

"I had my stereo on loud, so I didn't hear the screams that got others out of their cars. I saw those folks all get out though and then they all started to run. I couldn't see anything in front of us so I waited for a few seconds and then I saw more people running so I guess I just figured that it was a good time to get going myself. I grabbed my gym bag and ran away as fast as I could. It was then that I could hear the screaming behind me. I didn't dare turn around though. It just felt too much like one of those dreams where the bad guy is chasing you and he's just behind you with his ghoulish hand reaching out to you. You're keeping just out of reach and if you slow even a little, you just know that he'll get you. You know the dream?

"Anyway, me and this group of people were just running. Some folks started to slow down. They were all running out of breath. I'm in pretty good shape, but I wasn't expecting to be doin' no runnin' that early in the morning. So, pretty soon I was one of only five who were still going. It was me, another lady named Joan, and three guys. One of the guys had a big dog named Max with him. He was a great dog. We ran to the Carrs at Aurora Village, there at Northern Lights and Minnesota. We got there and the place was crazy. There were people running in and then running out with the craziest things in their arms. One guy was carrying a pile of cakes. He must've had at least five cakes. He just ran out, threw the cakes in his car, and drove off.

"Someone said that people were being directed to schools. Well, Romig Middle School was right there in front of us and down the road a bit was another elementary school, and it just seemed like a better idea to head further away from where we had started, so we hitched a ride with a fella driving a truck and he dropped us off at the elementary school.

"It was better there. People were still scared, but they weren't all panicked. The cafeteria staff brought out coffee and some snacks, and people were sitting around in the multipurpose room or the library. I chose the library, figuring that it would probably be carpeted. There were almost as many rumors and ideas as there were people at the school: a terrorist attack, an accident with some new weapon system out on Elmendorf, a new kind of rabies. And even the dead coming back to life, believe it or not. It all sounded pretty crazy to me. Still does, I guess.

"After maybe a couple of hours, I was out front smoking. One of the three cops there said that technically I was breaking the law, but he wasn't in the mood to enforce it at the moment. I promised that when everything settled down that I'd never smoke on school grounds again if he'd just let me off with a warning and to let me finish my smoke first too. He was cute, ya know, so it was nice talking with him. I'm sure that my mom would have approved of him. If he had tattoos anywhere, you at least didn't see them at first glance...not like Michael. We were just talking and then we heard this sound coming from down the road. I don't know how to describe it really. I mean, it kind of sounded like a...like a..."

"Freight train?" interrupted Jerry.

She pointed at him and continued, "Exactly. Just a few minutes later...well, you know. They showed up. The three cops, even the cutie that I was talking to, tried their best. They shot until they couldn't shoot anymore. I saw four or five of those things take down each of the cops. It was the most awful thing that I've ever seen. Luckily, Joan was there too and she grabbed my arm and pulled me away. I vaguely remember running to the back of the school with a bunch of other people. We went through an emergency door and then we were just running again. Max was with us, so I knew that his owner was there, but I didn't recognize any of the others with us. It was like a replay of earlier. Pretty soon our herd became a clan, which became a group. This time we ended up in a hotel down on Spenard. Those things followed us but we put enough distance between us and them to be able to get into the hotel and get onto the second floor without them seeing us. I guess there were enough other folks to be chasing that they didn't really notice that another had replaced our group.

"We hung there for a few days. There were eleven of us that got to the hotel, but there was already a small crowd of people hiding upstairs. We huddled together in rooms and waited. There was a little food in a couple of vending machines that we all shared as best as we could. We all hoped that the nightmare would pass as quickly as it had begun. Boy, were we in for a surprise. Early one morning, we all woke up to the sound of engines outside. We heard cars. Or, more to the point, trucks. These three big trucks were barreling down Spenard. I should have known better though. The trucks all had dealer tags and big signs still hanging on them. And they were all too shiny to have seen the kind of action that survivors would have seen. One of the men in the group, a high school teacher, went out front and flagged them down. As soon as I saw them, I knew that they were no good. They were whooping and hollering, probably not a sober one amongst them. I watched that man...that good, kind man who skimped on food to make sure that everyone else had enough to eat. He stood there and tried to talk to them. I saw him shaking his head once and then again. He looked over his shoulder up at us and I could see the look in his eye. We'd made a mistake.

"They shot him while he was still looking over at us. He fell down holding his right leg. While he was there on his back...defenseless... they shot him again. This time in his left leg. One of them, what I guess was their leader, asked the teacher something. The teacher shook his head again. I couldn't really hear him, but I could tell that the teacher was crying. And if I was to guess, he wasn't crying because of the pain in his leg. He was crying because he couldn't believe that people could be so ugly. And then that son of a bitch pushed that poor, good man over with his toe and stood over him for a second or two. Must've made him feel like a big man. Coward just stepped over him and had one of his toadies finish the job. I wasn't at the window anymore to see where the bullets hit. Joan and I were running again. I hadn't run that much in...well, ever. Joan was older than me by a few years but I think she was in a helluva lot better shape than me. We were a good team on the run together.

"We had to go through the main lobby to get to any of the first floor exits and those guys were already coming in through the front doors. It was as chaotic as when those monsters got into the school. Only this time, our attackers were a little more discerning. They were only going after the women. Any man they happened to grab or who happened to get in the way was stabbed or shot or beaten. I never knew that a gun could be that loud or echo in your ears for that long. It was terrible.

"We were starting to head down a hall...we were almost there, when one of them got a hold of Joan's hair. She had this pretty red hair, pulled back into a long braid. He yanked hard, hard enough snap her backward and knock her off her feet. She fell with a thud and didn't move. When I looked down at her, I saw a couple of the other girls already on the floor with those guys crawling all over them. They were screaming and begging for help but I felt helpless to do anything. Eric, Max's owner, pulled me along. He kept saying that we had to get away. Just concentrate on getting away.

"Well, the joke was on the rednecks. I guess it was the screaming or the gunshots, hell, it doesn't really matter what was responsible. Those things...those monsters started to arrive from both sides of the street. They just started to wade into the mayhem that was still erupting in the hotel lobby. I felt horrible for those girls who were on the floor. First to be brutalized and then to be butchered...it was too much for me to even think about. Who knows? Maybe those bastards had already killed the girls. I didn't hear any truck engines getting away, so I'm hoping that the cocksuckers got theirs in the end.

"So, we were back down to five of us...actually six if you included Max. We ran away from the main road and back into a neighborhood. We just wanted to get away and find somewhere safe to rest. We didn't see any more of those things for a couple of days but we did see some people back amongst the houses. Mostly we saw faces peeking over cedar privacy fences or folks scurrying like scared rats from place to place. I guess we must have looked like rats ourselves. We did finally get ourselves into a house to hide for a bit. There was still some food in the pantry too, so we all got a bite to eat other than junk food. I don't think Chef Boyardee ever tasted so good.

"Locking the front door was about as far as we went in securing the house. I know that it was a mistake now, but we didn't know what was happening yet. There wasn't any cell service, no power, no nothing. We only knew that things just seemed to keep going from bad to worse every time we turned around.

"We had only been in the house for a couple of days...I think. I've gotta be honest here. I've lost any sense of time without my daily and weekly schedules. I think we were only there for a couple of days but, hell, we could've been there for a week for all I know. I know that I spent most of the first day sleeping and then eating and then sleeping again. I use the term "sleeping" very loosely. I think I spent as much time staring at the ceiling as actually sleeping. Every time I closed my eyes I either saw Joan with that filthy, greasy piece of shit on top of her or that poor young cop at the school as his head was gnawed from his shoulders. When I did sleep, it was because my eyes just refused to stay open any longer. I'd like to say that I felt rested after I got back up, but the truth was far from that."

"Art was there, and me, Eric, another guy named Vic, and an older woman named Nancy. It was in the middle of the afternoon when we heard this horrible moaning outside. There were three of those things in the road outside. I guess Vic had had enough so he ran out with a baseball bat to...I guess take them on. He did alright too. He hit the first one on the side of the head and the thing just fell down. It didn't get back up either. It just crumpled down and was done. The next one he hit in the chest and that one fell too. He started to square off with the last one but they were too close to one another for him to swing the bat. He jabbed at it with the end of the bat to put a little space between the two of them. He had just about gotten enough room when the one that he'd hit in the chest grabbed his leg and tripped him up. Vic fell over backward but kept fighting. From his back, he hit the one lying next to him with the bat again, but the thing just rolled over on top of him. The other one grabbed one of his kicking feet and started to chew on his ankle. What none of us could see was that there were some more of those things coming up the road and as Vic screamed louder and those things moaned deeper, the ones coming started to move faster. They weren't necessarily running, but they were moving at a good trot. And now they knew where we were hiding. We ran into the backyard but there was another one of those things out there. It grabbed Eric and was trying to get a good angle to bite Eric's neck or shoulder. Max wasn't having any of it. He jumped onto the thing's back and started to bite and claw at the thing. That was enough for Eric to break free. By then, Art had picked up a shovel and hit the thing in the head with the blade. He just split the thing's head in half.

"Eric was okay and we were just about to make a run for it when Max started to yelp. He cried and moaned like I'd never heard a dog do before. It was terrible. The dog retreated into the corner of the yard and started to vomit. It looked like it was mainly blood that was coming up but I didn't really get close enough to check. I was already following Art and Nancy over the fence. Eric was still with him though. He tried to soothe the dog but poor Max was beyond consolable. And then he just got quiet. He was lying on his belly with his snout buried under him. Eric was rubbing Max's shoulders, and that's when Max turned on him. Max let out this deep growl and snapped at Eric. He moved away from the dog, and tried to talk to him. He was speaking as softly and as tenderly as he could, but Max continued to growl. The dog shook his head like he was trying to lose a ringing in his ear or something, but he didn't make any move to attack. Eric just kept talking and was still talking when Max got real quiet and then lunged at him. Eric was caught completely off guard. The dog tried to bite Eric's face but Eric fought him off, but Max was able to latch onto his wrist. He tore into him, using his teeth like a saw. Eric's flesh was just flayed open, and then Max stopped and backed away. He shook his head again. I think he was trying to fight it, ya know? Max started to whimper again as he struggled. Eric didn't wait around though. He got himself over the fence and fell onto the ground. He was already getting dizzy from the blood loss.

"Max shook all over and ran over to the fence. It was Max again. You could just see it in his eyes and just like that, he changed again and started to bark. He started to throw himself into the fence. I think it affects animals differently than it does humans. I didn't know it then, but now I understand that it's some kind of virus or an infection or something that's been spreading all of this. After seeing Eric, I guess it just kind of made sense to me that there was some kind of virus that killed the people and then something happened that brought them back. Only, it wasn't *them* that got brought back. Because it wasn't Eric that stood back up in the next house we found to stop in.

"We got to another place and hid upstairs. We tried to take care of Eric, but he just wouldn't stop bleeding. He barely had any color in his face and we were nearly carrying him by the time we got in. He was drenched in cold sweat but he didn't have a fever. It was creepy. We laid him on a couch upstairs and tried to make him comfortable. There were some crackers in the kitchen and some odds and ends, so we grabbed a bite while he rested. Nancy grabbed a handful of cookies from a package and went back into the living room. She stood there for a second without saying anything. She was just looking down at Eric. I saw her whole expression change all at once. She just said, 'Eric's gone,' and she started to cry. She barely knew him, but she was crying for him like it was her son or something.

"When Eric leapt back to his feet, she jumped back. Hell, we all jumped back. She called his name, but then he pounced on her like she was cornered prey. I guess that's kind of what she was, really. She let out a couple of screams, the second one just turned into a hollow, wet noise that sounded like she was swallowing her own voice. I think it's the worst thing I've ever heard. And on top of that to hear Eric chewing hungrily. He was kind of grunting with each bite.

"Art and I didn't stick around to be second courses. We ran out the back door and through the yard. We ran the rest of the day and most of that night. I don't know about Art, but I just wanted to get as far away from Eric and Nancy and Vic and Max as my legs would take me. I'm pretty certain that I saw more people here and there, but not a one did the slightest thing to help. It bothers me now, but right then I didn't really concentrate too much on it. I guess those folks were just too afraid to do anything and I can't really fault them for that. If I was somewhere that I thought I was safe and thought that maybe help would be coming, I don't know for sure what I'd do either.

"We ended up here a couple of days ago. It seemed safe and no one seemed to be around. It felt a little like being on Mars or something. Like it was some kind of ancient civilization; one whose inhabitants had long since left."

She paused to fish some more chocolate out of the jar she was holding. "Is this the end? I mean, I guess what I'm asking is, is this happening everywhere or just here? Does anyone know how it all started?"

Neil shook his head, "No. I don't think this is happening anywhere else. At least not yet. And I've been told that it started with a small boy and a small bite that appears to have awakened something that's been asleep a long time and probably should have just stayed that way." He looked over at Jules and Danny who were barely listening. They knew the story and had heard it all before.

"What about you, Art?" Kim asked. "What's your story?"

Art scarcely looked up at her when he said, "The beginning is a little different but it's the same ending. What does it matter anyway? All that does matter is that we're standing here in a parking lot when we should probably all be dead already. What does it matter where I started running from? I mean really, what difference does any of it make anymore? I was the fucking king of Siam."

He threw his mostly empty jar of ice cream topping out across Raspberry Road. He walked over to the far side of the parking lot and stood there. It was obvious that he was crying by his body language. Everyone just watched him, an uncomfortable silence gliding amongst them as they stood motionless.

# CHAPTER 13

Claire asked from the back seat, "Where are we headin'?"

Dr. Caldwell answered without taking his eyes off of the road in front of them and the houses, streets, and trees on his side, "We're going to see about camping out at Kincaid tonight. With as little as we've seen on this side of the city and especially in this little corner, it seems safe over this way. We're goin' out to the Chalet looking out over the Inlet."

She nodded. "Yeah, I know that place. I went to a wedding out there once. It was beautiful but a little windy. Do you think it'll be safe?"

Dr. Caldwell turned around this time and said, "Nowhere's safe anymore. You've got to understand that or you won't make it through this. You've always got to be on your guard." To everyone in the van he said, "We all have to be. And we have to watch out for one another."

His cold seriousness chilled Claire's warm memories. She resented him chasing away the single best memory and thought that she'd had in weeks. The wedding and raucous reception memories were replaced by the stark and unpleasant realities that she and everyone else had faced over the past few weeks. Of course the doctor was right, but still...why did he have to bring her down again?

They drove by the Kulis Air National Guard Base entrance. On the other side of the chain-link fence and wide open gate, the deceptive calm stretched out of view. Neil looked over at Dr. Caldwell as they passed but the doctor, sensing Neil's hopeful glance and the slowing of the vehicle, shook his head and pointed to the parked vintage cargo plane further down the fence line. Its sides were shredded from people kicking through them. It appeared as if some people had taken refuge inside, only to be discovered and then trapped. The victims kicked their way through the thin sides of the aircraft and were most likely overwhelmed as they emerged. There were clothes strewn all around and other evidence of a horrible struggle around the stationary craft that suggested whoever had been there was there no more.

They passed a small stone marker announcing their entrance into the park. The straight road gave way suddenly to sharp turns cutting in amongst the trees, winding its way back to a clearing with a large parking lot and a two-story structure overlooking the lazy high tide of the Cook Inlet. It was normally a great view and the clear day, again under more normal circumstances, would have had them all excited for such a treasure of the late summer-early autumn weather. Next to the chalet, a fairly abrupt slope led down and away into a large open field.

Neil said, "I guess we're here. Let's see if we can get ourselves into the chalet. It'll probably be warmer in there and I think we can bring one of those trash cans upstairs to light a fire on the balcony."

"And burn what?" Emma snapped, her voice irritated.

Neil said without a pause, as if he was accustomed to the attitude, "Wood. What else?"

Emma looked away toward the tree line, which sat a fair distance from the chalet and asked, this time as much as a bark as actual speech, "You expectin' one of us to gather wood from over there? There's no knowing what's out there, is there? We don't know what's out here at all."

She was right. He was assuming gathering wood or any other once mundane task continued to be so. He couldn't allow complacency to cloud his judgment. Was he willing to go in there to retrieve wood? There was no telling what dangers were waiting behind the trees. His casual assumptions could have cost a life.

He felt that familiar chill slither down the length of his spine and curl under, tickling his testicles into retracting for safety. They could just get inside and hope the closed windows and doors would be enough to keep them relatively warm through the night. It wouldn't be snug, but they could probably make do. He tried to imagine the dark stillness of the woods but was stung with the wretched memory of his closest encounter with one of the zekes. It had held him close enough for Neil to be able to smell the stench of death clinging to its clothes and lurking on its wet, rotten breath. In the dense woods, it was unlikely Jerry would be able to deliver the same quality shot from his hunting rifle as he had on that occasion. Jerry's precision was all that saved Neil that day not long ago. He physically shook as the next wave of chills coiled itself around his spine. How could he expect anyone to do what he himself was too terrified to do?

He was about to say as much when Dr. Caldwell said, "I can go. Malachi, you're a hunter right? Familiar with the woods? How about lending a hand? Maggie, you've got room in your backseat. Can you bring your car a little closer so we can load it up? It'd make it so that we could bring enough wood to last us through the night. It's going to be bad enough, no point in freezing if we don't have to. You in?"

Malachi looked at Maggie and both nodded hesitantly.

Dr. Caldwell smiled and said as soothingly as his bedside manners training would allow, "Look, Maggie, you don't even have to get out of the car. You just wait inside your locked car and keep the engine running if you'd like. When we come out, unlock the back door so that we can pile the wood in. Malachi and I will keep an eye out for one another while we're out of sight. It'll only be a few minutes. Believe me, I don't want to be in there any longer than we need. It'll be okay. Trust me."

Jerry was reminded of all the jokes in which politicians, attorneys, or even used car salesmen used that phrase. Trust me. He was able to stifle his chuckle, but decided to step away just to be safe. He and his hunting rifle found their way into the now opened doors of the chalet. He went out onto the second floor balcony, looking out over the sloped open field immediately to the north of the building. With the rifle raised to his shoulder, he peered through his hunter's scope. He was amazed at the clarity of the images as they appeared to him through the magnifying lenses. As opposed to an indistinguishable line of trees, he was able to pick out specific trees and branches. He could read Maggie's license plate as clearly as if he was standing next to the car: HLYRLR.

And then it hit him. "Holy roller. Jesus, this lady is a freak."

He watched the three of them drive down the path leading away from the parking lot. At the base of the winding driveway, they stopped abruptly. He didn't much like watching the good doctor disappear into the woods, but he had to admit that having some distance between Maggie, Malachi and himself made him much more comfortable. He'd seen and heard Malachi's disconnect and agreed with Neil that Maggie was hiding something. She'd avoided directly answering any questions and seemed to only be telling partial stories that served her own ends. What she had said, though, was enough for him to be wary of her both coming and going.

# CHAPTER 14

Dr. Caldwell had always thought of the woods as a quiet place. On that afternoon, it was as silent and as peaceful as a crypt. The forest was made up of narrow, white barked birch trees with equally thin limbs and branches still holding tight fisted to the small leaves starting to show all of their colorful autumn personality. Mixed in amongst these trees were their taller, fuller cousins, wearing thick conical coats of fragrant green needles. A few birds here and there chortled lightly, but there were no songs; only avian warnings shared well above the two men's heads. The quiet was at once menacing and comforting.

The two men walked side-by-side, their feet crunching an uncomfortably loud marching tune in the drying foliage. They had no tools to cut anything down, so they were relying on whatever scraps the forest floor had to offer. They walked solidly for several minutes before Dr. Caldwell finally said, "Okay, that's far enough. Let's find us some wood and get the hell outta here. Maggie's likely to get spooked and leave us in a lurch out here if we're not careful."

"She wouldn't leave us," Malachi said defensively. "Maggie's no coward."

"And she's no fool either. If she gets to thinkin' that we ran into trouble, she could just think it wiser to go back to the chalet or just hightail it outta here altogether. It's really got nothing to do with being brave or cowardly. It's a survival response. The whole fight or flight mentality kicking in, and sometimes we can't control it."

Malachi didn't know if he agreed with the doctor, but he appreciated that the man was speaking to him like he was an equal. It was the first show of respect he'd seen from anyone in a long time. It felt nice and made him feel like he was important.

He watched the doctor gather handfuls of sticks into his arms clumsily until, trying to pick up the last small branch he could reach, the doctor dropped most of what he was carrying. Malachi smiled for a moment and felt really good.

He went over to the doctor and motioned for him to stop. Malachi sifted through the collections of branches and dried twigs until he found a long, thin, and still partially green branch that was slightly longer than all the rest and set it aside. He then piled most of what the doctor had collected atop the lone twig but turned them so as to be perpendicular to it, forming a close approximation of a plus sign. "Now watch," he said. He found both ends of the twig under the rest and pulled these ends together until he could fashion them into a knot. He was left with a good-looking bundle of wood that made it easier to carry larger amounts of fuel for the fire.

They worked out a system in which the doctor gathered the wood while Malachi bundled it. They only spent a few minutes, but they were able to gather four very large armfuls of wood. With the wood bundles clutched under each of their arms, the two men ran out of the woods toward Maggie's car.

At first Maggie was worried. They looked like they were running so fast. Was something following them? She started the car with a single thought suddenly coming to her. *Is this the moment?*

Then she realized that there wasn't anything on their trail and that they were just excited about their haul of wood. She unlocked the door as they approached and they tossed in the wood, turned and ran back toward the woods.

They quickly got back into the routine. Dr. Caldwell tried to find better-sized pieces of wood this time, but even the most mature trees were still only a scant few inches in diameter. The pickings were slim, literally. He was walking over with one of several armloads of wood when Malachi suddenly shot up and stood stock-still. Dr. Caldwell followed the other man's lead and froze in mid-stride, his eyes widening when he realized why Malachi had stopped. He had heard something. Maybe he was seeing something too.

Dr. Caldwell was finding it difficult to control his breathing, especially when he heard a not too distant crunch. He hadn't moved and he was pretty certain that Malachi hadn't either. There was something else out here with them. His mouth was suddenly a desert experiencing a drought. He couldn't swallow, which made his breathing even more desperate and loud.

Malachi reached to his holster and drew his pistol. The doctor was still too stunned to move. He prayed to himself, *please let Malachi shoot straight*.

There was another crunch, this one even closer, then there were several more. Dr. Caldwell felt nauseous, a horrible burning rising in the back of his throat.

When Malachi lowered his weapon into a firing stance, Dr. Caldwell was ready to break into a sprint if only he could remove the concrete blocks that seemed to be affixed to both of his feet. He wanted to move, but he just couldn't. He couldn't even drop the sticks that were lying across both of his outstretched arms.

When the moose appeared from behind one of the robust fir trees and sauntered past them, both men were silent at first. It was Dr. Caldwell who laughed first but Malachi was quick to follow. Dr. Caldwell dropped his load of wood. "I think this is about enough, don't you? If it doesn't last through the night, well so be it. I've had about enough of the woods for one afternoon. How about you?"

Malachi, putting his pistol back in its holster, nodded and, still laughing, said, "I just about peed my pants. Damned moose probably knew what he was up to. Just messing with us. But yeah, let me get these ready to move and we can get outta here."

Back up at the chalet just a few minutes later, Malachi's description of the doctor's face and his own intense fear of the moose solicited roaring laughter. The mood for the rest of the afternoon was light and pleasant. Everyone's bellies were full and the sun was warm. Without the terror that still lurked in the city waiting to pounce, it would have been a very nice day for all of them; a teasing reminder of how things had been…before. It was a relief for all of them to momentarily forget the sorrow and the loss that had gripped all of their lives so tightly these past few weeks.

As night descended and the temperature dropped with the setting of the sun, the bundles of wood that Malachi and Dr. Caldwell had collected were combined with pieces of wooden furniture found throughout the chalet to make a pair of warm fires around which they all gathered. To most of them, it wasn't much different than camping. They talked about mundane memories and even shared jokes with one another, trying to keep the laughter flowing whenever possible.

# CHAPTER 15

It was very late—or very early, depending upon one's perspective—when Jerry woke Neil. Jerry had agreed to work the latest watch shift and Claire had elected to keep him company. They were standing next to the lone metal trashcan that still had a fire burning in it when Claire looked at Jerry and asked, "Can you hear that?"

Jerry suddenly realized that he could, but it was that same sound that he felt as much in his chest as he did in his ears. They weren't alone. He squinted and struggled to pierce the night, but the darkness was impenetrable.

Jerry whispered, "They're out there but I can't see a thing."

"Do you really think it's them?" Claire asked.

"Yeah, it's them. Either they're not that close yet or there're only a handful out there."

"You some kind of a pro or something? You've lived through an apocalypse before have you?"

"No. But I'd guess you to be about what...nineteen?"

"Exactly nineteen. Is it that obvious? And what the hell does that have to do with anything?"

"We've got a working theory that their moans, when heard in small numbers, vibrate at a frequency that affects ears in different ways depending upon the age of the listener. You've got young ears so you can hear it. Me too, but I bet most of the others can't. Not yet anyway."

She looked at him quizzically, doubtfully. She was set to ask him about his theory when Danny appeared and asked, "They're here aren't they?" He was massaging his chest and making a face like he was suffering a very bad case of heartburn.

Jerry said, "Good timing, kid."

"What?"

"Never mind. Yeah, I think you're right. I was trying to figure out how many and how far off they were. Can you go get Neil?"

Neil was outside in an instant, still wiping sleep from his eyes. Meghan, of course, was fast on his heels. "What's up? Kid says we might have some zekes out there."

"Yeah, they're out there."

"How many do you think?"

Danny answered this time, "There's just a couple out there and I think they're still out on the road but they're getting closer."

Jerry added, "If we wait too long, like, let's say, until dawn, they're going to draw more of them to us."

Meghan, just catching up to the conversation, asked, "What are we talking about here?"

Neil said, "Jerry's right. We gotta deal with them now. No fucking around and nothing fancy. They're not clever. They'll just come right at us if we bait them a little."

Danny suggested, "We could use the car headlights. It might even blind them a bit. Slow 'em down maybe."

Jerry and Neil nodded, congratulating Danny on a good idea. It was definitely time to get everyone up and moving, just in case. This was going to take everyone's help.

A moment or two later, the entire group was awake and gathering themselves. To Claire, Art, and Maggie, it appeared as if this was a well-rehearsed activity. Of course the truth was far from it. If nervous tension and fear could be tapped as energy sources, there was enough in the room to light up most of Anchorage. They were well armed but they were all amateurs in these matters. Dr. Caldwell and Malachi were the only ones in the group who had actually received weapons training, so all the guns in the world didn't give any of them any special edge when it came to using them. Neil grabbed his shotgun and put on the dark blue jacket with the deep pockets filled with shells. He was also carrying a forty-five caliber semi-automatic pistol. Dr. Caldwell was similarly armed, as was Malachi. Jerry toted his hunting rifle and a smaller caliber revolver that he tucked into his belt.

It was decided that Meghan would drive the minivan and Maggie would drive her own car. Meghan was carrying her own sidearm while Maggie declined to carry any firearms herself. The two vehicles were parked on the opposite side of the chalet, away from the approaching undead. They didn't think there were any of the things on that side of the building, but they all emerged from the back door at the ready. The two vehicles were started and moved slowly around to the front of the chalet with the shooters, Malachi, Dr. Caldwell, Jerry and Neil walking slowly between them.

The children were escorted onto the balcony and told to sit on the folding chairs set next to the burn barrel. Once out there, Danny said to his chaperone, Kim, "They're getting closer."

"Jesus kid, that's creepy. But I think you're right. I can hear them now too."

Emma, Claire, and Art, also armed with pistols, were inside the chalet, but downstairs by the front door. When they had first arrived earlier the previous afternoon, they all decided to bar the all glass front doors with a rolling rack of folding chairs and tables. It was heavy, and when locked into place, very difficult to move. They hoped that if the things were to find them and make it up to the chalet, that the heavy rack would help to secure the front doors long enough to allow them to escape.

Art said to the two women, "Maybe we should just make a run for it. What happens if there are too many of them out there? Who the hell put Neil in charge anyway? What makes this guy qualified to lead us?"

Emma, not looking away from the unfolding drama in the parking lot, said, "It's dark and dangerous outside. If there are only a handful of them, it probably just makes sense to deal with them so that we can move out of here when it's light enough to see. If there are too many of them out there, Neil will get us outta here. He's good. He's kept us all alive this long. Just be patient."

As she finished her sentence, the first gunshot cracked the quiet with its report.

Out between the two vehicles, Jerry operated the bolt-action slide on the rifle at his shoulder and said, "I got one. Pretty sure I got him through the head. He went down and isn't getting back up."

Meghan had the passenger side window down. Neil leaned in. "I think that's far enough. Now roll up this window and let's wait for them."

Meghan, whose hands were quivering, nodded and swallowed hard. She fumbled with the window control a few seconds before figuring out how to raise it. She started to look to her left now to make sure that none of the things were trying to swing up and around them. It was dark, but she was able to see a little further with the help of the van's high beams, despite being pointed in a different direction. The bright setting of the headlights cast enough of a cone of light so as to illuminate the space to either side of them.

Maggie's driver side window was already up. She saw Meghan come to a stop and followed her lead.

Neil asked Jerry, "Can you tell how many are out there yet?"

Looking through the scope, Jerry said, "I can see at least five and maybe more, but I think that's about it. I think we're lucking out right now. We can take these few."

Dr. Caldwell asked, "And then what? We know that these gunshots are going to attract attention from more of them. How much time will we have until more of those things show up?"

Jerry fired his rifle again. "Damn! Only got him in the chest."

Dr. Caldwell said, as if to reassure the other man, "Under different circumstances, that would be a good shot. Don't be so hard on yourself."

Jerry's rifled kicked again. "That got 'im. What were you saying Doc?"

"Never mind."

Jerry said, "They're moving much slower now. They seem more like Romero's zombies. Sorry, zekes. Still trying to get used to the new name. Maybe the decomposition theory was right. As they get further into decay, they'll become less and less mobile. This group is getting closer though. Get ready. I can still see five, so maybe we've got close to ten of them out there after all."

Neil started to chew on his lower lip. He could feel his heart rate begin to climb and his breathing begin to quicken. Dr. Caldwell could sense Neil's anxiety and said, "Let's all relax a bit. Keep a sharp eye out and we'll be okay. We can't let them get around behind us. If we start getting overwhelmed or hemmed in, we haul ass outta here."

They could all hear a faint, deep moan, as it became a kind of hungry growl. There was also a dragging shuffle, probably feet coming from out of the darkness. And then the ghouls were upon them. The zekes were just out of reach and fully in view within the glare from the headlights. Meghan screamed involuntarily and hid her face. Neil, distracted, peeked into the van to make sure she was alright. He didn't see the female fiend emerge from the light.

Dr. Caldwell did, though. He pulled the trigger on his shotgun and half of the woman's head disappeared. The beast spun around violently and collapsed in front of the van, just out of reach of Neil. The doctor pumped another twelve-gauge shell into the firearm's chamber and prepared to fire again.

This time Malachi was the shooter. His semi-automatic shotgun didn't require any action on his part to reload between shots. He fired once, hitting one of the things in the chest, which set it back slightly. He then fired again and removed the beast's scalp. He pivoted slightly and brought down another with a single shot.

Now brandishing a sidearm, Jerry fired the revolver three times, apparently hitting nothing. He backed away a few paces and stopped. He had never been so afraid in all his life. He couldn't concentrate and, therefore, couldn't aim at this close distance. It was different to be shooting at these things through his scope and with enough distance between him and them that he was largely out of harm's way. Fighting them up close like this was an entirely different experience. He could see them more clearly, even in the dark. He could smell their rank odor and hear their horrible guttural sounds.

Neil fired his shotgun and another one fell, closer still. Jerry said, "I think there's still one more out there."

They all paused and held their breaths trying to hear anything at all. Jerry said as he raised the rifle, "Yeah, here he comes."

And out of the darkness came another one. It was wearing a police officer's uniform. The ghoul's left hand was gone at the wrist and his left ear was just barely still attached, having been all but chewed from his head. Malachi backed away and lowered his weapon. He was shaking his head and mumbling unintelligibly to himself.

Dr. Caldwell stepped forward and pumped a lethal round into the beast's head, bringing it down in an instant. He looked over at Malachi and asked him, "Did you know him?"

Malachi didn't answer at first. He just stared at the fallen officer. Without looking back at the doctor, Malachi said, "I didn't know him well, but I...I knew his face more than anything."

"I'm sorry, Malachi. I don't think there were any options though. He—"

Walking away with the shotgun propped over his shoulder, Malachi interrupted him, "Yeah, I know. It couldn't be helped. He was one of them."

Malachi was more caught up in seeing the police uniform than anything else because he could imagine himself lying there instead of the other man. He wondered how it had happened in the first place. Was the man doing his duty and helping others or was he just trying to get away and got cornered? It had been ingrained in him that the police force was a brotherhood...a fraternity that bonded each to the other. He wondered to himself how many other police officers were still around. Was he the last of the brotherhood, or were there others still fighting and trying to preserve the peace?

And then he remembered, the man's name was Collins. Sergeant Collins. He'd met him at a couple of public safety functions and recalled liking the man. Between his larger than life size and his booming voice, he was someone that everyone recognized and could find in any crowd. And none of that mattered now. There he was, lying amidst a pile of rotting corpses in an empty parking lot of an abandoned city. He wondered if there was any hope of escaping Anchorage alive.

He tried to stave off the horrible misgivings that were taunting him then. He had gotten used to feeling somewhat normal again. He and the doctor had bonded in the woods while they gathered wood and it felt good to have some connection to someone again. But like a bad connection on a cell phone, he felt the bonds begin to fade into a garbled echo, barely recognizable for what it was. He walked back to the chalet and was surprised to see his father looking out at him from inside. The older Ivanoff was standing inside holding a can of beer. He wasn't waving to him or showing any real emotion. He just stood there watching and waiting. Malachi lowered his head as he walked and tried to ignore the image, the memory...the ghost. He wasn't sure what he was seeing at the moment and just hoped that it would go away. There was no comfort in that face from his past. There was only pain and distrust.

Back at the cars, Jerry, Neil and Dr. Caldwell were still standing their ground in case there were still more of them. Dr. Caldwell leaned down and removed the dead police officer's belt. The man's sidearm was still in its holster.

Neil said, "I think that's all of them. Maybe we should get back inside and start getting ready to move out of here. I'm sure those gunshots will bring more of them our way."

Jerry asked them rhetorically, "Was this really just the first day since we left our safe house?"

Dr. Caldwell, who was tightening the police belt around his waist said, "Yeah. What a first day, huh? I wonder what tomorrow has in store for us?"

# CHAPTER 16

The next day found them driving away from Kincaid Park. Maggie and Malachi, driving in Maggie's beat up Volkswagen, were following Neil and the rest of the group packed tightly in the minivan. The mood in the van, though not joyous, was much lighter than the day before. There was a general sense of possibility amongst the survivors for a change.

"I can't believe we got them all. And it seemed just so easy," Jerry commented. "You were right, Neil. They did just come right at us."

Dr. Caldwell breathed deeply. "This is no time to get complacent," he said flatly. "There was just a few back there. What happens when we run into a big group of them?"

"Hey, Doc, why you gotta go rainin' on my parade? Can't a guy be happy for at least a little bit? I know we're not outta the woods yet, but it felt good to kick some ass for a change."

"Yeah, I know. I guess I'm just being a bit of a pessimist is all. Sorry. You're right. It did feel good to be on the dealing end of things instead of the receiving end."

Art asked, "How much ammo do you guys have?"

Meghan answered, thinking about all the boxes of bullets and guns taken from her store, "Several thousand dollars worth."

"What?"

"Enough. At least for a while."

"And then what?"

Claire said bluntly, with that irritated tone again, "Enough for today and we can worry about tomorrow when it comes."

Art corrected her, "You mean 'if' it comes."

Meghan interrupted, "Talk about rainin' on someone's parade. I think you and Doc need to spend some time apart."

Art got quiet again and stared out the window at the passing trees, houses, and cars.

"What did you do, Art? Before, I mean," Neil asked.

"You mean before the end of the world?"

"Yeah."

"I was a real estate agent."

Meghan said to that, "Oh. That explains the gloom and doom. You sell anything lately?"

"Well not over the past few weeks," and he rolled his eyes as he looked over at Meghan.

Not taking the bait but still feeling a little mischievous, she continued, "Not many buyers lately?"

"No, the market is kind of...dead."

Neil moaned from the front and said, "Now that was bad and I know a bad pun. I kind of made a name for myself at meetings in the office for them."

Art asked, "So where are we headed?"

Dr. Caldwell asked, "You got a house you need to show or something?"

"Yeah, in sunny Hawaii and as far away from here as I can get. No, I was just curious where the next stop was."

Neil said, "I think we need to get over the Knik and head north. I think that's where the army is. At least, that's the direction they were headed last time we heard any news."

"And how long ago was that?" Claire asked.

Dr. Caldwell answered, "When all of this started."

Art disbelievingly asked, "And that's the best plan that we can come up with?"

Meghan, irritated with Art too now, asked him, "You got any better ideas?"

Art didn't answer and chose instead to look back out the window.

Neil changed the direction of the conversation slightly. "Before we get away from the city I want to make sure that we've got everything we need. And that includes gas."

"So, we goin' shoppin'?" Claire asked. "I always loved to shop, even when I didn't need anything."

Jerry asked, "And what about now?"

Claire sniffed her shirt. "If my shirt smells this bad, I'd hate to think what my socks and my underwear smell like."

Jerry's faced reddened slightly with the mention of Claire's underwear. He said, "Thanks for the image." The continued and enticing vision blooming in his mind caused him to blush even more.

"Ah, don't mention it."

Neil added, "I don't know about the rest of you, but away from the fire last night I was a bit chilly."

"Yeah, and it's only gonna keep getting colder," Dr. Caldwell noted.

"Maybe it would be worth the effort to do a little shopping," Neil said. "Where to though?"

Jerry said, "Well, if there have been other survivors like the scumbags that Claire and Art ran into on Spenard, they may have cleaned out a lot of obvious places."

Meghan said, "I wouldn't count on Fred's for supplies."

Neil added, "Or Wal-Mart, Target, Carrs…"

Emma asked, "Are we in a rush to get somewhere?"

"Why?" asked Dr. Caldwell.

"Maybe it would be worth the effort to swing by each of those. You never know. Maybe the infection swept through quickly enough that some of those places didn't get hit. It's probably worth the look, ya know?"

Neil nodded his head. "You're right. Doc, give Maggie a shout and let her know the plan. I think we'll shoot down Jewel Lake and then go across Dimond. There are lots of options down there."

Everyone seemed in agreement, or at least any dissent was not forceful enough to warrant comment from anyone. Dr. Caldwell called Maggie on the two-way radio and told her the plan.

She smiled when she heard the details. She had been to Dimond a few days ago. It was a mess and swarming with those things. She'd just barely made it away herself, and there would be some new ones down that way now. Oh the possibilities. She needn't do anything.

The Carrs grocery store at the intersection of Dimond Boulevard and Jewel Lake Road didn't look very promising. There were dozens of cars parked haphazardly in the parking lot, some quite literally atop others. Many of the store's large windows were either shattered or missing. Much of the building's facade was scarred with blackened wavy streaks of soot.

Meghan thought aloud, "What the hell?"

"People, scared and looking for help," Dr. Caldwell surmised, "flocked here because it was open and well lit."

To which, Jerry added, "And that's what drew Them here too. I wonder how long it took?"

Moving beyond the scope of that question, Neil said, "I wonder if there's anything of any value still in there?"

Emma, leaning forward to get a better look out the front window, said, "I wonder how many of those things are still in there?" She pointed to a single ghoul walking toward them from the parking lot. It wasn't moving fast. In fact, it was hardly able to move at all. The thing was as stiff as a cadaver.

Neil and Dr. Caldwell looked back at her and wondered the same thing. It would be dark in there. Even with the light coming in through the front and with their flashlights, the cavernous depths and corners of the store would be frightening. With the one staggering through the parking lot, they could count on more of those things being inside. Maybe they would luck out and that thing was just a late arrival who missed all the festivities and there wouldn't be others. That was a lot of maybes and they couldn't bank on maybes. There could well be a time in the future in which a maybe would be as good as it got, but for the time being they could play it safer. There were too many opportunities for something bad to happen in there, so Neil was leaning toward just moving on.

It was several minutes of sitting at the intersection while they considered what to do. Finally, getting fed up with just sitting, Maggie barked into the radio, "We goin' in or what?"

Still watching their lurking and slowly approaching predator, Neil said to Dr. Caldwell and everyone else in the van, "I'm thinking we move on. What do you think?"

The doctor suggested, "We can always come back. That might even encourage any others still inside to come out. Makes for much easier picking."

"I hope you're right."

Neil turned the van onto the broad empty lanes of Dimond Boulevard and headed east. Ahead of them was the true commercial district of Anchorage with a string of stores, strip malls, and culminating with the Dimond Center Shopping Mall. It all started with a Fred Meyer store that shared a parking lot with a Burlington Coat Factory. There were cars there too, but the numbers were far less intimidating and the destruction, though present, wasn't nearly as dramatic. For one thing, there didn't seem to be any evidence of a fire.

As they slowed, Maggie's voice came across the radio, "Why we stoppin'?"

Dr. Caldwell answered, "I think we're going in for a closer look."

"I thought we were goin' to the Dimond Center?" Maggie's voice seemed doubtful somehow, maybe even a little desperate.

"Why the hell would she want us to go to the Dimond Center?" Jerry asked the people in the van. "Talk about a zeke magnet."

Dr. Caldwell said into the radio, "I think we should be able to get what we need right here. We can always head down that way if we still need to…but we're going to start right here. Copy?"

Again from the radio, "I just thought…"

Jerry shook his head and leaned back into the seat. "I don't know what she was thinking. If she has been surviving all these days and weeks, then she knows what attracts those things. How could she possibly be that clueless?"

Art said, "I think she's just as scared as the rest of us and is trying to help out any way she can. I can't imagine that she would actually want to see any of us hurt or worse. She just sounded scared to me. How can you say that?"

Jerry shook his head again and started to say something but thought better of it. He wanted to say that he thought Maggie was a complete loon and felt that she was trying to get them all killed. He didn't know why yet,

**Sean Schubert**

but he was convinced that she fully intend to see all of them dead. Maybe he was just being paranoid, but maybe a little paranoia was what was keeping them all alive. It was no longer his practice to argue with people though, so he let Art have the last word. Maggie didn't sound scared to Jerry. She sounded desperate, like someone sounds when a plan unravels.

# CHAPTER 17

They pulled into the parking lot and drove slowly toward the store entrance. There weren't a lot of windows on the facade, so most of the store's interior was obscured from view.

Art said, "It's going to be dark in there too. How is this any better than Carrs? Maybe Maggie's right. Maybe we should just head down to the Dimond Center. I was in there once when the power failed and all the lights went out. It was dark but it wasn't that dark. The big skylights on the ceiling above the ice rink lit up that side of the mall really well."

When no one seemed to be listening to him, he ended with, "That's an option is all." And then he fell silent again.

Neil emerged from the quiet with an upbeat, "I've got an idea."

He steered the vehicle blithely through the random cars and shopping carts scattered across the otherwise empty parking lot. He pulled into the covered lane just outside one of the main entrances and then drove up and onto the curb, angled the van into the glass doors, then turned on the van's high beams.

There was some comfort in being able to see something inside the otherwise dark store, although the lights had about the same effect as trying to put out a house fire with a squirt gun; sure every little bit helps but....

It was decided that Meghan would go in because she was familiar with the standard Fred Meyer layout after having spent the last few years working at one. Dr. Caldwell, Neil, Jerry, and Art were to go in as well. They got out of the van and gathered themselves into a circle, each checking his firearm and the flashlights that they would carry with them. Malachi, standing next to Maggie's car, checked the load in his Glock and then made his way over next to the doctor.

Kim climbed out of the back of the van. "For Christ's sake! It's gonna take more than six people to grab what we need from this place. I guess I'll go too, but if I get killed, Neil I am going to be really pissed off."

Also getting out of the back of the van, Claire said, "She's right. Where do I get a gun again?"

Emma, sitting at the wheel of the van, pulled a small automatic from the glove box, along with a pair of extra magazines filled with shells. "Here. Do you know how to fire and load this?"

Claire took the pistol and held it out in front of her, targeting the liquor store sign across the street. "Haven't got a clue. Until earlier today, I'd never even held a gun before, but I've got to say that I kinda like it."

"Malachi, can you give her a very brief introduction to safe firearm handling?" Dr. Caldwell requested.

The former police officer strode over to the young woman and walked her through a thirty second tutorial on how to load and fire the pistol. He showed her the safety switch and told her to leave it in the safe mode until she needed to fire the gun.

When Malachi was done, Dr. Caldwell said to her and everyone else, "We're not here for revenge or to start a war with those things. If we run into trouble, try to get away. Use the gun as a last resort. If they are in here, then there are probably more of them around. Gunshots will only attract more of them to us and that's not going to help in the slightest."

Echoing those sentiments, Neil said, "Okay, let's get in and get out as quickly as possible. We'll work in teams of two. We need food and drinks, more ammunition, batteries and anything else that looks useful. Emma and Maggie, if either of you see any of those things out here, lay on your horns and wait for us."

There were nods all around. Claire stuffed her pistol into the front pocket of her University of Alaska Anchorage sweatshirt and stood next to Jerry. For his part, Jerry elected to leave his hunting rifle in the van and was sporting two pistols instead.

And so they entered the store, with the van's lights casting a cone of light into the immediate entrance and shadows across the deeper aisles and walls. Neil could feel his breathing already start to quicken. He and Meghan made their way to the electronics department at the front of the store. Amazingly, most of the flat screen television sets, Blu-ray and DVD players, and video games consoles were gone, along with most of the movies and video games from the walls. The glass cabinet at the front of the area was still intact. Inside were digital cameras and video cameras as well as more of the two-way radios. Neil broke the top pane of glass and reached in to grab out those radios. He also grabbed a couple of digital cameras and a digital video camera. He stuffed those into the empty backpack hanging from one of his shoulders. Meghan was deeper in the department and was loading every battery she could lay her hands onto into her own duffel bag.

Kim and Dr. Caldwell went to the sporting goods area to look for needed supplies. Not surprisingly, most of the guns were gone from the racks and about half of the ammunition as well. There were a couple of pistols and smaller caliber rifles scattered on the floor as well as several boxes of ammunition. Ignoring the guns themselves, Dr. Caldwell started to pick up the boxes of shells.

Kim asked, "You gonna get those guns too or do you want me to grab them?"

"No, I think we've got enough guns. Hell, we've got some that are still stacked under the seats in the van that haven't been used yet. It's bullets that we might be needing down the road."

Kim countered, "Grab them all. You never know what we might need tomorrow."

Hoisting a .22 caliber semi-automatic carbine onto his shoulder, Dr. Caldwell conceded, "You're right."

They went into the aisles and found some dehydrated camping meals and some more backpacks into which they loaded a lot of what they found. They also grabbed some more binoculars and multipurpose knives. Dr. Caldwell located several pairs of gloves and some camouflaged stocking caps as well. Kim had her hands on some battery powered Coleman lanterns when she saw what appeared to be a dried slime trail left by a slithering red snail. The crusty ooze led away from the Sporting Goods Department further into the store.

She stopped and grabbed the doctor's arm. Using the flashlight they carried, they both examined the rust colored mess on the floor. Dr. Caldwell pointed the beam of light in the direction in which the trail disappeared but couldn't see anything. He drew out the new automatic pistol from the holster he had taken from the fallen police officer and which he was now wearing.

"Should we go take a look or do we just get the hell out of here?"

Kim had no answer. Looking over her shoulder, Dr. Caldwell saw another possibility. He reached over her, taking the light aluminum baseball bat in his hands. Liking the feel of the bat, he grabbed three more and slid them into the top of one of the backpacks he was carrying.

"If those things move as slowly as the ones that we saw earlier this morning," Dr. Caldwell said reassuringly, "then I don't think we have that much to worry about."

Kim's eyes were as big as saucers as she processed what he was suggesting. Looking at the bat in the doctor's hands, she said, "If you don't mind, I don't plan on letting them get close enough to me to be able to use a bat." And she held up her pistol for him to see.

"No problem. Let's go check things out. I guess we should give everyone else a heads up too, huh?"

"And how in the hell are you gonna do that?"

Dr. Caldwell shrugged his shoulders. "It's not like we're in a library."

"Evvvvv'ryboooooodddyyyyyyy! We might have some trouble near Sporting Goods!"

At first, his voice danced like a spelunker's around the distant walls and corners of the store. For all of its kinetic enthusiasm, the voice seemed to be without a partner. There was only silence.

A moment of utter terror followed as the realization of the grim possibilities occurred to them. They stared into each other's eyes and waited.

And then Neil's voice cut into their worry with, "It's all clear up front."

From over near the Automotive Department, Art shouted, "Not sure in Auto Parts. Got some blood but no bodies...yet."

There should have been one more update, but an encroaching quiet was all that followed Art's update.

Neil asked of the store, "Jerry?"

Jerry and Claire were neck deep in the grocery section. They had a shopping cart that was rapidly filling up with large, family-sized bags of rice and dry cereal. There was a mix of canned fruit, vegetables, and meat on top as well. They had been busy and efficient, working together to hit both sides of each aisle into which they had gone.

They were in their third aisle when they heard a shuffle coming from the soda aisle next to them. Fast on the heels of the disturbing sounds, they felt the familiar vibration of fear that tickled and teased their insides uncomfortably.

All of Claire's color, what little Jerry could see in the scant light of their flashlights, faded until she resembled a mime. She whispered in her quivering voice, "If I could, I'd be pissing my pants right now."

Jerry's parched lips and arid tongue were making it impossible for him to speak. It didn't really matter. He wasn't quite sure what he'd say anyway. He looked up and then down the aisle in which they stood and tried to come up with ideas...any ideas to help them stay alive.

*Think! Think! Think! C-mon Jerry. You can do this.* "Okay. There's only two ways they can come at us. That means you watch that way and I'll watch the other. We can get through this."

"What? Are we just gonna settle down here and make a life for ourselves here among the canned foods?" Her fear was making her ramble. "Sweetie, you're such a romantic. What girl wouldn't dream of—"

The shuffling noise was moving down away from them, making Jerry's side the most likely from which it would emerge.

Jerry whispered, "Don't panic."

With worried tears coursing down her dirty cheeks, Claire forced a smile and said, "Panic? Who's panicking? I'm cool as a cucumber."

"Switch off the safety on your pistol."

Claire, who was already pointing the gun out toward whatever targets decided to make the mistake of appearing before her said, "Thanks. Seems like one of those things that I should've remembered the cop showing me, huh?"

She swallowed hard and tried to slow her breathing. She was painfully aware that she was making quite a bit of noise, but try as she might she couldn't calm herself. Her heart was thumping a frenetic beat that she imagined was acting like a homing beacon for their stalker.

The trembling beam of Jerry's flashlight shined an unsteady light out into the darkness. The shuffling footsteps had stopped and now Jerry and Claire felt like patients waiting in a dentist's chair. They knew the shot was coming and were anticipating the moment.

With Claire pressed against him back-to-back, Jerry could feel her shaking and could sense her fear. His was there too, restricting his breathing with its icy grip. He wondered if she could feel his fright as well.

He tried to get a handle on his emotions and asked, "Where did it go?"

A single bead of sweat threatened to drip from his nose after having traveled from his forehead; Jerry barely noticed. The truth is, Jerry would likely have scarcely noticed a massive coronary at that moment. He couldn't peel his eyes away from the danger that lurked just out of view. He was contemplating moving forward a little when he noticed the tip of a shoe that was protruding just beyond the bottom of the grocery shelves to his left. He touched the back of Claire's shoulder and then pointed toward it.

"Now what?" she breathed.

His voice cracking slightly, he whispered, "How the fuck should I know?"

"Well—"

Before either of them could say anything else, there was a flurry of movement that was in and then out of the flashlight's cone of light. Jerry was then aware that there was another light that was shining across his beam. He settled back onto his heels slightly and waited. He was pretty certain that zombies did not attack one another but was definitely certain that they didn't use flashlights to help them see in the dark, so he relaxed a little.

When Dr. Caldwell and Kim appeared, he smiled and lowered his pistol back down to his side. And when he saw the bat in Dr. Caldwell's grip he nodded and said to Claire, "I think we're okay."

On the floor but obscured from view by the darkness again was laid out an already decomposing corpse that, until just moments before, had been stalking Claire and Jerry. Its largely ossified skull had nearly disintegrated beneath the weight of Dr. Caldwell's heavy swing. The creature had hardly made a sound or any move to defend itself from the attack. It just reached out toward the doctor, allowing him to dispatch it without much fuss.

Dr. Caldwell cautioned, "Keep your eyes open and stay alert. If there's one, there are bound to be more wandering around in here."

Both Claire and Jerry nodded, but were relieved to know that the immediate danger had passed. Jerry said, "Thanks Doc."

Dr. Caldwell smiled and said jokingly, "That's all right, kid. After seeing your shooting with a pistol last night, I kinda' figured you could use the help."

Jerry cocked an eyebrow, to which the doctor replied, "Don't get me wrong. You're dead on with your rifle, but I think your sidearm marksmanship needs some work."

"Don't worry sweetie," Claire said, "I'm sure you'll get lots of practice."

"Yeah, I guess I'm kind of dreading that."

Kim continued to look around nervously. "You guys done?"

Claire nodded. "Just finishing up. Looks like a lot of stuff has already been nabbed by looters."

"You mean like the one that Doc just laid out?"

"Somethin' like that."

"Well, let's get this show on the road then. It's probably not the best idea to hang around here any longer than we have to."

"Agreed."

Back out at the van, the new ammunition was stacked with the old in the back behind the last bench seat. The new sleeping bags and camping supplies were piled onto and then bungee strapped to the roof. The food they were able to grab, which seemed like so much more in the cart, was placed on top of the ammunition and extra firearms in the back. Looking at it then, Claire and Jerry wondered what had happened to all the food they had grabbed.

Jerry said mockingly, "I guess when you're shopping for two the cart looks a helluva lot fuller than if you're shopping for an army."

"Should we get some more?" asked Claire, afraid that her suggestion might actually be heeded and she might have to go back into the store.

Meghan said, "No, I think maybe we should hit Burlington over there and get us some warmer clothes and coats. No point in overstaying our welcome or stretching our good luck too far. We don't have enough of that to go around as it is."

"She's right," Dr. Caldwell added. "We should probably keep moving."

Art and Malachi had, meanwhile, busied themselves with filling up the windshield washer fluid reservoirs in both vehicles and then checking the oil levels in both as well. Most of the automotive supplies they had pilfered were forced into the trunk of Maggie's car, sandwiched between spare fuel cans and Bibles.

# CHAPTER 18

They could have walked to Burlington Coat Factory, and during friendlier times they probably would have. With things as they were though, caution dictated that they never stray far from their wheeled lifeboat. So, they drove.

They pulled up in front of the clothing store and went through largely the same routine as at the previous store. In pairs, they made their way cautiously inside. Danny watched them as they walked into the store and disappeared.

Danny and Jules, both sitting on the middle bench seat of the van, had taken to silently watching most events as they unfolded. Unfortunately—or perhaps fortunately, one can never be sure of these things—they were never entirely certain what was going on, but always seemed to show that they wanted to understand. There was, however, a degree of relief in not having to participate in every decision, but sometimes Danny felt like an afterthought...the proverbial third wheel, though he'd never have put it in such a way. The distance was starting to become more apparent. In his own way he realized that he and Jules were a burden, and that bearing that burden was something that these people could decide was no longer in their better interests to bear. They weren't, after all, family.

When it was quiet and the fear was being held at a distance, like today for instance, it was then that he started to think about his family. He missed them and the quiet moments afforded him the opportunity to be reminded of them. He had thought that he was too old to miss them anymore; that he had grown up enough that he could get by on his own. The separation from everything and everyone that he loved and had taken for granted only proved all too well how painfully wrong he was.

It was troublesome for him that he couldn't remember his mother's face or his father's voice. Of course, the memories of both of them were strong, but they were feelings more than actual images for him. It didn't matter really; the feelings were bittersweet enough. He was disappointed that the pictures he brought with him on his mother's advice "in case he got a little homesick" were still in his backpack which was still sitting at the cabin near Seward in which he was supposed to be vacationing with the Housers. What a tragic turn of events. Never, in all of his former camping trips, sports camps, or family vacations had home seemed so impossibly far away.

The sadness had nearly taken him over when he realized that Emma was looking at him in the rearview mirror. She smiled and tilted her head a little. "You okay?"

"Yeah."

"Miss home?"

"Yeah."

"Me too."

"I thought you lived here in Anchorage?"

She looked out toward the road and beyond, seeing things that weren't actually in sight. "I don't know what this place is anymore, but it sure as hell isn't home. I don't think it ever could be again. Not for me."

They were both quiet for a moment or two when Emma asked, "You got a dog?"

Danny nodded his head. "Yeah. His name is Romie. Roman to be exact."

"I've never heard of a dog named Roman."

Danny smiled. "My mom and dad just found him roamin' around the yard and they decided to keep him. So they just called him Roman."

Appreciating the rehearsed nature of the reply and that the story likely originated with his parents, Emma smiled warmly. "What kind of dog is Romie?"

"A Golden Retriever. He's a great dog and loves to play. He can catch better than almost any other dog."

"I like dogs. You can count on your dog when you can't count on anyone else. Whoever said that dogs are man's best friend was right."

Danny nodded and drifted away in memories of Romie. Playing in the back yard, tossing…well, anything for Romie to run down and bring back. He was a great dog. And in remembering Romie and the great backyard at his house, he was surprised that he was suddenly visited with visions of his mom and dad in the backyard with him, remembering a barbecue from earlier in the summer.

He could almost smell the coals on the grill as they cooked themselves from black to grey. His Uncle Justin was there with his cousins Sydney and Stuart. They were twins but were a boy and girl, a fact that always confused him. He thought for sure twins either had to be two boys or two girls, but in the end it didn't really matter. It was just great to have them in his backyard and to be playing. They climbed into the clubhouse his dad built for him and alternated between playing war and playing house. Sydney didn't mind being the princess in the castle being defended by Stuart and Danny, but she definitely preferred being the mother or the teacher of the two boys.

Danny's favorite time of the night was when his uncle brought out the fireworks he'd brought with him. Of course Danny's mother immediately went into "worried parent" mode when she envisioned the pyrotechnical injuries that were sure to follow. Uncle Justin assured her over and over that nothing would happen and then shot her a concerned look when Sydney burned her finger on a hot sparkler. That just about ended the fun, but then Uncle Justin brought out the big rockets and Roman candles and whatever else he had in the wooden crate filled to overflowing with colorful cardboard packages.

Danny's mom was much more comfortable with these items because Uncle Justin was the only one who handled them and lit them, allowing everyone else to stand back at a safer distance. The red and blue and green and purple fiery flowers that raced into and then blossomed in the sky were spectacular and seemed to go on and on.

When the evening ended, Danny said a very tired good-bye to his cousins and Uncle Justin. He and his dad then sat down in front of the television to watch some of a movie before Danny was sent off to bed.

He missed his family and Romie more than ever, but it was nice for the memory to visit him. He looked over at Jules. She was sleeping again. She seemed to sleep an awful lot lately. And when she was awake, she was always tired and yawning.

It was about then, with Jules snoring peacefully and Danny remembering wistfully, that Emma looked into the rear view mirror and noticed a trio of ghouls emerging from the Fred Meyer entrance from which they had just departed. Once again, Emma was amazed at the clarity of Neil's foresight.

He had instructed Art and Jerry to move some of the shopping carts into a kind of barricade in front of the doorway. And now, those carts formed an excellent barrier behind which the fiends were trapped. They banged themselves repeatedly against the shiny metal rolling baskets but lacked the necessary problem solving capabilities to realize that they could just lie themselves over the carts and pull themselves free. For that matter, if the three of them were to work in concert, they could probably move the carts far enough away as to make a large enough opening through which they could all shuffle. Neither appeared to be forthcoming though as they merely banged into the carts futilely, spun in a hopeless circle, and then banged into the carts again.

If she weren't so disgusted by their appearance and behavior, the scene might even seem comical. *Next on America's Funniest Zombie Videos…* She doubted Fox had the sense or the taste to realize what a bad idea that would be. With the right marketing though, anything's possible. Just look at *American Idol*.

She lifted the radio and said calmly, "Neil, we got some friends caught up on your shopping carts over there. Nice idea by the way."

There was a pause and some electric snow that was suddenly broken by a concerned voice, "Are you all right? We're on our way back out."

"Relax. They seem to be pretty well contained right now, but I'd say let's not dawdle. No point in pushing our luck. Just get what we need and get back out here."

"Give us five minutes."

"For you sweetie, I'll give you seven." She set the radio back down next to the silver pistol on the console between the seats. "Danny, wake Jules will you? And then you better get your hands on a gun yourself. I know it's a lot to ask you, but two guns are better than one. And I think I know just the one. Why don't you get into the back there and start grabbing some of the guns from under the seat. I want you to get a rifle. It's kind of small, but it's definitely a rifle."

Danny shook Jules awake and then followed Emma's instructions. He reemerged from the back with a very trim camouflage-colored rifle. It had a fairly short stock and a very narrow barrel. On the bottom of the rifle was a stubby clip magazine. The gun was exactly the right size for him. His eyes were wide and slightly dazzled.

Emma said, "That was the kind of gun that I shot when I was about your age. My brother had one and used to target shoot with it all the time. It barely gave any kick at all and shot really straight. At least that was what he used to say. I remember shooting it and all I could think of was how loud it was. But even that wasn't too horribly bad. I'm guessing that it needs bullets put into that clip, so why don't you climb under there and find a box of twenty-two caliber shells. I'll show you how to load it and how to fire it, but hurry up. There's no time to waste."

# CHAPTER 19

As soon as his hands touched the small rifle, he felt different...special, like a grownup. But peering through the magnifying scope attached to the rifle stock, he felt powerful and fierce. When he focused his aim on one of the zombies banging himself to no avail against the simple shopping cart barricade, his heart quickened and his fingers buzzed as if he had just touched a live wire. He smiled, held his breath, and pulled the trigger. *Click.*

Emma patted him on the back and said, "That's good, Danny. Now, when there is actually a bullet in the gun, there won't be much kick but the sound might startle you at first. It sounds kind of like a big firecracker."

"Cool."

"Danny, you seem like a smart kid, so I don't want to talk down to you, but I think I ought to at least say that this gun is a very dangerous thing and the present circumstances don't change how dangerous this thing is. Do you understand what I'm saying?"

Danny looked her in the eyes and nodded. He understood. He also understood that, even under the present circumstances, his parents would never entrust him with a firearm. He doubted that his parents would have one for themselves. They didn't like guns and wouldn't have one in the house. He'd heard them talk about that many times with friends, family, and neighbors.

Many of their neighbors kept guns in their houses; most were for hunting, but some kept them for home defense as he'd heard it put before. It just made sense to him that people would keep a gun in the house. He could never figure out why his parents had been so adamantly opposed to the idea. Why wouldn't you want to defend your home against intruders...whether they were burglars or zombies? He just couldn't figure it out and current events had encouraged him to question it even more.

There was the time when Mark Little got his dad's gun down from the top of the bookcase. When he jumped down, Mark dropped the gun and it went off. No one was hurt, but he did kill one of his mother's nice planters and a struggling Ficus tree. Everyone agreed that Mark was lucky and that his dad should have done a better job of securing the gun. And there were the stories in the newspaper that he saw when he was looking for some easy but juicy Current Events topics; stories about teenagers being prosecuted as adults in the shooting deaths of friends or suburban homes being robbed by thieves looking for guns to sell.

Regardless, when Emma handed him the ten round clip and he clicked it into position, he felt more like a part of the group than ever before. Now, he could contribute something rather than just always taking.

He was probably the most happy when Neil saw him standing next to the van. Neil saw the gun, wrinkled his brow and tilted his head and then gave Danny a thumbs up gesture. Danny was so proud of himself. He slung the rifle over his shoulder and stood next to the van as a guard while the others loaded the gear into the quickly diminishing space in the back of the van.

They all had jackets now, and the heavier coats were packed away for later use when the temperatures dropped further. They had food and water, more ammunition for their firearms, and some baseball bats for close-up protection.

Meghan surveyed all of this and then turned to Neil. "So, I guess that's about it. We ready yet?"

"Almost. We still need some gas for the rig."

# CHAPTER 20

Unfortunately, the vehicles in the Fred Meyer and Burlington Coat Factory parking lots did not yield much gasoline. Most of the fuel tanks were close to empty or were bone dry. They were able to fill one five-gallon can and partially fill a second, but that was far from comforting for all of them.

When they got back on the road and started putting some distance between themselves and Anchorage, they'd need much more fuel, and the likelihood there would be filling stations between here and salvation was slim to nil. Unfortunately, the Tesoro gas station on the northwest corner of the parking lot was a blackened ruin. It appeared as if someone had already tried to pilfer the gas from the underground storage tanks but had actually blown himself or herself up in the process.

Meghan asked as they stood in the parking lot, "So now what? Can we make it with this much?"

Dr. Caldwell shook his head. "No. This might be able to get us out of town and maybe on our way to Fairbanks and the Interior, but we'd run out in the middle of nowhere and then be on foot. Doesn't seem like the safest bet to me."

Maggie stood on the edge of the discussion. She wanted to offer her suggestion but waited for the right moment. She didn't want to sound too eager and arouse any suspicions. The conversation swayed back and forth, shifting between opinions and strategies. Claire even suggested that perhaps they should just find another hiding spot in Anchorage to 'wait out all of this.'

All of the talk went back and forth until finally, Neil asked, "How 'bout you, Maggie? You have any ideas or know where we can get some gas?"

Maggie smiled a little and looked over all of them at the eastbound Dimond Boulevard. "I don't know about gas for sure, but I do know that there are dozens and dozens of cars that way...toward the Dimond Center. It looks like a parking lot just up the road. I'm sure with that many cars, you...I mean we can find all the gas that we need."

"Are you sure?"

Maggie nodded her head and pointed. "Everything that you need is down that way."

Jerry asked suspiciously, "What about...you know...*them*? Are there zombies down that way too?"

Maggie shrugged her shoulders, "Aren't they everywhere now? I mean, they were in the store behind us and they didn't seem to pose much of a problem for you."

"Yeah, taken in ones and twos we can handle them, but how many of them are there down that way?"

"We won't know until we go there, now will we?"

Jerry didn't like the way that she answered his questions without really answering anything. It was like watching a politician at a press conference coming clean about the latest scandal. She could talk and talk and never really say anything. He wanted to press her, but knew that ultimately it wouldn't yield anything but more frustration. Besides, she was right. They had been handling themselves well lately.

Emma asked, "Maggie, you've got a bunch of gas in your trunk. Can you share some of what you have with us?"

"Find your own. I worked hard for what I got."

"I'm sure you did, but doesn't it make more sense for us to share what we've got and work together?"

"What do you mean share?" demanded Maggie, suspicion in her eyes.

"Oh, I don't know. Like maybe, the food that we have that we've shared with you. And maybe the protection we shared with you last night at the park. You know, things we gave to you and did for you because it was the right thing to do."

"I didn't need nothing from you. Just because you gave me some of your food doesn't mean that I didn't have none of my own. I was doing just fine without all of you and now you want to take my gas."

Neil interrupted, "Nobody's taking anything from anyone."

Emma wasn't satisfied though. She continued, "Well what about Christian charity? Isn't there a vestige of decency that is taught in your *Bible*?"

"How dare you question my faith! My belief in God is steadfast and loyal. How could someone like you know anything about faith anyway? Malachi has told me all about you and the poison that you spew."

"Malachi told you about me? Well let me tell you a couple of things about your hero Malachi there—"

Malachi jumped in to defend Maggie. "Shut your mouth you Jezebel! You've got no right to ask Maggie for anything. Why would she give gas that is fueling the Lord's message to you...a non-believer just trying to avoid her fate."

"Fate? *Fate!* Don't go using pagan words that you don't understand."

Again, Neil interrupted the exchange. "Stop it! This isn't getting us anywhere."

Emma wasn't through though. Even as Dr. Caldwell was pulling her away, she spat, "Your Malachi there? He's a coward and a rapist. What does your goddamned book say about that? Huh? No amount of faith can change that. You disillusioned—"

Dr. Caldwell turned her and said to her, cutting her off, "Emma! This isn't helping."

Over his shoulder she shouted, "Hypocrites! You pick and choose what you believe from your book and then belittle the rest of us when we question your motives or your actions. You disgust me! And *him*, he belongs with those things over there. He's a monster and doesn't deserve to be wearing that uniform or that badge!"

With that said, she pushed Dr. Caldwell away from her and walked away. Danny, still standing next to the van, walked away too and stood next to her. By then, she was bent over at the waist and shedding hot, angry tears. She was so enraged she couldn't see straight and was afraid that she was going to vomit at any moment.

She said quietly to Danny, "I'm sorry, Danny. I guess I kind of lost my cool."

Danny didn't say anything. He was thinking, however, that he agreed with Emma. Why wouldn't Maggie share any of the gas she had? It just seemed like a safer thing to do. They could fill up both cars with what she had and then get moving. They could get away from all of this and leave it behind them. He wasn't sure about the Christian charity thing that she had said. He didn't remember a whole lot about that from church. He remembered coloring pictures and eating snacks at Sunday School. He remembered the stories about Noah and Job and the Garden of Eden. He remembered singing songs. That was about it for him. Maybe Christian charity was what the adults talked about while the kids were downstairs in the classroom.

He put his hand on her shoulder and looked over at the Fred Meyer entrance. Those things were still there and the buzzing in the air was getting louder. "I think we should get going again. The sound is getting louder so I think more of those things are coming this way."

"What?"

"I can hear them. They're coming."

"Hey everyone, the kid...I'm sorry, *Danny,* says that he can hear them coming. We should get moving."

Jerry nodded and agreed, "Yeah, I think he's right. I guess I was hearing it too, but didn't pay enough attention to realize what it was. Those three over there are probably acting like a homing beacon for more of those things."

Without having resolved anything, the group split up and went to their respective vehicles. They were moving again without any real direction, but Neil was relieved that the confrontation was brought to a temporary close, if not to a more permanent solution. It felt good to be moving again and to put the parking lot and anger behind them.

Emma sat in the back and didn't say much. She was still angry but she was quiet again. She kept looking behind her at the car following them. She imagined turning herself around in the seat and firing her pistol out the back window at Maggie and Malachi. In her mind's eye, she could see their car swerve and veer off the road out of control. Her thoughts didn't get any darker than that. She knew that her fury would subside and that these ugly musings were neither realistic nor healthy, so she closed her eyes and tried to let go of the hostility.

When she awoke, they were stopping near what looked like a parking lot but she knew that it was actually a street that cut through Midtown in Anchorage. She was unaware that she had dozed and woke feeling a little disoriented.

"What are we doing?"

"We still need gas," Jerry replied.

# CHAPTER 21

They sat for a few seconds in the stopped van without anyone saying a word. Danny lifted his new rifle from the floor in front of him and laid it across his lap. He was ready but it didn't seem anyone else was.

He looked over at Jerry and Claire, and then to Emma and Kim. They all looked exhausted, like his mom and dad did every Christmas morning after all the presents had been opened.

Claire asked no one in particular, "So we have to do this, huh?"

"No," Neil said flatly. "We don't have to but we'll probably be on foot soon if we don't. What do you prefer?"

She didn't need to answer and neither did anyone else. Regardless of the need, there didn't seem to be much enthusiasm in collecting the gas. Their failed attempt to siphon gas from the collection of vehicles at the Fred Meyer parking lot didn't inspire much confidence. Of course, there were a lot more cars here and a lot more possibilities.

Jerry finally said, "Okay, let's get going. We work in teams again?"

Dr. Caldwell said, "Yes. Two teams of three. One spotter, one siphoner, and one toter."

Neil said, "Okay, how about—"

Dr. Caldwell cut him off. "How about you stay with the van this time. You can find the bungee cords in the back and get the top ready to load the full cans. Meghan, you stay at the wheel in case we have visitors and have to get out in a hurry."

Neil started to protest but his fatigue caught the words in his chest and buried them beneath his momentary relief. He felt guilty about sending folks off on an errand of his choosing, but even the guilt couldn't find a voice.

Malachi was out of Maggie's car and joining the group as it formed next to the van. Dr. Caldwell began, "Okay, how about Emma, Malachi, and I..."

Emma, still not ready to be near the police officer challenged, "Yeah, that's not gonna work." She could have outlined all the reasons why, but she didn't feel the need to open that argument again; at least not there on the street.

"Okay, how about Jerry, Emma, and me. And then Kim, Art, and Malachi. We each take a couple of the large and a couple of the small cans with us. There's no messing around out here. We get what we need and we get the hell outta Dodge, okay?"

Everyone nodded his or her head. Malachi nodded his head too, but he shot a concealed sneer over at Emma. Since his wife, he didn't think he had ever had the same feelings of animosity toward anyone that he harbored toward Emma. She dug at him every time she could and he was getting tired of it. He hoped there arose a time in the future where she really needed help...*his* help, and he would just turn and walk away. He hoped that she begged for him to save her. He could see her surrounded by reaching, grabbing, clawing hands and hear her voice calling out to him to save her, but he wouldn't. He would smile down at her and revel in her desperation. The thoughts made his head swim for a moment and he teetered on his heels a bit.

Dr. Caldwell asked, concerned, "Malachi, you okay?"

"Yeah, just tired I guess." He looked over at Emma who was walking away and was relieved that she didn't see him start to swoon.

Each group walked up to the closest cars and, of course, there was no fuel in either. The same was true of the next and then the next pair of cars. Several cars later, Dr. Caldwell found a tank that was nearly full, based upon the fact that they were able to siphon out enough gasoline to fill two of the five-gallon plastic containers and start on one of the smaller three-gallon jugs. As he looked around the car, he noticed that there were no keys in the ignition, while in the previous cars there had been keys.

He called out to the other group, "Hey, look at the ignitions of the cars. If there aren't keys there, then we stand a better chance of getting gas."

Art nodded as he looked into the next driver's side window. He wasn't expecting the spectacle in the front seat that he saw. There, sitting slightly hunched over into the passenger seat, was a decaying corpse. Clutched in its discolored right hand was an automatic pistol.

"Jesus."

Kim asked him as she walked up, "What? What'd you find?"

Art just stood there looking down at the dead body. It was a woman who appeared to have been heading to work based upon her professional dress. She still had a cup of Kaladi Brothers coffee in the cup holder on her dash. On the seat next to her lifeless hand was a wallet opened to a family photo and next to that was a cell phone.

Kim looked in the window and gasped, surprised that after all that she had seen, she could still be startled. "Do you think she could be one of them?"

Art was already shaking his head, "No. I think she did it to herself."

Malachi was standing there now, but was not offering any comments. He was looking around at the other cars and trying to stay focused on the task at hand, which, for him, was becoming increasingly more challenging. Staying moving as he was seemed to be helping, but there were cracks in his reality that were separating him further and further away from everyone else, including his new friend Maggie.

Kim asked, "Why do you think she did it?"

"It could have been anything, given the situation. Maybe she was trapped and scared. Maybe she was already planning on doing it and it just seemed like the right time. Maybe she was on the phone with the family in the photo and heard those things getting to them and she couldn't bear it. Hell, does it really matter?"

"The keys are still in the ignition, so she's got nothing for us."

Kim looked at him in disgust. "That's a little cold isn't it?"

"Would you like me to say a prayer for her and for every corpse we come upon? That's a lot of praying."

She thought about it and responded, "No. I guess not. I just...I'm just afraid that the longer this goes on, the less sense of humanity we seem to be holding on to."

"I get what you're saying, but I guess I'm just more interested in being alive than in retaining something like my humanity. When we've gotten through this I promise to say a long prayer for all the people that we come upon but until then..."

Kim nodded her head and moved to the next car. "Hey, no keys. Maybe we'll get lucky."

Art snorted. "In a different time and in a different world, getting lucky had a whole different meaning."

"Just like a man. Even now on the eve of extinction, all you can think about is sex."

"Hey, you're the one that brought it up."

"Did not."

"Did too."

"You're impossible."

"I like to think of myself as just complicated...complex...an enigma to be unraveled but never solved."

"Is that a line that you've used before? Because it sounded rehearsed."

Art smiled. "Yeah, and it worked more than it didn't. Does it really sound rehearsed?"

Kim just chuckled and opened the car door to release the gas tank lever.

There was enough gas in that car to partially fill one of the five-gallon gas cans but that was all. They moved deeper into the line of cars and farther away from the van.

Jerry shouted to them from the other side of the car-choked street, "We've filled all of our cans, so we're taking them back to the van. We'll go grab some more cans and be right back."

Back at the van, they filled the vehicle's tank with one of the five-gallon cans and most of one of the three gallon cans. Neil said to Dr. Caldwell, "I'm already feeling better about this. Maybe we do stand a chance of getting out of here after all."

Dr. Caldwell felt the relief in his gut too. "Yeah, I think we should go back out there and refill these two cans. Do we have any other cans in there?"

"No, we've just got water jugs that we grabbed from Fred's. If we get the other group's gas cans back here and refill yours, I think we should be okay. That's a lot of fuel, especially since the van is full again. That will buy us a lot of miles."

"But will it be enough?"

"Only time will tell. Besides, there are bound to be other cars out there. Hell, so far things seem to be going much better."

Art, Kim and Malachi came upon a couple more corpses in cars while they searched. Apparently, the first woman who took her own life wasn't alone in her decision. In another car, a woman had taken an overdose of some kind of medication, the empty bottle of which was still sitting in her lap. And in the car next to that, a man had done similarly as the first, by shooting himself in the head. His suicide was much messier, as he had used a much higher caliber pistol. The inside of his window was stained a dirty, disgusting brown.

The three of them came to a big Ford pickup truck and paused. Kim said with concern, "I think we're getting a little too much distance between us and the van. Maybe we should call it quits and head back."

Art agreed. "Okay, let's check this big truck out and head on back."

"Deal."

They popped open the gas tank and started to draw out the gas. They filled one of the three-gallon tanks, deciding to fill that first because they hadn't had much luck so far in filling the bigger ones. Working together, they were able to lift and balance the empty can so that the short rubber hose could reach the opening. They stood there, each doing his or her part, as the malodorous but essential liquid filled the plastic container.

Art said to Malachi playfully after several seconds of quiet, "Kind of reminiscent of standing at a urinal isn't it?"

Kim asked, "Excuse me?"

"Well, there are certain things that guys do and don't do at urinals."

"And?"

"I guess standing here without saying anything and listening to liquid pouring into the can just made me nostalgic for those simpler times when I guy could stand quietly and pee at a public restroom."

Malachi, of course, hadn't said a word but instead cocked an eyebrow at Art. He didn't like talking about things as personal as that with a woman around. It just didn't seem right; like he was breaking some kind of established rule of politesse.

A few seconds later, their smiles faded after hearing a rhythmic clicking that appeared to be heading toward them. The sound started very faint but grew with each moment.

Art looked at Kim with a question in his eyes that Kim actually asked, "What the hell was that?"

"I don't know but I don't see anything. If it was one of those things, it seems like we should be able to see them long before they get close to us. Let's get this can full and then get on back. We can just say that we got all the gas that we could."

Kim, still looking in the direction of the sound, asked, "You sure?"

"Have you ever seen one of things sneak up on anyone? I think Neil's right; they don't plot and plan. They just come right at you. I don't think an ambush is something they could manage."

"Okay, let's just get this done then."

Malachi adjusted his hands slightly so that he was still able to support the can with one and get the other to his hip holster. He didn't remove the pistol yet, but having his hand there made him feel slightly more comfortable.

The sounds grew louder and seemed to expand, as if there was more than one source creating the racket. And then they could hear a growl, though they all agreed that it wasn't the same sound emitted by the zombies. It was more naturally animalistic.

Art shook the can a little. "We're almost done. Let's get ready to move."

They all wore concerned expressions like familiar masks that are never out of reach. Kim looked down at the hose, which was moving and threatening to emerge out of the top of the can as the container neared capacity.

When Art suddenly turned and ran, it caught both Kim and Malachi by surprise. Kim raised her free hand and was barely able to balance the gas can and keep it from toppling onto the ground.

Just a heartbeat later, Malachi saw what had spooked Art. A pack of dogs was almost upon them. The dogs were a variety of breeds and sizes, but one thing they all shared in common was a look of bloodlust that preceded them.

Without warning, Malachi stepped back and pulled his pistol. In so doing, he forced Kim to try and hold the gas can herself, which she was unable to do in the position in which she found herself. The can fell heavily to the ground but not before landing squarely on Kim's foot.

"Owwwwwww fuuuuuccckkkkk!!!!"

Kim still hadn't seen the dogs, but she knew that trouble was fast approaching. She took a step, trying to follow the now fleeing police officer.

Her first step though delivered a chorus of pain that rippled through her legs and up her spine. Her vision, too, was colored with tiny florets of pain, dancing like imaginary fireworks before her eyes.

She fell to her knees and was finding it extremely difficult to get back to her feet. She forced herself up onto her one good foot and tried to hop, but she was too off-balance to take more than a couple of steps before she fell again.

She screamed, "Helllllp meeeee!"

Malachi turned to see Kim sprawled on the ground with her hands reaching out to him. He started to step toward her but then saw the dogs that were nearly upon her. Malachi fired his pistol three times, bringing down the closest of the dogs. Even after having done that, he was still frozen in place.

The terror in his eyes matched the same that was in hers. They looked at one another for a mere second but that torturous second seemed to stretch on and on, seeming to span a lifetime. His furiously pounding heart demanded that he act; Kim was doomed if he didn't. His feet felt planted though. He tried to force them up. He tried, but he just couldn't. His fear was making him lightheaded and that only contributed to the already formidable presence that paralyzed him. His mouth opened and closed as if he was trying to speak, but the words didn't find a voice. He teetered forward on the balls of his feet, but then he leaned back and straightened his stance slightly.

Kim could see all too well that Malachi wasn't coming to help her. The fear was palpable all around him. Even her panic-filled voice desperately screaming, "Nooooooooooooo! Don't leave meeeeeee!" couldn't break the wall.

Malachi turned and ran back toward the van. Dr. Caldwell and Jerry met him at the edge of the line of cars.

Dr. Caldwell asked, "Malachi? Where's Kim? What's out there? Where's Kim?"

Too ashamed to even speak, Malachi pointed out toward the cars and toward Kim's cries. He felt sick and weak. He needed to sit before he collapsed. He couldn't handle the emotions that were gripping his chest and clouding his eyes. He wasn't sure if he was crying or not but it didn't really matter, he couldn't control it anyway.

Art said from already in the van, "Dogs. We were attacked by infected dogs."

"Where the hell is Kim?"

Almost in answer to that question, three hurried gunshots rang out from somewhere amidst the cars.

Malachi shook his head and then hurried on over to Maggie's car. He climbed into the passenger seat, closed the door, and bowed his head into his hands.

Neil jumped into the driver's seat of the van. "Let's get loaded up. There's no time to spare. They're still coming. Listen!"

And when they all stopped speaking, they could hear the approaching growls and something more. They could hear Kim. The anguish and the agony made her words close to unintelligible, but hear the words they all did.

"Nooooo!!!!!. Ohhhhhh Goddddddddddd!!! I'm not readddddyyyyyyy!!! Ohhhhhhh Jesuuuuussssss!!!! Nooooooo!"

There was a final gunshot and then all they could hear were the growls from the dogs that were now within sight. There were a variety of breeds and mutts coming at them. Some were big and some were small, but they all shared the same savage, aggressive appearance. They were no longer man's best friend by any stretch of the imagination.

The van's doors closed as the first of the dogs cleared the line of cars. The animal didn't even hesitate. It threw itself against the side of the vehicle with a thud and then stood up to do it again and again and again. With each impact against the door, everyone in the van jumped.

Meghan and Emma both said to Neil, "Just go."

Neil shut his eyes for a second. The sorrow was as heavy as it ever had been, but he couldn't find tears. The reservoir of his pain was as arid and salty as the Dead Sea. He put the van in gear and steered them away.

# CHAPTER 22

In the van heading toward downtown Anchorage, the questions came fast and furious.

Meghan demanded, "Art, what happened?"

"We were just getting gas and those dogs...they snuck up on us. It all happened so quickly. I just..."

Claire finished with a bit of a snarl, "You just had to save your own ass. Isn't that right? You got scared and left her, didn't you?"

Stung, Art didn't bother to even look at her. "I did all that I could. She just couldn't keep up. If I would have stayed with her, there's no telling what would have happened. What could I have done?"

Meghan looked at Claire and stifled her next comment. She could see that Claire was holding resentment toward Art that wasn't only stemming from this incident. There was something more going on. She looked over at Emma who was casting sideways glances over her shoulder at the car following them. Meghan already knew about the animosity Emma bore for Malachi.

Meghan said, "Art, tell me exactly what happened."

"What does it matter? She's gone and no amount of my telling you how it happened is going to change that."

"I just need to know."

"Okay. We had to go into the cars kind of deep to find enough gas to fill those cans. And then we found a big truck with two tanks on it and one seemed to be pretty full, so we started to fill the cans. The gas was only coming out so fast, though. So we just stood there trying to fill up as fast as we could."

"Who was doing what?"

"What does that matter?"

Claire interjected, "Just answer the goddamned question!"

Art started to vocalize a response to her barb, but bit it off still in his throat. "Kim fed and held the hose into the can while Malachi and I held it up."

"Held it up?" asked Meghan for clarification.

"Yeah, the truck had a lift package on it, so the tank was up kind of high. We were just standing there talking and filling the tank when the dogs attacked us. They were just there all at once."

Emma, sitting in the backseat next to Claire, thought to herself that if Kim was only holding the hose in the mouth of the can then it is only logical to assume that she would have been the first to be on the move. She dismissed her suspicions, however, as merely being products of her distrust of Malachi. She didn't bother to mention her thoughts out loud. She looked over at Art to see if she could detect any malfeasance. The side of his face held no clues whatsoever.

Refusing to look anyone in the eye, Art asked, "What does any of this matter?"

Dr. Caldwell, who had been sitting quietly but listening intently, said calmly, "Because, Art, if we know what went wrong this time then maybe we can avoid the same mistakes in the future."

"Mistakes? What mistakes?"

Meghan, her distrust on the rise now, asked, "You tell us? How did it all go so wrong?"

"What do you mean wrong?"

Claire shouted, unable to contain her frustration any longer, "She died you fool. She's dead and you were with her. You were there."

Seeing his opportunity to turn the tables, Art shouted back, "That's right. I was there. I was putting myself at risk while *you* stayed back here at the van...safe. Who the hell are you to judge me? You weren't out there when those goddamned dogs were coming at us, were you?"

Claire wanted to shout back at him but she could see that it wasn't going anywhere and now she felt like she may have disrupted Meghan's questioning enough to let him off the hook. She couldn't know for sure that Art had anything to do with Kim's death, but when he appeared from the line of cars well before the cop she couldn't help but wonder. And now, he seemed to be getting awfully loud and adamant about some pretty basic questions, but this wasn't going anywhere, so she dropped it.

Art too dropped it. He was satisfied that he had deflected blame from himself. While Art knew that he could have done more to help Kim, he was also fairly certain that in so doing he might have put all three of them at risk. As it was, two of the three of them had made it out and, in his mind, he felt that perhaps his actions had saved his and the police officer's lives. If Art hadn't recognized the danger and taken to flight, then those dogs might have caught them and they'd all be dead. In fact, his running probably saved everyone's lives because his sudden appearance put them all on alert. Would they have been loaded into the van already had he not warned them? And yet, these women and that doctor were berating him. Who the hell was he kidding? Art could see right through doctor's ploy. He didn't want to know how to make them all safer the next time something like that happened. No. He was fishing for any excuse to blame Art for Kim's death and that was clear.

Well, to hell with him. Art had dealt with people like that all his life; people who would twist and distort every detail of what everyone says just to prove themselves right. Kim's death wasn't his fault and he wasn't going to let anyone try and figure out a way to blame him for it. He figured the best thing for him to do was to not give them any fodder with which to work. He leaned back into the seat, crossed his arms, and closed his eyes. If he was asleep, even if he was faking it, they couldn't ask him any questions and use his answers against him.

Neil hadn't said a word. As he drove, he watched in the rearview mirror as the dogs tried to pursue them. Several had stayed with them for a bit, but in the end the two vehicles proved to have too much speed and too much stamina for the dogs. One by one, they slowed down and then stopped the chase.

As the infected dogs disappeared behind them, Neil relaxed his foot from the gas pedal a bit and started to breathe normally again. With the immediate danger gone, he surveyed the cabin of the vehicle. Down Meghan's cheeks spilled silent tears and in her eyes was a very familiar sorrow. To Neil, Kim's death felt like losing a family member and judging by Meghan's tears, she must have felt the same way. All the passion and anger and accusation melted away with each salty drop.

# PART II

# CHAPTER 23

Downtown Anchorage resembled many cities of similar size and age. There was a multi-lane thoroughfare or two; there were some good-sized office towers with names like Key Bank and ConocoPhillips at their tops. The government buildings and courthouses were large granite structures that seemed to serve as landmarks for navigation as much as they did actual civic function. Usually, the streets were mostly clean and the shops were mostly open. The restaurants were typically busy and the several hotels were absolutely hopping during the busy summer tourist months.

Once away from the city center, Anchorage was as beautiful and well plotted as any city. The Delaney Park Strip, just south of downtown, ran for several east-west blocks and served as a median separating the commercial from the residential portions of the old city. Amongst the small houses and cottages with finely groomed yards, flower gardens, and yard swings, it was easy to forget that a bustling commercial district that catered to tourist needs was just a handful of blocks away. Adding to the fairytale quaintness, it was not unusual to see a horse drawn carriage with sightseeing passengers skirting the edges of these largely idyllic neighborhoods. It was as peaceful and safe a place as its residents desired.

Of course, that had all changed for the inhabitants on that fateful morning several weeks ago. People, young and old, fled the vicinity like every other corner of Anchorage. And like the rest of the city, the vast majority of those people, both young and old, met their doom while trying to escape it. The chaotic desperation that had claimed most of the city's inhabitants visited itself upon this peaceful corner as much as it did everywhere else. There seemed to be no escaping it.

The amazing thing, though, was that after the people had left, the peace had returned. The once quiet streets were quiet again, even more so than before. The flowers continued to grow, as did the grass. There were children's toys, Big Wheels and bicycles, scattered in several yards but no laughing, screaming children to ride them. Yard swings, if gently nudged by a breeze, still swung but there was no resting gardener to enjoy them.

As the two-car caravan made its way through the neighborhood, there wasn't a voice to be heard from any of the survivors therein. To most of them, speaking seemed as irreverent as skipping through a cemetery. They watched each passing house and wondered about its past occupants. Had they made it out alive?

For Neil, seeing the absence of any human life in such a uniquely human setting was more than a little disturbing. None of the movies he had seen that depicted such events came remotely close to delivering on the intense sense of loss that he was feeling. He brought the van to a rolling stop for no reason other than the fact that he was feeling so overwhelmed.

No one in the van spoke for several seconds. They just looked out at the abandoned houses and the empty lawns, much as Neil was doing. Meghan placed her hand on Neil's shoulder and massaged his tense muscles slightly. He barely acknowledged it.

Claire whispered, "Are we all that's left? Is everyone else really...?"

Jerry finished her thought when she trailed off, "Dead?"

Without a hint of humor, she continued, "Well kind of, anyway. There aren't even any of those things. It's just so..."

Dr. Caldwell stepped in this time and said, "Eerily peaceful."

"Yeah."

The radio connecting them to Maggie's car chirped loudly, startling all of them. "Why are we stopping?"

Neil lifted the radio to respond but set it down without saying a word instead. He looked in the rearview mirror and saw Maggie with her hands raised and her shoulders hunched. He wanted to point out how annoying he found her, but decided against saying anything. There was already enough doubt circling Maggie, much of it his own, and he didn't need to add to it. Dissension in their ranks wouldn't serve any useful purpose for any of them. Besides, the tension in the air was all but palpable since Kim's death. It was obvious Claire, Emma, and Meghan had more or less made up their minds that Art was at least indirectly responsible for losing her. It was also apparent that Claire was not completely forthcoming in her reservations about Art. Neil wasn't entirely sure what she was hiding or why, but he could see in her disposition the vague outlines of a buried secret.

Jerry had maintained his silence. Neil could see that there was more going on with Jerry than before as well. He was infatuated with Claire and that was setting the young man off balance a bit. So now he and Jerry shared something in common; both were finding themselves falling in love at a most inopportune time. Nothing like falling in love on the verge of the end of existence.

Neil was finding himself relying more and more on Jerry. The kid was smart, despite what he would have everyone believe about himself. He was also very resourceful, having been able to make do and even thrive under the current conditions. What Neil liked about him most, though, was that he could count on Jerry to always be there. It probably didn't hurt that Jerry had saved Neil's life while they were still hiding in the house in South Anchorage. Jerry had become quite adept at using the hunting rifle. His cool-headed attitude and sure shot aim made Jerry a very capable sniper.

Neil was as thankful for Dr. Caldwell as he was for Jerry. The doctor brought a level of calm to most decisions and discussions. Dr. Caldwell was older than the rest of them in the van and had experiences and training that helped him maintain his cool under most circumstances. The doctor had shared that he was a war veteran, having served in Iraq in a medical unit during the height of the most recent Middle Eastern conflict. He also related that the events of the past several weeks were responsible for his dismissing most of what he thought he knew about medicine, physiology, and trauma care. Nothing like having the dead rising to shake your unshakable faith in science. Was this what it was like for the all powerful clergy when the scientists of the Enlightenment began to introduce physical laws based upon science to explain the universe, thus debunking an eternity of natural phenomenon being attributed to gods of various stripes? He could understand why they reacted so coldly and sometimes lethally to such suggestions. It had to be disheartening to contemplate the possibility that all or most of what you had learned was now in doubt.

Of course, none of the doctor's combat experiences really prepared him for the terror that had virtually wiped out Anchorage either, but then there wasn't training that could have done that anyway. Maggie and possibly Malachi might argue that receiving training at church in the Lord's Word is the only training that could prepare someone for what was happening, but Neil was a little skeptical about the nature of that training and for what one might be prepared. He wasn't certain if Maggie was an End of Days believer or some kind of apocalypse seeker, but her brand of Christianity didn't seem helpful or healthy to Neil. He hoped that perhaps the doctor might still retain some of his combat skills training and be able to pass it along to the rest of them. That was training that would hopefully benefit all of them. Malachi's peace officer training with firearms and other self-defense techniques would be useful as well, but Neil was more than a little suspicious of Mal's capability in imparting any of that knowledge on anyone.

All of this was running through his head when he heard little Jules in the back say, "Maybe he can help us."

Meghan asked her, "Who sweetie?"

"That man over there walking his dog."

All of the adults looked back at her and said, "What?"

"There. Look." She pointed down the road at an old man who was walking along the sidewalk. He had a dog on a leash in front of him that was sniffing at fences and bushes along their route. They conducted themselves as if it was just a Sunday morning and they were out for their daily constitutional.

Confused, Neil looked all around the houses of this section of the neighborhood. He had never felt more like he was somehow caught up in an extended and disorienting nightmare in his life. Could this be real?

Meghan nudged him from behind, "Go check it out."

Still dumbfounded, Neil sputtered, "But, but..." and turned the van toward the old man.

The dog walker stalled and waited as the unknown vehicle strode up next to him. His hair was as white as fresh snow while the thin beard on his face was a slight mixture of salt and pepper, with the salt definitely imposing itself over the darker patches of pepper. He looked over at the eager faces looking at him from inside the van. He revealed neither relief nor caution with his expression. Neil thought to himself that this guy is probably a hell of a Poker player.

Dr. Caldwell lowered his window, smiled, and said amiably, "Afternoon."

The old man smiled back. "Afternoon."

There was a pregnant pause filled with questions and confusion for all of them. The old man, still smiling, said, "There aren't many of those things around anymore, but staying in one spot for too long still isn't a very good idea. You folks want to come back to my house for a little respite? I don't have much but I'm willing to share."

Still caught up on the old man's nonchalant attitude despite what had happened and was still happening in the city, Dr. Caldwell was at a loss for words.

Meghan decided to step in. "We've got food and water and other supplies too. But your house sounds wonderful. Is it safe?"

"I'm standing here ain't I?"

"Good point," she said, smiling and nodding.

Dr. Caldwell asked, "You want a ride?"

"Thanks, but no. Moe and I need to finish our walk first. We can meet you at the corner of Eleventh and P, if you can wait for us."

# CHAPTER 24

Back at his house, the old man introduced himself as Mr. Truman Holton, "but please call me Charles."

Claire asked, "Oh, is that your middle name? My dad didn't like his first name so he always went by his middle name. Most of his friends went his whole life without knowing that they were calling him by that instead of his real name."

"No, my wife, when we first met, decided that I looked much more like a Charles than a Truman. To her Charles seemed just as dignified but less stodgy than Truman and it just took. I've been Charles for more than sixty years."

"Oh."

Emma clarified, "And your dog's name is Moe?"

"Actually, he's my wife's dog and his name is Mowgli but we've always called him Moe."

Dr. Caldwell took his turn to ask, "And your wife, is she here somewhere?"

Before answering, Charles suggested they go downstairs to talk. He said, again, that he hadn't seen those things around much, but that there was no point in inviting disaster.

The basement was as big or bigger than the upstairs. There was a large sitting room with a pair of couches and a plush, well-used recliner. A hallway leading away from that main room revealed at least three doors, one of which was open to a lavatory complete with a shower. The other two doors were closed, but it was surmised that one was likely a utility/laundry room and that the other could be a storage room or possibly a spare bedroom. In one corner of the main room was a small kitchenette complete with a deep freeze that hummed as if it was working.

Charles seated himself in the recliner as if it was his throne and Moe, a trusted thane, plopped himself on the floor to Charles' right.

Dr. Caldwell, sitting on one of the couches, asked, "About your wife? Sorry to pry? I'm just curious if there are others still alive."

"No no no. I understand completely. Moe and I lost Lucy to lung cancer three years ago. Didn't we boy?"

"Sorry."

"Yeah, it was the damnedest thing. Woman never touched a cigarette, she rarely drank especially lately, and she was a hell of a lot more active than me. And she's the one who gets the big C. I guess there's just no telling for sure what fate has in store for us until it's already sprung. People have said that God has a strange sense of humor about things. I always wondered if her death was the punch line to some cruel joke or was it still coming. Well, I did wonder and all this happened. It's probably just as well anyway, Lucy wouldn't have liked this at all. She would have reminded me at least that this is why we should have moved south when we had the chance."

To Moe he said, as he rubbed the top of his head, "Mama wouldn't have liked this at all would she boy?"

The dog lifted his head into the massaging touch and opened his mouth in satisfaction. Mowgli was obviously not a young dog but it was also apparent that he wasn't a senior either. He appeared to be a well-behaved adult with more than a little Australian Shepherd in him. He was primarily black with a white patch on his chest, some white on his face around his eyes and one of his ears, and then some scattered brown patches on the lower third of his legs.

Jules, who was on the floor, said, "He's named Mowgli just like the little boy in *The Jungle Book*?"

"That's right. My wife loved Disney and named everything with Disney names. She even named our car Thumper because it kind of clicked and thumped when we drove it."

Jules smiled. "My favorite is *Beauty and the Beast*."

"Our vacuum is named Beast. It's a big, heavy, loud Kirby. And upstairs, in the front window, is a big Peace Lily that's named Belle."

Jules eyes lit up and she smiled. This was the most alert anyone had seen her in days. She stood up and walked around the room, eyeing all the different items and trying to guess what name could possibly be assigned to each. Her steps and pace were reminiscent of one of Disney's many princesses as she glided from place to place humming a quiet tune to herself.

Charles watched her for a moment or two and then stood himself. "I might have something that you'd be interested in," he announced, and then he disappeared down the hall and went into one of the closed doors. Moe stood and walked over to the hallway too, though he stopped short of walking into the room as well.

When Charles re-emerged, he was carrying a golden satin princess dress with sparkling sashes and glittery, puffy sleeves. "I think this is just about your size if I'm not mistaken. This was a favorite of our granddaughters but they're all too big for it now. What do you think? Would you like to try it on for size?"

Jules was speechless. She had never seen anything so beautiful in all her life. It was even prettier than the ornate wedding dress her cousin had worn in the only wedding that she had ever attended. She nodded her head enthusiastically.

A little later, with Jules spinning and dancing around the room like a euphoric princess, the talk returned to Charles' survival to date.

Charles looked at all of them and began, "Moe and I have a routine. He likes to be walked in the morning and then evening so that's what we have always done. We tended to go out before everyone else was up and moving about because it was just easier; less distractions for old Moe. We get up, get dressed, and walk ourselves around the neighborhood. He relieves himself and I get some exercise. Doctor's orders.

"That morning, it started out like any other. We got ourselves up and out the door. Nothing seemed amiss. We just went about our business like usual. The neighborhood was quiet, but it always was early in the day. Again, that's why we walked then. It was still dark when we got home, and that's when things started to happen I guess.

"At first, we heard a few sirens and then a few more and then a few more. It was like the whole city was burning down or something. I didn't smell smoke, so I thought that maybe one of the big banks had been robbed or something. Well, Moe doesn't much like the sound of sirens, so he and I went downstairs to watch some TV and read the paper. Hell, I figured that if something was happening, being downstairs was probably better anyway. Boy was I right.

"We were watching a little CNN when the program was interrupted by an emergency news update. Some yahoo from one of the local news stations started going on about a disturbance of some sort in Anchorage. He started talking about looting, arson, and killing and how the authorities were trying to get the situation under control. They showed some video taken from a news helicopter that was circling over the university. Looked like a riot to me. Not that much different than what you might see from a protest from Iranians angry at their government again.

"They couldn't tell us for certain what was happening, only that civilian and military authorities were doing what they could to restore order. From the video shots they were showing, it didn't look like the civilian authorities, at least, were having much luck at stopping anything. There were police cars all over the screen but nothing seemed to be working. Those folks just kept coming.

"Pretty soon, the helicopter wasn't just over the university. They were showing shots from all over Midtown and then, all of a sudden, the screen went to a test pattern and that was all the TV was going to tell us. I went upstairs to make sure that the front door was locked. I started moving as much food downstairs to this fridge as I could. I grabbed blankets and some books. I didn't know how long this was going to last or how long we would be stuck down here, but I'd never been through a real disaster before so I was just guessing. Lucy and I didn't move here until 1965, so we missed the big quake of '64, which I guess would have been a bit of a warm-up."

"At that point, no one really knew what was happening. While I was upstairs during one of my trips to move supplies, I saw Mrs. Gardner across the street. She was loading up her car with...well, with stuff. She loaded in some photo albums—she was so proud of those, a suitcase full of clothes, and some other odds and ends. I just kept watching her and wondering if maybe I should be getting out of town too. When I looked around at this old house though, I just couldn't bring myself to leave it. Me, Lucy, and Moe were just too comfortable here. So Moe and I stayed. We watched Mrs. Gardner and most of the neighbors leave. For a short while, the neighborhood was more hectic than it had ever been. Even on the nicest of summer days, I don't know that I've ever seen that many people in the street. And then they were all just gone.

"The folks on the radio tried to stay calm and cool, but you could hear in their voices that everyone was just plain scared. They didn't sound like they knew any better what was going on than the folks on TV. They started telling people to go to some of the safe collection sites...schools mostly. Moe and I, we just got ourselves comfortable downstairs and decided to wait it out.

"Early on that first day, I decided that it might be safer if I was to put a lock on the door at the top of the stairs. I took one of the deadbolts from a door down here and put it on the door. With that on, we started to settle in a little. I guess I must have dozed off because the next thing I remember was waking up to total quiet. I looked out those small windows over there to see out into the street. They sit right at ground level and, as you can see, are really too small to let anything in or out except a little sunlight. You know how I said that I had never seen the streets so filled with people before? Well...I didn't see anyone. I looked up the street and down, there wasn't so much as a hint of anyone still around. I had one of those Vincent Price *Last Man on Earth* moments.

"You folks know what was happening probably better than I did at the time. All of a sudden, there just wasn't anybody around anymore. We stayed downstairs for the next few days. I was already a bit of a hermit, but at least before I could watch people doing their daily activities. The only thing to watch during those days was the grass grow."

Charles could tell that his audience was reliving those same first few hours and days themselves in their minds. He could tell that the memories for all of them were less confusing and more traumatic than his. They had seen up close and personal and lived through what he had only seen glimpses of from cameras in hovering helicopters and heard about from radio reports.

He decided that his experiences from early on paled in comparison to theirs and that they probably didn't need to hear all of the mundane details of how he spent his time.

The room was quiet though. The gentle hum of the freezer was the only sound in the room. It was the hum that encouraged the questions.

Neil asked, "Do you have electricity?"

"Well, yes and no. I have a generator upstairs in the garage that's keeping the freezer running and lets me turn on the stove every now and again. After I went through all the gasoline in my car, I just went around and found all the other cars in the area and have been running it off of that since. I haven't needed to take that much gas so far, but I know where the cars are and know where I can get gas when I need it. I usually turn it off at night and then turn it back on during the day. I figure the freezer should be able to keep itself cold when I'm not going in and out of it."

"So what all do you have in the freezer?" asked Jerry. "If you can share a pizza, I think I would be willing to be your slave for all of eternity."

"No. No pizzas. It's mainly halibut, salmon, and moose with a little caribou and some vegetables from the garden."

Emma asked, "Garden?"

"Oh yeah. It was Lucy's garden but Moe and I have kept it up over the years. We've got tomatoes, potatoes, carrots, cabbage, and some other odds and ends out there. Lucy showed me how to can vegetables a few years back, so I've got shelves of jarred vegetables in the storage pantry and even some cranberry, blackberry, and raspberry jelly in there. If we're quick about it, I can show you out back if you'd like. There are quite a few raspberries still out there."

Emma, still distracted with his inventory, asked, "Cranberry jelly?"

"Sure. You want to try some? I've got a jar over here in the fridge."

Neil asked, "I thought you only ran the freezer?"

"Oh, I do. But I keep re-freezing water bottles and cooling packs to keep in the fridge so that I can keep some of that chilled too. I figured it would be a long time before Fred Meyer was going to open again, so I'm trying to make everything last as long as possible."

Neil had thought he had been clever and resourceful, but now he was seeing true resourcefulness. Charles was amazing. He did not strike any of them as someone who was trying to scratch out a basic existence with only survival in mind. He was living well...as well as could be expected. Looking around the room again, Neil found himself wondering at the level of comfort in which Charles had surrounded himself. Neil looked at the cleaned and drying dishes sitting next to the sink in the kitchenette, at the garbage can next to the stove, and at the dog food dish next to that. He looked at the neatly arranged books and magazines on the shelves along the wall and at the blankets folded and sitting along the top of the couch. There were some candles and flashlights on the couple of end tables in the room. Nothing was out of place and nothing seemed out of the ordinary. Really, the only things in the room that looked slightly out of place and dirty were the group of survivors that were Charles' guests.

That one fact was more than a little embarrassing to Neil. Here was a guy who was older than any of them by decades and he was doing a much better job of taking care of himself and his surroundings than all of them combined. Sure, it could be argued that a single person requires less food and less maintenance, but a single person only has himself to rely upon as well.

What would Neil have done if he were alone? Could he have made it this far all by himself? He doubted it. And then he remembered the day when he and Tony started the fire down the block from their safe house. He got himself up and over a fence only to be confronted, grabbed, and threatened by one of the ghouls. The creature had Neil in his clutches and had it not been for Jerry, Neil would be one of them now. That memory still chilled Neil's thoughts and made him in even more awe of Charles.

Dr. Caldwell asked what Neil and Jerry were thinking, "What about...you know...the zekes... zombies...those things? You've obviously seen them. When did you first start seeing them?"

Charles sat back in his chair and thought. A hint of emotion crept onto his face and landed squarely in his eyes; eyes that were as grey as time. He took a deep breath before he began, "Sorry. It's just this is really the first time that I've had to talk about those first few days. Moe doesn't ask me a lot of questions and when he does it's usually about either eating or going to the bathroom.

"The street lights still worked through that first night but they only light things up so far. I think I started seeing them then. There were just a few, and in the dark they kind of looked like normal folks who were just in a bit of a daze. I guess I wasn't the only one who decided not to leave, because ole' Jaspar from down the street, he went out to see if he could help them. Maybe he thought they were just in shock or something, I don't know. I could tell that they didn't seem right and it wasn't shock. They just weren't right.

"As soon as Jaspar came into the light, there was this horrible noise and they took off after him. Jaspar was old, so he wasn't running anywhere. He held up his hands but they didn't stop. They just came at him. In the glow from the street light they didn't look human anymore as they went to work. It looked like something you might see on Discovery or...." He looked at Jules and Danny and stopped himself short, "Well, you know what happened.

"I heard his wife scream from further down, out of the light, and those things were after her just like that. She must have been up at the house still, because I heard some banging and then some shattering glass. There was a scream and then nothing. I hoped she had a heart attack or something before they got to her. Betty...Beatrice, had a bad heart. The next morning though, there was Beatrice, in her pink nightgown, wandering in the street. She was a walking nightmare. She wasn't a thing of grace and beauty when she was alive, I gotta be honest, but she really was a monster. The thing that I think bothered me the most, though, was that her little yappy pain in the ass white dog was still following her around like she was still in there. I'd hope Moe would have better sense.

"The next day I woke up and looked out the window there and didn't see anything. Beatrice was gone and so were all the others. Of course, I couldn't see much from those windows, but what I did see was a lot of nothing out there. A little later in the day, I saw my first group of survivors. They were running. There were about six of them, maybe more. They looked like they were just ordinary folks, but they looked so scared. They stopped right out there by the street lamp. It looked like they were just resting; trying to catch their breaths. I wanted to go upstairs and tell them to come inside, but I just couldn't. I was too afraid.

"It looked like two of them started to argue about which way they should go. One pointed north, into downtown, and the other pointed west, toward the airport. Maybe they were being tracked already or maybe it was their raised voices. Regardless, they all stood up at once and the fear already in their eyes became panic. Two of the women, girls really, started to cry.

"I might have still had time to help them. I could have told them to run over here and they could have hid in the basement with Moe and me, but I didn't. Instead, I watched them start to run that way up the street and then all of a sudden they came running back the other way. They disappeared from my sight and so I didn't see what happened, but then I heard the screaming. I honestly don't know what happened to them. They might have gotten away. I haven't seen any of them around since, if you catch my meaning.

"I saw a handful of others over the days, but it's been quite some time since the last group. In fact, the last one I saw was a single woman. She looked like she was in a bit of a daze, but she was still alive. I saw her at least a couple more times after the first too. She would just wander in the street and then disappear again. My guess is that she's moving from house to house, if she's still alive."

Jerry asked him, "What about lately? Have you seen any people or any of those things?"

Charles nodded and continued, "I've seen those things a bit but we've been able to avoid them mostly."

Neil tilted his chin and said, "Mostly?"

"Well, Moe still needs to go out. I didn't really want to turn Lucy's house into a latrine. I didn't want to catch hell from her for an eternity when it was my time to join her. So, after the first few days, Moe started to go out back but I could tell that he wasn't satisfied with this arrangement. I got myself a tire iron and decided to take him out."

Meghan asked, "A tire iron?"

Charles answered, "It was the best I could do."

Jules asked, "Weren't you scared?"

"So scared that my knees were knocking with each step. That first walk was short and sweet. He went out, took care of his business, and then we got ourselves back home. This went on for a few days but then we decided to be a little braver. We took a walk around the whole block. That was our routine for a couple of days, maybe a little more. When you're spending as much time alone as I have, details start getting a little murky.

"I guess we were feeling a bit cocky because we decided to let our guard down a little and almost ran smack dab into a group of three of them. Lucky for me, they didn't walk any faster than me. And we were able to lose them, but now I knew that there were some of them around. And they knew that we were around too. Almost ruined a perfectly good thing."

Dr. Caldwell asked slowly, "So are they still around then?"

"In a manner of speaking. They're really not much of a threat anymore."

Jerry nodded. "I get where you're goin' with that."

"Probably not, actually. I decided to go out on my own one morning. I didn't want anything to happen to ole Moe here and I didn't want to get tangled in his leash or anything. No offense, Moe, but I think you would have been a bit of a liability. I went out with my tire iron and not a clue as to what I was doing, but I knew that I needed to get rid of them or they'd end up getting rid of me. It didn't take long to find them. They were standing out on a corner. It looked like they were just waiting for the bus or something. They were just standing there. It was the damnedest thing. They looked like grey statues or something, only every now and then one of them would shake from their feet up to their heads and out to the tips of their fingers. It looked like maybe they were each in turn stepping on the same exposed live wire and getting a little jolt of electricity. I think that bothered me more than the way they looked, or even smelled for that matter.

"I got their attention, which didn't really take more than me rounding the corner. While I was still headed toward those things, I saw that Jackie Gordon's garage door was open. So, on my way back I decided that maybe this would be my chance. I knew that I couldn't outfight them. Hell, I was fighting with the tire iron just to keep it in my hands. Those things get heavy after a bit. Anyway, the garage is a detached model that used to be someone's shop and Jackie's late husband Tye did some modifications to it. One of the things that he'd done that he was most proud of was rigging a release in the back of the shop right next to the backdoor. The lever was just a really big switch and when triggered, it was a manual release for the garage door to come down. They had an automatic garage door opener, but he was a tinker and it came in handy when the garage door was outta repair.

"I guess none of that matters. What does matter was that I led those little buggers into that garage, shut the front door and let my self out the back, locking them inside. With a can of Tye's spray paint that I swiped from one of the shelves as I made my way through, I painted a warning on the front of the garage. Just in case anyone ever heads back this way. I'd hate for the wrong person to open that garage door and get a nasty surprise."

Neil asked, "And so you haven't seen any more of them since?"

"No. Moe and I have been pretty much the only ones around in several days. It may have been more than a week since I locked those things up. You wanna see our garden now?"

They went out back to check out the garden and just get some fresh air. Using a ladder, Jerry climbed on top of a little storage shed in the far corner. From there, he could see into most of the adjoining yards and beyond. He could also see up and down several streets. It was a great vantage point, but even better than the view was what he didn't see. He didn't see any of the predatory undead creatures that had been stalking them. Charles was right; there really didn't seem to be anything or anyone in the vicinity. Still, Jerry found himself scanning the backyards and streets over and over again as the others picked raspberries and other late odds and ends from the garden.

The raspberry bushes covered the entire back fence and were popping with the little red fruit. For Jules and Danny, this was the best time they'd had on their vacation to Alaska yet. There was something special about picking fresh anything from a plant and eating it right on the spot. They savored each sweet, juicy bite.

While the others enjoyed the backyard, Dr. Caldwell and Neil moved the van into the backyard through a large vehicle sized gate. With the gate closed and Jerry in his "crow's nest" observer position atop the shed, the back yard seemed like a fortress, safe and secure. For the first time in a long time, Neil felt like he could relax for a bit.

# CHAPTER 25

Malachi sat in the open air of the backyard and thought to himself that this was probably how Adam felt on that first day. This was no Eden, but it was closest thing to it that he'd seen in a long time. He leaned back in his folding lawn chair and soaked in the scene. Other than a grill, the afternoon had all the trappings and leisure of a holiday barbecue. There was food and laughter and, more importantly, no fear. It was as if the seven-foot cedar fence that wrapped itself around the yard like a pair of protective arms, held all the horrors of the past several weeks at bay. Of course, as he sat and reveled in the day, he was sitting away from most everyone else. To him, it was just safer, in case none of what he was seeing or doing was real.

Charles had brought out a couple of packages of smoked salmon from the freezer. The packages were passed around to each of the very eager guests in the backyard. Jules and Danny sniffed at the strips and then declined to eat any but everyone else dived in hungrily. The two kids busied themselves with eating the raspberries and then going back to pick more. While they worked on the harvest, they each ate the peanut butter sandwiches that Meghan made for them.

Art and Neil were busy at the back of the van. They were unloading some of the food and most of the blankets and extra clothing and carrying it into the basement. It had been decided that the group would stay for a day or two with him while they formulated a new plan. Hoping to assuage some of the guilt he felt for not helping the others that he'd seen, Charles elected to open his sanctuary to these strangers.

He was watching Art and Neil work and found himself amazed at the stacks of food and material they were removing. He moved over next to the van and peeked inside. When he saw the supplies in the back, he let out a sigh and said with obvious relief in his voice, "Boy, you folks sure travel in style. I was afraid that maybe I was gonna hafta feed all o' you. But look at all of that."

With a hint of false offense in his voice, Neil asked, "What kind of houseguests do you think we are? D'you think we were just going to eat all of your food and then leave you high and dry? I've got something for you in here too. Where is it?"

Neil lifted a canvas bag filled with cans and moved it aside. He pulled a plastic container from under the back seat. "Ahhhh. Here it is." He opened the opaque tub to reveal a variety of handguns and boxes of ammunition. He lifted a small, stubby nosed revolver and a box of shells and handed this to Charles. "You look like a Smith and Wesson man."

Charles took the firearm and weighed it in his hand like the statue of Justice holding her scales silently. He didn't say anything for several seconds. Neil wasn't sure whether he was having an emotional response to the gesture or if it was maybe something more. The gun was sitting *on* his hand more than *in* his hand, and this fact was not lost on Neil.

He asked tentatively, "Is everything okay, Charles?"

No response except more silence. He was thankful that enough was happening around them that no one else was paying any attention to their interaction. Neil could see now that Charles' quiet was memory induced. He could see the past in the old man's somber, distant eyes; a past that was steeped in forgotten memories.

"Charles?"

"Sorry. I just...I...uh...haven't held a gun in my hand in over fifty years."

"I didn't mean to...I didn't know."

Charles smiled as reassuringly as possible and replied, "How could you? My kids don't even know."

"What happened?" Neil was imagining some accident or possibly a crime involving a gun. Perhaps Charles had been a police officer or a security guard and he was forced to use his weapon.

Charles asked as he looked up at the sky, "Have you ever heard of the Chosin Reservoir?"

Neil started to say that the name wasn't completely unfamiliar to him but stopped himself short. Instead, he shook his head and let Charles continue.

"I was in the Army in 1950. I was part of the Army of Occupation in Japan. It was easy work and good pay. I was only eighteen, hell, just *eighteen*, and I was seein' the world on Uncle Sam's dime. And then, all of a sudden I found myself aboard a troop ship headin' to Korea. Who the hell had ever even heard of the damned place before '50? I eventually got assigned to the 32nd Regiment of the Seventh Infantry Division. We were called the Queen's Own. I know, I know. It's kinda funny to think that a US Army formation could carry that title but we did. It had something to do with the unit coming originally from Hawaii and having some traditional queen there first call us into service. I used to know the story pretty well. I guess because I was pulled from my original unit—an anti-aircraft battery—to supplement the 32nd's infantry roster, I didn't have the same connection to the unit that the other guys had. Hell, I was so new that I didn't even have a name yet. I was just, *Hey new guy*.

"By the time I came ashore, most of the major activity was over and we were just offloading and marching inland. There had been some fighting when the first wave hit the beach, but I guess we scared the North Koreans pretty good because they just bugged out in a hurry. That was September and it was already starting to get cool at night and staying cooler in the mornings before the sun had a chance to warm the air a bit.

"It was unpleasant where we were and compared to the comfort of Japan it was downright miserable, but I was lucky to not have fought in the Pusan perimeter defense. They almost lost it and quite a few young boys like myself saw their last days during that battle. But then the enemy broke and it was our turn. We hit the tough yellow bastards so hard that we pushed on up that peninsula right north of the 49th Parallel, all the way into North Korea.

"And then it started to get cold. I think the Koreans got the worst of it, but it still wasn't comfortable. On the drive north, we'd see their frozen bodies all along the roads as we chased them. Most of them looked like they just laid down with their rifles and went to sleep."

By this time, Danny had joined them and listened intensely. There was just something about war stories and boys; like mosquitoes drawn to warm blood. Danny's grandfather had fought in 'Nam, whatever that was, but never talked about it. He looked it up on the Internet and found out some basics: where it was fought, who fought, and for how long, but his grandfather's silence on his experiences was most frustrating. He eagerly awaited each word, reveling in Charles' adventure.

Charles continued, "We came to a place called Hagaru-ri, a kind of crossroads for mountain roads and passes on the southern end of this huge valley smack dab in the middle of some of the most inhospitable terrain in all of Korea. In Hagaru-ri though, we got all loaded up with supplies, ya know, like extra ammo and dry rations and things like that. And then we knew that something big was coming because we got treated to real food. It wasn't world class cuisine mind you, but it was a helluva lot better than the dehydrated pig droppings we usually got."

This latest comment brought a chuckle from both Danny and Neil. Even Charles seemed to be pleased with his wit.

"It was late November and as cold in those Korean mountains as any winter day in Anchorage I've ever felt, and I've lived more than half of my life in here. We didn't know it then, at least not yet, but we were at a place called the Chosin Reservoir. I guess it's a pretty big manmade lake, but it just looked like the world's biggest ice rink to me. I couldn't imagine it ever being warm enough in that valley for that damned lake to thaw. Man it was cold there.

## Containment

"Unfortunately for us, it was at the Chosin Reservoir that the Chinese decided to push back on behalf of their North Korean communist brothers. All at once, an entire Chinese army was in the valley with us and they were all about business. They weren't necessarily well armed or even well led, but there were just so damned many of them. By then, we had been designated a Regimental Combat Team, which is just when you take a bunch of infantry and then throw tanks, cannons, engineers, and anti-aircraft units in with it. The theory was that an RCT could operate independently in the field indefinitely so long as supplies continued to be delivered…a mini-army unto itself. The problem we had was the same problem the regiment had when it left Japan; we were understaffed. We had only one of our infantry battalions, about a third of our operational strength. We were tough, well armed, and well supplied, but there just weren't that many of us.

"That's not to say that we were the only good guys in the valley. There were some ROK, sorry, South Korean soldiers, some British soldiers, and a helluva lot of US Marines. Believe everything you ever hear about how tough those guys are. From their generals on down, they are a burly bunch and always spoiling for a fight.

"Unfortunately for us, most of the other fellas were on the western side of the reservoir and we were on the eastern side. The Chinese decided to hit both sides at once. When you outnumber your enemy by more than two to one, attacking like that is possible. The first few hours on that first night were bad. I was in the First Battalion and further north than any other units. There were somewhere between three and four hundred of us in the line and we got hit by a few thousand Chinese infantry. They just poured out of the darkness like bad news and drove us back. Colonel Faith, our CO, was really the reason that more of us didn't die on that first night because he was everywhere, telling us to keep our heads down but keep fighting. He just told us to hold until first light and then the air corps would come and kick some ass.

"Believe me, I forgot all about the cold on that first night. I was part of a Forward Observation team. It was our job to spot the enemy and then call for artillery support. We would use the radio to adjust their fire for better accuracy and effect. Because of this, we found ourselves higher than and more forward than most of the other units. Me, our officer, a Lieutenant Dan Greene, and Sergeant Ansel McGuire had been attached to an under strength infantry platoon. We were on a hill that had a good view of the roads and choppy fields approaching our positions. We called in fire all around us until we realized that we'd been cut off. That was a horrible feeling.

"Up to that point, the riflemen and machine-gun teams seemed to be holding the enemy at bay well enough to allow Lieutenant Greene to call in what they called danger-close fire support. Some of the explosions were so close that the heat was scorching the hairs in my nose. I wasn't sure what I was supposed to be doing. Maybe I was just another set of eyes, I don't know. What I can say is that I tried my best to be as small in my hole as I could get and stay out of the way of the bullets zipping by overhead. I only found courage to fire my rifle when Lieutenant Greene ordered me to do so and even then it wasn't something that I jumped at doing. Hell, those crazy Chinamen were trying to kill me. I could hear it in their voices; they were that close. I popped up and just started pulling my trigger. I didn't pick targets. I didn't have to. They were pretty much everywhere and I don't think they knew where I was at first. I shot until my rifle didn't have any more bullets to shoot. I reloaded and did it again and again and again. I lost track of how many times I repeated the process. There just wasn't time to think about things like that. I was probably making more noise than anything else. I couldn't imagine being an infantryman, whose primary job was to be in those kinds of situations…hairballs we would call them…and then sort them out. No thank you.

"And then there was a blast so close by that it knocked my helmet clean off my head. It's hard to describe those first few seconds immediately after. There was a ringing that wasn't just in my ears. My whole head and even my chest were ringing. I had blood running down from my nose and out of my ears, but I wouldn't figure either of those out for quite some time. I guess it's fairly common to have that after suffering a concussion like I did from the explosion.

"Anyway, I looked up and the lieutenant was gone. He was just…gone. The radio was there on its side and still squawking, but the lieutenant had vanished without a trace. They never did find his body. Sergeant McGuire was hit too but he was still alive…for the time being. Shrapnel had hit him in the arm, chest, and face. He was bleeding pretty badly but when I tried to help him, he just pointed to the radio and told me to keep calling in fire.

"I grabbed the radio transmitter and tried to answer the questions that were coming through, but the ringing in my head made it nearly impossible. I could hear faint noises but couldn't make out what was being said. I finally just told the other end that the lieutenant appeared to be dead and that I would continue to adjust fire.

"When the radio went quiet, I thought that would be the end for us. Luckily, the entire battle had moved on. It was like we were forgotten in the Chinese infantry's haste to close with the main force's position. There was still shooting and fighting, but it was well behind us by then. I can honestly say that I've never seen anything like what I was seeing all around our little hill when first light broke. The rocky fields all around us were carpeted with the bodies of dead Chinese soldiers. I don't know how many I shot personally or how many were killed by the artillery that I personally directed. I felt sick all over though. Until recently, it was the closest thing that I've seen that resembled hell on earth."

Charles paused and looked at Neil and Danny. He shook his head at the memory, as if he was seeing it all for the first time again. By this time, Meghan had joined them as well. She was standing next to Neil with her hand hooked under his crossed arm.

The old man looked at her and smiled warmly but then he looked embarrassed. Neil could tell that he wasn't accustomed to talking about his experiences in the war at all and was even less comfortable talking about them in front of a woman, especially one he didn't know.

With the smile still on his face, Charles looked at Meghan who, to Neil at least, seemed to be glowing in the sunlight. Neil could tell that Charles was seeing it too and was also aware that Charles could tell Meghan and Neil had become a couple. To acknowledge this fact, Charles looked at Neil smiled and winked.

"I didn't realize that I had been monopolizing the conversation for as long as I had. Where are my manners? Your generosity must have just taken me by surprise. You always hear about disaster bringing out the worst in people. I have firsthand experience with it from back then. I guess that it's still true as well that disaster can also bring out the best in others."

Neil blushed and lowered his head until his chin rested on his chest. Meghan leaned over and whispered in his ear, "See, I'm not the only one who's seen it." She smiled and kissed his cheek lightly. This did nothing to diminish the bright red from his face. It wasn't like Meghan to show any real affection in front of others. Truth be told though, Neil couldn't imagine anything that could ever feel as velvety soft against his stubbly cheek as her lips did at that moment.

He looked back up at Charles who was watching Meghan walk away. He said to Neil, "You got it bad don't you?"

Neil pointed his finger at himself and in a half-hearted show of being flabbergasted said, "Me? I don't know what you're—"

"Can it son. Remember, I've got a few years on you, so I know what to look for. And I looked the same way when Lucy used to kiss my cheek. So don't try and convince me otherwise. Got it?"

Danny, who was still standing there, smiled and even giggled a little. He liked Charles and he liked Neil looking so happy. Danny also liked that he could stand there and be included in any conversation. It wasn't anything like back home when the adults would stop speaking any time he would approach them. He was feeling more like one of the grown-ups every day.

He looked around at everyone in the yard. Jules was still over by the raspberry bushes along the fence. In the gold dress Charles had given her, Jules really did look like a princess. Emma had braided her hair and adorned it with some of the late blossoms from the flowers in Charles' garden. He couldn't hear her, but he could tell that she was singing something softly to herself. He wondered for a moment what would happen to Jules when they got back home. Would some distant relative come and take her away? He hated to consider that. He had grown very protective of her and was wondering if maybe she could just come and live with his family. Maybe there wouldn't be anyone in her family who would want her. Maybe if he went home as a hero, he and Jules could just tell the authorities that she was going to stay with him. Maybe.

Claire had joined Jerry on top of the shed. She was sitting down with her arms behind her and her legs stretched out in front of her. Jerry was standing next to her and still scanning the neighborhood all around them. When Claire motioned to Jerry to sit next to her, however, he was quick to heed her command. Danny was starting to see the same expressions on Jerry's face when Claire was around as when Neil was near Meghan. Danny chuckled to himself at his newly discovered insight into human behavior. His understanding of what was happening between both couples made him feel more like an adult than ever.

# CHAPTER 26

Maggie and Malachi chose to sit in the kitchen through most of the gaiety. They sat largely in silence with not even the gentle hum of electric appliances to cut into the heavy quiet. For Malachi, the stillness was welcome. He valued peace, especially since his life had been so devoid of it for as long as he could remember. In the silence, there was always the threat of his torturous memories assailing his thoughts and threatening his calm, but on that afternoon the quiet was without judgment...without accusation or blame. It was merely peaceful.

Still looking out the window at the others, Maggie said calmly, but with a sneer crouching behind her facade, "You know that God loves you, don't you?"

Malachi nodded his head.

"You know, too, that He has a plan for all His children, don't you?"

Malachi nodded again.

"Do you know your plan, my son?"

Again Malachi nodded, trying to preserve the quiet. He'd heard that said many times over his life; that God has a plan for everyone. No one, however, had ever asked him if he knew his or if he understood his role in a greater plan. Somehow, he had always assumed that someone would just tell him one day. He had always hoped that someone would reveal it to him. So far, he had been left painfully ignorant of any of it.

He spent those next several seconds after Maggie's question staring more at the thin lacy white curtains than through the window. The yard beyond was obscured by the veil, like a body beneath a funeral shroud. The people lost all identity; they were just nameless, faceless people going about their business. He watched them move around beneath the sheer cloak.

He remembered a day long ago and another veil similar to this. The face beneath was familiar but he could barely make out the details beneath the cloth. She lay there on the bier while others stood beside her and cried. They touched his shoulder gently, some rubbing his back as they moved on and took their seats in the room. He didn't understand then how much pain was growing inside him. He swallowed it down long ago and it became something different: anger. That anger, both with the world in general and with some of their companions even then relaxing in the backyard, faded into the thin white cloth in front of him.

He was still wearing his police uniform and was never more aware of that fact than at that very moment. He started to remember things...promises...oaths. The remembering was painful and its clarity was actually confusing to him. The oaths seemed out of place to him...foreign somehow. Had he taken them? Was that actually him in some long ago forgotten life?

He touched the cold, metal badge on his chest. He saw his mother. He could see her eyes and her approving smile peering out from beneath the veil.

He stood up from the table and, without uttering a single syllable; he walked out of the kitchen and into the backyard. He grabbed a lawn chair from the neatly stacked rack hanging on the back of the house and joined the others. The voices around him were soothing, despite his still feeling uncomfortable. He knew that he wasn't quite right yet, but for his mother he could try.

Maggie watched him go in equal silence. In the ring of moisture left on the tabletop by her water bottle, she traced a cross and whispered, "That's right. They'll all be somewhere better soon enough. The believers and the non-believers will all finally see. And so will you, my friend. You half-wit. You pagan trash. You'll see. And it'll all be better for everyone soon enough. You can only run for so long from the Truth and from the deliverers of His message."

She removed a small folding knife from inside her jacket pocket and held it out in front of her. "Truth" she said to herself and used the blade to open a small incision on her forearm. She watched the small rivulet of blood form and then course down her skin. Like a tigress cleaning her young, she ran her tongue the length of her arm, lapping the salty red fluid from the wound.

"Truth. Truth is the blood of the lamb," she quietly sang, the soft tune echoing like a symphony in her head.

# CHAPTER 27

The first night in Charles' basement was fairly pleasant, all things considered. The air inside was cool, but absent was the crisp edge the air outside carried on its shoulders. Between the food that Charles contributed and some of the supplies from the van, they enjoyed a veritable feast.

After dinner, they all played board games and told stories to one another. Charles shared with Emma and Meghan some of his wife's cherished photo albums she had created over the years. They looked at both black and white and color photographs of national landmarks and family occasions, a life of happiness documented on film.

Following Malachi's guidance, Art, Jerry, and Neil cleaned and oiled some of their preferred firearms, talking and laughing as they did so. Danny watched them, knowing that he would need to clean his own rifle in the not too distant future—after it had gotten some use, of course. The switch in Malachi's mood pleasantly surprised even Jerry. He and Dr. Caldwell agreed that moments of levity and stability were not uncommon with people suffering mental illness and that they should continue to be vigilant when it came to Malachi. The break, however, was nice for all of them. They also appreciated his knowledge of firearm care. None of them would have even considered for a moment the need to perform such essential maintenance.

Maggie ate her meal quietly but did smile at the frivolity and generally good moods that everyone seemed to have. After having eaten, she chose to open a Bible and read from it rather than join in any of the games or discussions.

When it came time for everyone to go to sleep, Charles retreated to the bedroom down the hallway and everyone else tried to make themselves comfortable on the couches and floor around the main room.

Lying on the floor next to Meghan, Neil stared up at that the dark ceiling. His mind was filled with images, memories, and waking dreams that became harder and harder to control as sleep began to overtake him. His last coherent thought was, *I hope this can last.*

The next morning, Jerry woke with a start. He shot straight up and sat there on the floor for a moment or two while he tried to remember where he was. He looked down at Claire, who was still curled up next to him and holding onto his hand. His chest warmed as an involuntary smile spread across his face.

The room was still filled with the sound of deep, sleep-filled breathing. Someone's nose was buzzing slightly with each exhaled breath. He looked around at the others, trying to distinguish everyone in the dim light of the early morning. He stretched and yawned, thankful for feeling rested again. He smacked his lips together loudly and rubbed the sleep from his eyes. He looked around again and realized that something seemed slightly amiss. He immediately looked around in a panic but found Malachi still leaning against a wall in the corner, still asleep.

Jerry stood up, lying Claire's hand back at her side, and wandered over to the small window looking out across Charles' front lawn. The light outside was faint but growing stronger by the minute. He didn't see anything that stood out to him as being wrong out front. Maybe it was just his imagination. He found his water bottle and took a short drink from it, mindful of preserving whatever water they still had.

Standing in the kitchenette, he realized what was wrong. He could see the soft glow of the rising morning on the wall of the staircase leading down to their room, which meant that the door at the top of the stairs was open. He felt his heart skip a beat and his skin went cold. He held his breath for a few seconds as his eyes darted back and forth across the room again. He didn't want to make too much noise in case there was some threat lurking upstairs, so he tiptoed through the sleeping bags and their occupants until he found Neil.

He shook the other man slightly. "Neil. Neil. You've gotta get up," he whispered urgently. "Neil!"

Neil opened his eyes, saw Jerry looking down at him, and knew immediately that something was wrong. He leapt up to his feet, grabbing the pistol that was lying next to him in the process.

With a whisper he asked, "What's wrong?"

Jerry motioned toward the stairs and said, "The door upstairs is open."

Neil looked around. "Maybe Charles and Mowgli went out for a walk and decided not to wake us."

"I don't think so. I don't think he would have done that to us. Besides, he would have at least shut the door at the top of the stairs. Don't you think? I mean, he wouldn't just take off and leave everything open like that. He's smarter than that."

"You're right. Get a gun and let's get everyone else up. Quietly."

Jerry nodded and did as he was told. Neil crept over to the stairs and looked up. Sure enough, the door at the top of the stairs was open. It wasn't just ajar like someone had forgotten to latch the bolt into the locking position either; it was wide open.

"Shit."

As Neil made his way up the stairs alone, he was reminded once again that he was not cut out for the hero business. He didn't really think of himself as a coward but he also couldn't believe for a moment that a hero's heart would be beating as quickly or as loudly as his was at the moment. The sleek automatic pistol clutched in his right hand was visibly trembling and offered little comfort to him. He stopped on the last stair before emerging into the room above. He held his breath and leapt through. He spun around right and then left, trying to see everything at once so as not to be surprised from behind. He could smell the cool morning air in the house and then realized that the front door was standing wide open as well.

He ran over to the door and slammed it shut, spinning again on his heels terrified that his latest move might have drawn unwanted attention to himself. His breathing was coming in very quick, shallow breaths, like a fish out of water struggling for air.

Coming up the stairs, Dr. Caldwell asked, "Neil. How are things looking up there?"

Neil looked around the living room and didn't see anything necessarily out of order. He appeared to be alone. Of course, he hadn't checked down the hallway or even out in the kitchen and dining room.

"Neil?" the doctor's voice this time was a bit more concerned than before.

Forcing his voice to raise louder than the whisper that it wanted to be, Neil answered, "So far so good. The front door was open too, though. We better look around and make sure."

"Okay. We're coming up. Hang tight."

Neil let out a long breath that he could clearly see due to the cooler outside air that hung in the room. *What the hell happened?* It was just a scant few seconds before Jerry's and Dr. Caldwell's faces emerged from downstairs. They looked around slowly and nodded to Neil, who was still standing with his back to the now closed front door.

Jerry said, "It's cold."

"Yeah. The backdoor might still be open. We should go check that next. How is everyone downstairs?"

Dr. Caldwell answered, "Alright, I think, but a little shaken. Maggie's gone."

"What?" and then Neil pivoted over so that he could see out the front window. Her car was gone too. "Son of a bitch. What about Malachi?"

"He's still down there."

Neil nodded. "Let's figure out what happened after we check the house. I want to make sure that none of those things is wandering around up here lookin' for breakfast."

They checked the back hallway. Luckily, Charles had chosen to close the door for the bedrooms and bathroom on the main floor, so the checking didn't take very long. The backdoor was as wide open as the front though. Despite the status of the doors, the house still seemed to be clear and was secured again almost immediately.

Standing in the kitchen, Jerry looked out a window into the backyard and saw that the van's doors too were standing wide open and some of their supplies had been removed and dumped on the grass.

Standing next to the van a few moments later, Jerry said to the other two men, "It looks like she took what she wanted and left the rest. What about the extra guns under the seat?"

Neil answered, "She didn't know about those, I don't think, because the tub is still under the seat."

And then, from the back of the van, Dr. Caldwell said, "She took the extra gas and the empty cans."

Not willing to believe the heartless actions, Jerry asked, "Are you fucking kidding me?"

Dr. Caldwell came around the van and asked the other two men, "What about the gas in the tank? Did she leave us anything?"

Neil answered, "I'd have to go get the keys to start the engine. I think that'd be a helluva lot easier than anything else. I'll be right back."

"Agreed," said Dr. Caldwell.

Just a minute or so later, out of breath from having run downstairs and back again to retrieve the keys, Neil was sitting behind the steering wheel of the van. He turned the key in the ignition and nothing happened. He tried again and again nothing happened. Nothing; not even a single attempt at coming to life.

Neil looked up and noticed that the dome light overhead wasn't on despite his door being open. "Curious."

"What?" asked Jerry.

"I think it's the battery."

"The battery?"

"Yeah, I think she might've drained the battery because the car is dead. It's not even turning over and it's never had problems like that in the past. Maybe she turned on the headlights or something. Hell, she left the doors wide open, maybe that was enough to do the trick. We don't know how long she's been gone."

"Yeah. Why don't we take a peek under the hood? Either of you guys know anything about cars?" Neil asked as he pulled the latch to release the hood.

Both Dr. Caldwell and Jerry shrugged their shoulders and then disappeared behind the raised hood.

Dr. Caldwell said before Neil had even gotten out of the driver seat, "I'm no mechanic but I can see at least one problem."

"Oh yeah?"

"Yeah," and he held up several of the cut and slashed pieces of a wire. "She killed the battery cables and it looks like that wasn't all. We're missing some other parts and there are definitely some pieces of something other than battery cables in here too. Shit, she took all the spark plugs too!"

"What are you sayin' Doc?"

"Like I said, I'm no mechanic, but I'd say that we've lost this patient and there's no bringing her back."

The kidding, in fact all the humor from each of them, melted away with the realization that statement engendered. They were going to be on foot now.

# CHAPTER 28

"You folks are more than welcome to stay here. Me and Moe don't have much to offer but we're willing to share."

Meghan looked at Neil, wanting to hear his ideas. He was a good man and a smart one too, and she trusted him. She doubted any of them would have made it this far if it hadn't been for him. He was always so doubtful of himself, but when he made a decision things tended to work out. Meghan knew that Kim blamed Neil for Tony's death but she couldn't see how it possibly could be laid at Neil's feet. It was precisely because of Neil's planning that they all hadn't ended up that way. If it was left up to the rest of them, they would have probably stayed in the house until those things got in and then it would have been over for all of them quickly.

"You are too kind," Neil said to Charles. "Your generosity is greatly appreciated. I just think that we would end up being a bigger burden on you than you know. When winter hits and supplies are really scarce, you aren't going to want to have as many extra mouths to feed."

"Don't think of yourselves as a burden to us. We'd like the company."

The offer was very appealing. It would be so nice to just stay and hope for the best, but Neil knew deep down that staying just wasn't the right thing to do. For one thing, Maggie knew about the house and what was there to stop her from leading back an army of those things like some perverted Pied Piper? Maybe if Neil and his group were to move on, she would just leave Charles and Moe alone. For a moment or two Neil thought about the prospect of leaving Jules and perhaps even Danny with Charles but then he saw an image of Charles keeling over from a heart attack and Jules and Danny being left to their own devices to survive. He just couldn't do that to them. There had to be help somewhere out there; some vestige of civilization that was still clinging to survival. They just had to find it.

He was all set to say that when Jules said quietly but to all of them, "I wanna go home. I don't wanna be here in Alaska anymore." Quiet tears and gentle sobs followed her words. "I want my Mommy and Daddy and Martin. I wanna go home and have everything be the way it used to be."

Emma lifted Jules in her arms and hugged the crying child to her chest. Everyone wanted to hug her and tell her that it would be all right.

Charles saw that they were resigned t leaving, and that it was futile to convince them otherwise. "What can me and Moe do to help you folks get ready to move on then?"

"I don't know why we don't try and find another ride before we leave. It's safe here and Charles doesn't seem to mind us being here. Can someone please explain it to me?" pleaded Claire.

Almost apologetically, Jerry replied, "Really, this place only *seems* safe. Sorry, Charles. Safety is a bit relative at this point. This place isn't any more or less safe than anywhere else. I mean, there's just a single bolt lock on the door at the top of the stairs. If those things got in upstairs, there wouldn't be any holding them back. They'd just slam themselves against the door until it gave and then this refuge would become a trap without a way out. Charles has just kept a low enough profile to keep himself from being noticed. In fact, I wouldn't be at all surprised to learn that we...that our being here has actually threatened his...anonymity. More of us in one spot means more sounds and more smells. We could be acting like a stronger and stronger magnet to the zekes still wandering around town."

Meghan had never considered that a possibility. They could actually be ruining this nice old man's last refuge. She was suddenly feeling a little guilty about the sanctimonious attitude she had assumed when Neil decided to give the majority of their pillaged supplies to Charles. It wasn't even that she didn't necessarily want to give him the cans of food and other supplies. It was just difficult to part with anything these days and she was afraid that they might give away the wrong thing. Of course it didn't make a lot of sense to tote around all that canned food on their backs. Her knowing that didn't really make it any easier though. She had helped carry all of it inside nonetheless.

And now, with Jerry's latest postulation, she was glad that she hadn't said anything about which she would be publicly embarrassed.

Jerry continued, "We can look for a new car or something on the move. We're bound to find something. Besides, Charles already said the only cars in a several block radius don't have keys in them."

Charles added, "And I drained most of the gas from all of them already too. Sorry."

Neil shook his head, "You don't have to apologize for that. Any other ideas or questions?" The room was silent. "C'mon people. This can't be just left up to me. What do all of you think?"

Claire said, "I think we should stay here, but you guys seem to know what you're doin', so I'm in."

Neil let out a single, half-hearted chuckle, "Don't kid yourself. There are no experts for what is going on. We've been lucky, that's all. Jerry's thoughts about those things aren't absolute. There was no training or preparation for any of this. We've been learning as we went, and only time will tell whether the lessons learned are helpful or not."

Dr. Caldwell interjected, "I think we're all just safer when we stick together and watch out for one another. I think Neil and Jerry are right about staying on the move though. Out there, we'll find more cars, more food..."

Art chimed in, "And more of *them*."

The doctor, not fazed by Art's comment, continued. "Perhaps. But how long before they find us here and then we're forced back on the road on their terms and not ours? We still have ample sunlight and enough supplies that we can carry to keep us moving for days to come. I think if we are going to be back on the road, I'd rather go now than later. And Neil, I think we should head north. We can get onto Elmendorf and then cut east toward the Knik Crossing. Who knows what we'll find on the military base?"

Art added, "Yeah, who knows for sure? How fast will we be able to move with two kids in tow and our backs loaded with stuff? If we get into a chase with those things, we're screwed. Has anyone considered that?"

Claire shot him a look from across the room, started to speak, thought better of it, and then let go with, "Art, shut the fuck up! You act like you'd be lookin' out for anyone other than your own ass! You don't care about these kids any more than you care about anyone else sitting down here."

Art looked stung. He took in a deep breath while she spoke and then let it out in his defense. "Listen to you, you hypocrite. If you hadn't followed me and done exactly what I did, then you would never have made it. You aren't any better than me or anyone else who's still breathing. Instead of accusing me of being somehow less of a person than you, maybe you oughta be thanking me. I can't believe how stupid you can be and how deluded. Jesus Christ! Look at you over there, smug and secure in your opinions of yourself. You ran just like I did and you'll do it again. When all is said and done, it's every man for himself. At least I'm adult enough to admit it. So yeah, I am primarily interested in saving my own ass. Are you willing to tell me that you aren't?"

She shook her head.

"Bullshit! When we're being chased and those things are right on our heels, are you going to be willing to carry that little girl there and slow yourself down? I don't think so and neither will any of the rest of you. You'll just keep on running and try and not hear her screaming for help. Afterward, you'll convince yourself that it was for the best anyway. You'll swallow your guilt—or maybe not—but you'll still be alive and that's what matters. That's what we all want."

"I don't want it at any price," Claire spat. "I'd never abandon this little girl." She paused and looked over at Jules and then at Danny, "Never. I'd give up my own life before I'd do that. Do you both understand?"

Art sneered. "Oh yeah? What about Joan? Your friend back at the hotel? When she was grabbed, did you stop to help her?"

Claire shook her head and tried to hold back the tears, "That wasn't the same."

"Why not? Wasn't she your friend? Hadn't she saved your life? The only difference here is that she was an adult and these are kids. You ran then and you'll run again. You'll see. All of you will. When the fear fills your thoughts and pure instinct takes over, the only thing that you'll be able to do is run."

Claire was crying by then and shaking her head as she stared at the floor, "You're wrong." She whispered emphatically, "You're wrong."

Art stood up and went up the stairs, saying as he did, "We're making a mistake. You'll all see."

# CHAPTER 29

They decided that it made the most sense to leave the next morning so that they would have a full day of sunlight in which to move. They packed backpacks full of cereal bars, water bottles, various survival supplies, and ammunition for the guns they elected to take. The backpacks were heavy, but there was a sense of security in their weight. Everyone, including Jules and Danny, carried supplies on their backs. Despite the still warmish days, they also each wore extra layers of clothes, so that vital backpack space would be available for the other necessities.

At first light the next morning, they all rose and headed out the door. Charles and Moe walked them out across the Park Strip and into the edge of downtown.

Neil and Charles shook hands. "You look out for them and everything will be all right," Charles said as he looked over Neil's shoulder into the deserted streets of downtown Anchorage. "If you get into a fix, make your way back here. Moe and I will keep an eye out for you."

Neil nodded and said, "Thank you so much for all that you've done for us. You'll never be forgotten, and if we do find a way out of this mess, we'll be sure to come back for the two of you."

"You just worry about getting yourselves to safety. Ol' Moe and I will be just fine. Won't we old boy?"

Jules left Emma's side and ran to Charles. She wrapped her little arms around his legs and hugged him tightly. He placed his palm on the top of her head and stroked her soft blond hair. "Now you run along, Jules, and keep an eye on these folks for me and Moe." She looked up at him but didn't say a word. He looked back down at her and smiled. With that, she ran back over to Emma and took her hand.

As they walked away, Charles and Moe turned themselves about and headed back to their home. Neil wondered if maybe they were making a mistake by leaving. There was a sense of security back at Charles' house. He knew, though, that the security was more than likely a mirage that could be shattered at any given moment; like the security that all the residents of Anchorage who had lived and worked in the buildings to either side of him had embraced for so long.

The air stirred as they made their way into the city proper. There were large professional buildings to either side and the empty cavernous barn of the new convention center in front. Whatever isolation or desolation any of them had felt in the suburban sections of the city paled in comparison to wandering the stark emptiness of a city as large as Anchorage. The grey city streets, typically packed with walking pedestrians and driving motorists, were as vacant as a tomb.

Neil was careful to put them on a course to detour them around the Transit Center, the public transit hub of downtown Anchorage. He didn't know if they should suspect pockets of zombies anywhere, but he figured it just made sense to play it safe and avoid places to which people might have fled and then been trapped. He was only guessing though. There were no sounds or smells or anything really to help his decisions; only gut instinct.

Marching in a single file line down the middle of the street like a claustrophobic parade, the column of survivors kept a vigilant watch on windows and doors and alleys and cars and.... There just seemed to be an endless list of threats and traps all around them. Neil was concerned that the farther they went, the deeper into danger he led them.

A flutter of movement from a recessed doorway caught all of their eyes. They gathered themselves into a tight circle while Neil and Jerry went forward, weapons at the ready, to investigate.

Neil suggested as they walked forward, "Use your scope and see if you can make anything out."

"I already looked through," Jerry replied, "but there are potted plants and walls in the way."

Breathing deeply and letting it out slowly, Neil nodded and continued ahead. There in the doorway was a group of ravens. He remembered that a group of crows was called 'a murder', and wondered about the name applied to a group of ravens. The two species of birds seemed to share so much in common. It was of little consequence that Neil didn't know a group of ravens was called 'an unkindness' because both names seemed fitting under the circumstances. Whether it was a murder or 'an unkindness,' the birds, black as nightmares, were picking away at something on the ground that was still out of view.

"What is it?" Meghan asked from back in the group, startling both Jerry and Neil.

Neil raised his hand as they cleared the last of the obstructions. The brown, blood-stained and shattered bones of a corpse, mutilated and dismembered, were being picked clean by the fluttering scavengers. There were tiny bits of clothing on the ground around the body but, other than a blizzard of bird droppings, not much else was present.

Again Meghan asked, "What is it?"

Neil and Jerry jumped again at hearing her voice. They looked at one another for just a second and then Neil said, "It's nothing. You guys just keep moving on up the road. Just some birds getting into some old trash."

Jerry said quietly, "I think maybe we should get away from these birds. If they're carrying the infection, there's no telling how it could affect them. Remember the dogs."

Suddenly very concerned, Neil raised the shotgun in his hands toward the birds and then backed away with Jerry. *And this is only the first block*, Neil thought to himself grimly.

And thus began the not-so-enthusiastic journey through the barren remains of a city ravaged and claimed by a plague.

# CHAPTER 30

Have you ever been somewhere that you could have sworn you'd been before, but try as you might, you can't seem to make anything about it seem familiar? That was happening with every step as the group of survivors marched slowly into the heart of Anchorage. To Meghan, it reminded her of the time she came home from school and found a man in their kitchen who sounded like her dad, was wearing her dad's clothes, and acted like her dad but was missing his trademark mustache. It was the weirdest thing. She was set completely off balance by the alteration. It actually took her a couple of days to truly get used to the new look. She wasn't sure that an entire lifetime would afford her enough time to get used to the "new" Anchorage. Only thing was, Anchorage's mustache hadn't been shaved off; it had been ripped viciously from its face. The mangled mess remaining could never again look as it once did.

Walking in a generally northerly direction, Jerry suddenly stopped when he caught a whiff of an unfortunately familiar stench. "I think I can smell 'em. Yep. It's definitely them. That's an odor that sticks in the memory."

Dr. Caldwell asked, "Coming from where?"

"I don't know but it's not that strong. Either there's just one of 'em or they're not too close."

Claire almost cried, "I fucking hate this. Why didn't we find a car first?"

Jerry said over his shoulder, "We're gonna be okay. Just..."

At that moment, from the building to their right, a window several floors up shattered into a thousand glistening shards of glass and rained down on the street next to them. And quickly on the heels of the glass, three of the undead beasts fell to the pavement with a horrible wet slapping sound. The three were piled one atop the other and still writhing, tangled and mingled like worms in the bottom of a can.

Claire did cry this time, "Oh sweet Jesus."

From the top of the pile, the first of the zombies finally got its hands under itself enough to raise up to its feet. Its movements were stiff and seemingly inorganic, like a living statue...a golem come to life. Its skin, an ashen, lifeless grey, was drawn tightly across its facial features, starting to recede slightly from its eyes. It didn't look real and it certainly didn't look like it was once a human being. When its jaw lowered, it exposed a mouth utilizing a hit or miss approach with teeth. There was a molar missing here and an incisor missing there. This incisor was cracked in half while that eyetooth had been honed into a threatening point. Its first steps were no more fluid or natural than any of its other movements.

As it stepped forward, the second one from the pile arose in much the same fashion as the first, though this second one had been a woman, under better circumstances. The third didn't seem to be moving at all. Perhaps the fall had crushed its skull and ended its misery.

Malachi stepped forward and fired two shots in quick succession into the closest one. The first shot took off its still lowered jaw and the second shot caught it just below the eye. The impact from both rounds hurled the beast tumbling head over tail backward where it came to a motionless rest, looking more like an abandoned pile of rags and trash than a body.

The second one, wearing a dress and one high-heeled shoe, didn't seem to even notice that its accomplice had been dispatched. It just came awkwardly forward with its emaciated arms extending out toward them. Its horrible, hunger-filled moan reached out with its own icy fingers to tickle their spines. Neil, firing from his hip like a Hollywood action movie hero, hit her across her right upper chest and shoulder. She spun and twisted to the ground, but with a grunt and a series of audible pops and clicks from her shifting bones, she rose back to her feet and continued forward apparently unfazed.

Without a word, Malachi brought her down with a single pull of his trigger, the bullet finding its way through her forehead and out the back of her skull.

"Thanks, Malachi."

"Don't mention it." He wanted to say that he hoped that those three bullets would start him on the path toward trust again. Malachi, however, would never have been able to fully verbalize that sentiment. It wasn't that clear even for him. How could he possibly be able to communicate it to someone else?

Jerry said, still leaning back on his heels, "That's not what I was smellin' and I can hear them now too."

"Them?" asked Claire, a grimace spreading across her face like a very aggressive rash.

"Yeah."

"How many Them?"

"A few...at least." Claire moaned.

Dr. Caldwell said, "So maybe this isn't going to be as easy as we'd hoped."

Art sneered under his breath, "I knew it. Now we're fucked."

Forgetting the acid that was building in her stomach like a toxic storm, Claire shot him a look and very nearly growled at him. "Don't worry, Art. I'm sure you'll find a way to get yourself through this."

"Stop it goddamnit!" Neil spat. "We don't have time for this."

Meghan asked, "So now what? Do we wade into there and hope that Jerry's "few" is really just a few? Or do we go back around and just hit another pocket somewhere else?"

Art interjected, not even attempting to disguise the contempt in his voice, "Or we could just go back."

Neil repeated, "Or we could just go back."

Everyone looked surprised and a little confused.

He shrugged his shoulders and said pointedly, "Folks, mine aren't the only ideas here. Going back is definitely an option. I personally think that going back to Charles' now would be selfish of us and draw the damned zekes right to him. I think it's nice to have that refuge behind us if we need it, but I think it should be a last resort. We can go back to another house and board it up like we did before. But also like before, I think it would just be a matter of time before they sniffed us out and then we'd have to escape again but this time on foot. At least now, we're moving on our terms. I will say though, that the longer we sit here debating it, the more danger we're in."

"Why don't we go into one of these buildings and see if we can get a better view of our surroundings?" Emma suggested. "Maybe then we could choose a way through town."

Dr. Caldwell smiled. "Now that's a great idea."

She smiled doubtfully. "It is?"

Neil nodded and replied, "I think it's a helluvan idea. I'd say the one where our friends here came from is off the list, but what about one of the others nearby?"

Meghan asked, "How do we know which one?"

Malachi said, without changing his expression or looking away from the road ahead, "Locked doors."

"What?"

"Look for locked doors."

Dr. Caldwell, again beaming, said, "You're a genius, Mal."

Without any further delay, they ran across the street to a tallish, nondescript, giant rectangle of a box with a door on the front building. The big glass door was locked and looked unmolested.

Jerry suggested, "We could go around to the back of the building. I think there's a parking lot, another entrance, and some office windows on the ground floor back there. I think we should go in one of the windows. Even if we break it, we can close and bar the door of the office the window is in. Regardless of what we do, I think we need to do it now. They're probably just around the corner up the street."

Meghan said, "Then why the hell are we still standing around talking about it?"

Just a few minutes later, they were climbing the stairs to the top floor and a possible view of the streets and open spaces around them. There was a certain sense of security about being back inside but none of them were fooled into believing that they were actually safe.

Even with flashlights and the scant light coming in through windows, it felt like they were journeying deeper and deeper into a cave. Appearing to be both following and preceding, their footsteps echoed the entire length of the stairwell, prompting them on more than one occasion to pause and determine that they were still alone in the building. The silence that ensued each time they stopped was worse than the cacophony of sound that preceded it.

Out of breath and sweating, they arrived at the top floor to find the door was locked. To make matters worse, there wasn't a window on this door as there had been on the doors behind them.

Claire asked, "So now what?"

Neil leaned his shoulder into the door and pushed as hard as he was able but there wasn't even so much as a shudder by the door on its hinges. He and Jerry stood back away from the door and threw themselves against it with much the same result. They were about ready to do it again when Malachi's hands found their shoulders and restrained them.

"Why don't all of you go back down the steps a couple of flights and let me have a go with this," he said, holding up a shotgun.

Neil, smiling in the dark, said, "Now why didn't I think of that?"

"I'll need someone to hold a flashlight up here but everyone else can wait down there. You folks might want to cover your ears. It's gonna be loud in here."

He was right. It was loud. Their footsteps were nothing compared to the roar from the gun. Luckily, however, it worked. Malachi and Dr. Caldwell kicked the door, which swung back and forth on its hinges, trying to mimic its rustic cousin, the saloon door.

The hallway into which the door opened led to several larger conference rooms that were positioned on each corner of the building's top floor.

Dr. Caldwell said, "I think we've got pay dirt here."

Emma mused playfully, "What, you a miner now?"

"Ya gotta have a hobby."

"And yours is mining?"

"No."

"Okay, now I'm totally confused."

"I prefer to think of it as suspense rather than as confusion."

"Whatever it is; I'm there."

"I watch a lot of History Channel and lately they've run some shows about the history of mining."

"Lately?"

"Well, you know. Before, when GCI cable wasn't on permanent hiatus."

From down at one of the conference room doors, Jerry said, "I think this is the one. Door's still locked. Malachi, you want to do the honors?"

Malachi stepped up and eyed the door for a second or two. He took a deep breath and exhaled loudly as he pounded the bottom of his foot hard against the door just above and to the right of the door handle.

The door flew inward heavily, slamming with a thud against a comfortable looking chair parked a little too far away from the long, heavy, dark table that sat in the middle of and dominated the room.

Jerry shrugged his shoulders and said with a smile, "Ya gotta give it to him. The man's got a way with doors."

Neil smiled and entered the room. It had a solid two walls of windows looking out over much of downtown Anchorage. As he approached the window he said over his shoulder, "You guys have gotta see this."

If he didn't know any better, he could have mistaken what he was seeing for a very well attended but subdued rally for grey people. There were hundreds of the ashen skinned monstrosities loitering in and around an intersection at which sat an open parking lot on one corner. The mass of ghouls didn't move much. Every now and again, the crowd was collectively affected with tics and spasms that sent arms into the air and heads turning and twisting. It was one of the most inorganic things he'd seen them do to date, aside from the killing and eating of anyone and everyone around them that is.

As Jerry and Malachi stepped up, Neil said, "I guess it's a good thing we looked before we leapt, huh?"

Jerry dropped himself into one of the very soft looking plush office chairs situated around the table. The chair swiveled awkwardly as he turned himself to get a look out the window. Now seeing the spectacle, Jerry leaned forward in the chair to truly take in the scene below.

The few seconds of awed silence was cut when Jerry remarked, "How did anyone get anything done having a meeting with this view? Jesus, I don't think I'd be able to concentrate on a thing being said up here."

Leaning back and with just the slightest hint of a smirk on his face he asked, "Did you say something, Neil? What about jumping?"

"Funny. So now that we can see better, I guess we won't be heading that way. Better to learn that from up here than down there. What about that way?"

From behind them Meghan asked, "What's down there?"

Jerry said, "I think it speaks better for itself than we ever could. Come hither."

Neil laughed and said with a warm smile, "Boy, that chair has really had quite the affect on you. Hasn't it your majesty?"

"Let's just say, my good man, that I could get used to having the finer things in life."

"You don't say."

"You could too if only you worked as hard as I did when I was a young lad. I started out with nothing...and yet here I am today...at the top of the world. Well, at the top of this building anyway."

Neil rolled his eyes and started to step away. He asked Meghan, "Where is everyone else?"

"There are clean bathrooms up here with toilet paper and water in the bowl. Where do you think everyone else is?"

# CHAPTER 31

Using the conference table as it was intended, the entire group found themselves sitting about the dark oaken monolith to discuss their options. The discussion had ebbed and flowed; the few ideas truly embraced by everyone examined and evaluated from every possible angle.

Art still persisted that going back was their best option. Unfortunately, that was the only opinion he shared...and shared and shared and shared. Even Jules felt like he was being a little obsessive and repetitive. She probably would have even said he sounded like a broken record, if she had been familiar with the expression.

"Okay, okay," Claire said. "We get it. You think we should go back. We hear you loud and clear. Since none of the rest of us agree with you, maybe you should just stop bringing it up or take off by yourself. Nobody's gonna stop you. You can head on back and be safe if that's what you want to do." Claire spoke in her typical fashion that she reserved for Art alone. She simply did not like Art and she didn't care who knew, including Art. "Why don't you do something constructive for a change, like shut up?"

Art's glare was full of poison but he declined to respond to Claire's barbs.

Trying to defuse a bomb that had already detonated, Neil asked, "Other suggestions?"

Dr. Caldwell said, "How about the Atwood? The Performing Arts Center? And we could use the sky bridge to go across to the Egan Center."

Meghan asked, "Won't the Egan be bad too?"

"I don't think so and neither should the Atwood. With the new Dena'ina Convention Center opened, the Egan kind of lost its status as a primary civic collection point. I mean, how many events have switched to the new joint already? How many concerts or whatever have any of you been to at the Egan recently? Any? I know most of the conferences that I attend, if they aren't at one of the area's hotels, they are usually at the Dena'ina lately. It's all about new and shiny when it comes to hosting. And the Atwood is just a big theater. It has no emergency appeal or function to my knowledge. I think we should be good at both places."

Emma finished with, "Okay, but how do we get there? We can see the bastards over there, but there's no telling what's on the other side of those buildings there. For all we know, there could be groups of those things at every corner...in every alley...everywhere."

"It's probably better that we just assume that," Jerry said. "What's the saying, hope for the best but plan for the worst?"

Neil added, "I think that should just be our motto from here on out."

With the exception of Art, who merely held his dissenting opinion to himself, everyone agreed that, without any other options seemingly available, Dr. Caldwell's suggestion made the most sense. They plotted a course that took them from building to building until they reached the Atwood.

# CHAPTER 32

On the run again...

They emerged into the back parking lot of the building to find a trio of the fiends loitering amidst the yellow parking stripes. The awkward, stutter-stepping nightmares came at them like faded and weary but persistent salesmen. And they weren't going to take no for an answer. Meghan screamed when she saw them, stumbling awkwardly backward into Claire who also screamed.

Malachi stepped forward with his pistol at the ready but Jerry interrupted with, "No! Don't use a gun. It will only draw more attention to us."

Art asked sarcastically, "You want us to use bad language?"

From behind them, Dr. Caldwell said, "No, I think these will do," and handed Neil an aluminum baseball bat.

Neil said as he walked away from the group, "Get the kids back inside. They don't need to see this." To Dr. Caldwell he said, "How we going to do this Doc?"

"Don't think. Just act."

Dr. Caldwell swaggered out into the parking lot with the bat in one hand. To Neil, he looked like a gladiator...a warrior from days gone by, going into battle with his club. He tried to emulate the same confidence and fearlessness, but was afraid that he just looked like he was acting. The doctor got closer to one of the ghouls, leaned himself forward on the balls of his feet like he was preparing to swing at a pitched baseball, and swung. As the bat made contact with the thing's head, a metallic clang echoed between the buildings. The beast's head rolled to one side, its neck clearly broken with the first swing. Dr. Caldwell didn't hesitate for even a second. He swung the bat again; this time taking off part of the scalp. Into a crumpled heap of rotting flesh and tattered clothing, the zombie fell.

Neil held his breath, partially to try and control his breathing so as not to hyperventilate and partially to reduce the amount of the stench that he could smell. He thought he was ready to swing, but he couldn't get himself to do it. He hadn't been in too many physical altercations in his life. Whenever a situation seemed to be brewing toward a fistfight and a possible opponent confronted him, he always found himself resistant to throwing a punch. He could stare the person down, but most attempts at actually fighting brought on a nearly uncontrollable hysteria within him that all but immobilized his hands at his sides. This same feeling was what was staying his hands at the present moment. Even when the thing had its hands raised toward him and was approaching him threateningly, he was finding it difficult to hit it.

Dr. Caldwell was busy trying to square off with the third and final ghoul and was, therefore, not available to help. Neil backed away a little to buy himself some time. He was slightly distracted with the memory of having been clutched by one of the things several days ago. He shook his head, trying to stave off the helplessness that was threatening him. Why couldn't he do this?

It was getting closer with each passing second. Neil was feeling like the fly caught in the spider's web again; just waiting for that lethal bite.

Meghan watched him from inside the glass doors. "Jerry, do something," she urged.

Jerry nodded and stepped back outside. He walked over toward Neil, who said dispassionately, "I've got this one. I'm just..."

Jerry responded, finishing Neil's thought, "...making him suffer a little."

"Yeah. Suffer."

Neil got both of his hands on the bat, swung it in a high arc over his head, and brought it down with a powerful executioner's swing onto the top of the demon's skull. The creature gurgled slightly as its cranium was crushed down between its shoulders, losing all shape and function. Watching it slump silently backward, Neil said, "Thanks."

"You got it. I think we should get moving. I can hear them coming toward us again."

"Yeah. You're right. No point in wasting any more time here. Let's get outta here. Now."

Disengaged. That would best describe Neil's mood for the next several...actually, he wasn't really certain for *how* long. He felt like he was living in a series of frightening and somehow connected images, like he was stuck on the reel of a stop motion camera. He remembered pounding footsteps against damp pavement. There was Meghan running close behind him. Her face was strained and desperate. Was everyone else still with them? Where were the children? Were they keeping up? There was another sound, more distant but building. It was more footsteps; a lot more footsteps. They were being followed...pursued...*hunted*. He was prey fleeing for his life with the rest of the diminishing herd.

The running was accompanied by shouting and arguing. Someone, a man, suggested something but someone else, a woman, disagreed. They fought on the run, like two cowboys having a gunfight from the backs of racing horses on the prairie.

There was frantic, terrified sobbing as well...all around him. He may have even been a part of that but he couldn't be sure. He saw doorways and windows, abandoned cars and a crashed bus, but none of it registered as anything that even approached reality. Stop motion photography, after all, was something to be watched and not something to be survived.

And then there was quiet again. They were back inside. Where? There was arguing and protests, but he couldn't follow. He wasn't even sure about the voices. Maybe that was Dr. Caldwell or it could have been Jerry. It came from behind him.

Another voice. He looked up to an audience of faces waiting for the show to begin, and what he was slowly realizing was that he was the main attraction at this carnival. He rolled his eyes from left to right, his head barely moving.

"Well, Neil? What should we do?"

The question registered this time. What should we do? That was an excellent question. To his dismay, he discovered that his well was empty. He was about to shake his head and admit to as much when the pounding of fists against the glass doors separating them from the outside menace steeled his one thought.

"Let's find a back way out and get the hell outta here and quick. We gotta keep moving. We gotta put some distance between us and them. Just keep moving."

They ran down the wide hall into one narrow corridor that led to another. They passed doors but didn't see any way out, just more offices or bathrooms or storage rooms or whatever. They started to turn right again and then Neil saw it. On the wall high above another door was an Exit sign.

There was no time to pause; no time to be careful. Behind them, the large glass doors and windows of the office building finally gave way and came crashing to the floor, and in poured a reeking wave of bloodthirsty beasts hot on their tail. Everyone ran through the door, which was then slammed shut, hoping to be that barrier that might finally stem the tide.

Dr. Caldwell said, "I don't think this door is going to hold them for very long. We better keep moving."

They all agreed on the run as they headed north up an alley that emerged onto Sixth Avenue. They could see the Atwood up the road a few blocks, with nothing but empty street between them and it.

They started to slacken their pace a little to which Neil said emphatically, "No! We can't let up! Keep moving! We don't have the time to catch our breaths now! We gotta get somewhere safe first."

As he was saying this, they all heard the familiar sound of rage-filled footsteps pounding behind them again. They knew that if they could get into the Atwood Concert Hall before their pursuers saw them, then perhaps they could gain some distance and a modicum of safety. The casual confidence they all had when they first entered the city was faded and gone. They were desperate refugees again trying to stay ahead of the storm.

They ran to the first set of doors they saw and, not surprisingly, they were locked. Jerry said to all of them, "I think we should keep moving to the doors around the corner."

Claire, with wide, questioning eyes, demanded, "Why the hell don't we just get inside before it's too late?"

"We don't want them to follow us if we can avoid it, and right now, they'll see us go in. Maybe if we get into a door around the corner, we'll lose them for a bit. Outta sight outta mind."

Dr. Caldwell decided for all of them, "Let's just move. He's got a point but this is no time for a discussion. Go!"

The crowd of ghoulish pursuers was getting closer with each second. They weren't running at them, thankfully, but their single-minded pursuit was persistent. They just kept coming relentlessly forward as a single, angry, mob.

At the next set of doors, Jerry used the butt of his rifle to break an opening in the door. The task wasn't as easy as Jerry had imagined. The glass was tempered and shatterproof.

After watching several vain attempts, Meghan ordered, "Step back." She raised the pistol in her hand and fired a single shot just above the door's outer handle. The concrete alcove in which they were standing magnified the crack of the gunshot. Neil, shaking his head trying to relieve the ringing a bit, looked at Meghan with surprise. She shrugged her shoulders and smiled. "Someone had to do somethin'."

Jerry again used the butt of his rifle, but this time he banged it just above the small opening. The wooden rifle stock went through the hole, making it large enough for his hand. He reached inside and pulled on the horizontal handle, thus releasing the locking mechanism from inside.

With the door open, they all piled into the hall's main lobby. The room was cavernous, with ceilings reaching several stories above where they stood. To Danny, it resembled some of the big churches he'd visited with his parents. As they ran up the wide staircase to the next floor, he looked over his shoulder at the door through which they had come. Outside, the first of the zombies were just passing. They seemed to be going right by the door. They didn't seem to be following them; at least not yet. They did, however, seem to be moving much more quickly than it had appeared from a distance. It wasn't quite a run, but he would have called it at least a jog or a trot. Any illusion he may have been harboring about being able to outrun these things needed to be rethought. They were still very dangerous and should not be underestimated.

Jules who was standing on the step above him tugged his shoulder. "C'mon, Danny, we gotta go. We gotta keep up or they'll leave us." Jules' eyes betrayed her fear of being abandoned and forgotten. She'd heard Art's protests and his warning to the others about bringing her and Danny with them. She would have liked to stay at Charles' house but she thought that Neil and Jerry might still be able to get her home. Now, with those scary things chasing them and all the adults acting so frightened, she didn't want Art's prophesy to become a reality.

Jerry came back down the steps to where they were standing and said reassuringly, "Don't worry you two. Nobody's leaving anybody. Got it? We do have to keep moving though."

Danny smiled up at Jerry. "It looks like your idea is working. They're going right by us."

"We can't get sloppy then," Jerry cautioned. "We gotta use this extra bit of time. It's important that we keep moving so that we can stay safe. Let's go."

Jules and Danny both sprinted up the staircase, taking a couple of stairs at a time. They beat Jerry to the top and followed the others as they ran toward the doors opening into the sky bridge that spanned Fifth Avenue.

Standing in the enclosed footbridge, they all paused and looked down. On the street below them, hundreds of the beasts were beginning to congregate. Jerry remembered once visiting a zoo featuring a large shark tank with a walkthrough breezeway that allowed visitors to see the sharks from a fish perspective. It was fantastic and a little claustrophobic. That was how he felt now. Like a spectator at a zoo looking at dangerous carnivores still in their cages, he looked down at the fiends on the street below.

The things barely resembled human beings anymore. For the most part, their flesh was starting to pull tighter and tighter across their bones as the moisture in their skin and muscles diminished. Most of them still bore the horrible wounds that had originally claimed their lives, though they were now crusty and as brown as rusted metal. Their clothing resembled the tattered rags that one might find covering the abandoned and forgotten furniture in a long condemned tenement building.

Emma stood quietly as they watched the throng below. "I can't stand to watch this anymore. I'm so afraid I might see someone that I recognize...well, would have recognized before all of this."

Dr. Caldwell asked them, "Shouldn't we just keep moving?"

They made their way across the elevated corridor toward the doors that opened into the Egan Convention Center.

"Wait a minute," Neil said, "I might have an idea here. Take a look inside. Are there any of them in there?"

Jerry pushed the unlocked doors open and peered inside. He disappeared for a moment or two and then was back. "It looks clear. What're you thinking?"

"I want everyone to hightail it outta here and I'm going to see about trying to get those things' attention on me up here. Maybe we can get them distracted enough that we can get away without them even knowing it."

Meghan looked skeptical. "What do you mean, you're going to get their attention?"

"Don't worry, I'm not going to do anything stupid. I'm just going to make some noise so that they're all looking up here at me and then I'm going to sneak away. They're not that bright or even that aware. They probably won't even notice that I'm gone. I'll catch up to you guys in just a minute or two. Find the back door of the Egan and then wait for me. I'll be along in a few."

Meghan, not fully convinced, asked, "Wait a minute. They don't even know we're here. Why don't we just sneak out before they figure it out?"

Dr. Caldwell answered, "We've seen those things and how focused they can get. If Neil could draw their attention up here and then get away without them knowing it, they could still be looking up here waiting for their meal for as long as time and their decomposition allows. I think it's worth a try."

"Why does it have to always be Neil?"

"Because it's my idea. I wouldn't feel right asking someone else to do it. I'll be safe up here," Neil assured her. "Besides, we've got the walkie-talkies. I'll stay in touch."

"You goddamned better!"

"I will. Now get outta here." Neil held up his radio and Dr. Caldwell did the same.

Despite his reasoning, Neil wasn't entirely convinced that he should always be the one to set his ideas into motion. It seemed like every idea they had was his. It was starting to get exhausting.

A noise from the Atwood Concert Hall behind him drew his attention. He walked over toward the large double door to look back inside. He could definitely hear movement; most likely footsteps. "Shit."

He ran back into the sky bridge and started to speak frantically into the radio, "They're in the Atwood. I'm on my way. Where are you guys?"

In a crackly, static-laced voice, Dr. Caldwell responded, "We're almost at the back door near the elevator. We'll wait for you."

The sound behind him was getting louder. Thinking better of drawing any more attention to himself, he elected to not pound on the glass wall of the sky bridge and instead just make his way toward the rest of the group. He wasn't convinced that his plan would have worked anyway. If the things saw him running away into the Egan, they might have just chosen to follow him and then they wouldn't be any better off than they were now.

What he didn't know and couldn't have known was that with the absence of the normal sounds of the city to obscure it, his own pounding footsteps as he ran down the sky bridge were heard clearly in the street below. When all was said and done, he did draw attention to himself but the eyes looking and the ears listening to the sky bridge overhead were very aware that the source had gone into the Egan. As a singular force, the entire group of zombies moved out of the street and against the glass walls of the Egan Center. It was just a matter of time before the glass gave way to the pressure and they would be through.

Neil saw all of this as he ran through the Egan Center lobby. He felt like he was a fish on display in a large aquarium being viewed by hungry predators. "Well that didn't work."

When the first window shattered and came crashing down in a storm of sound, he rounded the corner toward the exit. Jerry was still there holding the door but everyone else had already departed.

Jerry asked, "We still good?"

"No! Get movin'! I'm right behind you!"

The echo of pounding fists, slapping palms, and scratching nails against the windows behind him had spread across the entire glass front of the building by the time he was passing through the door.

Jerry said in awe, "Jesus! Jesus!"

He let the door close and joined Neil who was already running after the others well ahead of him. The explosion of sound that followed the breaking of all those windows was something that could be felt as much as it could be heard. It startled all of them to a stop.

Claire ducked down as if anticipating the approach of flying shrapnel and debris. Of course, Art sneered at her and even chuckled to himself.

Meghan saw it and thought to herself that this was no time to be petty. Neil was still a bit behind them, but at least now she could see him again. She took an awful lot of comfort in that. Neil just seemed to be able to keep them at least one step ahead of tragedy all the time. Forget about the fact that she was finding herself falling for him more and more every day. She was even convinced that had she met him outside of the current circumstances she would have felt the same way. Granted, her engagement would have been a bit of an obstacle, but then again, they weren't outside of the current situation.

Her comfort quickly turned to concern when she saw Neil waving frantically and shouting, "Runnnnn! Runnnnnnnn! Get outta sight! They're—" That was when she heard the dull thuds of angry fists against the inside of the door from which Neil and Jerry had just emerged. Those things were right behind them. Luckily, Jerry and Neil were close to a full city block away from the Egan Center, and, unfortunately, still almost two blocks away from Meghan and the rest of their party.

It didn't appear that the two men were in any immediate danger, though there was no time to dawdle. When the door exploded outward, its hinges buckling and sagging from the force, she felt that familiar chill in her heart that dried her mouth and soaked her palms.

Then she realized that there had been so many of the undead creatures on Fifth Avenue in front of the Egan Center that they had spilled around the edges of the building. They were even then coming up the streets on either side of the Egan and heading straight for them.

Neil yelled again, "Go! Run! Gooooooooo!!!"

Realizing that there was no way they would catch up with the others before they were cut off, Neil and Jerry adjusted their course so that they would be running straight away from the oncoming crowd rather than traversing across it. They were running up a street that, upon crossing the next street, started to slope down slightly as it started its descent toward the Ship Creek area and the Alaska Railroad Depot. Neil and Jerry had the same thought. There was a large Hilton Hotel at the end of that patch of street and its multiple entrances and exits presented the best opportunity to possibly lose their stalkers. Neil hoped that he and Jerry would be able to keep the attention of the horde on them and allow the others to get away. He knew it would be much easier for the two of them to evade and escape than it would be for the larger group. Even so, it wasn't going to be easy. There were so damned many of them and they seemed to be multiplying. Both Jerry and Neil quietly hoped that the Hilton wasn't already crawling with the abominations.

Neil could plainly hear and feel the vibrating buzz that preceded the undead and impregnated the air with its presence. To Neil, it was the same sensation one might experience while sitting on a vibrating chair that was shaking too much and for too long. It left him feeling disoriented and queasy. He was thankful that he was only able to feel it when there were so many and so close. Poor Jerry, Claire, Danny and Jules were much more sensitive to the vibrations and were subject to the nausea almost constantly.

Still on the run, Neil peered over his shoulder to assess the situation. There were literally hundreds and possibly more than a thousand of the demons behind them now. They seemed to be intent on following Jerry and him, not even aware of the other group. There was a strangely comforting and unsettling sense of satisfaction in that. The fiends didn't seem to be capable of running any longer, but their pace was much more than a casual walk. They moved with a purpose and that was the hunt.

The walkie-talkie still gripped in his left hand began to squawk. He had completely forgotten about it.

Never slowing his pace, breathlessly he shouted into the radio, "Say again."

It was Meghan. "We're safe. We're away and no one's following. How 'bout you two?"

"Still trying to get away," Neil said. "Gettin' there. I'll give you a shout when we're clear. Find a safe spot to hide."

"Be careful."

Remembering that it was a cell phone chirp that had given away their last hiding spot, Neil was careful to turn off the radio and slip it into his jacket pocket. To Jerry, he said, "They've gotten away. Now it's our turn."

Starting to sound winded himself, Jerry answered, "I didn't realize we were waiting for our own turn." He smiled over at Neil as they continued down the street.

# CHAPTER 33

Running was fast becoming a fact of life. Even so, Dr. Caldwell wasn't any happier about doing it again. He looked back behind them and was relieved to see an empty street. They weren't being followed. Neil and Jerry had thankfully drawn the throngs of undead after them, buying time and distance for everyone else. He would have liked to slow his pace but the fear that was twisting his stomach into knots was propelling his legs forward.

Malachi was still leading the pack. He was, at that moment, kneeling behind a small sport utility vehicle sitting in the middle of the road. He had his sidearm drawn and held in a ready position in front of himself. He peeked up over the back of the vehicle and scanned the street in front of them.

On the street, the sidewalks, and tucked into doorways were the shattered and mutilated remains of scores of Anchorage's former residents. The undead had set upon them like locusts upon crops, leaving so little of their victims as to prevent reanimation. Even their bones had been splintered and broken as the fiends devoured the marrow within. Tiny bits of shredded clothing and personal effects, such as wallets and purses, were all that identified these piles of rubbish as skeletal remains.

Watching Malachi, his mannerisms and disposition reminded the doctor of images of police officers from television crime dramas. Officer Ivanoff had just fallen into old habits and training, as if there was the slightest possibility that the threat to his safety was from some perpetrator's gun.

As each bisecting avenue crossed the street ahead, increasing numbers of cars were packed tighter and tighter together. To Dr. Caldwell, it looked like a giant rodent maze. Wrong turns; dead ends; and of course the unknown, hidden things that lurked somewhere within the turns or on the other side. What to do? Where the hell was Neil?

And then Malachi made a move. The former police officer ran from the back of one vehicle to the next and then to a newspaper-vending box. He paused and looked back at the balance of the group, still trying to follow. His breathing was slightly labored and short. With his dirty sleeve, he wiped away the running beads of sweat from his brow. Again, he surveyed the street and the deadlocked press of cars and trucks.

Perspective, and how it changed one's vision of the world, was an amazing phenomenon and not lost on Dr. Caldwell. Malachi didn't see the maze that Dr. Caldwell saw; or at the very least, he wasn't overwhelmed with the imagery. He just let his instincts and his training do his thinking for him. This, of course, wasn't all that different than the little white rat's behavior in the lab. Perhaps his actions were a little more complex and calculated, but otherwise very comparable. It was of little consequence, however, as the rest of them fell in behind and followed the police officer, trusting in his judgment.

The next street up was C Street, and straddling it was a large, abandoned People Mover public bus. Around the stalled mass transit vehicle, a pocket of tightly packed cars and trucks had formed an impassable barrier.

Dr. Caldwell said from behind, "Malachi, I think we should stop and catch our breaths at the parking garage up ahead there. Maybe Neil and Jerry will be able to catch up with us then."

Meghan, of course, appreciated that comment and the sentiment more than anyone else, though she was clearly not the only one who was noticing Neil's absence. The further they had gotten from Neil, the more anxious her thoughts and fears had become.

From Meghan's side and trying to comfort despite struggling for air herself, Emma said, "He's alright."

Meghan held up the now static-filled radio and let her grief take her. She shook her head and tried to speak but the knot in her chest was restricting her communication to pantomime. She shrugged her shoulders and accepted Emma's sympathetic embrace.

Emma peered over Meghan's shoulder at Dr. Caldwell's questioning look. She forced her mouth into a partial crescent and gave him a half nod. She didn't know if Meghan was going to be able to keep it together or not, but the reality was that it didn't really matter. They were going to keep moving regardless. Meghan's state of mind would not and could not figure into that simple fact.

Malachi was now leaning himself against the rear corner of the bus and peeking around it. He was pleasantly surprised to find he was keeping his wits about himself. He could still feel some lingering hostility and raw anger toward Emma, but even that was becoming more nebulous, like the fading memory of a dream after waking. Each moment still held unspeakable terror for him, but dealing with these new horrors and not those of his past was helping him stay alive. He had seen neither his loving mother, nor his angry father, nor his sad cousin in days. He missed his mother but was thankful for the absence of the other two.

There was just enough room to maneuver himself along the side of the bus. Dr. Caldwell, by that time, had leveled his shotgun into a firing stance and was watching every step Malachi made. He looked into car windows and in the minimal gaps between cars, while he continued his own, careful pace forward, on the lookout for anything that seemed like a menace waiting to pounce.

When the hand suddenly appeared in the bus window above and slightly behind Malachi, he almost choked. He brought the twelve-gauge shotgun to his shoulder but hesitated for a better target. He knew that shooting the thing's hand off would do little more than create a noise to attract more of them. If he was going to shoot, he wanted it to count.

And when the hand slid the window open slightly, he was, to say the least, confused. They had all agreed that the zombies didn't seem to possess the faculties necessary to perform even the simplest, most rudimentary of tasks, and yet, the window was clearly opening.

Malachi backed away and looked decidedly spooked. The words, "Help us," drifting out of the bus caused both of the men to jump back in surprise.

They looked at one another. Dr. Caldwell said with a hush, "Are they alive?"

He was answered by an equally wispy, "Please," emanating from inside the bus like a distant echo.

Emma and Meghan were now approaching, each sporting a pistol in clenched fists.

Dr. Caldwell looked at Malachi then said to the women, "There's someone...something in there. Malachi and I are going to go check it out and we need you two to watch out for...anything...unusual."

"Unusual?" Emma smirked. "Okay, Doc, I'll let you know when anything *unusual* happens. Oh, sorry. *If* anything unusual happens. All things considered, the lines separating usual and unusual have been kind of blurred over the past few weeks. I mean, what do you—"

Dr. Caldwell cut her off abruptly. "Stop! We don't have the time right now for this. Just be on the lookout, okay? Don't let anything sneak up on us or you."

"On it." Her demeanor lost all condescension just like that.

Malachi and Dr. Caldwell wasted no time. They vaulted over cars and, on one occasion, went through the still open doors on both sides of a minivan. Once at the entrance to the bus, they tried to look in the windows but found them covered with what appeared to be cardboard. The mystery was still contained within. And then like Pandora opening her box, the door labored itself open with a series of clicks and clanks.

There stood a man whose gaunt, emaciated frame needed to add some weight in order to qualify as a wraith. He smiled wearily but said nothing.

After a brief pause, Dr. Caldwell asked, "Are there others with you?"

The man nodded slowly. His eyes were struggling in the sunlight. Still he said nothing.

The doctor didn't want to pressure this obviously tortured soul but he needed him to understand the urgency of the situation. "We can help but we have to go now. Do you understand?"

A distant gunshot captured both of their attention and seemed to add the exclamation point to the doctor's statement. Standing there, Dr. Caldwell was able to smell the horrible rot that filled the air of the bus. It was a mixture of death, sweat, and feces being swirled together into a potent aroma. He wondered how anyone could possibly exist in such conditions.

There were two others with him; another man and a woman. All of them shared enough in common with Holocaust survivors that Dr. Caldwell found himself inspecting their arms in search of the telltale black numbers, dashes, and letters.

The other man was an older black man whose greying curls were only slightly lighter than his sickly looking skin. He smiled as he descended the bus stairs and almost stumbled when his feet hit the pavement. He apologized for his misstep and the involuntary grab onto Malachi's arm to prevent his plunge. "I'm sorry. I've spent more time crawling around on that damned bus than I have on my feet in…actually, I don't know how long it's been. Guess I still need to get my sea legs under me."

The woman coming behind him did fall. Dr. Caldwell was suddenly very concerned about her mobility, or lack thereof. Her legs weren't much bigger around than the typical mop handle. The doctor got a hand under her arm to hoist her up. To him, she didn't feel like she weighed much more than a mop either. She was likely in her fifties, about Dr. Caldwell's age, but she had the physical affect of an elderly senior. She seemed weak and vulnerable, a lethal combination that could prove problematic for all of them. He was relieved when he withdrew his hand and she was able to stand on her own.

The first man to greet them and the last off the bus was younger than the other two. He also appeared to be much more fit, though his muscles too had suffered and atrophied from the conditions they'd had to endure recently.

He drew in a deep breath of air, savoring it like fine wine. He closed his eyes and exhaled with gusto. "I forgot what air could smell and taste like. All I've had to breathe for as long as I can remember has been shit and death, death and shit. Poison with every single breath."

The other new man shot a look in his direction and said defensively, "It worked didn't it?!"

Meghan asked, "What worked?"

The woman answered, "It was Daniel's idea. He thought that maybe if they couldn't smell us and we didn't move around enough for them to hear, then maybe we could be safe."

"No such thing as safe anymore," Art commented from behind them.

Again, the other man said, "Well it worked and we were safe. Weren't we?"

Seeking clarification, Meghan asked the man who insisted that whatever had worked, "So you're Daniel then?"

"No. He's still...he's still..." stammered the woman, unable to complete her sentence.

The first man finished for her, "He's still on the bus. He died a couple of days ago."

Emma asked tentatively, "Was he...?"

"Bitten? No. He just went to sleep one night and didn't wake up the next morning."

"What do you think caused it?"

His voice meandering like a long Alaskan summer day, the first man answered as he looked up at the cloudy sky, "What does it matter what caused it? He's dead, just like the rest of them."

"We haven't eaten in days," the woman continued, "and the water ran out about three days ago. A few of us tried to drink our own urine but then that stopped too. I think it was just hope that had sustained most of us these past few days. I just knew that someone would happen along; well, someone that didn't want to eat us, that is."

Dr. Caldwell said, "We've got some food and water but I think we should get off the street. Emma, can you conjure up some granola bars and water or something? Anything that can be chewed on the go."

"Sure."

The parking garage was a short jaunt up the street. Though agonizingly slow, they moved as quickly as the three newcomers would allow them. Luckily, they were able to get up to the third level of the parking deck without incident.

In getting to the parking structure and then up the winding driveway to the third floor, they heard two gunshots and then nothing else. It was both worrisome and promising. The gunshots could only be from Neil and Jerry, which meant that they were still alive but it also meant that they were still in trouble.

From their vantage point, they could see back up the street from where they had come, the most likely route the two men would take to reunite with the rest of them. Meghan alternated between holding the radio to her ear or to her mouth, with which she would plead for any response. None was forthcoming.

Dr. Caldwell, meanwhile, had gone up to the top tier and was using the binoculars to get a better view. It didn't look good. There were still hundreds of the things moving up the street in the direction that the two men had traveled. They weren't moving as fast as the others who were originally on their heels. They were probably just chasing the group that was chasing Neil and Jerry. They weren't nearly as animated or as alert, though they were every bit as frightening.

He decided that it would probably be wise to do some looking all around them and maybe even check out their next step. He looked around at the top tier of the parking deck. There was no roof and no cars, so it was more or less a one block by one block open-air parking lot.

He'd only been up here once before. It was Black Friday, the day after Thanksgiving, and he was pretty certain that everyone had decided to come to the Fifth Avenue Mall for whatever big sale at which his wife was also determined to be. They grabbed one of three remaining parking spots in the whole garage. It was cold and slushy and earlier than he wanted to be awake. He was miserable that day and complained almost the whole time.

He could remember that day like it had just happened. He remembered the petty resentment that he felt toward his wife for making him come. He was suddenly ashamed of himself and longing for his wife. He walked over to what he thought had been the spot in which he had parked that morning. He stood there and remembered his wife and the life they'd had together. It wasn't perfect but it was good. They shared more laughter than tears, but they shared it all. No longer optimistic about her prospects for survival, he thought about her last moments. It was agonizing for him to think that she likely had to suffer so much and was alone in doing so. He said quietly to the wind, "Oh honey. I'm so sorry." He could feel the grief begin to wrap its rough, hot hands around his heart, but then he heard, "Sorry for what?"

He pivoted around, expecting to see his wife, and instead saw Emma, who was walking toward him. He shook his head and said, the pain forcing a slight crack into his voice, "I was talking to...thinking about...remembering...my wife."

She paused for a moment, not sure whether he wanted the company or not. Despite her feelings for him, she didn't want to impose herself or be a nuisance. She had actually come up to the top at Meghan's urging because it didn't make any sense for any of them to wander off alone. She'd eagerly complied with Meghan's request, and even went so far as to try and convince herself that she was going after the doctor because it was sensible, and not because she wanted to be in his company all the time.

She suddenly felt like an interloper, as if she had interrupted a private conversation between a married couple. She was all set to turn on her heels and walk away when he looked up at her. "Memory is the weirdest thing," he said, "and it sneaks up on you when you least expect it." He wanted to say more but he just cracked a difficult but seemingly reassuring smile for both of them.

She could sense that he was still hurting and wanting to say more. What could she possibly say that would bring any solace? It was especially difficult for her given that she was more and more convinced that she wanted to be the one for which he held special, random memories. She was becoming the "other woman". It didn't matter that his wife was likely amongst the ranks of the undead currently wandering the city.

"Meghan thought it would be a good idea if I...if you weren't...I can just go back down if you want to be alone."

"No, no. It's fine. I just wanted to check out where we're going to be heading and see if I might be able to catch a glimpse of Neil and Jerry."

"D'you think they're going to make it?"

With the toe of his shoe Dr. Caldwell fiddled with a small pile of sand. While he made lines in the fine grains, he said, "If you're asking me if I think they have a chance of getting back to us, I'm not sure. There are an awful lot of those things down there. Neil is pretty smart and Jerry is good too, there are just so damned many of them. I guess I don't know that there would be a whole lot of value in waiting for them for too long. I don't think it would be wise to mention this around Meghan. Is she going to be able to make it?"

Emma shook her head doubtfully. "I don't know. Maybe. She's seeming pretty desperate right now."

"Is there anything any of us can do?"

"Yeah. Can you make all of this go away and have things go back to normal again?"

Again appreciating her humor, the doctor smiled. "Sure. And then I can solve the mystery of cold fusion and the gift of immortality."

She smiled at him. "Meghan will keep up. She has to. What choice does she or any of us have? Now how is our next move looking? Gift of immortality?"

# CHAPTER 34

Heading directly north from the parking garage was a street that became a bridge connecting downtown Anchorage with its neighbor, Elmendorf Air Force Base, part of Joint Base Elmendorf-Richardson. Midway across the bridge was what appeared to be a pair of military Humvees that had attempted to hold back the surge and had met the same fate as every other roadblock.

Leading up to the two-vehicle barricade, Dr. Caldwell could see a swath of discarded clothing, luggage, children's toys, and the odds and ends of a populace on the run for its life. He'd seen similar sights during his tour in the Middle East; refugees fleeing the fighting in search of a peaceful stretch of real estate where there wasn't shooting and dying all around. The sad truth that Dr. Caldwell suspected and even accepted was that in this conflict there was no such place. The dying and suffering was a self-perpetuating mess that never stopped pursuing these refugees. They could count themselves lucky if it didn't precede them to where they were running and was waiting for their arrival.

He couldn't see to the far side of the bridge to the security checkpoint, but he suspected that it would just be the same as everywhere else. He was fostering the lingering, perhaps teasing, sense of hope that the military training, organizational capabilities, and armament of the security forces of the joint military bases would have somehow enabled them to be successful where everyone else had failed so miserably. That hope was already fading. Seeing the abandoned Humvees and the disarray all around and behind them didn't help matters. Was there hope for any of them anymore? It was becoming ever more difficult for him to hold at bay his pessimism regarding that question.

During the Gulf War, he'd seen and heard that sense of ever impending doom with soldiers engaged in the day-to-day meat grinder that the conflict had become during his deployment. Some of the men just seemed to come to terms with the fact, in their minds, that the battles and the killing and the death would never end. In fact, most of the men, once true combat exhaustion had set upon their nerves and their emotions, accepted the fact that death was inevitable and usually waiting around the next corner or on the next patrol. The numbness to which combat fatigue led was both a blessing and a curse. And Dr. Caldwell understood that all too well. Yet, there he was, with the proverbial Novocain dulling his senses and his judgment.

He fought back his doubts, at the very least for the moment, because he was preparing himself to go deal with Meghan. They couldn't afford to wait much longer. It had been some time since Neil and Jerry had led the horde away, and it was becoming less and less likely that either of the two men were going to re-emerge. As much as it pained Dr. Caldwell to think it and even accept it, it was a reality that they couldn't ignore.

He and Emma made their way back across the top floor of the parking deck. They stood there for a few more minutes, hoping for any sign at all that the two men were still alive. There hadn't been any gunshots in quite some time and the mob of creatures down the street had moved out of sight. A few stragglers, primarily undead beasts whose bodies had been mangled enough in dying as to impact their mobility, were still lingering in the now largely empty street. They seemed lost and confused, like sheep that had been separated from the flock.

"I think we should go talk to Meghan," he said to his companion.

From behind both of them, Meghan, who was walking up the ramped driveway, asked, "Talk to me about what?" She was still holding the radio, which was singing its static-filled tune, firmly in her right hand. At every slight interruption in the empty atmospheric white noise, Meghan's eyes would not too subtly cast themselves down toward the device and then look back up hopefully.

Dr. Caldwell looked into her eyes and was about to speak when Meghan interrupted him. "Don't even suggest that we're leaving him. None of us would have ever made it this far without him. We owe him some time."

"I know how hard this is to hear, Meghan, but we have to deal with reality. We both know that we can't stay here indefinitely. We have to face the facts. I don't like it any more than you do."

"Then give him more time. He's still out there. He can make it back. We wouldn't be here without him. How far do you think...?" The tears welling up in her eyes and the heated pain in her chest robbed her of voice. She crumpled down against the concrete wall and let the powerlessness and the desperation take her. She hung her head and let her eyes be raging storm clouds to the pavement below her. She forced out, "We can't. He can't."

Dr. Caldwell found in his reserves of past training the capacity to remain calm and reassuring. He said as soothingly and honestly as possible, "We can't let his sacrifice be meaningless. We have to keep moving. Even Neil would agree with that. Wouldn't he?"

Not looking up at him, Meghan shook her head. Dr. Caldwell, though, could tell that she wasn't denying it; she was merely struggling with accepting it. She managed to say, "Not him. Not him too. I don't think I can take it."

"Maybe we can help each other, because I'm having a hard time too," Dr. Caldwell admitted.

"You? Why?"

"With Neil gone, who do you think everyone is going to expect to have all the answers and ideas that are supposed to keep us alive? And I don't think I'm nearly as qualified for the job as Neil, or even Jerry. And hell, I was an officer in the military. I commanded troops in the field. Well, not really. I was a surgeon, but I was in command. In this situation I'm totally out of my league, but that doesn't matter because everyone is going to look to me regardless. What kind of weight do you think that puts on my shoulders? Christ, if I thought we could wait here for those two, do you think I'd be in a hurry to bug out? We just have to think and do what's best for the group...for all of us...for those two kids. We have to think like Neil."

"The next step in Neil's plan was to get across the bridge and onto Elmendorf. Maybe we should stick to Neil's plan."

All at once, Meghan stopped sobbing. She sniffled a couple times and took a deep, calming breath. "Doc, would you look one last time please?"

Without betraying the sense that he was just doing it to placate her, Dr. Caldwell agreed. "Of course. I do think we owe them and us that. Wish me luck."

Emma leaned down and rubbed Meghan's shoulders and back. This led to a warm sympathetic hug and more tears. She said into Meghan's ear, "C'mon, we can get through this if we work together. I know it hurts honey."

"I can't believe this is happening...again," Meghan sobbed, "These damned zekes are really putting a harsh on my love life." She let a painful laugh escape, followed by a couple more sniffles.

Without taking the binoculars from his eyes, Dr. Caldwell leaned forward as if to get a more focused look and said calmly, "I think I see them."

# CHAPTER 35

When Jerry and Neil had been separated from the rest of the group with both a proverbial and literal city's worth of zombies fast on their heels, Neil was afraid his nightmare was going to finally catch him and drag him into the darkness. There were moments when he didn't see how the two of them were going to make it out of the predicament alive.

They ran north on E Street, which tilted slightly downward toward the Hilton Hotel. The front windows and large glass doors of the luxury hotel were shattered and blanketed the floor with a million little prisms. Jerry led them into the hotel and beckoned Neil to follow.

"If we can get them into the hallways, maybe their numbers will slow them down. We can put a little distance between us and them."

Neil nodded and said as he struggled for breath, "Yeah, but we can't lose them entirely. We need them to follow us so that they don't follow the others."

Jerry nodded and took a right in the lobby. In the hotel, the walls amplified the ghouls' groaning. Jerry ran up some stairs, down a hallway, and then back down some other stairs. Some of the walls were ashen black like the coals in the bottom of a barbecue grill. Other walls, especially down a particularly cluttered hallway, were fouled with smeared rust colored handprints. Down this corridor, some of the guestroom doors had been forced from their frames and were lying uselessly on the floor. Left to his own devices, Neil was convinced that the maze into which they were running deeper and deeper would merely swallow him into its seemingly endless depths. He felt like a Dickensian child who inadvertently wandered into a Nineteenth Century manor's shrub maze and was lost forever. As it was, Neil was thankful that his partner knew his way around, but was a little worried that they might be heading toward a dead end.

Jerry, seemingly sensing Neil's reservations, said as he ran, "I used to work here before I went to school for nursing. I did room service for a bit and then maintenance. Got to know the place inside and out."

Neil nodded again and felt much better about their prospects. Soon, they were back out on the street. The streets all angled down, pointing toward the industrial park, which got its name—Ship Creek—from the fish-rich waterway that cut down its middle. The area was home to the main depot for the Alaska Railroad, a fairly new hotel, and several support businesses for the Alaska tourism industry. On the far northern edge of the area was the once bustling port of Anchorage, and above it all was a bridge that connected Anchorage to the Government Hill area and the main gates of Elmendorf Air Force Base.

They rounded a fence and ran through a large staging yard with several box vans still awaiting cargo that would never be loaded. Using one of the vans as a stepped vaulting aid, Neil and Jerry lifted themselves over the ten-foot high chain link security fence into an adjoining parking lot. The mass of zombies packed into the yard were cornered and fairly well tethered into place by their own single-mindedness. They reached and clawed through the hundreds of fence openings, trying futilely to close the distance between themselves and their prey.

Of course, there were still hundreds more of the ghouls to offer chase, so any sense of satisfaction was fleeting and gone as soon as it appeared.

"Hell, about another ten yards like that," Jerry quipped, "and we'd have them all locked up."

Neil tried to laugh, but was finding it more and more difficult to take in enough air to be able to breathe let alone laugh. His legs too were starting to feel weak and rubbery. Exercise had not been a priority for him before this cataclysm and now he was regretting it. Maybe that would have made a good selling point for the Alaska Club: "Come work out and stay in shape. You never know when you might be chased by zombies." Regardless, he was starting to worry their pace was unsustainable. If they got caught out of steam and out in the open…if they were overwhelmed…. They needed a different plan.

"Jerry, I don't know how much longer I can keep this up," he huffed. He looked over his shoulder and was somewhat comfortable with the distance that was growing between themselves and the band of followers behind them. Most of the creatures were moving at a slower, shuffling pace, but they never slowed and never tired. Neil was reminded of the pursuit scene from *Butch Cassidy and the Sundance Kid* and Paul Newman's line, "Don't these guys ever give up?"

The younger Jerry knew that Neil was right and was feeling the burn himself. His breathing too was becoming shallower and shallower as they continued. He pointed to another long building and suggested that they head for it, hoping to perhaps lose their pursuers and maybe even catch their breath for a few moments.

They ran from pavement to grass and back to pavement. Upon hitting the pavement for the second time, Neil's feet were momentarily confused by the surface changes and sent him sprawling to the ground. His right hand hit hard, opening a nice road rash on his palm and wrist. He banged his right knee on the hard ground too, sending a desperate message of pain through his nerves to his brain. He got himself up but the pain made walking difficult and running all but impossible. He limped forward, looking over his shoulder at the horrible mass that was getting closer to him with each step. He could feel the impact point on his knee throb. He forced himself to keep moving forward and motioned to Jerry to get himself to safety. Jerry, of course, ignored him and instead got his shoulder under Neil's right arm and hand and then helped Neil. They were moving much slower than they had been previously but were still staying ahead of the relentlessly pursuing predators.

At the building, they went around back and found an open loading bay. Luckily, the bay was up high to accommodate loading and unloading cargo and pallets from trucks. The stairs leading up the bay were fairly well blocked by a stack of boxes that had fallen on its side. From the bay's loading platform, Jerry heaved over some empty heavy wooden pallets and further blocked the stairs. He realized that the front of the building held many windows, but if the things continued their mindless pursuit and just followed them to the back then perhaps they would have enough time to move to the other end of an internal hallway without being detected. Perhaps.

From the loading area and the attached warehouse section of the building, the two men retreated deeper into the structure passing through a threshold into a well-kept office area with soft-carpeted floors and lightly colored walls. Seeing that there were windows looking out from the offices to either side of the hallway, Neil and Jerry dropped to their knees and crawled, careful not to be detected.

"How's your knee?"

Grimacing slightly, Neil answered, "I think it'll be alright but this crawling around shit isn't helping." Sensing Jerry's worry, Neil added, "Of course, I'd just as soon endure a little pain as opposed to the alternative."

They came to a set of stairs and decided that going up might work to their advantage. They crawled slowly upstairs, avoiding the stairwell windows as they went. Pausing to look through one such window, Neil only verified what he already suspected. As a reeking, grey wave of rot, scores of the beasts shuffled around to the rear of the building. Mindlessly, they followed the surge, which was becoming penned tighter and tighter into the already packed loading area.

Once upstairs, the two men were back on their feet and trying to find an open room or office in which to catch their breath. Thankfully, they hadn't seen any of the telltale signs of the struggles that they had seen in other buildings and houses all over Anchorage. The edifice had the appearance of an office closed for the weekend.

The relative peace that the hall engendered supplanted the misgivings and the chaos that seemed to grip everywhere else the two men had run. The men's pace eased somewhat, as did the nervous looks around. Not since they had left Charles' house had they felt so comfortable. And then Neil remembered regretfully that they had just departed Charles' residence earlier that morning. It had already been a long, arduous day, and it was only going to get longer and harder. Hopefully, their haven would not become a trap.

From his backpack, Neil produced bottles of water for himself and Jerry while Jerry found some pepperoni sausage sticks and small packages of lemon sandwich cookies.

Chewing hungrily, Neil said, "Ya know, I never liked these damned Slim Jims before, but I don't know that I've tasted something so good as these little bastards right at this moment. Delicious little foul creations."

Jerry was chewing on a second sausage stick. He nodded but then gestured with his chin toward Neil's pocket. "Maybe now would be a good time to give them a shout and see what's up."

Still trying to catch his breath, Neil nodded and reached into his right hand jacket pocket. It was empty. Then he reached into his empty left hand pocket. He patted himself front and back, becoming increasingly frantic as the seconds passed.

He sighed and hung his shoulders, shaking his head as he did. "It's fucking gone. It must have dropped out...hell, it could've fallen outta my pocket anytime."

"So, there's no way that we could possibly know where they are and they have no way to know if we're still breathing?"

"Pretty much."

"And the hits just keep rolling in. So, we're on our own."

"For a time anyway."

Jerry wadded up his Slim Jim wrappers into loose balls and tossed them across the hall. Looking at the wrappers as they slowly unfolded themselves, he said, "They're not gonna wait around for us. Why would they? They needed to put some distance between those things and them and that just meant making a getaway. Didn't it? They're long gone."

Neil considered the younger man for a moment and thought about what he was saying. It did make sense that Dr. Caldwell would lead the others away as fast as he could, but there was something about the doctor that led him to believe that there were other options that might take precedence. For instance, they could make their way across the bridge and onto the Air Force Base and leave notes and markers behind to point the way toward them. Then there was the possibility that Dr. Caldwell would be waiting for them more or less where they had parted ways. He thought about Meghan and wondered how she was doing. He'd promised that he would stay in touch with them on the radio. The device had limited range and capacity, making it less than ideal, but it was at least something. And it was lying uselessly on the floor of the Hilton Hotel or in the middle of the street or something.

"Is there any way at all that maybe…"

Jerry shook his head and barked, "They're gone. I think we've just got to face it. Meghan. Claire. All of them."

"I've gotta believe that they're still there, Jerry. They've just gotta be."

"Why? What makes you think that we'll ever see them again?"

"Because the alternative really sucks, that's why."

Jerry turned that over in his mind a few times while he fought with a couple slivers of sausage stuck between his teeth. He couldn't stop thinking about Claire and getting back to her. He imagined Neil and him getting away to nothing and always being on the run without a single hope of seeing anyone else ever again. Neil was right and he knew it. Even if they weren't destined to see the others again, they could at least try. "Okay. You're right. Do you ever get tired of being right all the time?"

"I think you'd have a long line of people who'd disagree with you on that one, starting with my parents and ex-wife."

"Still?"

"Well, a few weeks ago I think you would've had a lot longer line than now, but my parents are still alive down in the Lower Forty-Eight, and my ex-wife would probably hate me from the grave."

"Pretty rough divorce?"

"Let's just say that I wouldn't be surprised to see her attorney out there leading the zombies so that he could squeeze a little more of my life out of me as a final compensation to her for having married me in the first place."

"Jesus. That's rough."

"Ancient history now."

They got up and went to the end of the hall. There was a small window that looked out onto the opposite lot from which they had come. From the window, it didn't appear that there were any of the ghouls waiting for them in that direction. Rested and partially fed, the two men were feeling much better than when they came into the building. Like a pair of athletes preparing to start a marathon, they stretched their legs and checked their gear.

As they stood in front of a door leading out into the lot they had inspected from above, Neil said confidently, "I think we've got this. If we can get out without making much noise, maybe we could sneak away without them even noticing."

Jerry nodded. Neil nodded back and put his hand to the push door handle. "Ready?" Again Jerry nodded, exhaling a deep breath.

Neil pushed the door open and was immediately grabbed by a filthy, grey hand that clawed at him violently. Hitting and pushing as forcefully as his fear would allow, Neil was able to finally break the thing's grip and force it back. It was a man who was wearing the blue denim uniform of a delivery driver. The one good hand was already reaching back toward Neil while his other mangled limb was still swinging uselessly at his side.

There was another of the fiends just behind him; this one a woman in a business suit of sorts. The front of her throat was a mutilated mess of decomposing, frayed flesh that revealed the small bones and deteriorating muscle tissue of her windpipe and gullet.

Neil didn't hesitate for the slightest instant. He leveled the shotgun in his hands and fired. The blast opened a large hole in the man standing in front of him and sent him sprawling on top of the woman. With his second shot, Neil hit the man again, pressing him further into the woman until they were knotted enough to allow Neil and Jerry to get away.

As they started to run again, Jerry said, "So much for getting away quietly. Where to?"

"Hell, I don't know. Just run!"

They could hear the horde behind them get excited again and start to shuffle toward them. There was thankfully some distance that separated them now so that the two men didn't feel the need to maintain a sprinting pace. They were able to settle into a more long distance trot of sorts.

As they continued east, the buildings became more tightly packed and the streets more clearly defined. The two of them ducked into another building and waited long enough to let their pursuers unknowingly run by and disappear out of sight. When they felt like it was safe to start moving again, they went back in the direction from whence they had come. They found a staircase cut into the side of a grassy incline and used that to get back up to Third Avenue and downtown Anchorage. With the threat behind them still in the Ship Creek area, Neil and Jerry were able to slow their pace somewhat and catch their breath.

Just minutes later, they crested another set of stairs through a retail center and were back up on Fourth Avenue within sight of the B Street parking garage. Standing on the now vacant street, Jerry looked down the road and saw what was undeniably Dr. Caldwell standing atop the parking garage and waving at them.

Jerry nudged Neil with his shoulder. "You were right again my friend. And thank God for it."

# CHAPTER 36

They were circling her slowly, deliberately, repeating over and over again, "Zombie. Zombie. Come to life." And then they started to count down from ten to one. The voices were children's but the faces were those of Dr. Caldwell, Emma, Claire, Art, Jerry, and even Neil. They were looking at her, the playful menace in their expressions darkening with each pass. Their voices started to jumble themselves into a confused, twisted echo.

Meghan was aware that she was lying on her back but try as she might, she couldn't rise up or even change positions for that matter. She was at the mercy of the swirling voices around her. She was terrified and helpless. The fear was not alone however. She felt her anger slowly start to simmer, building pressure and heat like a biological crock-pot, until her blood threatened to boil in her veins. The taunting fear faded, gradually pushed away by an overwhelming hunger that sent crackling jolts of unexpected sensation into her seemingly lifeless extremities. The hunger fueled the anger and the anger gave anima back to her limbs.

All at once, she was on her feet again, only she wasn't sure who she was anymore, or *what* she was. The only certainty that she felt was the hunger. She needed to feed. She could smell...prey; delicate, tempting, and near. She could smell life and all of its juicy, salty possibilities.

"Zombie. Zombie. Come to life," continued to echo around her in the voices of children. She lashed out with her hand and brought it back empty. She reached again and again and each time her attempts were fruitless. Finally, her clutched fist brought back a squirming, squealing little creature...a pig perhaps. She barely even paused to consider it before her gaping maw was chewing into it. The raw, briny bits of flesh spilled down her throat only half-chewed, filling her stomach and still the hunger persisted.

Her quarry was limp and lifeless, cold and uninviting. She tossed it aside and realized it was the body of a child. It was a beautiful blond-haired girl she knew. It was Jules, and instead of being horrified at her choice of prey, all she could think to do was find Danny and do the same to him. She spun around looking for the second child. She could smell him. She could almost taste his scent it was so strong.

The hunger, gnawing at her from the inside out, was driving her mad. She heard herself make the voracious grunts and growls of a predatory beast. She saw another face. She knew it, not that it mattered. She must feed. She must always feed. But she did know it. Wasn't his name Neil? He was special once. Yes, he was Neil. He was trying to talk to her; to tell her something. He was motioning to her but she couldn't hear him for the other voices. "Zombie. Zombie. Come to life."

The voice was becoming more prevalent as her vision again began to fade until there was only his voice. She still couldn't understand it but she could hear the words; it was more than just gibberish.

Meghan's eyes fluttered slightly and then she saw Neil looking down at her.

"You awake sleepy head? I thought you might be having a nightmare because of the noises you were making." She sat up abruptly and hugged him.

"You okay?"

"I will be in a few seconds. Just hold me please."

Neil didn't say anything more. He knew what was going on. They all had nightmares and day-mares and even still awake-mares. It was hard to escape when you were living day in and day out through a reality that trumped most nightmares.

# CHAPTER 37

Meghan, trying to shake away the sleep that was still lingering, asked, "How long has it been? How long did I sleep?"

Neil told her that it had been just over twenty-four hours since they had all crossed the bridge onto Elmendorf. She wasn't quite certain what she had been expecting, but more of the same wasn't it. She held onto hope that with her next waking moment, she would be greeted with a smile and some genuinely good news.

As he held Meghan and tried to will away the terror that tormented her behind the veil of sleep, Neil remembered those emotional moments. The joy of reuniting was eclipsed by their persistent survival needs. They needed shelter. They needed to keep moving, and so they had.

The bridge might as well have spanned the River Styx, allowing access to the Gates of Hades and the unknown perils of the Underworld. They marched slowly, looking in every direction but down. Below them, amidst the idle businesses of Ship Creek, was the pursuing horde to which Jerry and Neil had given the slip.

Once across, Dr. Caldwell fully expected to be confronted by new horrors. It felt like they were journeying into some new Hell, another of Dante's wicked Circles with fresh torments. Anti-climactically, it just appeared to be more of the same. Perhaps that was Hell enough.

At the main entrance of the Elmendorf side of the joint military base, the guard building had been reduced to a blackened pile of ashes, charred lumber remnants, and crumbling, scorched bricks. Lying around the ruins of the building were several mostly decomposed bodies. Most of the flesh from these corpses had been picked cleanly from the bone, leaving the skeletons to begin to shed their copper tones of blood and tissue for the white of the bleaching sun.

As if the Nature Gods could sense the mood of the group, the sky began in fits and starts to empty its Stratus buckets onto their heads. It was as if a giant celestial sponge was being wrung dry above them. Soon the drizzle became a downpour so that all of their heads, their clothing, and their gear were soaked and dripping.

Jules and Danny were the only ones in truly rainproof jackets so, thankfully, they were spared the discomfort and chill of being drenched to the bone. Poor Gerald, Dave, and Evelyn, the survivors from the bus, were all ill prepared for the weather and were, consequently, miserable. None of them had anything more than what they had been wearing those several weeks ago when they'd been forced into the survival marathon still currently being run. There was, unfortunately, not much extra clothing or jackets to be shared, but that which could be shared was. So, the three suffered through the autumn shower and felt their body temperatures and their immune systems drop along with the moistened air temperatures.

As they passed through the gate area, Meghan pointed out that a fair distance up the main road there were a handful of camouflage-clad fiends loitering, waiting, wanting. The things were mostly still, standing like deadly statues waiting for divine life to be breathed into their ruined bodies.

Jerry hoisted his scoped hunting rifle to his shoulder and peered through the telescoping lens. He placed the black cross-hair on one of their heads but paused when Neil touched his arm. "They don't know we're here and by the time they start heading this way we'll be on ours. No point in drawing any more attention to us than we have to."

Jerry nodded and put the rifle back over his shoulder. He then removed the automatic pistol from his hip holster and checked that it was cocked and loaded. "Right again."

Neil smiled. "You're gonna give me a complex."

Claire asked, "What the hell are you two talking about?"

They both answered as they started to walk away, "Nothin'."

It was late afternoon by then and the prospect of traveling in the dark with the unknown all around did not appeal to any of them, so they made a priority of finding shelter for the night. Following the road on which they were already traveling, they soon found themselves in the midst of base housing. The neighborhoods on Elmendorf were no different than the neighborhoods through which they had passed everywhere else in Anchorage. Aside from the empty shell casings from spent bullets and the random discarded clothing and luggage, there was a serenity clinging to the residential streets.

In short order, they found an open two-story home that would suit their purposes. With exhausted legs and weary minds, they made themselves comfortable on couches, chairs, and beds. They eagerly invited any change from the lethal monotony of running and hiding, running and hiding, running and.... It was a draining routine that was not too different from that of prey species on savannah of Africa or the tundra of Alaska.

**Sean Schubert**

It was in one of the bedrooms that Meghan had woken with such a start after her nightmare. She never liked waking up in unfamiliar surroundings, especially after having a bad dream. Luckily, Neil helped to chase away her fears and discomfort.

She whispered into his ear, "Can you lay down with me for a bit?"

Without a word, he swung his legs up onto the bed and leaned back. She then laid her head on his chest and snuggled up close to him. Not long thereafter, they were both asleep and trying to steal away the little bits of rest they could find between nightmares.

# CHAPTER 38

Deciding that it would be a good idea to check out their immediate surroundings to search for any supplies or other helpful items, Dr. Caldwell, Malachi, and Gerald all left their newly found refuge at first light the next morning.

For each of them, the experience was like entering another country or possibly walking on the moon. While there were houses and cars and yards and all the other trappings of a modern community, the lack of any people—or even animals, for that matter—added a discomfiture that they could never quite overcome. Despite the drizzle that persisted, there should have been children in yards playing and dogs barking and adults driving or moving about in some fashion.

Watching with wary eyes all around them, the three men walked down the middle of the street. Behind every door, every tree, and every corner they knew that danger could be waiting for them.

"So what are we looking for anyway?" Gerald asked.

Dr. Caldwell answered, "We'll know it when we see it."

"So, nothing in particular?"

Again, Dr. Caldwell shot back, "I can't think of anything that's not in short supply right now."

Momentarily departing from his typical behavior, Malachi interjected, "Not water. Not now anyway."

Gerald finished with, "Yeah. That was a helluva idea Neil had. Who would have thought about draining the hot water heater into our empty water bottles?"

They nodded at one another but didn't say anything else. Gerald wondered if perhaps there was a bit of jealousy or competition with the doctor in regards to the younger Neil. He couldn't tell for sure, but the doctor's short answers made him suspect that there might be some issues between the two men. He also wondered about the police officer. There was just something about the cop that didn't seem right all the time. He often seemed emotionally distant and disconnected from the others in the group. Physically, the police officer was rarely in the same room with everyone else, which none of the others seemed to mind. It was a weird dynamic to be sure. He looked first at the doctor and then at the police officer, wondering about his observations and whether or not he, Evelyn, and Dave had made a mistake by coming along with them.

The excitement of having run into living people again had just made them all so hopeful that any hesitation about going never rose to the surface. On the bus, it had been miserable but they felt safe and somewhat secure, if a little hungry and uncomfortable. Perhaps the good doctor and his friends would have just given them some of their food and water and moved on their way. Maybe he and his two bus mates could have waited all of this out. He'd made a life of waiting and watching and hoping that things would get better for himself. Why had he chosen to change? He was a black man who'd grown up in a white man's world. Sure, things had gotten better over the past few years, but he was still black. He couldn't wish that away no matter how hard he tried. And it wasn't just about color. It was about attitudes and expectations; it was about prejudices and fears, both his and others'; and it was about missed opportunities and discarded dreams. He'd learned the art of keeping his head down and his mouth shut to get by in corporate America. Nobody wanted to hear his ideas anyway. If he could keep his comments to himself, the comfortable paychecks would keep rolling in and he could maintain the quality of life that he wanted for himself.

Now, there he was walking down the middle of a street that was as foreign and intimidating as the desert to a polar bear. It was quiet though; the only sound that of water dripping from awnings and down gutters. With each step, the three men seemed to ease a bit.

"Neil's a smart one," Dr. Caldwell said. "He seems to really be in his element in all of this."

Somewhat surprised by the comment, Gerald pressed for more information. "Is he former military...security?"

"Nope. Mortgages."

"Mortgages?"

"Yeah. Some mid to low-level nobody who was never considered anything but replaceable. Kind of sad really. He's a born leader, but I bet he'd never say it. And his old bosses never saw it. What a fucking wasted opportunity for them."

Gerald was decidedly able to relate to that sentiment, having spent a lifetime wallowing in the quagmire of disappointment and missed opportunities.

They were spiraling out from their new hideout. The streets, like the houses, all looked the same. There was a distinct "Stepford" quality to the neighborhood, everything perfectly laid out and planned. The absence of any people contributed to the otherworldliness of it as well. It was like an unused television or movie set that was awaiting the word "action" to bring all of it to life.

They turned another corner and were on their return trip when they spotted an olive colored Humvee on its side in the front yard of one of the houses, this one a yellow shade. The driver, obviously not buckled in safely, had been pitched through the now shattered windshield. The body, of course, was absent, having likely been set upon by the ghouls as soon as it hit the grass. Maybe he or she was still unconscious when the transformation from human being to midmorning snack took place.

In the yard, however, where the body should have been was a metallic black object. Triumphantly, Dr. Caldwell announced as he peered through his binoculars, "That's what we're looking for."

"What?"

He smiled. "Better hardware."

Dr. Caldwell and Malachi picked up their pace to a light trot and covered the distance to the wreck much quicker than the slower and more laboring Gerald. The doctor raised the M4 military assault rifle above his head like a trophy of victory. He checked the load on the magazine and confirmed what he suspected: it had never been fired.

Smiling again, he said, "This will even the odds a bit in a pinch. Let's check out the Hummer to see if we've got any other goodies."

Forgetting, or possibly disregarding his training in the excited moment, Malachi was already atop the vehicle before Dr. Caldwell shouted, "Fuck! Malachi! Check inside before you go diving in. No telling what might be waiting inside."

The police officer was already reaching for the door handle when he drew his hand back as fast as the gasped breath that he swallowed back down his throat. The rear passenger window was down and immediately in front of him. He felt exposed and helpless staring down into the dark on the other side, not knowing what horrible torments could be harbored in the shadows.

Dr. Caldwell pulled a lever on the side of the new firearm and readied it for action. "Malachi? You okay?"

From inside, Malachi's ears were tickled by the slightest suggestion of sound and he froze. He was struck with an intense vertigo that caused him to falter. Across his mind, like a crackling tempest spread the words, "Oh no. Not him."

But it was indeed his father's voice that said again, "What's wrong, Mal? You gettin' into trouble again? Does Daddy need to take you out back?"

"What's wrong, Mal?"

Who was speaking that time? Was that the doctor? Or was it...? He looked up to confirm that there was indeed a doctor who could be talking to him. His grip on reality, like his grip on the side of the big vehicle, was loosening dangerously. There *was* a doctor, but the look that Malachi shot to

Dr. Caldwell was full of the confusion and doubt that had been dogging the police officer. The doctor hadn't seen the look for some time and was concerned to be seeing it again.

Malachi shook his head and forced himself back into focus. By that time, Dr. Caldwell had come around to the front of the Humvee and was pulling the shattered windshield from its frame. He said quietly, "It's okay, Malachi. I'm here. We'll do this together."

Gerald wasn't quite sure what was happening, but the doctor's demeanor made him uncomfortable at once. There was something going on that was spooking the doctor and not knowing what it was that was causing it was bringing on a new fear for Gerald.

He whispered to Dr. Caldwell before the doctor had climbed in through the now glass-less window, "What's going on?"

"Just watch out and make sure that nothing sneaks up on us. We'll have this thing checked out in a sec."

"But..."

"Don't worry. Just keep an eye out. Okay?"

Gerald backed away and pivoted around to see their surroundings again. The houses all around them seemed to be looking at them now. They were no longer empty buildings. They were creepy, soulless creatures that seemed to be circling and threatening them.

From inside the Humvee, Dr. Caldwell shouted, "Got it!"

He re-emerged from inside with another of the firearms, a pair of metallic green latched boxes, and some other odds and ends all stuffed into a camouflaged pack. "Okay, let's get our asses back to the others before anything happens. Malachi, you coming?"

He jumped down from the vehicle without a word. Carrying their newly found equipment, the three made their way back to the house. All three of them, Malachi included, walked with a much-deserved swagger. Today was about good news and they'd be the bearers of it.

# CHAPTER 39

A couple of days passed without incident while the group debated their next move. They ate, rested, and talked. With each passing day, the nights grew a little longer, a little darker, and a little cooler. The days too were becoming cooler as the rain and damp weather persisted.

Unfortunately, the house did not have a fireplace, so a small Coleman grill was brought from another backyard nearby and a constant fire was kept burning to generate a little warmth. That creature comfort, however, was fleeting and confined to the room in which the grill sat. The rest of the house was slowly but steadily yielding to the encroaching cold.

"So, what'd you do before all this?"

Meghan, walking from downstairs to up, at first didn't realize the question had been directed at her. She retraced a couple of her steps and asked, "What was that?"

Art stepped forward from out of view and said, "I was just wondering. You're just so...fit. You must've been an exercise instructor or something with a body like that."

"What?"

"I mean...I don't mean to be too forward or anything, but don't you think you've got a great body?"

Starting to feel quite flustered, Meghan sputtered, "Well I...you know...I don't...," and then she trailed off, not entirely sure how to answer that question.

Art let a slick, well-practiced smile play across his face. His eyes not too subtly took an elevator ride from her feet to her head and back down again. "Trust me. You are a very attractive woman."

Meghan was embarrassed as the flushing red of her breached modesty filled her cheeks.

At this acknowledgment, Art's smile stretched onto his bristly cheeks, revealing two rows of glistening pearly whites that all but reflected her face back at her.

He walked away with a bit of a swagger and left Meghan confused as to what had just happened. He walked up the stairs that she had been trying to climb before the exchange, leaving her motionless down by the front door.

At the top of the stairs but just out of sight in the hallway stood Dave, the younger and more robust man from the bus. He motioned to Art and the two walked quietly into a bathroom toward the end of the hall.

Dave said in whisper, "Man, you are smooth. I mean, wow. That was impressive."

Art shrugged and smiled, pleased at the observation.

"No. Really. That was very...slick. And believe me, I've seen some things in my day. Isn't she with...?"

Art nodded. "If I've learned nothing else, it's that things, love included, are temporary and just commodities and properties to be leveraged and sold to the highest bidder."

"And you've just upped the ante?"

"Exactly."

"Whatcha got in mind?"

"Just a little more say in how things are done around here is all."

"There's definitely something to be said for being the master of one's own destiny and if you can do that and convince that sweet young thing to be at your side, hell, I'd call that a good day."

"Exactly what I was thinking."

Dave leaned forward. "You got any other moves you're planning?"

With the same smile uncoiling itself just above his chin, Art said, "I'm just getting started."

# CHAPTER 40

Danny threw the dice and moved his token seven spaces around the game board. He did this with all the interest of a teenager forced into attending a three-day insurance sales seminar. The little green piece representing Danny on the board didn't show any more interest in the game than he did. It came to rest silently and unenthusiastically, waiting on the next roll of the dice for its chance to move once again.

With a whine, Jules buzzed, "I liked the games at the other place better."

Danny didn't answer her and instead chose to push the dice toward her. Ignoring them, Jules continued, "I like my games at home better too. I miss home. I just wanna go home, Danny. When are we gonna go home?"

"Just roll the dice, Jules. It's your turn." Danny wanted to be at home too, but seeing how far and how thoroughly the catastrophe in Alaska had spread he had begun to wonder himself whether home would be waiting for them at all anymore.

"I don't wanna play anymore. I wanna go home."

Again, Danny was forced to imagine home and what was waiting for them now. Were his parents still alive? Was anyone back home still alive or were they like all the other people out there that were bent on killing and terrorizing? It was long past time for this nightmare to end. His affect was becoming as flat and pale as the morning skies. He was only playing the game to burn the hours until it was time to sleep again. He looked over at Jules and saw that she wasn't in the mood to wait to sleep. She had simply lay back and closed her eyes in frustration. He was amazed at how easily she could embrace her slumber. It was typically much harder for him to find the peace to slip into an actual restful sleep. When he closed his eyes, he still saw his friend Martin laying across the seat in the minivan those many days ago. Sometimes, he saw Tony, who had been killed trying to help them get away from their first hiding place. It didn't seem right to him that a person of his age would have seen so much and such cruel death.

Danny finally decided that perhaps sleep was an option worth pursuing for himself too. Right there across the glossy Milton Bradley game board, he spread himself on his stomach and wished for sleep to find him.

About twenty minutes into his nap, when his mind wandered somewhere between sleep and awake, Danny thought he heard somebody walk into the room. Their voices defied detection as they spoke in hushed, hissing whispers. Danny was reminded of the times in which his parents had ventured into his room after he'd gone to bed but before he had truly embraced sleep. He would lie there with his eyes closed feigning sleep. Usually, possum playing led him to sleep's embrace. Maybe his parents knew this. Maybe all parents knew this. Maybe it was a game that they all played without ever really knowing that the other was playing. These thoughts, mixed with the voices, played themselves across his mind, like flashes of color and light...a neural pyrotechnics show exclusively for him.

And the old trick worked yet again because it was several hours later when he found himself being shaken awake by Jules.

"Danny. Danny. It's dinnertime. Get up, Danny."

"Okay, okay. I'm awake." He rose from his belly with game tokens and cards stuck to his face and in his hair.

Meals still tended to be good for everyone, especially because there seemed to be such an abundance of virtually everything. There were plenty of proteins, starches, and sweets. They even managed to still be holding some cans of fruits and vegetables. Drinks were usually sports drinks, sodas, or water.

This meal was no exception. They ate heartily and shared the rare smile and even rarer laugh. Mealtime was when everyone was at his or her best. Some ate out on the back deck under the grey but dry skies, while others ate at the glass top bronze table inside.

The only one absent was Malachi, who had taken to his solitude again. His interaction with others was reserved solely for Dr. Caldwell, but even that was very limited.

The reclusive police officer had withdrawn again and isolated himself from everyone else. His behavior was still worrisome, but it was also viewed as much less of a threat than before. This, of course, stemmed from his recent reliability and his keeping to himself his extreme opinions about others. He was still considered and referred to as creepy in conversations between the women primarily, but even they, Emma included, recognized that his contributions had kept them all alive at one point or another.

While the others ate that night, Malachi retreated to a small bathroom situated in a hallway on the ground floor next to the unfinished utility room. It was in a dark corner of a dark hallway, lit only by the fading pale light of the evening sun and a lonely creeping strip of flickering light down near the floor.

He sat on the closed toilet and pressed his hands together in front of his face. His silent prayers were being given voice by a series of grunts and whimpers. Even through his clenched, trembling eyes, Malachi could see him.

"That's right, Mal. You should be prayin' for the things you done." The air in the dark room became rank and foul all at once, tainted with the foul waste that was collecting in the bottom of the un-flushed toilet bowl below him.

"You been a bad boy again, Mal?"

Malachi cracked open his eyes slowly to reveal the confines of the small room. He'd chosen the room because it seemed so small that even a floating spectre wouldn't be able to find enough room in which to taunt him. He was relieved when he didn't see anything but the dancing shadows of the minuscule flickering light of the single burning candle on the sink counter top.

He became acutely aware of how badly he was sweating when a rivulet of beaded perspiration streamed down his forehead and onto his cheek. He swabbed away the salty liquid with hands that were as moist and heavy as kitchen sponges.

The sorrow surprised him at how quickly it overtook him. When the tears and quiet sobbing struck, he lost near total control of himself. He leaned forward and planted his forehead onto the wall.

The wall was cold and firm; solid and real. Maybe it could bear some of the heavy regrets and lingering pain that were overwhelming him. He pressed into the plaster even harder, feeling the uneven pattern and ridges imprinting themselves on his skin. The pain, like the hard wall, was real...tangible.

When the wall didn't seem strong enough and with nowhere else to lean, he tried to turn inside. He tried to find the strength of his faith. He saw a string of pastors and Holy Fathers from his past and even managed to remember some of their voices. But from them, all he could hear were words and no power. They could well have been speaking Aramaic for all he knew. It didn't matter because the words were as empty as politicians' promises; they said them because they were paid to do it.

He squeezed his temples to the point of pain in search of some buttressing strength. When he sought strength and faith and power from his past or his mind, the faces he saw and the voices he heard were those of his mother and his grandmother.

It was to them that he clung when the violence began, aimed first at them and then later at him. Despite the anger and the betrayal and the bruises and cuts, his mother's smile was ever present in his memory. Sometimes, he wrapped himself in the red warmth of her smile where no hands, no words, and no thoughts could harm him. It was a sanctuary he had always carried with him, but one that was becoming increasingly more difficult to find in the tangle of memories and torment that was his mind.

"You know she didn't even want you don'tcha?" the voice asked. "At first all she could think about was seein' someone and makin' you go away. And then she tried to give you away, but no one wanted you. Even when you was a baby, people could see that you were going to be a bad boy. Even as a baby...."

With desperate, pleading tears and a trembling face, he forced out of himself with a shudder, "You're not real. You're not real. Just go away. You're not real."

"Oh, I'm real, Mal. I'm as real as you...cuz I am you. Don't you get it?"

Malachi swung around as deftly as he could in the minuscule space. The candle's flame leapt into the air as if it was trying to make a run for it, but in the end elected to stay on the comfort and security of the wick. The cast shadows followed the flame's lead, trying to flee from the foul smelling box of a room, but they too retreated when the candle decided to cancel its emigration, shadows being only as brave as the light that leads them.

Nothing. The room was empty, save for him and his lone companion: the candle. He sat back down and nearly squealed when his father's unshaven face was suddenly just inches away from his own. "You were a mistake, Mal...an unwanted mistake. That's why all those things happened to you. No one wanted you; not even your own mother."

Malachi shot up from his toilet seat and flung open the door. He very nearly fell forward through the door but caught his balance at the last moment. He backed away from the open bathroom door and the little flame that seemed so distant and alone, his eyes darting left and then right to make sure that he wasn't being pursued.

He was at least maintaining a better sense of where he was and not confusing the present and the past. The voices and the faces were as real as those of the people upstairs, though. If he tried, he just knew that he could reach out and touch them if he wanted. Maybe that was what he needed to do. Maybe it was up to him to push them away and punish them the way they had done to him all those years ago.

He could feel all the fear becoming anger. Then, at the height of his anger's boil, he remembered his past's evangelists and their fiery sermons. He remembered the sense of righteous understanding and that there were absolutes in life. There was a simple yet powerful comfort in knowing that there were rights and wrongs on which one could count, as well as good and evil from which one could be damned.

And then it hit him. He knew what he needed to do. Every house should have one and hopefully this house would be no exception. He ascended the stairs and found a small bookshelf that had more knickknacks than books but didn't find it. He went to the coffee table that had been moved into a corner of the living room and dug through the magazines and picture books and still no luck. Of all the books he might find, he couldn't imagine that he wouldn't come across this one. He stopped in the middle of the room and thought about it for a moment, while everyone in the dining room stopped eating and stared at him. He was utterly oblivious to their gazes.

Where could it be? He spent several seconds thinking and considering and then he remembered seeing them in people's bathrooms in the past. With urgency in his step, he made his way down the narrow hall on the main floor and stopped at the entrance to the bathroom. Although this room was larger and was lit with several candles, he couldn't help but feel the tenuous hold of fear from his encounter in the other privy downstairs only moments before. He held his breath and waded in, hoping that his search would yield success quickly.

He looked in drawers, in the basket next to the toilet, and in the small linen closet and still found nothing. He finally looked in the least likely of places, the cabinet doors under the sink where one typically finds personal hygiene items, cleaning products, and extra toilet paper. He used his small pen sized flashlight from his belt to be able to see. At first, there was only what he expected, but behind the stack of toilet paper rolls he caught sight of a dark covered book. He pulled the tower of paper down as if he was Godzilla on a rant in a toilet paper roll version of Tokyo and there it was, waiting for him.

He hugged the book to his chest and breathed much easier. He opened the cover and began to read quietly but aloud, "In the beginning there was only darkness...."

# CHAPTER 41

Jerry tried peeking through the long narrow window next to the large double doors but couldn't see anything. Between the darkness on the other side and the opaque cloudiness of the treated glass, it was no use. He wasn't able to see anything. He tried the handle but already knew that it would be locked. Why would this door be any different than the majority of doors they'd encountered?

"Why the hell are we stopping here?" demanded Art.

Meghan admonished him with, "Irreverent much?"

Neither pausing nor softening his tone, Art continued, "You in the mood for prayer?"

Thinking to himself that he liked Art less and less, Jerry was able, after considerable effort, to avert launching into the rant that was threatening to leap into the fray, a rant that was something of a constant for him in his past.

The past tirades were typically characterized more by humor than by aggression, but they usually surfaced as a response to someone else's aggressive posturing. He found that when someone else was already provoked and on edge, it became that much easier to poke fun and taunt the person. His mouth got him into altercations, both physical and vocal, on numerous occasions, but he never seemed to learn from his past dealings and then had to accept the consequences which often included bruises, several suspensions from school, and lost jobs.

He was likely considered by most of the adults in his life to be a smart-assed slacker who was better at picking apart others' problems than he was in solving his own or making anything of himself. And the thing was, they were right. He was all that and more...or would that be less? No matter. There was a line from an Everclear song that summed him up nicely: *"I am a loser geek, crazy with an evil streak."* Yeah, that was him alright.

All that changed, and all at once. No one, not even he, saw it coming or would have predicted that he would ever have chosen the path that he was traveling. Maybe it was his friends from college, home for the summer, bragging about their exploits and living the life that he wanted for himself. Maybe it was that he was sick of always being broke and having nothing to call his own. Maybe he was sick of living under his parents' roof and living by their rules and standards. Maybe it was just all about timing and he was due. It didn't really matter.

He enrolled in a school out in the Valley where the training was good and the staff was great. He was able to see a different option for himself that wasn't easy but at the very least it would be his own. A lot of what he was taught was stuff he already knew, but hearing it again at that moment just seemed to help him remember and understand.

Not since he was a little kid had he sincerely applied himself to any endeavor. He had never known how it felt to work and accomplish something worth doing. It was a feeling that was as intoxicating as any drug he'd taken. The difference was that he was paid for this feeling and there wasn't any nasty next day hangover. He found that he was good at providing care for people and that getting paid to do that was a hell of a lot more satisfying than cleaning car interiors, or bussing tables, or anything else he'd ever done. The other thing that he learned was that when he didn't run his mouth every time he felt the urge, people were more inclined to listen to him when he did speak.

And it was all because of these realizations that when he turned around, he said to Art, "Some churches kept food pantries. Give me a little credit. I'm trying to think like Neil."

"I'm in," Meghan proclaimed. "Maybe we'll find a clean toilet for a quick pit stop."

Jerry joked about her seeming obsession with toilets, and she shot back her own jocular parry.

Art interjected on the heels of the exchange, "Funny and beautiful. Definitely a keeper."

Meghan rolled her eyes and blushed. Jerry thought to himself that he really didn't like this guy. They got into the church only to find the only doors leading away from the main hall were also locked. Using his rifle's butt as the universal door opener, Jerry forced each of the other doors starting with the one displaying a bathroom sign. The third door led to a shiny tiled hallway and a set of stairs that went both up and down.

Art suggested, "Split up and cover twice as much ground at once?"

Jerry immediately shook his head and asked, with the irritation in his voice far from masked, "Have you never watched a monster movie? Christ man! That's the first rule. You never split up! A single person is easier to kill than a pair or a group. How have you survived for so long being such a novice?"

"I was just thinking and—"

"Well stop, you dill hole. Not knowing what you're doin' can get you killed and I'm okay with that. But it can get her killed and me too and that just isn't gonna fly."

"I just figured...."

Jerry shook his head and said bluntly, "Don't. The figurin's already been done."

Art started to open his mouth and then stopped when he caught Jerry's glare. Jerry's demeanor surprised Meghan as well. She'd never seen him act like that before and it was catching her off guard.

In Art's defense she said, "Jerry, we all should have a say in this. His ass is just as on the line as yours. What if you're wrong?"

"If I'm wrong, you can tell me you told me so. But if he's wrong, ain't none of us going to be telling anyone anything."

"He's just trying to help."

"Well he's not. Let's go." Jerry started walking down the hallway toward the stairs. He turned back around and said, "You want to have input? Fine. We goin' upstairs or down first?"

Trying to play the victim and possibly garner a little more sympathy from Meghan, Art said half-dejectedly, "You've made all the decisions so far. Why would you stop and ask us our opinions now? It's only our lives you're directing."

Not willing to bite, Jerry simply answered, "Fine. Upstairs it is."

They checked the offices, small meeting rooms, and closets upstairs and found nothing. The place was still mostly orderly and neat, as if the rooms were still expecting their normal activity to resume at any moment.

Standing in the empty upstairs hallway, Art snidely commented to no one in particular, "Well that was time well spent...for all of us." He walked back toward the stairs and started to make his way slowly back down to the main floor.

Jerry stopped dead in his tracks and balled his fists at his sides. He closed his eyes and let go a deep, animated breath while he sought to calm the anger that was starting to boil and displace any coping mechanisms that he'd developed in the past couple of years. Meghan touched his shoulder and said softly, "Let it go. It's just his way."

Jerry thought to himself so loudly that he was afraid Meghan could hear that Art's way was going to get Jerry's foot planted in Art's ass. It had been a long time since Jerry had hit anyone in anger or frustration, but he could feel those old instincts threatening to surface again.

They stood on the brink of descending into the dark unknown of the church basement. Moving halfway down the stairs, Jerry peered into the darkness trying to discern anything that might be down there. It was no use. Jerry had never seen such darkness in his life. He pulled his flashlight from his pack and tried to cut the darkness with its beam.

There was another hallway and some more rooms behind closed doors. On the walls were Sunday School pictures colored and hung proudly by the children who used to come there on the weekends while their mothers and fathers attended services upstairs. The temperature downstairs was decidedly cooler and damper, like a cave. Jerry thought to himself that he hoped they didn't disturb whatever bear might be hibernating down there.

He whispered, "Get your flashlights."

Meghan took hers out and added its illumination to that of Jerry's. Art was quiet for a moment and then admitted, "I don't have mine with me."

Both Jerry and Meghan looked over at him with their mouths opened questioningly. Meghan asked for both of them, "What?"

"I didn't know that we'd need them. I thought we were just going to be looking in houses. Captain Jerry didn't let on what his intentions were."

Jerry had had enough. "You lazy, self-righteous, self-centered, cowardly sack of shit!!! You do nothing but whine and complain about everything and set yourself up as some wayward victim who doesn't have any say about anything and when you get the opportunity to contribute and to do something for yourself and everyone else you drop the ball." Jerry turned to face Art and started to ascend the stairs in his direction. As he did so, he handed his flashlight to Meghan.

"What was it that you were thinking? Was it that you were just being selfish again and a heavy flashlight might slow you down too much if you had to run? Doesn't it make you feel like less of a man to know that Meghan brought hers or that the punk kid brought his? Or do you not have any self respect at all?"

Meghan tried to intervene, "Jerry, this isn't going to accomp—"

Jerry stopped her short, "No, Meghan, not this time. Art, I've known people like you all my life. I think I might even have been on the road to *being* you at one point and then I discovered something that I was missing and that I can see you're missing too: dignity. You go through life doing just enough to get by and then hope that those around you will pick up the slack. You don't necessarily do anything wrong, but you only do enough right so as to stay above reproach. People like you make me sick."

Art crossed his arms defiantly across his chest and then asked without a hint of emotion in his voice, "You done now?"

Jerry stepped right up into his face and said coolly, "I'm just gettin' started so you'd better watch your ass."

Meghan finally successfully intervened, "Okay, Jerry. This isn't accomplishing anything. Let's go check out downstairs and then get back to the house. We're losing daylight standing here arguing. Let's get moving."

Jerry turned around and joined Meghan on the stairs. Art too started to come back down the stairs, but Jerry spun around and demanded, "Not you. You stay nice and safe up here. Fucking coward!"

"You better watch what you say to me," Art admonished.

"I'll say anything I want to you and however I want to say it. Got it? When you're man enough to pull your own weight....never mind, that'll never happen, will it? Fucking worthless sack."

With that, Jerry spun around and stomped down the stairs. The first thing he realized when he got to the bottom of the stairs was that he was inwardly envious of Art's position still in the light. It was the kind of dark where light seemed to be an intruder of sorts. Whether from the teasing darkness or the cool air Jerry didn't know, but the hair on his arms and neck all stood on end as he walked deeper into the gloom. Their footsteps on the tiled floor made faint, clicking echoes that preceded their progress.

The darkness was so complete, so overwhelming, that even the cones of light emanating from their flashlights seemed useless, like cutting water with a knife. The air, too, seemed unfriendly, stale, and cool as it touched their skin and filled their lungs.

Mostly, the doors opened into lonely classrooms, begging for the voices of children. Hanging on one wall was a construction paper cut out of Noah's Ark and on it were pasted pictures of animals cut from magazines.

Meghan wondered aloud, "I wonder if Noah was told to grab any humans on this go 'round?"

Trying to sound resolved and steady despite his quick, shallow breathing, Jerry said with a bit of a swagger, "Well, Noah had better stay the fuck outta my way. 'Cause I'm comin' aboard."

"This church got you a little riled or something?"

"No. Why do you ask?"

"I don't think I've ever heard you use language like that or get so...aggressive with someone before. And here, all of a sudden, you seem...unstoppable."

They were, by then, looking in the last room, which was a janitor's closet. If they were looking for cleaning supplies, they'd just hit the mother lode. As it was, the church was proving to be a bit of a bust.

Jerry answered her as they started to get back into the pale light peeking its reluctant head down into the blackness. "I guess I've always had kind of a weird relationship with church and God. I guess I believe in God, or at least *a* God. At one point, I really got into church and studying the Bible and all. That was right after I discovered death and how permanent and real it was. I think God helped me find meaning, in a way, but it was all rooted in fear. And after awhile, the fear wasn't enough so I drifted away.

"I don't really go to church except weddings sometimes. I think I've got a better grasp on God though, and especially on faith...at least my faith. I just don't like to talk about faith because it seems so personal and private to me. As for this church getting to me? No, not really. It's just another empty fucking building. I'd say it has more to do with our company than anything else."

"There you go again," joked Meghan.

Art, still standing at the top of the stairs, asked, "Anything?"

Jerry didn't even bother to look at him. Meghan shook her head but didn't say a word.

The three of them went back to the front doors and opened them unknowingly into a group of four awaiting zombies on the front steps of the church. Two of the monsters were little girls whose skin had greyed and whose eyes had yellowed but were still wearing matching pink pajamas. They lunged at Jerry and Meghan, who were both in front of Art.

Jerry was able to use his rifle to hold off the two in front of him. Using his rifle stock like a staff, he struck the little girl in front of him squarely in the face hard enough to shatter several of her brittle front teeth. Her head jolted back, sending her into the camouflage-clad soldier behind. Tangled and off balance, the two toppled onto one another and struggled to get back to their feet.

Meghan, meanwhile, had been surprised into a backward stumble. She was nearly on her back with the two zombies in front of her trying to follow her down. She screamed and instinctively raised her arm to fend them off, knowing full well that her exposed skin presented a very tempting and ripe target for the chomping mouths coming at her. She couldn't think; her fear was paralyzing her wits. She closed her eyes and just hoped that it would be over quickly.

Then she heard a distinctly metallic thud and she was being pulled free. She opened her eyes and saw Art getting ready to swing the heavy crowbar in his hand again. The little girl who had been almost upon her was now rolling back down the stairs to the street in front of the church. Her limbs flailed uncontrollably like the plastic arms of a soft, life-sized doll discarded by its owner.

Both Jerry and Meghan paused and looked up at Art who was brandishing the black crowbar like Arthur wielding Excalibur. The three remaining ghouls were not so distracted, though all three were teetering back on their heels giving Jerry and Meghan a window to recover.

Meghan hopped to her feet and Jerry pulled the pistol from the holster on his hip. He squeezed off three quick shots, all of which struck the two monsters directly in front of him. The remaining little girl with the now jagged front teeth caught one of the bullets in the head, taking off her right ear and much of the right side of her face and head, but didn't accomplish its intended goal of destroying her brain. All three bullets struck the man behind her and caused him to stumble down the steps behind him. Unsteadily and awkwardly, he rose back to his feet and started back up the steps.

Jerry kicked the mutilated little girl still in front of him and sent her head over heels back into the man at the bottom of the stairs. As she rolled down, they could hear her grunt and growl, sounds that were decidedly not human but definitely disconcerting.

He raised the pistol for another shot at the final beast that was still near them and inching steadily closer to Meghan. This time, the gunshot tore off the top half of his head and propelled him into the front yard of the church.

With just a second to spare, Meghan asked, "Now what? Do we need to find another way out?"

Jumping down onto the lawn himself as he spoke, Jerry said, "No. We just need to stay away from these two and get back to the house before we run into any more of them."

Meghan didn't need to hear anything more. She joined Jerry down near the lifeless and now motionless corpse he'd dispatched. Art wasn't sure. He felt like if they were holding the upper hand and could kill these two, then maybe they should. It would just mean two fewer of those things out there and that seemed to be a good thing to him. He was just as flustered as the other two, but hitting that thing with his crowbar had given him a jolt of confidence and power that was making it difficult for him to want to retreat. He hadn't really been a part of the melee out at the park and hadn't been able to experience enjoying such an advantage when facing the undead. The scales always seemed tilted away from them and it was more about surviving than it was fighting.

It was fairly intoxicating. He wondered if this was how soldiers felt after their first taste of combat. You're taught about right and wrong and where taking another human falls on that continuum. It's one of those primal laws that were fairly consistently adhered to by most civilizations. Yet, there he was; able to crush skulls with reckless abandon. No regret. No fear of reprisal. No consequences.

He was about to say they should attack when Meghan shouted, "Look!" and pointed. In the street now and a couple blocks away, a crowd of staggering and hungry beasts was starting to move toward them.

Jerry grabbed Meghan's arm and shouted, "C'mon. We gotta go! Now!"

Meghan said over her shoulder, "Art?"

"Right behind you," he said as all the bravado in his veins retreated.

They ran hard and fast, climbing a couple of fences along the way to put something more than just distance between themselves and the monsters now pursuing them.

They made it back to the house without encountering any more undead predators, but their arrival caused a stir. It had been literally days since any of them had seen any of the fiends, even from a distance.

When their breathing had calmed enough to answer questions, Evelyn asked them, "So they're still out there?"

Jerry nodded slowly and apologetically. "We're still not alone." To which both Meghan and Art nodded but realized that Jerry's pronouncement was enough.

Evelyn, already appearing healthier than when she had emerged from the bus, lamented, "I was so hoping that everything that had happened had all been a dream and I was finally awake again. It's just too bad. I really was starting to believe that it was all going to be okay."

# CHAPTER 42

Art dropped his pack on the floor and took a generous drink from the glass of lemonade. He stepped away, not even remotely aware Danny had moved twice out of his way, once to avoid being stepped on and once to not have the dropped day pack hit him on the head. He was just inside a door and reading a comic book. He was hoping to stay out of the way and felt like he had more or less succeeded until Art came home.

Danny was glad that Jerry and Meghan were back. He liked both of them and felt especially close to and appreciative of Jerry for saving his and Jules' lives. He didn't hear all of the recounting of the latest expedition out into the surrounding area but didn't feel like he was missing out on much either. Sometimes he was interested to hear about new finds or good hauls of supplies, but he didn't really want to hear about more of those things and about having to get moving again. He instead chose to remain in his reading position in the bedroom doorway.

He looked over at Art's pack and realized that it was open. Danny immediately spotted the little handgun. He knew not to touch them, but no one ever told him that he couldn't admire them. He reached into the bag and moved the big, black flashlight out of the way so that he could better see the pistol. It looked like something that he might see in a spy movie or a new Tom Clancy video game.

Art stepped up out of nowhere and grabbed up the bag. "Whatcha lookin' at?"

Danny said honestly, "Your pistol. It's pretty cool. I just saw it and was lookin' at it. I didn't touch it, I promise. I was just lookin'. Honest."

Art tilted his head to one side, sizing up the youth. Satisfied that he'd gotten the answer he wanted, he walked away without a word.

By that time, completely distracted and unable to concentrate on reading, Danny got up and went in search of either Jerry or Neil. They were like the cool uncles that kids at family reunions sought out. The two men were on the front porch talking. When Danny appeared, they paused for a moment to acknowledge him but then continued, using 'he', 'him', and 'her' instead of names. Danny knew about whom they were speaking because Jerry was just recounting in more detail the findings and goings on of the latest expedition into the surrounding area.

After ranting for a few more minutes, Jerry waited for Neil to respond. Neil nodded his head in agreement with whatever observation Jerry had made. "He's a tough one. I'll give you that. Not quite sure what's going on with him."

Jerry answered, "I don't like him one bit. And the way that he's been acting toward Meghan...it's just not right. I mean you guys aren't married or anything but everyone knows... Hell, he's out back with her and having her tell the story of his heroics right now. What a tool. The prick didn't bring his flashlight and sent us down into the dark without him. Before we left, just like before anyone leaves, everyone is supposed to make sure they have everything that we're going to need and that includes a flashlight. He said he had it and then when he needed it, he suddenly was without one. And then if we would have run into any trouble, he would have been safe from all of it. Coward."

Neil shook his head and corrected, "I don't know if coward is as fitting as opportunist really."

Danny couldn't resist, "You mean Art? Don't you?"

Jerry and Neil looked over at Danny, trying to decide whether or not they should confirm his assumptions. Neil said, "Danny, I don't know if it's good that you're listening to this. Jerry is just trying to vent a little...."

Danny blurted out, "He had a flashlight with him."

Jerry, surprised and looking more seriously at Danny asked, "He what?"

Danny answered after looking over his shoulder, "Yeah. Just now, when he threw his bag down, I saw his flashlight in his bag."

Neil wanted clarification. "Are you absolutely sure?"

"Yeah. When he threw down his bag on the floor, it was unzipped and I could see in it."

Jerry shook his head and looked at Neil, "That son of a...."

Neil wasn't done yet. "Could it have been anything else?"

"No. I saw his gun and wanted to see it better but didn't want to touch it. I know the rules. The flashlight was in the way, so I reached in and moved it. It's definitely a flashlight."

Again, Jerry said, "Son of a...."

Neil said, "Thanks, Danny. Once again you've come through for us." He touched Danny's shoulder and squeezed it gently.

And with that simple gesture, Danny again felt as connected and as important as he ever had in his short life. This was a definite departure from his experiences over the past several days. Ever since Art's tirade back at the old man's house and his referring to Danny and Jules as encumbrances, Danny had just felt on guard and especially sensitive to any and all comments about either Jules or himself. Who could blame him?

He was worried about their status as excess baggage for most of the others in the group and now, with the new people and their needs, there was even more of a risk that they could get lost in the proverbial shuffle.

It was an awful lot for a ten-year-old to have on his plate. It was probably just as well that he didn't fully understand all of it or the possibilities would have likely completely overwhelmed his young mind. Children weren't intended to deal in such horrific absolutes. There was no allowance for playful mirth, the true magical motor of childhood wonder, when survival was at the core of your every action and thought.

The connections he was making with the adults in the group and the responsibilities he was assuming for Jules were the most outward signs of his fading juvenile sensibilities. To Neil, although he was proud of the little guy, it was tragic what he'd had to experience and endure and how it was affecting him.

Neil was reminded of the African Boy Soldiers who were forcibly drafted and trained to fight for the various warlords of that continent. *National Geographic, Time Magazine*, or maybe it was Sally Struthers, did a story about the child soldiers of Sierra Leone or Rwanda or possibly Sudan. He just remembered the distant, gaunt expressions of those little boys, all about Danny's age, who were wearing green military uniforms and toting black military firearms in the photos. The pictures hadn't meant much to him at the time of reading, probably in a dentist or Division of Motor Vehicles office, because the faces all seemed so foreign and so different. That was all changing though; Danny was changing. He was unfortunately becoming their own boy soldier. Neil wondered if there was ever any going back.

Jerry asked, "So now what? What do we do?"

Neil wasn't entirely certain what his next step should be. If they were to confront him, Art could just deny it all and then get even more sly in his deceptions. He might also find ways to threaten Danny and Jules, and Neil would not let that happen. They needed to find some way to expose Art definitively to the others in a very public fashion so that he couldn't deny it or weasel out of it.

"This just seems like the plot line of some bad reality TV show or something," Jerry commented disgustedly.

Neil replied, "Yeah, but getting voted off of this island means a helluva lot more than just missing out on the cash prize at the end of the show."

# CHAPTER 43

How long had it been since he'd slept? The thought occurred to Malachi randomly and then was gone. His days were becoming a blur of fear and torment. He wasn't sure when he'd eaten last but the growling protests coming from his abdomen suggested that he'd stopped eating about the same time that he stopped sleeping.

Maybe he was becoming one of those things and the others just weren't willing to tell him. That was probably why they largely left him to himself, although he'd seen them out of the corner of his eye watching him and spying on him. Was he destined to butcher and kill and destroy like the unholy beasts stalking the streets of Anchorage?

What about his eternal soul? Would it be allowed inside the Gates if it was damned on earth? Eternal damnation? Was that really to be his fate? The fear added a sharp edge to the malaise and dulled senses of his cloudy existence but that was all. The fear was as hot and real as watching a fireplace video on a television screen. It was there, but if you didn't keep your eye on it, it was as if it just went away.

If only he could say the same about the specter of his father who appeared and reappeared seemingly at will and always with the same insults, the accusations, and the same threats. Malachi, on some level, understood that these appearances weren't real, but that realization was fleeting, pushed aside forcefully by the toxic mix of paranoia, psychosis, and exhaustion. He was finding it exceedingly difficult to be certain of anything.

"Why are you so sad, Mal?"

Was the voice in the dark garage real, or was it just in his head? The only light in the garage was coming from the small window on the door leading to the backyard. With the settling darkness outside, however, the light filtering in did little more than cast a grey pall over everything that hadn't already been consumed by the encroaching darkness; not even enough light to cast any definitive shadows.

Malachi was sitting on an empty five-gallon bucket with his back to a corner. He pressed his shoulders into the corner and scanned the garage for anyone or anything. He thought he saw something move across the window but he couldn't be sure. Oh God! Had those things found them?

He reached to his hip holster and unsnapped it. He was starting to rise when he heard, "What do you see, Mal? You still afraid of the dark?"

He looked over to his left and felt the cold, nauseating chill start at the nape of his neck and spill down his spine. His father, like a menacing gargoyle, was perched precariously atop a paint can sitting on the garage workbench. The old shade smiled at him and was all at once coming at him.

Malachi lowered his head into his hands, warming his face with his hot, deep breaths.

"Look at me when I'm talking to you, boy."

"I'm not a boy anymore."

"You talkin' back, boy? You need me to teach you a lesson again?" The hazy apparition reached out to him and Malachi recoiled almost involuntarily, hitting his face against the garage door and the metal tracks that guided the wheels for raising and lowering the door.

He could still feel the ghost reaching out to him, so he leaned even further, falling over into a stack of yard tools. The metal and wood hoes, rakes, shovels, and even a posthole digger fell on top of him with quite a clatter.

His father was gone, but his echoing laughter remained.

Just seconds later, the inside garage door was flung open and the darkness was flooded with several bright beams of light and some loud voices. "What is it?" "Did they get in here?" "What do you see?"

"It's only me," Malachi said apologetically. "I'm in here."

Dr. Caldwell's disembodied voice said, "Malachi? Where are you?"

Malachi finally freed himself from the tangle of tools and stood up. "I'm over here. Just tripped is all."

Dr. Caldwell's voice was now full of empathy and concern, "Malachi, you're bleeding. You okay?"

"I think so. I'm not...I mean, I don't..."

"It's okay, Malachi. Why don't you come inside and let me see about stopping the bleeding a little."

"No, I'll be okay."

"Malachi, I think you should get a look at it yourself then. You're bleeding pretty good. At least come inside and wash up a little."

Malachi let himself be led back inside where the doctor tended to the cuts on his face, his temple, and the side of his head. He also had a sizable welt on the top of his head where something had obviously hit him.

"Jesus, Malachi, you should be more careful. Those tools are a nasty bunch of characters. Maybe you should be hanging out with us instead."

The joke wasn't lost on Malachi. He even managed to crack a smile for a second. He said with some very welcome amusement, "Kinda like the moose in the woods, huh?"

Dr. Caldwell smiled and said in feigned protest, "Are you still giving me grief about that?"

"Nah. But it still kinda cracks me up is all."

"Well I'm glad that I can be of entertainment to someone."

"Doc," Malachi asked, "if something were to happen to me, you know, like maybe I got the sickness that made those other people turn into what they are, would you level with me and tell me?"

"I guess I'm not following you, Malachi. Do you mean, if you got bitten or something, would I tell you about it?"

"Forget it. Never mind."

"Malachi, you're not sick, but I think you should try to eat and maybe even get some uninterrupted sleep."

At first Malachi didn't answer. He just shook his head. He was having the hardest time finding his voice. He forced out the tiniest of sounds that barely escaped his chest, "I can't. I'm too...afraid."

Dr. Caldwell straightened himself up and tried to reassure the man, who was clearly struggling with something. "We will watch out for you. Those things won't be able to get to you. You should get some rest so that when the fight does come, you'll be able to fight back."

"I can't. It's not that simple."

"We're here for you, Malachi. Let us help."

Desperate now, Malachi pleaded, "But you can't protect me from *him*. He can wait. He's as patient as eternal time. He wants me."

"You'll never be alone. You'll be safe."

"Nothing's safe from him."

"Malachi, at first I thought you were talking God or Jesus. Now, I'm not so sure. This would at least be a different version of either of them than I've ever known. Even Old Testament God in all his wrath and vengeance, and death from above wasn't as bad as all that."

"He's no God and Jesus wouldn't have him."

"Who then, Malachi? Who is it who is so threatening to you?"

The conversation, if it could be called one, was over. At that point, waiting for a response from Malachi was like waiting for a winning number to be called on the Powerball Lotto or the elusive and infamous check in the mail; sure there's always that outside chance that it'll come but it's probably not worth anticipating.

Dr. Caldwell waited a second or two longer and then said, "Come with me, Malachi. Come up and get a bite to eat."

Malachi hesitantly followed Dr. Caldwell up the stairs. If Dr. Caldwell could get some food into his belly, maybe he could coax him into some rest too. The psychosis, dormant while they were moving, was returning in earnest and Malachi's exhaustion was only feeding it.

When the two men were back upstairs, Dr. Caldwell found a place to sit in the living room.

Neil asked him quietly, "How we doin'?"

Dr. Caldwell shook his head and admitted honestly, "I don't really know. I think it's important that he gets some rest and nourishment. I would have referred him to a mental health specialist long ago."

Emma got up from her spot on the couch and left the room. She still wasn't willing to entertain discussions about the police officer, especially if it led to showing him any sort of compassion. He'd tried to rape her and that was a fact. The rest of it was merely speculation and she had neither the stomach nor the tolerance to speculate when it came to him.

Still, she no longer felt threatened by him the way she had when they were first on the run from the hospital. That seemed so long ago; a lifetime ago, and getting further and further away with each dawn. She looked at herself and tried to remember the woman that she was. Her fingernails, once finely sculpted and manicured, were broken and worn and held the dirt of a refugee under them. Her clothes too were dirty and stained, and probably smelled awful, though she had largely become desensitized to such things. She didn't have a mirror but she didn't need one to be able to imagine the tired lines on her face or the grime that was settling there. She felt like a different person living in a different time.

She wandered out onto the back deck and watched Art, Dave, Meghan, Gerald, Evelyn, and little Jules talking out in the fenced yard like it was just another normal autumn barbecue. She couldn't hear them. They all seemed to be smiling and carrying on, though, neither of which interested her. She just stood against the railing and looked up at the sky, whose grey hue and cool disposition resembled the skin of the undead. It wasn't raining at the moment, but the suggestion was still in the air, which left moist, cool kisses on the skin.

Back in the living room, Neil looked at Jerry and Dr. Caldwell and asked, "So what do we do now? The zekes know that we're here, or at least are still around if they don't know our exact location yet. There's no way we can stay here much longer and not risk getting trapped again."

Dr. Caldwell looked over at Malachi sitting at the dining room table and eating his soup. "Seems like we've had this discussion before under similar circumstances."

Jerry lamented, "Yeah, but then we had a car as a way out. We're on foot now."

"All the more reason that we put together a plan before we get found out," Neil said.

# CHAPTER 44

Meghan rose earlier than anyone else. She rolled away from Neil's arms and stood quietly, hoping not to disturb any of the others sleeping nearby, and wandered out onto the back deck into the cool morning air.

Once outside, she found that she had risen before the sun. To the east, above the silent, hulking Chugach Range, the smoldering embers of the waking sun were just starting to cast a grayish purple glow behind the peaks. Like paint spilled on the canvas of the sky, the dull luminescence gradually spread itself up and out, crowding the dark purple bruise of the night out of reach.

"Beautiful," she whispered.

The voice behind asking, "What was that?" caused her to jump a little. Art smiled and asked again, "What'd you say?"

Meghan turned back to continue watching the growing hints of dawn and replied, "I said that, despite all that's happened and all we've lost, something as beautiful as this could still happen. If the sun keeps coming back day after day, then maybe there's a chance for all of us."

"Unless the sun just doesn't care or maybe it's just doing it out of habit—doesn't know any better and so just keeps doing its job day in and day out. I've known lots of people who did that in the past." Sensing that perhaps he was causing her to withdraw, Art corrected course. "I think I like your take on it better. It's more poetic and hopeful, both things that I've come to admire about you."

Still standing behind her, he placed his hand on her shoulder and rubbed it gently. When she didn't stop him or recoil from his touch, he let his other hand move to her other shoulder. He then proceeded to massage her shoulders, neck, and upper back in wide, searching circles.

Still looking away from him at the mountains, Meghan asked, "If we're all gone and there are none of us left to see it, will sunrises still be as beautiful?"

"Of course they will be."

She turned suddenly and looked at him with her piercing blue eyes. "How? If there's no one here to see, then how? And why? What would it matter if the sun never showed its face again and everything around us simply withered and died and the earth just became a lifeless rock like the moon?" She shook her head and held back the tears, though the sorrow was finding it easy to stamp itself across her face. "I'm sorry. I guess I was lost in the moment. I..."

Art cut her off by kissing her fully on the mouth. At first, she didn't do anything but accept his mouth against hers. He was warm against the still cool air of the morning. Not seconds later, she pushed him away and moved to the other side of the deck. She didn't speak or even look at him.

He whispered, "Sorry. I just...I guess I...sorry."

Still not looking at him she said, "It's okay. I guess I was sending out some confusing messages wasn't I? It's just that in the past few weeks, I've...we've been through an awful lot and I guess I'm as mixed up as I've ever been."

"You don't have to apologize. I probably stepped over the line."

"No you didn't. It's just better that it doesn't go any further than that. Okay?"

"I'll do my best but I can't promise anything. You're just special to me and sometimes it's hard not to express it. Can this be our little secret?"

"Yeah. In fact, it's probably better that this just stays between the two of us."

"Can't argue with that."

With that said, Meghan went back inside to find something to satisfy the growing hunger building in her stomach, leaving Art on the deck to himself.

When he was alone, he couldn't help but smile. He did like Meghan and hoped that, perhaps when all of this was over, somehow they would find a way to be together. If it worked out that way, he wouldn't complain a bit. She was lovely in both appearance and spirit, but the reality was that there were hundreds, thousands, and maybe even more women who fit that description. If it didn't work out with Meghan in the end, he was certain that he could find someone. For the time being though, he was pretty sure that he could count on her to be a friendly voice for him when he couldn't be there to represent himself in discussions.

# CHAPTER 45

*Still no sleep. Can't. He won't let me. No peace. Only rage; only fear. Why does he hate me? Why won't he let me sleep? I'm his son. Pain in my stomach. Is that him? Is he there cutting me from within? Have to stop it. Have to stop him. Need peace. Need sleep.*

*Mother, where are you? Why don't you protect your little Malachi from him anymore? Where have you gone? Am I forsaken? Have you turned your back on me for good? Have I not paid for my sins? Is there no redemption?*

*God, help me. Give me strength. I don't think I can do this anymore; not alone. Give me a sign. Show me the way. Is it blood you want? Please. Storm is rising, threatening. No end in sight. No rest. No hope. Can't keep this up. Won't keep this up.*

*If I'm to go to Hell, he's coming with me....*

# CHAPTER 46

Art and Dave wandered away from the others, who were distracting themselves in the fenced back yard and enjoying a brief respite from the damp autumn weather. Seeking privacy from prying eyes and listening ears, the two men stepped inside the back door that led into the garage.

"There's more talk about moving on again," Dave said. "What are we gonna do about it? It just doesn't make sense to me that we'd leave this place only to go searching for another."

"Who's talking about leaving?"

"The three guys who are always talking about what the rest of us are going to do. Who do you think?"

"When? Did they bring it up with you?"

Dave shot Art an incredulous look and wrinkled his brow with doubt. "No. D'you think they'd actually involve me? Those guys would no more have me around when they talk as they would you. It's definitely us and them, even if they don't know it yet. And right now, they're in charge and I don't see how we are going to change that. I mean, what happens to all of us if they're wrong and we leave anyway. What are we going to do?"

Art paused and peered out the window at the group in the yard. The little boy and girl were chasing each other around while the adults watched. Emma and Meghan were sharing a bottle of water. Art was pleased to see that Meghan wasn't standing in Neil's shadow as she normally was. Maybe she was re-evaluating the nature of their relationship, especially in consideration of how it affected Art's relationship with her. Because they shared a secret now, he felt like he held some sway over her.

He asked Dave, "Why does gold have value?"

Confused and doubting whether he heard it correctly or not, Dave asked, "Why does what have what?"

"...gold have value?"

"I would typically bite and ask why but what does the question have to do with anything?"

"It's not that profound really. Gold has value because people have arbitrarily assigned value to it. I think there might be valuations that cause the value to fluctuate from time to time, but really that just determines the degree of value at the moment.

"Some time long ago, probably before recorded history, some guy had this rock with a little bit of sparkle to it that he cleaned up, heated in his fire, banged into shape with another rock, and then rubbed and polished to a shimmer. Someone else saw his shiny, shaped rock and decided they wanted one too. And then the guy who found that first hunk and knew where more of it could be had became the first gold merchant.

"It's a soft metal that is easy to shape and never rusts or tarnishes. But really that's about all gold has to offer."

Dave laughed a humorless hack of a chuckle. Shaking his head and starting to question his own judgment in people, he asked, "Is there any other worthless information you'd like to pass along?"

"You're missing my point."

"Apparently."

Still looking out the window on the door, Art said, "The only reason Neil and his co-stooges are in charge is because the others have let them be. We just have to offer a better alternative. You know, give 'em platinum when the other guy offers gold. At least make them feel like you've got platinum, whether you've got it or not."

"So what're you gonna do?"

Art shushed him and looked into the darker corners of the garage. "I think there's someone there," he whispered.

"Who?"

Not seeing anything specific but feeling less than alone, Art said, "Probably that crazy fucking cop."

In the garage's darkest corner, furthest from the slither of light fighting desperately for its shrinking foothold on the wall, Officer Malachi Ivanoff was rousing from a senseless stupor; or, more to the point, he was shifting from one flavor of senseless stupor to another.

He looked up and saw, just inside the door, a pair of glowing wraiths clacking their fangs together as they whispered curses between one another. Their bottom thirds shrouded in shadows, the menacing figures seemed to float like bad dreams waiting to pounce on their hapless victim. He immediately knew that his father had sent them. He'd sent them for him, and they were conspiring and deciding how best to steal his soul and flee back to the dark pit with him in tow.

He tried to shrink himself into the same tiny ball that he became when he was a little boy and wanted to be unnoticed or forgotten. Sometimes it worked well enough that he wouldn't get new bruises to cover those that he'd received the day previous.

It didn't work this time, though, because when he tried, the glimmering translucent spirits heard him. He stood as still as he could, but they looked right at him, right through him. Like electrified, milky white opals, the beings' eyes cast about in the darkness fixing on him with predatory intent. One of the spirits barked some curse at Malachi in his demon tongue, the voice cold and poisonous.

Malachi bowed his head and held his breath. In a fleeting lucid moment, he doubted that any of it could be real. He tried to convince himself that there was no such thing as monsters but that conventional wisdom and the past reassurances of his mother were both nullified by the monstrous terror that lurked and waited for them all throughout Anchorage. Still, those creatures who had hunted them incessantly for weeks now, those zombies, were once men and women but had been driven to their current state by an infection.

Were there monsters now? That question, that doubt, melted away the last vestiges of his tenuous hold on reality. When he looked back up, he clearly saw monsters. They were two phantoms that had emerged from the depths of Hell to perform his father's bidding.

His eyes adjusting to the scant light, Art thought he could make out the shape of someone sitting in the corner but he wasn't entirely sure who it was. He asked into the darkness, "Malachi, is that you?" There was no response but he did think that he could hear breathing. The hair on the back of his neck and arms stood on end. To Dave he said, "I think we need to get out of here and carry on somewhere else."

Dave asked, "D'you think he heard us?"

Art shook his head and said dismissively, "Who the Hell's going to listen to him anyway? He's off his nut."

Dave agreed and turned to make his way out behind Art, but in doing so he nudged a pile of cans stacked atop a couple of boxes and the whole heap tumbled down with a crash.

On the heels of the ruckus, the deafening, echoing, raging reports from Malachi's sidearm caused both men to jump. The first couple of shots went wild, but then the police officer's aim found its mark. Dave screamed as bullets struck him in the chest, shoulder, and neck. He was flung lifelessly against the garage wall, and then crashed to the floor violently.

Malachi didn't stop shooting. He continued to fire his pistol until there were no more bullets to shoot. After he'd pulled his trigger a handful of times with no result, he returned the handgun to his holster and waited for a second. The stillness was surprising; the smoke from the discharged bullets forming a lingering, nose-stinging cloud.

They were men and not specters as he had thought. And now those men were on the floor in spreading pools of thick crimson that were seeping from their bodies. At once, Malachi knew what he'd done. He'd broken a cardinal sin of both his faith and his profession. He'd killed in cold blood. He'd taken lives that were not his for the taking. He also knew that his shooting would likely draw the attention of the creatures from which they were all hiding. He'd endangered all of them.

With his mind still taunting him, he ran through the house, found one of the new M4 assault rifles, and then bolted out the front door.

Everyone else, still in the backyard but now planted firmly on their faces following the sounds of gunshots from the garage, heard Malachi run down the street yelling at the top of his voice. He wasn't making any sense, just noise. His voice became fainter and fainter as the distance grew. Shortly thereafter, his voice was replaced with the rat-a-tat of the M4. Even the gunshots, however, seemed to be coming from farther and farther away with each passing breath.

Dr. Caldwell crawled to the door leading into the garage. The window, though still in its pane, was shattered and bore a small hole right in its center. He listened, his head cocked to one side. He heard breathing, panting really, like someone struggling for breath. There was no movement and no other sound.

"Is there anyone still in the garage?" he asked into the room. When no one and nothing answered, he made up his mind that he had to go investigate. From his hip holster, he eased out the big Smith and Wesson revolver that was always at his side. "Neil, I'm going in. Got my back?"

"Is it going to get me shot?"

"I was hoping for a simple yes."

"Yeah, I'm there. Jerry?"

"Already on my way."

Neil huffed while he crawled over to the door just behind Dr. Caldwell, "At least zombies don't shoot at you."

Before they could go, Art choked out, "He fucking shot us. He...." His voice was cut short by a sudden choking fit.

Dr. Caldwell couldn't wait any longer. He sprang up and ran into the garage. The air was scorched with the acrid remnants of discharged gunpowder. He stopped awkwardly, allowing his eyes to adjust to the much more scarce light. Neil, of course, didn't realize this and was into launching himself forward before he could alter his course.

Instead of entering the garage with poise and confidence, the two men tumbled forward in very un-hero-ish style, tripping over the fallen stacks of supplies that had been knocked over in the chaos. Neil clumsily punched the toe of his right boot into a large sack of rice, which bled little white beads from the plastic wound.

Still struggling to his knees, Dr. Caldwell called out, "Art? Where are you?" He looked around and saw a pair of legs emerging from behind a ladder and an unmistakable red pool. Neil was back on his feet and looking in the same direction as Dr. Caldwell. He too saw the legs. He was the first to step forward while Dr. Caldwell was still scanning the room.

Neil asked, "What are you doing?"

Dr. Caldwell said slowly, "He said 'he shot us.' I'm looking for the other...people that made up 'us'."

Neil nodded in understanding and picked his way through the mess. For all their efforts to organize and categorize, it only took one catastrophe to bring it all down around them and they were back at square one. Stacks of boxes had laid low piles of cans that had toppled over towers of bottles. There was dry cereal spread out and stuck to the floor by splashes of soda or juice. If not for the burnt smell of the gunshots, the garage would have been overwhelmingly sweet, approaching unbearable.

He got over to the pair of legs and rolled him over. "It's Dave, and I don't think he's breathing. No pulse either."

Dr. Caldwell yelled to Jerry, who was still standing in the doorway, "Go get the Med Kit! The one we pulled from that military ambulance."

Dr. Caldwell panned the garage again and then saw him. "Art's over there. Looks like he's breathing."

From outside and with a voice that was threatening to crack, Meghan asked, "What happened? Is everyone alright?"

Neil and Dr. Caldwell were leaning over Art, trying to ascertain the damage without adequate light. He was obviously hit; his clothes appeared as if they had been dipped in a vat of red dye and his skin had an almost glowing, pallid whiteness to it.

Meghan was much closer when she asked, "Need some light?"

"Yeah, that would be great," Dr. Caldwell answered. "Where's Jerry with my bag?"

"Right here," answered Jerry as he tossed the backpack-sized medical supply kit.

With the aid of Meghan's flashlight, Dr. Caldwell immediately tore into it, taking supplies and medications out in a furious pace. He cut Art's shirt off and decided that the blood was coming from lower. He felt around and found the wound. How could he have missed it?

The color was so absolute, so deep, that he had assumed that Art's pants were darker than they actually were. It took looking at his own rust-stained hands after he'd touched Art for the doctor to realize how badly Art was bleeding.

He had been hit three times. Under more normal circumstances, the wounds, though serious, would likely not be considered life threatening. Seeing the blood and feeling his frustration and helplessness to properly treat the injuries, Dr. Caldwell was reminded all too clearly that these were not normal circumstances.

The first wound was of the least concern. The bullet had punched a hole through the soft tissue on his flank and just above his waist, essentially poking a ink pen-sized opening in his love handle. There were no organs threatened in that part of his body and the heat of the bullet had partially cauterized the opening so as to limit the amount of blood loss. That's not to say that it didn't look bad, but the reality, as Dr. Caldwell knew, was that it was far from life threatening even with the most limited of care provided.

The second was more troubling as it was on his left leg below the knee. That hole was less round and more oblong than the other, evidence that the bullet had likely struck something else first and then careened into him as it traveled awkwardly end over end. Tiny flecks of white bone fragments near the surface of the oozing hole caught the light cast by Meghan's flashlight. They resembled small white-sanded islands in a sea of meandering red.

Dr. Caldwell thought to himself that neither the location of the trauma nor the presence of the bone fragments boded well for him. Art would likely be incapable of walking for the next few weeks.

Of course the third and final wound was the most problematic. It appeared that Art's hip had been pierced, which likely resulted in his pelvis fracturing. Without proper equipment, Dr. Caldwell couldn't ascertain the nature of the internal injuries that were conceivably received as a result of that injury; not that he would be able to effectively treat them anyway. Just the amount of blood that Art had lost was starting to really concern the doctor. They had neither plasma nor a clean, sterile environment in which to provide even the most basic care to their suffering compatriot. He felt as in control as a Civil War era field surgeon whose only option for many injuries was amputation and then prayer.

They moved Art into the hallway near the front door. They tried to make him comfortable with pillows and blankets while Dr. Caldwell directed them in first aid for each of the injuries. They applied pressure to slow or possibly stop the bleeding and the good doctor worked feverishly to clean the wounds of bits of bone and other external matter such as shreds of cloth and minute pieces of plastic and wood. If there was any good news at all on which they could build, it was that each of the three bullets had exited the body, meaning that Dr. Caldwell didn't have to go digging into the bleeding openings to retrieve any lodged offenders. There were both entrance and exit wounds for each injury.

Meghan held his hand and spoke slowly and reassuringly to him over and over. She wasn't certain that he was understanding or even hearing what she was saying, but she continued to do it just the same. She rubbed his forehead and his cheeks soothingly and tried to provide both comfort and distraction.

After several tense moments and a seemingly Herculean effort by Dr. Caldwell, they had nearly controlled the bleeding from each of the three bullet wounds, though the bandages pressed firmly against Art's hip were still spotting through the several layers applied. The dose of morphine administered to Art had also thankfully taken effect enough to let him rest.

Dr. Caldwell finally set back onto his haunches, tilted his head back, and let out a long, labored sigh. He looked over at Neil. "We've got to talk."

# CHAPTER 47

Obviously agitated and her emotions on the rise, Meghan demanded, "So what the hell are you suggesting?"

Dr. Caldwell, seeing Meghan's growing and animated concern, said as calmly as possible so as not to throw gasoline on the proverbial fire, "I'm not suggesting anything. I don't think any of us have suggested any course of action."

Defensively, she fired back, "No, but you did make it pretty clear that Art is going to be nothing but a burden and perhaps a burden not worth..." She couldn't finish.

"Meghan, all I said was that, because of his injuries, it is unlikely that I can do anything to help him other than try and manage his pain. Maybe help him be comfortable, but even that is going to be a challenge."

"Until he dies. You forgot to say 'until he dies'."

Ignoring her, Dr. Caldwell continued, "And also that it is unlikely that he would be walking any time soon, if ever again. We're talking Nineteenth Century medicine here. Either he is going to heal or he's not, but only time will tell."

Under his breath, Neil said to himself, "Something we once again don't have much of." He turned to Meghan. "Meghan, we have to think about all of us and which are the best ideas to keep us all alive. That hasn't changed. Remember when we left the house and we had to leave Rachel and Tony?"

"That was different."

"Only by degree and by personality. Is that more important this time? Is he somehow more special than Rachel? Or Tony?"

She looked at him with her eyes full of pain. Neil could see the conflict and the confusion. She turned and ran back downstairs just as the tears started to fill the bottoms of her eyes. She flashed one last watery look at him before she descended the stairs and then was gone. He considered chasing after her but his stung pride, like a heavy barnacled anchor, planted his feet to the floor.

As silent spectators, Emma, Claire, Gerald, and Evelyn watched the scene play itself out.

Finally, Emma said, "I'll go check on her."

"And I guess I'll go check on Art," Evelyn said.

Dr. Caldwell said, "Thank you ladies. Well played, Neil."

"What? Am I wrong?"

"Are you familiar with the phrase, 'it's not what you said; it's how you said it'?"

Neil rolled his eyes and shook his head. "You sayin' I was bein' insensitive?"

Nodding his head, Dr. Caldwell answered, "That pretty much sums it up, yes."

"Yeah. Came up a couple times during the divorce. I guess I'm defective in that department."

Jerry finally said, "So, back to the task at hand."

The big question that Meghan dreaded, as did all of them—including Neil—was what to do now. There was no doubt in any of their minds that their current and strictly temporary refuge had been compromised. The fact that they were about to be on the run again was no longer a point of debate and they all accepted that.

Malachi's shooting would act like a magnet for the zombies who had been seeking them out unsuccessfully for the past several days. The series of shots would help their predatory instincts to hone in on their position. Malachi's subsequent action in running down the road while yelling and shooting the assault rifle would help to detour them temporarily but they had no illusions any longer about staying there long term.

Dr. Caldwell wondered about poor Malachi. He couldn't be certain, of course, But Dr. Caldwell wanted to think that Malachi had realized what he'd done and how he'd compromised everyone else's lives and had chosen, in that moment of clarity, to do what he must to make amends. Dr. Caldwell hoped that Malachi was able to slay the ghosts of his past before they got him. The doctor was also keenly aware that if they were to delay too long, then the best of what Malachi had done would be outdone by the worst of his actions. If had Malachi just sacrificed himself to buy them a little time, then they had damned well better use it to the best of their abilities.

It was a familiar topic and a replayed discussion. They needed to decide a direction and a route. They also needed to decide what to take and how it would best be carried. It would have been much easier if they had a vehicle at their disposal, but that was obviously not an option. Wishing for a vehicle was as effective as wishing for a helicopter to come and spirit them away. Neither were realistic possibilities.

Throughout this exchange, Neil's voice was curiously and perceptibly absent. He nodded and listened, but his distraction was obvious to all of them. His input was as desperately needed as was his leadership, but neither were forthcoming.

He wanted to go to Meghan but what he'd do then, he didn't know. He could feel the divide that had been forced between them, and when he thought about that, he couldn't help the anger that he felt toward Art. It wasn't Neil's fault that he realized he really didn't like the guy right about the time Malachi went nuts. And now that Art had been shot, Neil's feelings toward him made him feel and look like a jerk. And that kind of pissed off Neil too. Just because a guy has been shot, doesn't excuse him for his actions. But Neil couldn't think of anything that Art had done really. He'd been difficult and a bit of a naysayer, but he hadn't actually done anything. Neil was certain that Art had been a....

If Neil was going to be perfectly honest with himself, he'd just have to admit that his dislike of Art was as inexplicable and subjective as a lot of modern interpretive dance. He'd also have to admit that he never really put any effort into getting to know Art as anything other than another set of hands with which to get things done. Their interactions had been limited at best despite having shared some fairly intimate space on occasion over the past few weeks.

In fairly short order, Neil was completely ashamed of himself for his foolish pride and his jealousy. His ex was right and now so was Meghan. He deserved every bit of their enmity, if that's what it was that he was getting. The world would likely end and all life extinguished before the mystery of Woman and her effect on man would ever be untangled by unworthy mortals. If there was ever a proof of God's existence, it is that there has to be one being in the universe that understands women. If not God, then who? Still, if he didn't show any jealousy, then he could be accused of not caring enough. With regard to women, Neil didn't see a whole lot of options to win.

His dad, probably the smartest guy he knew, would likely say something like: 'it's not about winning the game or even scoring points, it's just about playing the game and getting something out of it'. He said things like that a lot to Neil while he was growing up. Neil probably should have listened to him more often rather than think of all the ways in which his dad was wrong about everything. Once again, another missed opportunity that had been kicking him in the ass his entire life.

Badgering himself and second guessing everything that he'd done to date made him angry again, but this time the anger was more of a mood spoiler than it was anything else. He decided to let Dr. Caldwell deal with Art and for Jerry to deal with the others. Neil retired to a bedroom with Jules and Danny and shut the door. There were fewer questions with the children and those that were asked weren't nearly as taxing as those that he would face from the adults in the other room.

The debate continued and continued, resurfacing at every opportunity. Despite the high emotions and the loud voices, a decision was reached upon which they all could agree.

# CHAPTER 48

Gerald was completely sincere when he said, "Geez, Doc. That's impressive. They teach you how to do that in medical school?"

Impressed with his own handiwork as well, Dr. Caldwell nonetheless didn't want to sound cocky. "Nope. Scouts."

"Scouts...Boy Scouts, that is, wasn't too popular where I grew up. At least not in our neighborhood. I 'spect most folks just didn't have that much extra money for such things. Whatcha call this thing again?"

"It's called a travois. As I recall, the Plains Indians used them to move the sick or the hurt and sometimes even the old."

Gerald, always full of good humor, joked, "I think I may be a little of each I'm afraid."

Dr. Caldwell answered with a smile, "I think one travois at a time is about all we can handle."

Gerald asked, "So are we really going to be able to move him and us?"

Dr. Caldwell nodded reassuringly. "It's going to take all of us working together but I think we can. We can't stay here much longer. I just hope we have time to get ourselves prepared enough for the long road ahead."

Almost on cue, Jerry and Claire burst into the garage where Dr. Caldwell and Gerald were working. They'd just finished burying Dave in the backyard without any fanfare or even an audience. Nothing dramatic or the least bit consoling was said. Jerry's face was very serious and Claire's looked somewhat nervous.

The doctor asked, "What's wrong?"

Jerry looked at Claire and said with alarm, "The buzzing. We can hear the buzzing again. I think they're getting close."

"Shit. Have you told Neil yet?"

Jerry nodded. "Yeah. He's getting Jules and Danny together. Evelyn and Emma are helping gather together some last minute supplies."

"And Meghan?"

"She's still hanging out with Art," Claire said.

"Is he conscious?"

"In and out."

"When he's in, is he being quieter?"

Jerry shook his head.

Dr. Caldwell stood up from his creation and used his authoritative voice. "It's time then. We've got to get out of here while there is still daylight. Maybe we can get to another hiding spot before it gets dark." To himself, Dr. Caldwell muttered, "Maybe I can give him something to put him out and keep him quiet."

Neither Jerry nor Claire said anything to that. They just looked at the travois seemingly made of mop handles and bed linen. It seemed so fragile…too fragile to be able to transport a person. They could only hope that their concerns were unfounded; this hope was unfortunately in addition to the hope that transporting the stricken Art would not so hobble them that they'd all soon be meeting their collective fates. All of this would certainly be easier if they still had a vehicle.

When he thought about or, more correctly, pined for the minivan, he always thought about Maggie and her betrayal. He'd trusted her no more or less than anyone else and yet she had been allowed to hamstring them so thoroughly and so cleanly. How anyone who claimed to have any connection to Christianity, or any other faith for that matter, could do something so vile was a mystery to him. He'd known a lot of Christians in his day, and they were, by and large, good people and understood there existed a balance to expressing their faith and conducting themselves as responsible citizens; faith footed in absolutes and civic interaction based upon compromise. There were fundamentalists on both sides of that divide but he tended to ignore their extreme messages. This understanding struck him during his more philosophical quiet moments, which were becoming rarer as the days and weeks passed.

As it was, he'd made no effort to understand either Maggie as an individual or her motivation. He had neither the time nor the interest to spend considering why or how she could be so incredibly and ruthlessly hateful as to want to cause such suffering. His anger and resentment, not to mention his constant fatigue, overwhelmed any half-hearted attempts to seek revelation about her. He only reserved a dull rage and a distant hope that their paths would cross again.

Dr. Caldwell remembered the task they had just completed and asked, "You guys okay?"

Both of them nodded but said nothing.

Dr. Caldwell said quietly, "Thank you for taking care of that."

"Seemed a little cold to me," Claire remarked. "He may have been a bit of a jerk, but he deserved better. We all deserve better."

Dr. Caldwell bowed his head and said, "Amen to that."

# CHAPTER 49

Meanwhile, Neil, sitting in the bedroom with Jules and Danny, finished reading a book to the two kids. If asked, he wouldn't be able to give a single detail from what he had read. He was as disinterested and unengaged in the activity as was a traffic light on a timed schedule in the early morning hours. With neither cars nor pedestrians around, the light merely cycled through its trichromatic faces much the way Neil saw and read the words.

His distraction was evident to the children who had probably heard more personality and interest from the voice announcing airport security policies than they were from him. They listened politely, hoping to encourage future readings with perhaps a little more enthusiasm. Everyone seemed to be more on edge since the police officer hurt Art, but Neil seemed to be just the opposite.

If either Danny or Jules were a trained psychologist, they would have described Neil's affect as flat, if not a little depressed. He was just barely going through the motions of the day-to-day routine. Danny didn't like to see Neil that way. To him, Neil had firmly occupied a place of awe and power. He was the man who made the decisions that kept them all alive. He was the rock that all of them needed to hold back the flood of doubt and insecurity. But the rock was crumbling and starting to crack and it scared Danny to think that there wouldn't be that someone who could so decisively lead them. Dr. Caldwell and Jerry were both smart and were good at helping everyone, but neither of them had that special something that Neil had.

Thinking and worrying about it was starting to make Danny's head hurt a little. He closed his eyes and tried to will the pressure away from his temples. He was starting to feel a little queasy too. He didn't like all the anxiety from himself or the others, but it didn't appear as if things would be getting any better any time soon.

He was pondering what he might be able to do when Jules said to him, "My head's starting to hurt like my tummy."

Danny opened his eyes and said quietly, "Mine hurt too." He quieted his thoughts enough for him to realize that it wasn't the tension or the fear that was causing the discomfort; there was a familiar buzzing, a dull, low hum that permeated the air all around them. He immediately knew what it was.

He said to Neil, who was still staring blankly at the wall, "Neil, I think they're back."

Not looking away from his spot on the wall, Neil asked, "Who's back?"

"Them. The zombies...zekes...whatever you want to call them. I think they found us."

Neil nodded his head and said coldly, "Yeah, it was just a matter of time really."

"Shouldn't we go tell the others? Shouldn't we be doing something?"

Neil knew that Danny was right and felt the cold shame of his disregard cool his mood and his response even further. The memory of his failed marriage and his presently failing relationship with Meghan were weighing on him heavily.

He rose to his feet and stood still for a moment or two longer while Danny and Jules watched him, not sure what to do next. Silently, he walked out of the room and down the hall.

Jules asked Danny, "Are we gonna be alright?"

Danny nodded his head reassuringly and said as much for himself as for her, "Yeah. Neil will take care of us. He always has. I think maybe we should pack our stuff."

# CHAPTER 50

If asked, Neil probably wouldn't have been able to confirm that he was up to the task of making decisions anymore. In the swirling tempest of his self-loathing, he had no faith in his judgment or anything else of his for that matter. With his thoughts as heavy as hammers, he banged the martyr nails through his hands on his own self-imposed cross.

He slunk down the hall toward the others, who were running all about the house gathering supplies and figuring out the best way in which to carry the materials with them after they made their exodus to their temporary promised land. No one seemed to notice him coming into the room, at least no one appeared to look up and acknowledge him. Maybe they were all just being polite and not casting their accusing glares at him. Silently and alone, he walked out onto the back deck and looked out toward the east.

The mountains were engulfed in the heavy, grey clouds of autumn. Their peaks, rising just above the ashen soup, bore only the slightest dusting of snow, but there, plain as day, was the white evidence of winter's impending approach.

Bad news seemed to greet him at every turn. How did that happen exactly? For a while it felt like he had his act together. For a change, people were looking to him for answers rather than for a sycophantic nod. And the funny thing was that he always seemed to have the answers and was able to steer all of them to safety.

All of them, except for Tony, Rachel, Kim, and now Dave and Malachi. Jesus, maybe they were all just fools for listening and he was even more foolish for opening his mouth in the first place. It had probably all been sheer luck and it felt like it was starting to run out on them.

He spent the rest of the day mindlessly going through the motions of packing his gear and preparing himself to be on the move again. He did most of this in the back room with the kids and away from everyone else, in a self-imposed exile.

In the other rooms of the house, everyone else was frantically going about collecting supplies. As the pile of backpacks started to form alongside an arsenal of weapons at the foot of the stairs near the front door, everyone's mood began to match Neil's.

The days they had spent in the house had become comfortable and were beginning to become predictable. And perhaps most importantly, they all felt safe and somewhat secure. There was plenty of food and water again. With scavenged batteries, they even had some entertainment with music and handheld video games. The house had taken on a lot of the same qualities as a home; a welcome change for all of them.

Those warm feelings were all coming to an abrupt and disappointing end, a fact that had shaken their collective morale. If morose were aromatic, the air would be heavy with it. It was just lucky that their circumstances prevented any of them from dwelling for too long on their present reality.

And once again they all came to the harsh conclusion that there never seemed to be enough time. Stepping just inside the front door, Jerry yelled, catching them all by surprise, "Tiiiiiiime to go!! Nowwwww!! They're just up the road a ways! C'mon everyone! We gotta go!"

Emma was the first to the top of the stairs. Her eyes protested as loudly as cannons but all she could do was shake her head and pull her parka over her shoulders.

Meghan and Dr. Caldwell emerged from the downstairs bedroom now serving as a hospital ward for their lone patient. Rhetorically, Dr. Caldwell asked, "So soon? Really?"

"Yeah. They're quite a distance up the road and movin' slow." To Meghan he answered the question that was forming but hadn't been found by her voice yet, "And they're definitely headed in our direction. They came around a corner and then turned toward us."

She asked Dr. Caldwell, "Can we move him?"

"Safely? Probably not. But I don't see that we have much of a choice as it is."

With just a hint of emotion and a dash of hope, Meghan suggested, "We don't have to run. Maybe we could just wait it out. Maybe they'll pass us by."

"Are you willing to gamble that chance with all of our lives to save Art's? With your own? With Jules'? The cold honest truth is that even if we don't move him, there is a better than average chance that he's going to lose this battle anyway. He's lost an awful lot of blood and it doesn't seem to be stopping. And if infection sets in, there's really nothing I can do about that other than give him the little bit of penicillin that we've been able to scrounge."

Jerry said, "And I think as heavy as that blood scent is, it might just attract them to us anyway. I don't think there is any hiding from them."

"How many are there?" Dr. Caldwell asked. "Can we stand our ground? Maybe buy Art some time?"

"Dozens at least. Probably more. I couldn't see the back of the pack because of the fog, the distance, and because they just kept coming around that corner. Hell, there might be more of them out there heading our way from other directions that just haven't come into sight yet."

Dr. Caldwell lamented, "We never seem to be able to catch a break."

Meghan asked, "Where's Neil?"

"I don't know." Jerry shrugged. "I've been out front on watch for the past couple of hours. Last time I saw him he was upstairs."

Truly concerned for more than just the obvious reason, Meghan asked, "Is he alright?"

Jerry wasn't happy with Meghan's actions or her apparent decision to side with Art over Neil. He didn't even bother to conceal his disappointment saying, "I really wouldn't know. Maybe you should go ask?"

Trying to defuse the conversation a bit, Dr. Caldwell suggested, "Jerry, you better get back to it. And keep yourself safe. Don't get tunnel vision and forget to watch all around. As you said, there could be more of them coming from every direction."

"On it," Jerry assured him, and went back out front, this time with his rifle in his hands instead of on his shoulders.

Claire came down the stairs silently with her coat on and her backpack slung over her shoulders and went outside to join Jerry. She shot an accusing look at Meghan as she did.

Dr. Caldwell and Meghan returned to the makeshift hospital room. Once inside the cramped room, Meghan said, "I don't know what I've done. I didn't know I had done anything really. I don't remember choosing sides or one man over the other. I didn't mean to start some kind of internal feud. I guess I didn't even know that was happening in the first place. Now, I've got everyone mad at me and I've hurt Neil."

"And yet here we are," summed up Dr. Caldwell.

"Have I really hurt him that badly? I didn't mean to. Hell, I didn't even know that I was."

Dr. Caldwell only looked up briefly from applying a clean dressing to the still oozing wound just below Art's waist. He didn't say anything.

She continued, "How did it all go so bad so fast? If it matters, I don't think I did choose. I just saw someone who needed my help."

"Was that before or after Art had been shot?"

"What does that mean?"

"Can you hand me the scissors?"

Meghan lifted the medical scissors from the dresser and put them in Dr. Caldwell's hands. She asked him again, "Are you saying that...? Wait, what *are* you saying? Really, why should I feel guilty?"

"Do you?"

"Well yeah. Look at the mess that I apparently caused. How can I fix it?"

"Meghan, I don't claim to be a relationship guru. That's just not my specialty. I fix people when they're physically hurt. I can help mend broken bones and, hopefully, gunshot wounds, but I can't heal a broken heart or hurt feelings. I was never good at that sort of thing. Ask my wife." With that comment, the doctor paused and thought about what he'd just said. He hadn't thought about her in days, which brought on a degree of guilt. He thought about the last time that he had been insensitive to her and about his stubborn pride in refusing to admit it. He thought about how foolish he'd been and how he regretted not having gotten the chance to say that he was sorry for hurting her feelings.

He said to Meghan, "I can only say that the past few weeks has taught me that if you have something that needs to be said to someone that you care about, then you should probably say it before it's too late."

Meghan started to walk out of the room, but turned back to Dr. Caldwell. "But I don't know how."

"That, my friend, is just something you'll have to figure out for yourself."

# CHAPTER 51

He muttered under his breath, "Lord have mercy. This man is already heavy." Gerald was, of course, referring to the stricken Art. Jerry, Emma, and he were toting the travois like a three-handled stretcher, electing not to have it dragged behind a single person.

They needed to move faster and quieter than the traditional method would allow. For the moment, they were doing just that; moving fast and quiet. The distance between themselves and the likely hundreds of ghouls hot on their tracks was growing little by little. The tortured, hollow groans and the buzzing in Jerry's, Claire's, Danny's, and Jules' chests were becoming more and more faint. A couple of well-timed turns at a pair of corners placed their hunters out of sight but definitely not out of mind.

Emma said, "We're not going to be able to keep this up forever. My arms are already starting to hurt. And my legs, well let's just say our recent diet and my poor aerobic activity before all of this went down are not making my muscles like me very much."

To that Evelyn stepped up next to Emma and offered to relieve her of her duty. Emma shook her head and said in her best exercise instructor voice, "It's okay. I'll work through the burn. Thanks though. My point is that we're not going to be able to haul his ass around indefinitely."

Emma thought to herself that Evelyn was easily twice her age and her arms were no bigger around than Jules' were. Gerald too was older by just as many years. She could see the strain in his face as he struggled to maintain the pace while not dropping Art. Thankfully, Dr. Caldwell was able to sedate Art enough so that the jostling nature of his transport would not solicit the whimpering groans that would give them all away. As it was, Art was no more expressive than the fiends that were chasing them.

Stopping to catch his own breath a bit, Dr. Caldwell answered her dryly, "We have to find another hiding spot to rest up and maybe drop off their radar. That's all. It's worked before." He looked behind them at the empty street and finished, "Things are already starting to get better. See, we've left them all behind."

Emma answered, half-joking, "Easy for you to say. You're not acting the part of a pack mule." She smiled at the doctor and even managed a wink.

The joking and discussion came to an abrupt end as they rounded the next corner. In the middle of the street and staggering straight for them was another mob of perhaps twenty of the undead creatures. Their slow and clumsy gait gathered both steam and purpose as their enraged eyes caught sight of their approaching warm meal.

Claire, leading the others, shouted, "Shit!" and stopped dead in her tracks. Most of these things had once been soldiers. Their camouflaged uniforms were rank and filthy, decaying almost as quickly as the occupants were. The one nearest her was missing part of his left arm, though the rotting stump was hungrily reaching out toward her. Another of them was dragging behind it, like a modern electronic umbilicus, the wire and silent phone receiver to the pack radio set on his back. Each had been gnawed and mutilated to death. Claire took several steps backward to join the others who were standing as immobile and indecisive as she.

Neil, up to this point, quiet and avoiding having to do anything but follow the others, stepped forward with his shotgun to his shoulder and fired three successive shots. Like the first blasts of a pyrotechnic display at a Fourth of July celebration, the echoing roar brought all of them out of their stunned paralysis.

Neil could feel himself growl a little inside as he pulled the trigger. All three slugs found their mark, striking three different zombies, though only one dispatched its target while the other two merely created rust-colored holes on the others' chests that did little more than decorate the pair. He pumped another twelve gauge shell into the chamber and fired again, this time very nearly severing the head of yet another.

Dr. Caldwell shouted, "Back! We need to get back! Everyone!"

By then Jerry had started squeezing off rounds as well. He didn't need to use his scope, given the closeness of the range to his quarry, but he chose to use it regardless. The illusion of distance by peering through the glass eye probably helped to calm him and allowed him to focus on his target. He pulled his trigger and watched the scalp of one of them lift from its head and disappear in a horrid burst of brown. He lowered the rifle slightly and chambered another round with a quick action on the rifle's bolt. He pulled the trigger and another monster fell motionless to the ground. These things didn't seem to suffer or feel any sensation at all. It was just as if the lights were simply turned out as the things collapsed into the piles of decaying flesh that they should have been in the first place.

Dr. Caldwell again demanded as Emma, Gerald, and now Evelyn moved Art away, "We don't have time for this! There are too many! We've got to go! Come on!"

Neil looked back and said, "Go! We'll watch your back. Doc, you and Claire had probably better keep your guns at the ready. They seem to be converging on us from all around the base and the gunshots aren't going to help. There'll probably be more, so stay alert. We've got this."

"Neil, we can't separate the group."

He didn't answer that point directly but instead said as he looked Meghan in the eyes for the first time since their heated exchange, "Keep 'em safe. All of them. We got this."

"But..."

"Go damnit! We'll catch up."

Jerry discharged his rifle again, bringing down another one. The younger man said as he brought the rifle back to his shoulder, "Can you guys finish this later? Neil, I could really use some help here."

Another shot rang out, this one coming from neither Neil nor Jerry. The bullet caught one of them in the exposed part of the beast's upper chest in the space between its neck and shoulder. The creature, though not dispatched, was spun around, gurgling a nasty, wet sound as its gelled internal fluids filled its throat.

Neil, Jerry, and Dr. Caldwell all looked back to see young Danny with his rifle still at the ready. He pulled the pump action on the small rifle and shot again. This bullet hit the thing squarely in its chest, shattering its sternum as it set it back several steps.

Neil smiled at Danny but said to the doctor, "You better go before Danny takes them all and makes us look bad." And to Danny he said, "Nice shootin' there, Tex. Help the Doc keep everyone safe for me."

There was no more discussion. Neil and Jerry were once again on their own. Jerry fired again and realized he'd emptied the five round capacity of his rifle. He slung it over his back and pulled his pistol from its holster. "You know, I'm not very good with these things, don't you?"

Neil pulled the trigger on the shotgun again and then said, "Yeah, I know buddy. I think it may be time to get ourselves moving again before you prove that point."

Looking down the road from where their group had originally come, Jerry could see that the first group of zombies who had been tracking them were now coming up from that direction. Options were quickly being eliminated. He shouted to Neil, "We got more company."

Neil fired his remaining three shots into the nearest crowd of undead and then ran in the same direction the others had gone with Jerry fast on his heels. Trying to think ahead as they ran, Neil started to feed more orange plastic sheathed shells into the aperture on the bottom of the still hot gun. He tried to keep track but lost count almost immediately. Having anything in it would be of benefit he figured. He just hoped that he loaded enough to get them out of a pinch if necessary.

They were thankful for the fact that the now desiccated and decaying zombies were by this point unable to get beyond the pace of a serious mall-walker. Their limbs were simply too stiff to allow any fluid movement at all. There was some comfort in that but running into the new group of monsters created a new reason for alarm. And to drive that point home, they heard a not too distant scream followed by a pair of gunshots somewhere ahead of them.

They increased their pace as much as they could. Another shot, this one a little closer, raised the urgency in their steps still further. By then, they were close enough to hear and recognize the next scream as belonging to Claire.

They looked down each intersecting street they passed, searching for evidence of the rest of the group. They saw nothing; just empty pavement and abandoned houses. They finally came to a spot where the road turned to the right, heading east and directly toward the distant mountains. There, in the middle of the street, were four more of the creatures, all with their backs to the two men. Neil shot the first one, hitting it at the base of its skull. The creature very nearly did a forward flip from the blunt, violent impact. The three remaining zekes tried to turn, but Jerry's sleek firearm barked and spat feverishly and he quickly dispatched those. In only a matter of seconds both his pistol and the street were empty.

The two men paused, breathing heavily, their breath animated by the cold air into thin white clouds, reluctantly dispersing before their faces. Neil nodded and wiped the sweat from his brow. "Nice shooting."

Jerry choked out between labored breaths, "Where are they?"

Looking around and hoping to get the slightest idea from any clues left for them, Neil said despairingly, "I've got no idea. They could've gone anywhere but they couldn't have gone far. Besides, they'll hear our gunshots and know that we're following. I mean, the Doc knows that we—"

Jerry held up his hand and stood stock still with his ear turned toward the street. He looked around wide-eyed and asked, "What's that?"

"What's what?"

"I can hear something. It kind of sounds like..."

Neil was already pumping the action on the shotgun. He'd learned to trust Jerry's ears and his instincts. And once again, both of these attributes served them well.

There, amidst the coagulated carnage piled in the street, lay a fifth body; a body that had gone unnoticed previously. Neil could tell by the noises it was making that it was no longer human. He was all too familiar with the preternatural and predatory sounds made by the undead ghouls who now populated their city.

Both Neil and Jerry felt the terror in their chests burst into painful, heavy knots. This newly reanimating corpse was most likely from their group and could be just about anyone.

Still unable to definitively discern who it was, they were able to at least figure out that it was a woman based upon her clothing and size. It raised itself onto its hands and knees as its disorientation turned to ravenous rage. Neil was able to hear the new vibrations in the air this time. From the beast's mouth a steady, foul, dark fluid spilled onto the damp pavement.

Neil said with a mixture of regret and limited relief, "It's Evelyn. They got Evelyn."

The poor woman had been brutalized. Her neck had been sheared clean of any flesh, exposing both her trachea and esophagus; both life-giving passageways also severed. This was the cause of the fluid spilling from her gaping mouth, which continued even as she rose to her feet. Once she was up, the fluid found its original path back down the now open drains that currently comprised what was left of her throat. The air still in her lungs slowly tried to force its way up and out against the downward flow of bright red blood, causing a bubbling, sucking, red morass to form on her upper chest.

"Evelyn, I'm so sorry," Jerry managed. His words were just fading into the ethereal soup when Neil discharged the shotgun and ended their former companion's suffering.

Jerry said solemnly and honestly, "I'm glad you were able to do that."

"It was done before I could think about it."

"And now?"

Neil was already walking when he said, "Let's just leave it at that. C'mon, let's keep moving."

With the possible threats all around them seemingly multiplying, the two men were more on guard than ever. They were moving at a good clip, but not running. They couldn't chance it. Not anymore. One wrong move and they could end up like Evelyn.

They had traveled a couple of blocks further east when Neil said, "I think I see them."

Jerry asked, "By 'them' you mean...?"

"Up there, ya goof," and Neil pointed. "Use your scope if you can't see them."

Jerry was way ahead of him. Peering through the optic on his rifle, he said with a smile, "Yeah. It's them alright." He lowered the rifle. "Thanks, man."

Neil wasn't quite certain the reason for the gratitude and his expression must have betrayed this fact.

Jerry clarified, "I guess I didn't know that Claire meant that much to me. Getting back to her means an awful lot. Back there I was afraid that...well...it could have been anyone lying there in the street. It could have been her. I don't know for sure what I would have done if it was."

Recounting his own fears of the possibilities to himself, Neil said only, "Yeah, man. I get you completely."

# CHAPTER 52

Now away from base housing and moving along a road that had been cut through a thick forest of alder and spruce trees, the relief of not seeing the horde of undead hot on their trail helped them all to relax somewhat and fall into a much more sustainable pace. Dr. Caldwell and Neil were at the head of the column, Jerry and Claire were at the tail, and everyone else was in between taking turns pulling the travois. From either side, they could hear the gentle snaps and cracks of the falling autumn leaves, noises that at first made them all jumpy. The air was cold and moist, pinching their exposed cheeks and ushering in a chorus of stuffy, sniffling noses. As they walked, a thick ominous fog rolled in and obscured the road ahead and the forest behind the first rank of trees to either side. It was as if they were walking into an only partially completed painting with blank canvas all around the central focal point.

It was as quiet as a church on an early Sunday morning before services began. The fog, taking full advantage of the stillness of the air, waited and watched, anticipating the next act of the drama that was unfolding in its midst.

Not one for showing reverence to just anything, Claire said to Jerry, "I used to love the fog. It always seemed so full of mystery, and questions and possibility. I remember waking up early on school mornings when I was a kid and standing on the deck with my dad and watching the morning fog as it clung to the trees and bushes like cotton balls caught in the branches and leaves...like today." Claire paused and thought about her father, who had been dead for a few years by then, and then about her mother who, in all likelihood, joined him on that morning a few weeks ago when their living nightmare began.

Jerry asked, "And now?"

"I hate the fog," she spit like poison.

"Why?"

"Same reasons I guess. Now the unknown seems a heck of a lot more frightening than back then. Before it was just a matter of seeing what the fog was hiding. I knew every inch of my backyard during the day, but when the fog was there and I couldn't even see my swing set that had been there for years, it was like I was in some foreign place. Now, the fog and the dark and the unknown are just as likely to kill you as anything else." She looked ahead at Jules and Danny and lamented, "I feel so bad for those two kids. Whatever childhood they had is gone and it'll never come back. Even if—and that's a big if—all of this somehow sorts itself out, they'll never be able to go back to just being normal kids again. What hope do they have? What hope do any of us have?"

Jerry put his arm around her small shoulders. "There may still be hope yet. Don't give up. Not yet."

She looked at him squarely. "You say that, but do you really mean it? I mean, every time I turn around, there are fewer and fewer of us. That's what happened before you found us. When we started out, there were so many and then there was just me and Art. And now we've been whittled down to just a handful again. What happens if we're all that's left? What happens?"

Jerry knew that was, or could become, a very real possibility. They'd heard nothing from the outside world since this all began. He wondered about other extinct species and if they were able to begin to contemplate the end.

He wasn't a great student in school but he remembered a high school English class with Mr. Anderson. They read a book called *Grendel* that captured his attention. It was the story about a monster from another older book called *Beowulf*, but this more recent novel was told from the monster's point of view. At one point, Grendel happened upon an old dragon who was angry at the whole world because he was the last of his kind and was hunted merely because of who he was and what he represented. Jerry was really able to relate to the dragon's anger at the world and his fate. There were just far too many similarities between the dragon's reality and his own. The worst part was that the dragon could see into the future and knew that the end was coming and there was nothing he could do to change his fate. Perhaps there was some comfort for Jerry in not knowing the future. There was still free will and chance that needed to be figured into their situation, and to that he clung.

"I could've given up on hope back there when we had to...deal...with Evelyn. It was horrible. Before, when I pulled the trigger and put one of these things down, there was no connection. They were strangers. It wasn't easy because I couldn't help but think that it wasn't too long ago and that person could have been checking me out at the cash register at the grocery store, or helping me open my new bank account, or whatever. But at least I didn't recognize any of them. And then there was Evelyn. But even before we knew that it was her, there was this fear in me that it could have been someone else. Maybe even you. What I mean is that...shit. I'm not really good at...."

Claire smiled coyly and asked, "At what, honey?"

Jerry's head nearly swooned as he summoned the courage to say, "Claire, I have real feelings for you and for the first time in a long time, since even before all of this began, things, at least some things, seemed good. And what I mean by things is you. For all the bad and the ugliness that's been all around us, I think it's a helluva lot more bearable when I'm with you. And back there, when we didn't know who it was that they'd gotten, all I could think about was losing you. I just don't think I could take that."

Claire said softly and sincerely, "It was no walk in the park to have you gone either, I can assure you." She looked up at him from beneath the ever-present green and gold Seawolves cap and flashed a smile that warmed him from inside out and made their surroundings a little less foreboding.

He thought to himself that, yes, things were good for a change.

# CHAPTER 53

They plodded along slowly and quietly for some time. The hushed sounds of the forest all around them were the only sounds that accompanied their trek. Even the travois' legs, wrapped in socks, seemed to withhold their voices. They went on like this for more than an hour. Eventually even the fog grew weary of watching them and retreated further into the trees, exposing the empty, open road in front of them.

A very tired Jules looked over at Danny and whispered, "How much longer do you think?"

Danny shrugged his shoulders and wondered the same thing. He also was curious about their destination. Were they headed toward safety and perhaps more people? The constant fear, the terror, and the loss, along with the nagging exhaustion in his feet and legs were all starting to become a focus that defied ignoring. He was just a kid. He didn't have the same coping skills that adults in their many more years had developed. He just knew that he was tired and hungry and was ready to be home again.

Missing home, like his fleeting juvenile attention, came and went, but when it was in his thoughts it was hard to shake. The memories though were becoming more bitter with each passing day. The problem that was plaguing him was that he didn't seem to have the same recall of home or his parents as he thought he should. Their faces and their voices seemed like he was experiencing them from behind an opaque window. The basic essence of them was there, but it was just outlines and suggestions lacking any real presence. They were just masks, crude representations of the people and the things that were so important to him in a time not too long ago. He wondered if it was the same with everyone. Was it just easier to concentrate on dealing with the problems all around you if your memories weren't distracting you? The question was there and gone almost immediately as his attention was drawn to his left by a louder than normal leaf breaking loose from its arboreal mooring and tumbling awkwardly to the ground.

Every now and again, Neil would come to the rear of the their line to ask Jerry and Claire, as well as Jules and Danny, if they were hearing or perhaps feeling the tonal vibrations that were the undeads' calling card, but they had detected nothing. There was nothing around them making the slightest noise. Maybe it was just the fog forcing everything into a temporary slumber, but somehow it all seemed so different, so permanent and final. It was as if the air itself had become toxic and had poisoned the land to the point that life, all life, was unsustainable. It didn't help that the autumnal season was in full swing, shaking the leaves and the vibrant colors of summer from most of the trees within immediate sight.

They proceeded like this, shrouded in the silence of the grave, for several hours more. The morning had given way to midday, which was fading into a rapidly declining afternoon.

Neil peered over his shoulder to catch Jerry's eyes, but the younger man was too busy looking into the trees to his left. Jerry's distraction immediately raised alarms for Neil, so he turned abruptly to make his way back to inquire. He walked briskly, choosing not to run and cause anyone else undue alarm. He swept by the group walking with Art and didn't say a word or even make eye contact with any of them.

"Hey? We good?" asked Neil in a voice barely louder than a whisper.

Jerry, not fully aware that he'd been distracted, answered, "Sorry. I was just.... No, I don't hear anything or see anything. Sorry to cause you any heartburn."

"No, I'm sorry. I guess I'm just a little jumpy."

"Try decaf. I hear it helps to calm the nerves," Jerry teased.

"Yeah, I'll keep that in mind next time I'm ordering a cup. Smartass." Neil turned to resume his post at the lead position. He was just coming to Meghan's side, with whom he still hadn't been able to bring himself to talk yet, when Claire got his attention.

"Hey , Neil, I think we got a problem here."

Neil thought to himself that of all the phrases in the English language, he perhaps dreaded that one the most. Every time he heard it, it seemed that things typically went from bad to worse all at once. He said unemotionally, "What's going on Claire?"

Dr. Caldwell, meanwhile, raised the M4 assault rifle to his shoulder and assumed a very trained and professional firing stance in the middle of the road. He scanned left and right, careful to lower the gun's muzzle if he was pointing it anywhere near the others in the group. He breathed slowly, trying to control his emotions, especially the fear that was starting to percolate in his stomach.

Neil could feel his own blood pressure begin to rise in anticipation of Claire's revelation. He could surmise from Jerry's posture, however, that it was something other than the approach of a ghoul or a group of the monsters. He tried to glean from Jerry's eyes what it could possibly be but there was not the slightest hint because Jerry was looking down at the pavement.

Neil asked again, "What is it? The suspense is killing me."

Neil was still nearing them when both Jerry and Claire pointed to the ground. Then Neil could see the unmistakably new patches of dark fluid that had pooled in long, slithering stretches along their path. It didn't take much deduction to figure out that the fluid in question was blood and not much more to determine that it was coming from Art.

"Jerry, can you go up to the front and help keep an eye out? Claire, I need you to stay back here and do the same. Doc, can you come back here for a second or so?"

Everyone's agitation quickly peaked. Emma, who was pulling the travois, looked at Neil's concerned expression and then down at Art, whose face was absent of all color. He looked as pallid and lifeless as a sterile white hospital wall.

Dr. Caldwell pulled open the blankets that had been used to shroud Art into a warm cocoon. Even before the last layer had been peeled away, Dr. Caldwell could smell, hell he could almost taste, the briny aroma emanating and beckoning like Charon's otherworldly beacon from Art's seeping wounds.

He touched the other man's neck but there really was no point in it. Dr. Caldwell had seen death before; entirely too much before. Art was dead. There was no denying it. Somewhere along their journey, Art had peacefully drawn his last breath, exhaled it in a long, quiet hush, and then left this world.

The doctor looked up silently, shaking his head as he did. "He's gone."

Out of habit from a life that seemed he lived so long ago, he shared, with his silent but expressive eyes, a moment of acknowledgment with everyone standing around him. Regardless of anyone's opinion of Art, the realization that suddenly there was one fewer of them to continue forward was very sobering. They were now tops on the Endangered Species list, higher than even the African White Rhino. And as autumn started to look and feel more like winter, would there be a more appropriate season to contemplate the demise of one's own species?

Despite Meghan's and Gerald's quiet protests, it was determined that they would merely wrap Art tightly in his blankets and leave him under a pile of crisp leaves and small sticks on the side of the road. They stood quietly over the lifeless body, nobody willing to break the reverent silence. After a brief moment standing thus, they got back on the road and continued their trek east.

As they walked, Emma wondered aloud to Meghan, "I wonder if he was conscious?"

Meghan answered flatly, "No. I think the Doc had him pretty doped up."

"Damn. Died without even realizing it."

"We couldn't have him crying out and attracting the fucking zombies, now could we?"

"I wonder if it's better or worse."

"Dead is dead. It doesn't really fucking matter."

Emma asked seriously, "You still think dead is just...dead?"

A reluctant sigh escaped Meghan. "You're right. Maybe we and even Art should be thankful that in his case dead is just dead. I guess there's some peace in that at least."

"Meghan, I'm really sorry."

Her frustrations at the assumptions continuing to be made boiling over, Meghan bit as quietly as she was able, "For what? I wasn't with Art. I didn't want to be with Art. I don't know how any of that came about. To my knowledge, I'm not in a committed relationship with anyone at the moment since my goddamned worthless fiancé joined the ranks of the undead."

Emma, trying to quiet her, asked calmly, "And Neil?"

"I thought...maybe...I don't know. It felt like it and I think I wanted it, but maybe I just wanted it more than he did."

"Why do you say that?"

"I kind of thought that maybe he'd have put up some kind of a fight or something. But he just folded his tent and moved on down the road without even looking back. I thought maybe I'd been imagining it all along. Maybe it was just convenient for him to have me at his side in whatever capacity I was."

"What about now?"

"I was having one of those emotional moments a couple of days ago and thinking that I was missing Brian—my ex. But I think I was actually missing Neil."

"He's a good man, Meghan."

"I know, I know. But I've hurt him so badly. He barely even looks at me anymore, and I didn't mean to do any of it. Hell, I didn't even *know* that I was doing it. Seems like I should have been able to enjoy whatever it was that I did."

"He's probably just not sure what to do. You know how guys are. What's the word? Oh yeah, clueless."

Meghan smiled in appreciation of the levity and looked up at Neil, who had his back to her. She was glad, as they all were, to have him leading them again. He was good at it. She hoped that perhaps, since he was able to take up that role again, he might be able to find a way in his heart to see that she did care for him and wanted to be with him, despite how things might have appeared.

# CHAPTER 54

As the day yielded to evening all at once, the now bone weary survivors were just happening upon a traffic gate that allowed access to the largely open and inviting Glenn Highway, the lone artery north out of Anchorage. This stretch of highway was far enough north of the clot of traffic that contributed so heavily to the demise of Anchorage and its residents that there were fewer and fewer vehicles the further one looked away from the city. The essentially eternal gridlock of cars and trucks was behind them, leaving clear pavement and an unknown future in front of them. Not having the claustrophobically tight confines of the city stalking their every step was refreshing and perhaps a little unnerving.

Without the constant traffic typically seen along the highway and the accompanying sounds, it was as if the road was auditioning for a supporting role in a special about America's ghost towns.

Claire echoed everyone's sentiments when, after only a brief handful of steps along the shoulder, she remarked, "Kinda creepy."

With good humor at its root but a dash of snip for flavor, Emma responded, "D'ya think? Way to state the obvious."

"Just sayin'."

"I know, Emma said. "Sorry. I just can't help myself sometimes even after all that's happened. I guess old habits die the hardest."

Neil chimed in, "Speaking of which, I think we probably missed rush hour and the next one won't be comin' through any time soon. Maybe we should move out onto the road and put a little more distance between ourselves and anything that might be in the trees."

Without a word but perhaps a quick glance over the shoulder for each of them just to be certain, they fanned themselves across the road forming a moving line that bisected the northbound side of the highway. They didn't necessarily need to be on that side of the road but, as Emma suggested, old habits do tend to take the longest to die.

Dr. Caldwell said, looking back at the dwindling setting sun, "It might be wise to find ourselves a good spot to stop for the night in just a little bit...before it gets dark I mean."

"Anybody got any ideas?" asked Neil.

Jerry thought for a second and then decided to ask, "Anybody ever go car camping?"

Claire responded, "Who hasn't?"

"That was more of a suggestion than it was a question really."

Dr. Caldwell, in a classic game show voice, said, "We have a winner. An all expense paid trip to sleeping in a van or SUV along Alaska's great Highway One." He followed his announcement with "Ding! Ding! Ding! Ding!"

There wasn't the multitude of cars on this stretch of road as opposed to closer to Anchorage, but there were still a couple here and there. Maybe they would find a streak of good luck and happen upon a vehicle with space, keys, and fuel. Of course, that was a maybe as slight as a Pixie kiss and as rare as an honest attorney; not really a maybe to even be counted upon, but a maybe that did exist nonetheless. These were the kind of maybes that career politicians promised during stump speeches but had no intention whatsoever of ever fulfilling.

The first car they encountered was a small white Mercury wagon sporting the dents and dings of a well-used family car. Unfortunately, in the driver seat sat the desiccated remains of a woman, most likely the mother of the household. As Neil looked in through the closed windows, the woman's eyes cracked open and peered up at him. Her seatbelt restrained her movement and the locked car door held her in her roadside tomb. Weakly but hungrily, she began to move herself back and forth in her seat.

Neil jumped back from the car like he'd been hit with an electric current. "I'd say this one isn't going to do."

Emma asked, "What should we do with her?"

Dr. Caldwell asked her seriously, "What do you mean 'do'?"

"Well, we can't just leave her like this. She deserves peace as much as any of us."

Neil said, "The doors are locked and I don't think that it's wise of us to use our guns unless we absolutely have to. We can't afford to—"

Meghan interrupted him. "C'mon, Emma. Let's keep moving."

"But we can't just—"

"C'mon. We need to find a car soon."

Emma was starting to let her emotions get the better of her for the first time in a long while, but listened to Meghan and allowed herself to be grudgingly pulled away.

Neil said to Dr. Caldwell and Jerry, who were the only two still standing next to the car, "There's a dog in the back seat too. D'you see it?"

Jerry answered, "I do now. Looks like he was infected too."

Neil asked him, "How you figure?"

"He's got blood on his snout and those footprints on the seat in back aren't mud, I suspect. I wonder who infected who in there?"

"Does it really matter?"

"No. I guess not."

The next few cars were each inadequate or unsuitable in their own ways; too small, broken windows, or more corpses. It was looking like Jerry's idea, though borne of good intention and possibility, wasn't going to pan out. But then they saw it with its tinted windows and burnt umber paint beckoning invitingly in the strained and diffuse light of the fading overcast day.

It was a Toyota minivan sitting on the shoulder of the road. It was facing the wrong way on the highway, though that didn't seem to matter. Its fleeing former occupants had left its doors open. There was a child booster seat in one of the back seats and a backpack sporting a Star Wars *The Clone Wars* logo and Clone Trooper on it. Luckily, there were no corpses, but there were also no keys. The van would at least present a relatively safe place to stop for the night and one where they could get out of the elements and perhaps stay somewhat warm.

The air was already cool with the threat of moisture hanging in it. So far for today, the rain had somehow luckily been held at bay, but they knew that the somewhat dry weather would soon be chased away by its mischievous wet autumn sibling.

Jules, who had been quiet all day long, whined, "I'mmmm cooollldddd."

Meghan suggested to her that perhaps it would be better if she got in the van to warm herself.

"It's cold in there too. Can't we have a fire? Whenever we used to go camping with my mom and dad we always had a fire."

At first, no one said a word but then Neil said, "That's not a half bad idea. We haven't seen or heard those things since we got away from base housing. If we didn't have a big fire, we might get away with it."

Dr. Caldwell asked, "Might?"

"Jules is right, Doc. If we all get sick because we're all cold, hungry, and tired, where will we be then? I think maybe we should get ourselves some wood and build a small fire. Those things are moving pretty slow now, so if we see any of them we can just get back on the road and stay ahead of them."

In a quick discussion, it was decided that Neil, Dr. Caldwell, Meghan, and Emma would gather wood while the others would prepare a campsite of sorts around the minivan. Just to be safe, Jerry would position himself on top of the van to keep an eye on the surrounding area.

Everything seemed to be plotted and planned when Danny asked, "Can I go collect wood too?"

Emma said apologetically, "I don't know if that is such a good idea. What happens if you get lost out there?"

To which Danny replied, "What happens if you get lost? I want to help too and picking up sticks to burn is something I can do. Let me help, please."

Dr. Caldwell's raised eyebrow was enough of a message to Neil for him to say to the young boy, "Danny. You're right. You are perfectly capable of picking up and hauling sticks for us to burn. Thank you for your offer."

"Then I can go?"

"Of course you can."

Danny jumped up with delight, his smile curling delightfully onto his cheeks.

"Hold on there. We've got to lay out some ground rules first. You follow every one of my instructions to the letter. You are never out of my sight. And if I say run, you run fast and hard until I tell you to stop. Got it?"

"Got it."

"Okay, then let's get going. Gerald, Claire, and Jules…you guys going to be alright with setting things up without Danny's help?"

Gerald smiled. "It's not going to be as easy without Danny's help, but I think we can manage."

"Good. Then let's roll."

# CHAPTER 55

Danny, as were the adults with him, was surprised by how dark it was after a mere few steps into the trees, as if the light was too afraid to venture into the forest. The recent rains and damp air had done their jobs on the otherwise crisp, crunchy ground by making the leaves and fading foliage a silent carpet upon which to tread. The absence of any appreciable light or sound created the impression that they were walking into an enclosed room instead of the fringe of a national forest.

Following Neil's guidance, Danny gathered small fallen twigs and dry leaves that had gotten caught beneath larger sections of trees, thus having been shielded from the weather and left dry and usable for a fire. There were countless sticks and twigs but most were still wet and green, making them virtually useless for their purposes.

Each of them, Danny included, was carrying a flashlight, but the darkness out of reach of the limited cones of light just seemed all the more ominous and threatening, somehow defying the cosmic and eternal will of light itself. It just didn't seem possible. And yet, the darkness continued to press its case, confining their lighted area in a tighter and tighter ring. They never ventured farther than a few feet from one another as they set about their task. They worked silently, as if their voices too were intimidated by the gloom's advances. Like nervous birds gathering twigs for a nest, they picked through the undergrowth but always kept one watchful eye on the trees and the shadows all around.

In short order, they had accumulated quite a stash of fuel for the fire, despite the challenges. They were each toting heavy armloads and were heading back when they were all startled by the unmistakable sound of a footstep falling upon and breaking a stick. The crack and pop sent a rush of fear and adrenaline through each of their veins. They stopped as one and listened.

Emma asked nervously, awkwardly panning her flashlight around as it was balanced precariously between her forearm and her side, "Are we not alone out here?"

Remembering his and Malachi's encounter with the moose out at Kincaid Park those many days ago, Dr. Caldwell said confidently, "Probably just a moose. Why would one of those things be out here? There's nothing around. Where would he have come from? There's no reason that they would be out here."

Meghan answered, "Except us...you know, food."

There was another snapping, this time closer. The acoustics of the forest, however, made it virtually impossible to determine the direction from which the sound was coming.

They were frozen in their tracks, no one certain what to do. Dr. Caldwell finally said, "Okay, let's just head back. Doesn't matter what's making the noise if it's far enough behind us."

Meghan said, her discomfort evident in her voice, "That's as good an idea as I've heard in some time. Let's get goin'."

Forming themselves into a tight column, they started marching toward the edge of the trees, barely discernible from their current position. Due to their loads of timber, they only had three flashlights between all of them being used to illuminate their path. Meghan was reminded of her experience with Jerry in the basement of the small church on Elmendorf. There, the walls that delivered some sense of security contained the shadows; there were only so many places from which a predator could emerge. Here, death could come at them from every direction. She was barely able to swallow the putrid taste of fear as it churned and gurgled her stomach acids until they rose to the back of her throat.

Neil and Dr. Caldwell were carrying the largest stacks of wood, the more sizable pieces of dry timber piled across their chests. The two men were breathing in quick, harried breaths, the result of both their muscle strain as well as their anxiety. As it was, they sounded like a pair of steam locomotives struggling up a hill.

They moved cautiously, trying to use their limited light to its maximum effect. The trek back to the highway seemed to be impossibly long, a terrifying journey seemingly without end.

Unfortunately it was too late when Danny realized there was more than fear upsetting his stomach. The dread's presence was undeniable, but there was a tragically familiar underlying sensation, a buzz, that was making him more than a little queasy.

Danny was coming to that realization when the pale, tortured, seemingly floating visage of a ghoul appeared in his light beam. The creature was just a handful of feet away. The surprise sent Danny's flashlight to the ground and Danny onto his back next to it. He kicked his feet violently, trying to do a version of the backstroke on the forest floor. He was fairly certain that his panting was accompanied by his own terrified screams, but he couldn't be sure in the fog of his paralyzing terror of anything that he was doing or that was happening around him. Chaos gripped the moment too firmly in its clutches for him to be sure of anything.

Heeding Neil's advice, when he was finally able to get back to his feet, Danny started to run. He didn't care the direction or his ultimate destination; he just wanted to get away as fast as he could. The details could be worked out later when he no longer felt like a fleeing, hot meal ready to be served for dinner.

He ran blindly, somehow not running himself into a tree, until his chest hurt and the breaths just would not come no matter how hard he tried to draw air into his protesting lungs.

Any sense that he had about having felt fear before was completely dispelled when the awareness of his utter isolation in dark woods filled with monsters hit him. Without his flashlight, he didn't even have the comfort of that lone beacon. He stood still, as still as he ever had in his life, and looked around in the pitch black. He'd never known dark so complete in his life. There was neither moon nor street lamps to light the way. He began to shudder, the cold suddenly making itself a more equal partner with both the darkness and fear. He couldn't help the tears but he suppressed the sobbing that threatened to emerge as well, too afraid to draw attention to himself. The tortured seconds stretched themselves out into an eternity. He wanted to take a step and perhaps make his way back to the others, but he had no idea into which direction he should head or from which direction he had come. He had no idea what he should do.

With no options readily presenting themselves to him, he did the only thing that he could think to do. He sat down against a tree and wrapped his arms tightly around his frame, making himself into a little ball. He was sure to keep his feet under himself so as to keep his legs dry, but he got himself as close to the ground as he possibly could, hoping that any monsters that were still out there might just pass him without realizing he was even there.

He wondered to himself with a whispered doubt, "Why did I even come to Alaska?" He was then reminded of his friend Martin who'd asked him along on this journey to the north. Poor Martin. In his nightmares, he'd seen his friend's tortured face as he was carried into the hospital's emergency room, but that was about as far as his recollection extended concerning the boy.

He thought about Martin's mischievous smile and accompanying laugh whenever he was tickled with something he'd done or seen. Danny thought about sleepovers and birthday parties. He remembered early Saturday mornings at soccer fields and late Fourths of July under a colorful shower of bursting pyrotechnics. But as his mind conjured memories, he couldn't help but be visited once more by the image of Martin's greying, agonized face shortly before he succumbed to the sickness that had started all of this suffering. The tears that followed were as much for his lost friend as they were for himself.

He wished he had brought his rifle with him rather than having been talked out of it by Emma. She promised that the others were well armed enough to be able to protect themselves and him in the event of trouble. He knew that he should have kept it slung over his shoulder. Why did he let himself get talked out of it? At least if he was armed, he'd be able to defend himself. As it was, he was helpless and lost. He would probably never be found.

He pulled his arms from his sleeves and let his heavy parka become more of a tent for him than a coat. Maybe he would at least be able to stay warm that way. He remembered that he had stuffed some fruit snacks into his inside pocket in case of any emergency. He figured this was as much of an emergency as he could imagine, so he let his hands find the pocket and opened one of the packages. The sweet, chewy goodness helped him to momentarily forget his plight.

He sat there for quite some time, letting the peaceful moments pass as he appreciated the simple distraction that was tantalizing his mouth. There was no real point in considering what to do next, because he really didn't have a clue. If he was to try and find the others, he might just wander deeper into the forest and be lost forever or, worse, he might happen upon another of the monsters and deliver himself for dinner; no point in making it easier for them.

His imagination getting the better of him, he then thought about the possibility that the others might have joined the ranks of the undead. What would happen to him if there *were* no others anymore? They could all have fallen prey to their attacker, especially if there was more than one coming at them. He only saw the one, but he was so terrified and in such a rush to get away that he could have missed many, many more of them as they descended upon his friends. He could be the last of them still alive. And then what? He had no idea where they were headed or even how to get out of the woods to get back on the highway. Suddenly, his helplessness made room for its eager accomplice hopelessness.

By and by, Danny's ears were touched by a faint tickle, a teasing suggestion of sound without true voice. Danny's nerves, already twisted as tightly as a coiling steel rope, began to unravel. The tears were back, as was an involuntary moan that forced its way out of his chest. He began to repeat over and over, "I don't want to be here anymore. I don't want to be here anymore. I don't..."

The words were so distorted by the salty, wet sobs that it more resembled the garbled gibberish of some imaginary language rather than English. His eyes, filled to overflowing with hot tears, were blurred to the point of blindness. He chanced a nervous glance over his shoulder and his obscured vision saw a pair of glowing eyes coming straight for him. He turned away and felt his stomach drop into his boots. He wanted to run but couldn't seem to bring himself to get up and go.

He felt a hand on his shoulder and still he couldn't rouse himself from his paralysis. He was as caught as a moth in a spider's web. He swallowed hard and clinched his eyes as tightly closed as he could get them, hoping that he could just wish away this moment.

"Danny? You okay?"

He opened his eyes slowly, hopefully. It was a voice that he'd grown to trust and now he knew why. It was Neil and he was crying as much as Danny, as was Meghan, who was standing next to him. The man lifted Danny into his arms and gave him an emotional and affectionate hug. And Danny just let him, feeling as secure as when his mother used to do the same to him in the middle of the night after a nightmare. Neil seemed to possess the power to chase away the dark and all the terrors that lurked inside its concealing folds.

Through his own relieved sobs, Neil said, "I've been lookin' for you."

Danny couldn't speak. He just burrowed his face deeper into Neil's embrace, the utter terror that had been racking him only moments before fading with each deep breath.

Neil asked, "You think we can head on back to camp and the fire now? Or would you prefer staying out here for the night?"

Danny stated emphatically, "Let's go."

On their way back, Danny asked Neil, "Where's the others?"

Neil answered as they walked, "The Doc and Emma already headed back to the camp with the wood we gathered. I'm hoping they'll have a fire going by the time we get back there. I don't know about you but I'm starting to feel the cold air in my bones and I could sure use some warming up."

Danny smiled at Neil, satisfied that they'd all made it safely out of the woods. "What happened to...you know...the..."

"Oh him. The Doc was on him almost as quick as he was on us. He used his baseball bat so that he wouldn't make any noise and draw more of them to us. You were out of there so quick that no one noticed you'd run until you were already far away from us. You got some speed kid."

"Sorry, I just remembered what you told me."

"You don't have to apologize. You did great. I'm...I'm just glad that we could find you."

"I knew you would."

"I made you a promise before that I'd never leave you behind and I intend to keep that promise. Besides, Meghan here would not have let us leave without you either. She's rather insistent about that."

Danny looked at Meghan and smiled at her too. She wrapped her arm around his shoulder and hugged him to her hip. Danny was happy to see that whatever bad feelings there had been between Neil and Meghan seemed to be gone, or at the very least fading. He hoped that meant that maybe Neil could be happy again.

# CHAPTER 56

With the warmth and the dawn-like corona of firelight surrounding them, the haggard survivors waiting out the oppressive night felt some sense of promise that a new day would rise and with it the possibility that they were nearing the end of the six-week waking nightmare. They took turns standing watch on top of the minivan, but it was just one of those precautions that created a fleeting sense of security without actually making them safe, not too dissimilar to those measures taken by the Transportation Safety Administration at airports.

Danny and Jules retreated into the back seats of the minivan and curled themselves into a tight corner, trying to conserve and pool their collective warmth while they slept. The others joined them in irregular intervals as the adults also took turns trying to rest.

Late that night or, perhaps more accurately, very early the next morning, Neil and Meghan had occasion to be alone at the fire. To everyone, the two of them appeared to be somewhat reconciled, but they had yet to actually discuss the perceptible divide that had opened between them and seemed to not have been spanned yet.

The fact that she sat on one side of the fire and he on the other drove that point home quite tersely for her. She wanted to move over closer to him but wasn't quite sure if it was okay to do that just yet. He was talking to her again, but they hadn't actually talked yet. There was still a nagging cold between them that had nothing to do with the temperature of the crisp October air.

Hoping that perhaps her words would find a place closer to him than she was able to find for herself at present, she said, "I'm sure glad we found Danny as easily as we did."

"Yeah, I think we got really lucky tonight. That could've ended much worse than it did."

Meghan could sense the emotion in his voice. "You okay?"

Neil nodded and stirred the fire with a stick. He was quiet for several seconds but she could tell that he was searching for his words so she let the conversation move of its own accord. She was afraid that if she started leading, he might be deprived of his opportunity to actually share the feelings and the thoughts that were wanting to be expressed despite his apparently inability to do just that. Maybe if she were quiet long enough, the words would flow. It was both frustrating and wearying, but she stood her ground.

Finally he did speak, his words as quiet as his thoughts, "Thank you for helping me find him and helping me keep my promise. I haven't always been the best at the whole promise-keeping thing. I just don't seem to have it in me. But this promise was important. More important than any promise that I've ever made. I'm afraid that if I couldn't keep this one then maybe I'd never even bother to make promises to anyone else or even myself ever again. And a life without promises just doesn't seem like one worth living."

He paused as his fire stirring created a dancing cloud of glowing red embers that leapt up from the fire and danced like a band of aboriginal natives circling their campfires, celebrating the coming hunt. The little sparks sizzled brightly as they rose and then extinguished themselves like lightning bugs that've used up the last of their bioluminescence.

"Meghan, if I can do nothing else with the time still allotted to me in this nightmare of a life, I want to at least be able to know that I did right by those two kids. I wanna know that they'll live to be adults, and that I had something to do with it. I know that they aren't my kids but it kind of feels like they are. I've never felt this protective of anyone before; neither kids nor adults."

He surprised himself at the ease in which the words were coming. Before he could stop himself, he said, "I'm not sure what happened between us or even if there was an 'us' to begin with. Hell, I might have just been imagining it all along. I'm sorry though. I'm sorry for making you feel...well, I don't know how I made you feel exactly. I just know that you seemed to be very angry and I guess pretty disappointed with me. I think I got jealous of Art a little because he seemed to have your attention more than I did, but that isn't why I did or said the things I did. To be honest, I don't even really remember doing or saying anything that horribly bad, but I've never been that adept at recognizing my own stupidity or selfishness so I guess that's just par for the course as they say. I can say, though, that the things I did were done because I thought they were in the best interest of all of us.

"And now that it is all said and done, I'm not entirely sure that what I did was for the best. We've lost almost as many people as are still with us. We can't keep this up or there won't be a we to keep it up. Ya know? But really, other than those kids, you're the only one who I've wanted to keep safe and you don't seem to want to have anything to do with me anymore. I just don't think I know what I'm doing anymore. I'm second guessing every decision and that isn't good for anyone."

Meghan's face was partially obscured in shadows or Neil would have seen the smile mixed with the tears. She couldn't have been happier to hear him say the things he was saying about her, but the doubt in Neil's words pained her deeply. Neil had done everything he could for all of them. He'd almost always accepted more responsibility than all of the rest of them combined. He was willing to make decisions and, whether they were right or wrong, he was willing to do that for them and willing to accept the consequences of those decisions. He didn't deserve to be feeling the way he was. He deserved a debt of thanks from all of them. All she could think to do, however, was move herself around the fire until she was able to sit next to him and then lay her head on his shoulder.

"Whether you do or not," she whispered, "we all have faith in you and your decisions. You've gotten us this far and up the road a bit is help just waiting for us. By the end of tomorrow, I bet you won't have to be making decisions for anyone other than you and maybe me if that's still possible."

She paused and caught his surprised look as her words registered with him. She smiled softly, letting the satisfaction of what she was finally able to say for the both of them stretch across her face. Now facing him, she leaned forward and kissed his lips as softly as a feather. His lips were dry but as smooth and delicate as tissue paper. After several seconds, she withdrew and saw the surprised look on his face. She could tell that he wasn't disappointed but still she teasingly asked, "Sorry. Was that not alright? I guess I can refrain from...."

He didn't let the words finish before he was pressed against her again for another embrace. She could feel the warmth of his kiss radiating like a furnace from within her chest. It was a warming glow that neither the encroaching darkness nor the chill air could begin to cool.

When Jerry emerged from his nest in the van, he cleared his throat loudly, apologetically. The interruption stopped the kiss but it could never stop the affection. Meghan laid her head back on Neil's shoulder and hugged his arm tightly to her chest. After several quiet moments, she kissed Neil on the cheek and then took up Jerry's spot next to Claire in the van.

Jerry said as the van door slid shut, "Sorry man. I didn't mean to spoil the party."

Neil smiled as he continued to stir the fire. He said confidently, "Ain't nothing spoiling this party ever again."

"You guys must've done some talkin' I guess?"

"Yeah, you could say that."

"It's about fuckin' time, my friend."

Neil smiled at the young man. "You're right. Hey, I think that's the first time that you've called me your friend."

"Is that alright with you?"

"Man, everything just seems to be coming up Neil tonight."

"Well, my friend, I think we'd all agree that of all of us you definitely deserve a little satisfaction for a change. I'm glad to see you cheesin' the way you are. It makes the night a little less cold."

"I know exactly what you mean."

# CHAPTER 57

Neil was perched atop the minivan when the following morning finally dawned. To his damned near gleeful surprise, the sunrise was actually accompanied by sun, a celestial fixture that had been noticeably scarce over the past few weeks.

The Alaskan sunrise never ceased to amaze him and this morning was no exception. The rainbow sherbet colored skies filled the dark and white speckled bowl of night until all remnants of the purplish black were gone, awaiting its reintroduction with the sunset.

Neil thought back to his mornings at his office; the quiet predictability, the fresh coffee, and watching the sun emerge from behind the Chugach Range. He remembered those simple mornings waiting to see the beautiful and mysterious Lani, who worked for another company in the building, his cinnamon angel of morning, bounce into the building under his anonymous gaze. And, as if on cue, Meghan climbed from the van and looked up at him.

"Top of the mornin' to ya, ma'am," Neil struggled out with his best Texan accent.

"It's beautiful, if a little chilly. You wouldn't know that it's...."

"The end of the world?"

"You just know how to charm a lady sir," she chuckled. "How is it that I happened to get you all to myself?"

"That's my point exactly. This doesn't necessarily have to be the end of the world. Could it be that this is just our opportunity to start again...to fix what we got wrong the first time through? I mean all of us. Once this has all settled back down, maybe we'll be able to come back together again and figure out that the petty differences that kept us at odds with one another were all for nothing."

"Boy, aren't you Mr. Positivity this morning? Have you been listening to those self-help tapes again?"

"Hardly. Can you fault me for being happy and a little optimistic this morning?"

Teasingly, she said, "It's not like you got lucky or anything."

"You call it what you want and I'll call it what I want. That may have been the most romantically affectionate thing that's happened to me since my divorce and all it took to happen was the end of the world."

"I thought you said that it...?"

"Oh stop it for God's sake. Just can't let me be happy, can you?"

Neil knelt down from the van roof and kissed Meghan's warm mouth. The previous night's kiss, while arousing and nice, was somewhat surprising and, therefore, kind of awkward and sloppy. This one was more confident and much longer, involving more than just lips. When he pulled back, she suddenly leaned as far forward on her toes as possible and stole another playful peck.

She smirked. "I'm just razzin' you a bit. I'm a pretty happy girl myself. In fact, I was hoping to wake up early enough to be able to catch the sunrise with you. How's that for smitten?"

"You're just a few minutes late."

Still smiling, she said as she stretched, "I guess there's always tomorrow."

"Absolutely."

# CHAPTER 58

The Glenn Highway could very well have been the highway to Heaven or to Hell for all they knew. They started out early, hoping to make the most of the weak autumn sun. The going seemed much easier in the warm sunshine, despite the unsettling feelings of walking down the middle of the heretofore-bustling highway. There were no sounds to greet them. Mother Nature was as withholding with her voices as was the deserted world of man. Across the pavement, evidence of fall was able to collect itself without fear of the rush of traffic. Leaves, some damp and still somewhat green and others crisp and dry, splayed themselves on the warming ground.

The highway stretched out and disappeared into the distance in either direction. From the looks of it, the roadway could just as easily have been some lost relic cobbled together by a Roman Legion to service the vast reaches of the Empire. They walked along the forgotten highway heading north and away from the mayhem of the city behind them.

They walked for a time in silence. Jules wavered between skipping happily and dragging both her feet and her backpack sluggishly, the bipolar nature of childhood affecting her mood and her conduct.

On their right, they passed the charred and flattened remains of the highway weigh station. It appeared as if a pick-up truck had smashed uncontrollably into and through the small structure. The resulting fire had razed the building's humble walls to the ground. An Alaska State Trooper vehicle stood amid the ruins, several rotting corpses scattered all around it.

As they neared the scene, Neil and Dr. Caldwell paused and looked at one another. Dr. Caldwell said for both of them, "It's probably worth a look."

Neil said to everyone else, "Let's take a break while the Doc and I check things out."

Regardless of the circumstances, the prospect of taking a break interested all of them. Their bodies were feeling as worn as their clothes were looking. Insufficient sleep and not enough calories were beginning to take their toll.

The two men walked slowly, carefully approaching the carnage. Despite lying face down and not moving presently, there was always that not so outside chance that one of the bodies on the pavement would rise up and attack them suddenly.

Sure enough, as they stepped into the immediate vicinity, one of the corpses stirred and, missing its legs, started to pull its emaciated and decaying frame toward them. With disgusted awe washed across his face, Dr. Caldwell looked over at Neil and said, "We can probably walk around it just as easily."

"No one deserves to be like that though. It's really just mercy and needs to be done."

With a smile, Dr. Caldwell shot back, "I can think of a few people that wouldn't cause me any heartburn to see like that, but I get your point." From his backpack, the doctor removed his trusty and well-used aluminum baseball bat. With a single, forceful, silent swing, the abomination was dispatched.

Neil looked into the State Trooper Ford Explorer in search of, well, anything. He laid his hands on a twelve-gauge shotgun still in its rack. He grabbed as much as his two hands could carry and then leaned back out of the vehicle. He was still in mid-turn when he was suddenly struck with the gravity of his actions.

"Ya know, Doc, never in a thousand years would I have guessed that I'd be doing this."

"What're you talkin' about, Neil? You're a natural. You've got good instincts. You know exactly what to grab."

Nodding but not necessarily agreeing with his companion's simple assessment, Neil said for clarification, "No, what I mean is that I…I mean how is it that when I look at this hellish scene all I see is what's useful? I'm a fucking scavenger, picking over and around corpses for the scraps that the dead were polite enough to leave me. And you say that I'm good at it."

"Neil, things are different now."

"Not so different that I should so casually disregard death. I barely even noticed these bodies and there are quite a few. These weren't evil people who deserved the torment they got as the walking dead. And what about the poor Trooper who stood his ground here? What could have been going through his mind as he squeezed off round after round? Did he have a clue? Did he get a chance to say good-bye to the woman and child in the photo on his visor? What have we…sorry, what have *I* been reduced to?"

Dr. Caldwell was quiet for a second or two. He was looking toward Neil, but really he was looking through Neil. He was seeing all that Neil had seen and that he had obviously missed.

Lying near and even atop the carcasses were dozens of large black ravens who were as stiff as boards. As the carrion birds had torn at the toxic flesh, aggression motivated each successive peck more than did hunger. And with each new chunk of tainted tissue, the poison thickened in their veins until one by one they'd tilted over on their sides and died. They literally ate themselves to death.

"Neil, what would you have us do? And what do you expect from yourself? If we stopped for a eulogy every time we came across a dead body, where would we be? This is about survival. You can't forget that."

"Survival at what cost, Doc? Do you remember the old *Planet of the Apes* movie? The one with Charlton Heston?"

"Yeah."

"Those people that Heston and the other astronauts encountered before the apes showed up and started shooting...they were just animals, with the most basic of instincts. They didn't speak; they had no art and no culture. They had completely surrendered their humanity to their pursuit of their base needs, the most obvious of which was sheer survival. Is that where we are headed? Is that what we want?"

"I get your point, Neil, but maybe that's a concern for later."

"What happens if that was what those people's ancestors thought and said and did? Maybe they were just trying to survive and forgot what it was that set us apart from the rest of the animal kingdom."

"So what do we do then?"

"We just can't forget. We have to see all this and remember that these were people, same as us, at one time. We can't let ourselves, or especially Danny and Jules, become numb to the tragedy. We can do better and still not compromise our survival. I've gotta believe that."

Dr. Caldwell nodded and looked again at the grisly scene. Perhaps it was his military training or his medical background that had steeled his nerves to death and dying. He oftentimes didn't see a dead person, he'd only see a dead body, and he realized that there was a big difference between the two.

"Neil, you're right. We can do both. We can gather supplies as we find 'em and still show respect to the souls whose loss provided for our continued survival. It's going to be a challenge, especially for me, so we are going to need your help in remembering."

Neil finally allowed a sense of satisfaction to creep onto his face. "Thanks, Doc. If not to ourselves, we owe it to Danny and Jules and any other kids that are still out there. If this isn't the end of humanity, then I think it's important that we keep a tight grasp on it."

"Neil, what exactly was it that you did before the crash of civilization again? Because I don't think that I'm buying that you were some low-level nobody peddling mortgages."

Neil couldn't help but smile and said simply, "I think I got everything that mattered from the Trooper's SUV. Maybe we should get back on the move."

Dr. Caldwell looked over Neil's shoulder one last time. He counted thirteen bodies on the slowly warming pavement. He saw the vehicles and the destroyed building that had once served to protect the roadway and felt the sorrow and the loss that all of it meant. He saw what Neil saw and, though the loss of life pained his soul, he was relieved that he was able to acknowledge for himself that it was a loss for all of them and not just the handful of people whose lives had been prematurely snuffed out those many days ago.

# CHAPTER 59

They walked until well past noon before they came to the site of what appeared to be a significant battle between a military unit and the zekes. It looked as if both the north and southbound sides of the Glenn Highway had been straddled with concrete traffic barricades in an attempt by the military to do what the civilian forces in Anchorage had tried and failed to do: contain the mayhem. From a distance, the ground shimmered as if it had been paved in gold. In reality, they found as they got closer that there were thousands of spent shell casings carpeting the pavement.

As they drew closer to the battlefield, the air grew heavy with the reeking pungence of the hundreds of decaying bodies on the road leading up to and over the temporary and ineffective concrete wall. The presence of death, as undeniable and palpable as the sun, was all around. The bodies, the smells, the vehicles, like rotting relics themselves, all smacked of death.

Emma pinched her nose in an attempt to stifle the nausea that was starting to tickle the back of her throat. "Is there any way around?"

There wasn't, unless they were interested in doubling back and finding a way up onto the ridges that enveloped the road on either side. With the sun already reaching for its cap, the press of time was as distracting as the hell through which they were walking.

Luckily, there were few of the mangled corpses along the far shoulder of the highway. They were able to use this channel to pick their way forward and avoid most of the staggering gore. Neil and Dr. Caldwell paused at one point as they caught sight of more assault rifles lying on the ground. They looked at one another for a few moments while they contemplated wading into the morass. Deciding that the field would be treacherous to navigate, they opted to avoid the possibility of receiving a bite on their lower legs by an immobile but still very dangerous zombie caught in the tangle of bodies.

Breathing through their mouths instead of their noses to try and avoid the stench, they all found that the putrescence was prominent enough in the air as to have formed a taste that lay on their tongues like a pair of too tight pants that refused to be peeled away. The foulness, like a thick green cloud, threatened to impede their every step.

It was as if all the elements were conspiring against them. The sun, too, so warm and inspiring, had retreated behind the mountains and out of view, seeking its afternoon hammock as it awaited the arrival of its evening relief. The shade brought cooler air, which harbored a subtle threat completely foreign to the nature of the sun.

The shadows, growing as the sun waned, made watching the piles of corpses more challenging and raising everyone's anxiety. They watched the bodies so as to detect any sign of movement that could signal the rise of a threat.

Slightly skittish as they traversed what felt like the lion's den, they each in turn scanned the heaps of fouled corpses that would have certainly pleased the likes of Pol Pot. No incinerators or furnaces; no efficient gas chambers; just rotting piles of bodies and miscellaneous body parts bearing the violent trauma and torn flesh that only a battle could produce.

Jerry was the first to spy movement. At first he thought that it was just an optical illusion perhaps created by his taxed nerves partnering with the darkening and stretching shadows. When Claire saw it too, though, he knew what he was seeing.

"Neil, we got..."

His voice sounding defeated, Neil dryly finished for him, "A problem?"

"That too. But I was gonna say that we got movement over there."

With everyone else gasping and facing about, Neil, remaining calm despite the alarm bells that were echoing in his skull, said, "Yeah and that's a bit of a problem."

Claire was starting to repeat over and over, "Oh shit. Oh shit. Oh..."

Dr. Caldwell tried to settle everyone with, "They may be moving but they're not getting up. So long as they're on the road and we aren't, there's no threat. Just keep moving and watch the ones over close to us."

They moved in a single file line, careful not to get too close to anything along their path. At one point, they passed a soldier whose forehead was adorned with a dime-sized hole. His left arm had been partially gnawed and the right side of his neck was a brown and rust colored mess of torn folds of flesh. To Meghan though, all that caught her attention was that his nametag read: Taylor. That was her last name.

Surnames, such important concepts for so many people for so long, were now taking on completely different meaning. There was also the very real possibility that last names no longer had any meaning at all. Really, if there was only one Meghan, what difference was it whether her last name was Taylor or Burton or...she wasn't sure what Neil's last name was but that was certainly another possibility.

All at once, two things that stood out to her from her thoughts took her. The first was that she so readily and easily included Neil on the same list as her maiden name and the name of her fiancé, which was eventually going to be hers, had they married. The fact that she did it without hesitation was what struck her as so surprising because she was not typically so impulsive as to fall for a guy so completely and so quickly. And this despite the fact that she was had no idea of his last name. It started with a 'J', she thought.

The second surprise was the flood of memories that surged from behind the Taylor nametag. When Meghan was still a little girl, she became enamored with Elizabeth Taylor's life and career. She was amazed with the glamour and the sense of uber-celebrity, and Elizabeth Taylor was a shining and graceful member of the American aristocracy. Meghan watched all the movies she was able to, catching them on cable channels, from video stores, and bought the occasional movie online for harder to find titles. As she grew, the obsession subsided, though her passion for Taylor's films never dulled. When she moved to Anchorage, she decided that she was setting out on her own adventure like Taylor had done in countless Hollywood fantasies. And then she met Brian, who was so nice and handsome. She knew she had found her place when she learned that his last name was Burton. It just seemed like fate had happily smiled on her life. Taylor and Burton: one of Hollywood's great romances. He was definitely the one.

That was more years ago than she cared to remember. She had accepted her fate to be denied matrimony and had even gotten cozy with the idea. She was alright with staying a Taylor. And seeing it on the uniform of a dead soldier gave her pause, like coming upon your own name on a random headstone in a cemetery. It was unsettling and sent an unpleasant chill up her spine that uncomfortably tickled the base of her skull and her buttocks at the same time. She visibly trembled, catching everyone's attention.

Neil asked, "You okay?"

"Yeah, I just...I guess I kind of...Hey, what's your last name?"

"What? I mean, Jordan. Can we do this somewhere else?"

She smiled. "No. All better now. Thanks." She blew him a kiss and winked playfully. She walked on by, allowing Dr. Caldwell to move forward again.

Neil asked the doctor, "Doc, have you ever figured women out?"

Shaking his head, he answered, "Women to me are a lot like golf."

"Huh?"

"Meant to be played and not won, or, in a woman's case, not understood...just played."

"Thanks, Doc. You weren't, like, a specialist in advising patients or anything were you?"

"You'll see one day. It's not that far off."

"Yeah. I get ya. Did you happen to spend any time with my Dad?"

"What?"

"Never mind."

They moved around the pocket of death as quickly as possible. Just beyond, the rock walls to either side of the highway gave way to open land leading to the Knik Delta flood plain. To their right, on the south side, the mountains were still there, but several hundred yards off. On their left, there was nothing for miles.

Neil said confidently, "The Knik crossing is just ahead. From there...well, we can see where we can go from there. Maybe the military will still be there."

Dr. Caldwell had his doubts, but he refused to give them voice. If the Army was there at the bridge, or even anywhere in the Mat-Su, they would have seen or heard helicopters. The Army would have birds in the sky all the time to keep an eye on any movement in the vicinity. Of course there was always that possibility that the circumstances of the military's situation precluded that, but if that was the case then he wasn't sure if heading toward them was the best idea. The reality was that it was the best idea any of them had and they were on the brink of seeing whether or not the idea was going to pan out.

# PART III

# CHAPTER 60

Standing there on the bluff and having to face them was the hardest thing Neil had to endure since standing before the judge at the finale of his failed marriage. He, once again, was a disappointment to the ones who were relying on him most.

The hope had been that finding the Knik Bridge would somehow deliver them, as if the bridge itself contained some power to save. And like the Arthurian quest for the Grail or the conquistadors' search for the Fountain of Youth or the Lost City of Gold, this journey ended in failure.

From this vantage point, they could see for miles in either direction. The unfortunate thing was that it appeared as if they were looking out onto the moon's busiest highway during rush hour. There was, quite literally, nothing happening anywhere as far as the eye or a pair of binoculars could see. It would have been peaceful and inviting if they weren't aware of the cause of such superficial tranquility.

Dr. Caldwell suggested, "Maybe we should stay up here for the night. Isolated. Plenty of wood. I think we'd be safe."

Jules protested, "But it's windy and cold."

Emma agreed. She knew they had a tent in one of the backpacks but they couldn't all fit in it and, besides, it could barely be expected to provide much cover with its nylon walls. "Jules may be right. It's already cool up here and it's still early. Too big of a fire is just going to draw more of them to us. Maybe we should find somewhere else."

Jerry said, "That's gonna be tough before night falls. We can build a barrier and use the tent to contain the light and the heat. I think we should make do. Neil?"

Neil had barely heard any of the discussion. He was still distracted with their failed attempt at finding the end of the rainbow. He had placed all his faith and all of his focus on the bridge. He took the easy way out and sided with Jerry and Doc Caldwell.

"We're here. Let's make the most of it. We'll work in teams: some gather wood, some dig a fire pit, and some find the tent. Let's make the most of the daylight we've got left."

"Don't take this the wrong way," Claire said, "but why is it up to you? Why is it always you deciding what, where, and who?"

Neil shared a look that evinced no ego and no guile, completely disarming Claire. He said without the slightest emotion, "It doesn't always have to be me. Anyone can have this job...gladly, I might add. Up to now, nobody seemed to be interested." He paused and looked at everyone else this time. It wasn't a machismo challenge to the others, as his expression clearly communicated. It was a mantle that he hadn't sought nor would he miss. To prove it to himself and the others, he asked, "Claire, what do you think we should do? Keep in mind that the sun isn't just going to fade. It's going to go out almost as fast as flipping a switch. So we've gotta get somewhere quickly or risk wandering around blindly in the dark. You saw how dark it gets without streetlights. Where should we go? You lead and I'll follow for a change."

"I wasn't saying that. I guess maybe I'd just like to have a little say in this is all. I mean, it's all of our lives that are at risk here."

Dr. Caldwell said to all of them, "Sometimes committee decisions are good and sometimes we just need someone willing to step up and take charge. So far, that someone has been Neil, and I for one am thankful that he has because I don't think I would have been the best at getting us out of the jams that we've had."

Gerald, typically quiet and merely a spectator, interjected, "When Evelyn, Dave, and the rest of us first set out, there were dozens of us. We started out at the Public Safety building on Tudor, at the Trooper Station. Someone heard on the radio that it was safe there. We all came there individually or in twos and threes. At first, it was quiet. We all thought that maybe whatever was happening elsewhere in the city might not reach us. We had a bunch of cops there and thought that maybe they'd keep us all out of harm's way. In hindsight, that was pretty ignorant of us, but who could blame us for thinking that the police could keep us safe? That was their job after all. And who was better prepared to do it than them?

"When the mobs of those twisted souls started to arrive, we knew that the handful of police officers, even with their guns and their training, would never be able to hold those numbers off. They came at us from the direction of the hospitals just up the road.

"So we left. Remember, there were bunches of us and people from all walks of life. We went north up Boniface. It was everything we could do just to get away. I don't think any of those policemen were so lucky. They stood their ground and held them off so that we had a few seconds' start. We didn't know where we were going; we were just going. And those...things, they just stayed after us. They just kept running and running. They never get tired. Of course, you all know this by now but on that first day, we didn't know what to think.

"We ran up the road and came to the grocery store. Some of the folks thought that we should go in there and lock the doors and hide. Others wanted to keep running. Others just wanted to be safe and didn't care how or where that would happen. Nobody was willing to make a decision, so we stood there in the middle of the road with only minutes...maybe only seconds separating us from those things. We stood there and took a vote. Can you imagine that? Someone threw out the options and people stood there raising their hands like they were voting for class president or what snacks they should have in the afternoon after recess.

"A bunch of us didn't wait around to see the election results. We just decided to keep moving north. We hoped to maybe run into folks with cars or trucks who'd be willing to help. I wouldn't be at all surprised if those other folks were still debating what to do when they were overtaken. When we got to the northern end of the city but not quite up to the highway, we didn't know for sure which way to go. There was a ruckus out on the highway, so we decided to head into town. But it felt like we were a boat without a rudder, just drifting on the waves. We went from a democracy to anarchy in just so many minutes. It took Daniel to finally take the reins and steer us toward a safe haven. Actually, it was a series of what we thought were safe havens until we finally ended up on that damned bus where you found us. If it wasn't for him being willing to make what he thought were sound decisions, I don't think any of us would have made it.

"Things have settled down since then, but I think having a single person in charge when all is said and done has its merits. Neil, that's not to say that I don't think that we all shouldn't have a say in things, because, like Claire was suggesting, it's all our lives that we're talking about here. And Neil, whether you like it or not, you are that man, and I think it would just be in all our better interests if you got cozy with that fact, because every time you doubt yourself or your decisions you put us all in jeopardy. We can't afford you being all down on yourself because someone gets killed."

Emma said playfully, "Unless that someone is me. Because I gotta tell ya that I'll be super pissed if that happens."

Everyone smiled at her but looked back at Neil and nodded in total agreement with Gerald's summation. The older black man then zipped up his coat to close his collar around his neck and said, "I guess I can start looking for firewood if someone is willing to come along and help me out a bit. Claire?"

Realizing that all that was said was right, Claire nodded and repositioned her Seawolves hat on her head. All of them set about their tasks, preparing for the cold, dark night that was bearing down on them.

# CHAPTER 61

Electing to use a blue tarp instead of opening the tent, they were able to fashion a large roof over an area enclosed by stones and pieces of sod. They built a fire in the middle, which kept them all warm. It was a quiet night for all of them but it was restful.

The next morning arose slowly, the sun as reluctant to shed its warm blankets as they all were. Sensing the sun's hesitation, the clouds rolled back in, lowering the temperatures and the visibility significantly. The air was damp and uninviting.

A small but steady fire had been kept for whomever was standing watch. At this early hour, when night's chill still held sway over any warmth to be had in the still rising day, Neil was thankful for the enthusiastic flame. He was tempted to wake Meghan but Jules was sleeping snuggled up against her, and he just didn't have the heart to interrupt that.

So, once again, Neil found himself alone during the loneliest hours of the day. It was okay though; much better than it had been recently. Finding themselves out of the city, encounters with the undead diminishing, reconciliation with Meghan, or perhaps just being able to see another day's dawning could all have affected his mood. Regardless of what it was or wasn't, his load felt a little less cumbersome.

He pulled his backpack over to himself to get a bottle of water. He reached in and fished around the bag's chaotic interior and felt the concern rise back into his awareness. He was finally able to lay his hands onto a single sixteen ounce bottle. That was not welcome news. He wondered if somehow his bag had been shorted on bottled water to accommodate some other necessity, like ammunition or batteries. He hoped that was the case and that everyone else had more to share.

Jerry was the next to rise. As soon as he had sat himself on the ground next to the fire, Neil asked, "Sorry to start hitting you with questions as soon as you get situated, but how you doin' on water?"

Jerry leaned back, slapping his head with an acknowledging whack. "That's why it feels so much lighter. I might have one or two. You?"

"This is my last."

"Well, it's not like we're in the desert or anything. We can collect more, right?"

"Yeah, but we gotta boil it. Which means that we gotta get it and we gotta have a fire."

"You got a different idea?" asked Jerry as he carefully opened one of his water bottles. He sipped conservatively and then dutifully replaced the cap.

Neil didn't have any ideas worth mentioning, only concerns about what to do. The only idea that seemed to be forming was a possibility that he was having a hard time considering. He said finally, "The way I see it, we've got three possibilities. We go north toward the Mat-Su Valley and the Interior, we stay here, or we go back to Anchorage where we know we can find supplies."

"And...them."

"Yeah. And them."

"Why didn't you say anything about supplies or help when you said the Mat-Su?"

It was just instinct but Neil was fairly certain about his assumptions of what lay to the north. "They got across the Knik. That much is clear. If they got across, that means that the nearest force able to stand up to them is in Fairbanks at Fort Wainright. There's no way that those troops could have been mobilized and transported in time to check the hordes' advance anywhere nearby. I think they might have made a stand in the tight corridors of Denali Park. That means several days' hike before we might, and I can't stress that word enough, *might* find friendlies. And unless they figured out a different method of dealing with them, I'm afraid that we might be talking about the crossing at Nenana."

Jerry was nodding through all of this. "I can't say that I disagree with any of that. So why not just keep heading north and scrounge for supplies in Palmer or Wasilla?"

"The military may not have been able to stop them but I'm sure that their efforts at least slowed the spread somewhat. That would have bought Mat-Su residents time to get out and in getting out I'm guessing that they picked clean most of the stores already. There's a good chance that most of what we need is already gone."

"So, we get staying here or going back as our only options?"

Warming his hands near the small fire as much for effect as anything else, Neil asked, the doubt creeping into his words as they crawled out into the cool air, "I don't know about you, but that fire only did so much last night to keep me warm. How long you think we'll be able to stay out when it starts to get really cold and snow hits? Seems like freezin' to death isn't any better of an option than facing the same at the hands of..."

Neil caught Jerry's expression and corrected himself, "Well maybe in degree it's better but not in outcome. Either way, we end up dead. Besides, we can probably get water, but what about food? I'm not a hunter. You?"

"No, but what you're suggesting is nuts. No one is going to buy into it."

"I'm glad you put it that way, because that is exactly what it is: a suggestion. Claire was right last night. It doesn't always have to be my call."

"Neil, we trust you. It's that simple. You may say otherwise, but we can all tell that you're not just looking out for your own ass. You've kept us all safe and, probably more importantly, you've kept us going. We'd probably have waited in that house in South Anchorage or there on Elmendorf until we got boxed in and overrun with nowhere and no time to go. You saw the writing on the wall and made sure we had better options."

Neil shook his head and suggested, "I think that may just have been luck. I'm no brilliant strategist."

Without the slightest hesitation, Jerry disagreed. "No, that's not how I see it at all. Both moves were calculated, and they were the right decisions. So it sounds like you're thinking we should head back to Anchorage then?"

Claire was just emerging from under the tarp and heard the last bit of the last sentence. Through a yawn she asked, "I must still be waking up because it sounded like someone thought it a good idea to go back to Anchorage. That couldn't be right could it?"

Remembering her challenge the night before, Neil thought it wise to let Jerry do the talking, which he did. He laid it all out for her, just as Neil had done for him, and let her think about it. Once again, adhering to the mindset of the devil you know is sometimes better than the devil you don't, she agreed that the logic was sound, if terrifying and unpalatable.

"How you guys goin'ta sell this to everyone else?" she asked.

It didn't take much selling as it turned out. In fact, spying the "living" bridge through the binoculars discouraged any thoughts about proceeding north. No one was interested in tempting fate needlessly.

Emma commented as she peered through the binoculars, "I don't think I've ever seen anything more disgusting. They look like insects or something, slithering all over one another. I guess we should be thankful they're all tangled and can't get up." She lowered the glasses and asked no one in particular, "Back to Anchorage, huh?"

Dr. Caldwell thought for a second and then said, "There is another alternative that hasn't been mentioned."

Neil said thankfully, "We're all ears Doc."

"What about Eagle River? There was a, relatively speaking, fairly vibrant retail presence there. Maybe there's still something to be had by checking it out."

Emma asked, "Didn't you live there?"

"Yes. And our house is fairly removed."

Neil started to speak but only got out, "Doc, she's probably…"

"I know, I know. There's not a whole lot of hope but I think we might be able to get into Eagle River and find a safe place to hide indefinitely. If there aren't a lot of those things around then we might be able to find a place to stay for the winter possibly."

Neil said, "I think it's worth a look. What do you guys think?"

No one said anything for a few seconds and then Meghan chimed in with, "Let's do it. Maybe Eagle River was able to stay off of those things' radar. Maybe it's still safe."

And so, Eagle River it was.

# CHAPTER 62

The journey south was uneventful and anticlimactic. Plodding back over the same steps, including passing through the now familiar horrors of the failed roadblock attempt, felt wrong to all of them. This, despite the fact that their past lives had been based largely upon tracing and retracing the same routines day in and day out. Whether their feelings were justified or not were immaterial; the mood of the group was what it was, pure and simple.

Realizing that whatever perceived threats were minimal, Dr. Caldwell and Neil were more daring, wandering deeper into the road in search of anything useful. They found a couple of the soldiers' M4's under some bodies, but both guns were empty of ammunition and so covered with gore than neither men thought it worth the effort to carry them. Short of that, there was nothing of value to be uncovered within the short distance either man was willing to wade into the bog of bodies.

Wandering still further south, they chose to pause at Mirror Lake. Despite the day having no inspiration beyond a pale, grey, featureless sky, the lake was still beautiful. The water had a slightly curious ripple, asking questions of the breeze that teased its mood.

Dr. Caldwell said from somewhere far away, "We used to bring the kids down here for Saturday picnics. We had a small canoe that we'd take out...the kids and me that is, while Valerie got lunches together. Actually, the lunches would already be packed and ready but this was her chance to get a few peaceful moments to herself and it gave me the opportunity to be a dad for a few minutes. She was an awfully smart lady."

Emma asked, "What were their names? Your kids I mean."

"Jacob and Laura. Jacob's in his last year of college and Laura's in her first."

"The proud papa, huh?"

"Yeah, they're good kids." He trailed off with both his voice and his eyes.

Emma sensed his worry and tried to reassure him. "I'm sure they're okay. I mean, they're thousands of miles away, right? There's no way this thing could've spread down there already. Someone had to have figured this out by now. Figured out how to stop it. Don't ya think?"

The doctor had drifted away. His feet took him to the edge of the water, where he stopped and saw a canoe from the past with a father and his two children gliding effortlessly under the warm summer sun. Maybe Emma was right, but there was as much of an opportunity that she was wrong and the doctor could not ignore that possibility. The not knowing was as distressing as anything else. And getting this close to his home and his wife only made all of the emotions that much more powerful. He needed to know.

On the far side of the lake, near a docked floatplane, he could see a group of twenty or so people milling about with the unmistakable stilted gait of the undead. Getting everyone's attention, he pointed across to them. From this distance, the ghouls were not much of a threat, but their presence suggested that there was a possibility that more of them could be near, so Neil said to all of them, "This place isn't safe. Let's catch our breath and get back on the road. We still have a bit of traveling to do."

Claire said with a bit of a whine to her voice, "But we just got here. They're all the way over there. Can't we wait for just a bit? It doesn't even look like they know that we're here. Look at them. They're just standing there." Looking over at them more intently, Claire winced a bit and shook her head. She had to admit. Even from this distance the walking dead were horrifying.

Neil, looking over at them as well, countered, "I don't know about you, but I don't think I want to gamble with everyone's lives for an extra breather. Do you?"

Claire shot him an ireful look but didn't say anything. Neil, however, took the hint. He said, "What does everyone else want to do? We can wait for a bit and try to stay out of sight or we can get back on the road. I'm good either way, I guess."

Claire was a little surprised by the last thing he said because he sounded sincere. She looked at everyone and said almost apologetically, "I'm not trying to be the opposition here. I just think that maybe we should take our time when we can. If we're always in a hurry we might, I don't know…"

Neil was nodding the whole time, while everyone else just stared, listened, and waited. Finally, Claire said in exasperation, "Oh, never mind. Neil, you're probably right."

Quickly, Neil spoke up, "No, I think you're onto something Claire. If we don't need to be rushing, then maybe we shouldn't be. We have to conserve all our resources, including our own energy. It's not just about whether my legs are tired or not. It's about all of us. I would like to add, however, that we also are contending with time and the days are getting shorter. We can't afford to dawdle."

Meghan finally asked, "So what are we going to do?" And to Neil she asked, "Dawdle? Really? Who uses that word anymore?"

Neil ignored her ribbing and answered the serious question by looking at everyone with the question in his eyes rather than in his voice. Danny and Jules shared their own idea by fishing out some granola bars from their backpacks.

Dr. Caldwell, seeing the decisiveness of the children, said with a smile, "Finally, someone with some true, honest sense about them. Rome burned while Nero fiddled. There's no reason why we shouldn't eat a bit while we figure out what to do."

The quick snack effectively ended the debate; though not the vigilance. The perils of a common day were anything but common any longer. Not too long ago, the worst to expect was a frightful but typically not life threatening encounter with wildlife or perhaps having an unsavory vandal break into one's car while you were away. It had been quite a turn the world had taken.

Neil and Claire stepped away from the others to talk. Quite contrary to what she was expecting, Neil said that he appreciated the fact that she didn't just complain. When she disagreed, she offered reasonable alternatives. She was glad that he didn't think of her as another Art, someone who seemed to contradict the opinions of others solely because they weren't his opinions. She didn't want to be that kind of person.

The creatures on the opposite side of the lake, in time, started to move slowly around the far shore. It appeared that they had caught the scent of some prey nearby and were drawn to it. Jerry watched them as they began their instinctive trek and warned everyone that it may be time to be going again. In very short order, they were back out on the highway, leaving Mirror Lake behind them.

# CHAPTER 63

The North Eagle River Exit from the southbound Seward Highway is as nondescript of a stretch of inclined pavement as any other in the world; just a short road that led to a longer one. Why then, was everyone feeling so much anxiety as they approached it? No one spoke, which wasn't necessarily a strange thing as of late, but it also seemed as if they all were afraid to breathe for fear of upsetting some menacing presence that was just out of sight. From the highway, all you could see was the top of the road. There was no hint about what might be lurking there above.

As they, as if on cue, all stopped and waited, Jerry asked the ragged column, "We ready? Doc?"

They nodded as one, a chorus of heads signaling its silent consent. All eyes, however, were firmly on Dr. Caldwell. Their apprehension, aggressive and raw, was for him. They all knew what to expect and yet they all held onto the hope that there *was* still hope.

Starting with Neil, they pumped rounds into their shotguns and handguns. Jerry opened the bolt on his rifle and checked that a bullet was there. He locked the bolt back into place, loading the round, and then said, "Let's do this."

There was no bravado in their pace. Taking long, slow strides, they climbed the hill with all the vigor and enthusiasm of a sloth. When they did finally crest the incline, none of them were ready for the scene that opened up in front of them.

The Fred Meyer grocery store that once sat at the end of the road was now a twisted mess of steel girders and crumbling concrete, more resembling a modern art sculpture than a former retail outlet. A fire that devoured it from inside out had ravaged the store. This skeleton of a structure was attended to by a few dozen of the loitering undead, waiting outside the forever barred doors of the store like the dead waiting for their ride across the River Styx.

Meghan, a former manager of a sister store in Anchorage, breathed, "Jesus," a sentiment they all shared.

Looking through his scope, Jerry said, "I don't think they know we're here."

"Let's keep it that way," Neil said quietly. "C'mon, let's get our asses outta here before they ever get a chance to find out."

Looking at Dr. Caldwell, Emma asked, "Which way is home?"

Dr. Caldwell, hearing that familiar word with more warmth and promise than ever in his life, said hopefully, "We live down that road a bit and then up."

Claire asked, "Up. What do you mean by up?"

Gerald, who rarely spoke, said to everyone's surprise, "Maybe we should work out the details somewhere else folks. We may be wearing out our welcome." He pointed toward the zombies in the parking lot who were starting to show signs of agitation, likely brought on by the new scent of prey.

They were already walking when Neil asked the doctor, "You sure you want to go there, Doc? I mean..." He trailed off before he regretted suggesting anything.

Dr. Caldwell answered plainly without looking at him, "I have to know."

"Yeah. I guess I would too."

They moved as quickly and as quietly as they were able onto the adjoining road that led away from the former Fred Meyer and its grey-skinned loiterers. They were on the Old Glenn Highway with newly constructed houses on either side of them. Like in Anchorage, developers were desperate to clear and build on every available parcel of land, taking the maximum advantage of the limited prospects for such development.

Many of the housing subdivisions had winding streets that sloped down away from the main road on which they were walking. They also passed a growing number of the seemingly requisite features of suburban America: strip malls. Restaurants, tanning salons, specialty clothing stores...you name it, you could find it. They seemed to be everywhere, like invasive species of plants fertilized with our collective and insatiable demands for new gadgets and the latest gizmos. These buildings now sat idle, waiting for the next big sale.

As their elevation increased, the wind temperature noticeably decreased. No longer was it merely nipping at their cheeks and noses. Their legs and arms were starting to feel the cold through the layers of pants and jackets they all wore. Breathing too was becoming more of a chore.

They veered off the main thoroughfare and started up a road that very clearly continued to climb its way fairly steeply up the mountain. The pavement still in the shadows was icy and slick and their exhaled breath became much denser with the plummeting air temperature.

Dr. Caldwell's house was on a section of road that had started to twist and wind, trying to cut the steepness of the angle of incline. Each step was more and more laborious as they continued up. Access to his house came from a small road, without a road sign to announce its name. From off the main path of traffic, the narrow street meandered discreetly, using both a sharper than average turn and a large rock to conceal its very presence. Such a street would play hell with pizza delivery drivers.

The five or six houses on the street all sat on the left side with the right side offering an unobstructed view of the valley that cut itself between two Chugach peaks. They all stalled as they started down the doctor's street to soak in the scenery.

Neil said, "Jeez, Doc. You sure know how to pick a neighborhood. Look at that view."

"I have Val to thank for that."

"Which one's yours?"

"The fourth one up."

They walked slowly, hopefully toward the beautiful residence, the earth-toned facade looking peacefully out onto the quiet street and welcoming panorama. The first thing they noticed was that the front door was still closed, which was a good sign that they all noted to themselves. A nice Saab coupe was parked in the driveway, obviously his wife Valerie's car.

Jerry looked in the driver's side window and saw the keys still in the ignition. The car door was unlocked, so Jerry reached in to remove the keys. The car had been left running until it had burned all its fuel. Jerry didn't bother to mention that, as that was definitely not a good sign at all. She wouldn't have just left her car running unless she was surprised. Jerry thought to himself that she could have been surprised but had enough time to run away to safety. He rose up from the car and tossed the keys to the doctor.

Dr. Caldwell caught the keys with a metallic jingle and held his hand up, the keys dangling, for a second or two longer. He looked at the keys without saying a word. With the reluctance of the condemned walking up to the gallows, he dragged his feet up the wooden stairs of the front deck. He unlocked the door, something that helped to stoke the dying embers of hope in his heart, but before he could open it Neil stopped him.

Trying to hide his own apprehension toward the possibilities of what they may find, he said, "You may need to know, Doc, but let us check things out first. Please? We don't know what we're gonna find in there."

At first wanting to protest, Dr. Caldwell consented with a nod and stepped onto the far side of the spacious front deck. The flowers in the planters, though struggling against the cold, still did their best to show their colorful smiles. He said after seeing them, "She's gonna be pissed at me for not bringing her flowers into the garage. She's been taking care of these things like they were children. I'm sure I'll be in trouble for that, despite the whole end of the world thing. There were just certain things that I had to get done, no excuses. I guess I'll move these things down there in case she hasn't noticed yet."

Neil and Jerry both forced a nod and a smile and then turned their attention to the task at hand. They opened the door slowly, trying not to create any noise at all, but of course, the hinges creaked and moaned as the door opened. Dr. Caldwell said as he lifted the first planter, "Yeah, I was supposed to get some W-D 40 on that too."

Neil, allowing a very slight but uncomfortable chuckle to escape, said, "Don't worry about it, Doc. We can get to it later."

The house was a split-level of sorts with stairs leading away from a smallish entry area just inside the front door. The nature of the lot, as it was with all the houses on the street, was that it sloped sharply. The result was that the upstairs back door and the front door were both at ground level, with a large part of the foundation buried in the ground.

The stairs in both directions were carpeted with pristine white carpet. Out of habit, both men leaned down to unlace their boots so they could take them off, as was custom in Alaska. Neither of them got very far in the process and both came back up smiling at one another.

Jerry smiled and said, "Habits."

Neil responded, smiling as well, "Yeah, some just take longer."

The downstairs was dark and foreboding, so the two men opted to look upstairs first. Neil said to Meghan, "Watch our backs. There may be something downstairs that we can't see."

"What do you want me to do?"

"Just stand here with your gun ready and watch for anything that might come from down there. Danny, help Meghan."

Danny already had his rifle in his hands. His nod was eager and appreciative.

The large living room into which the stairs led was at the front of the house, its oversized picture window staring like a thankful eye at the view. From the living room, they walked into a formal dining room with a dark, formal dining table of finely polished hardwood. The room was separated from the kitchen by a slatted wood door that allowed some partial view of the room on the other side. They could see the outlines of cabinets and counter tops and the grouted lines of the tiled floor. They could also feel a cold draft that found its way from the kitchen and into the dining room through those same opened slats.

Jerry pushed open the lightweight door and let Neil through. Neil said in a hush, "So far so good."

They stepped into the kitchen, seeing the first evidence of things being amiss. The phone, an older model still mounted to the wall and sporting a long, coiling cord, was off its cradle and lying on the floor. And then they saw more than they wanted. The sliding glass door that led out onto the back deck was shattered into countless sharp prisms on the floor. They rounded an island of counters and a chopping block and saw the unmistakable brownish streaking stains on the tile and leading out the missing back door.

Someone, most likely Dr. Caldwell's wife, had been attacked and brutalized as she was dragged outside, probably kicking and screaming as evidenced by the house slipper lying on its side next to the wall. The white, fuzzy slipper too, had been spattered with gore on that long ago morning. It didn't appear she had gone down without a fight though. There was a large kitchen knife just outside the broken door and on the floor inside were two grey, very male looking fingers, or parts of fingers anyway. Any other attacker would have been discouraged and chased off. As it was though, her assailant likely didn't even register that it had lost two of its digits and just continued its assault with its remaining eight.

Neil swallowed hard. "Poor Doc."

"Yeah. How d'you think he's gonna handle this?"

"How would you?"

"What can we do?"

The two men returned the phone to its proper place on the wall and tried to clean up the stains on the floor but the stain was too old and the floor too porous. In the end, they elected to try and cover as much as possible with a rug they retrieved from a bathroom down the hall. The rug did its best to conceal the grisly remains, but the forensic pathologist's playground was larger than the rug's meager capabilities.

It seemed they were in the house for the better part of a day but when they came back outside they learned they'd only been in long enough to allow Dr. Caldwell to move his wife's planters.

From in front of the garage, he looked up at Neil as the two men emerged. Neil drew in a deep breath and shook his head. He wished he had better news, but alas, it wasn't to be.

Something happened to the doctor's face then. Once vibrant and energetic, disguising his age and wisdom, all at once his eyes lost their vitality and the stubble on his cheeks suddenly looked more ragged and silver. His skin lost its elasticity and chose to hang from his jaw rather than tighten itself across his cheekbones. In that blink of an eye, he became an old man.

When Neil and Jerry re-entered the house, this time with the others in tow, they felt more like intruders than before. As they ascended the stairs, each looked over his shoulder to the trailing Dr. Caldwell as if to get permission to continue. They were guests, after all.

Dr. Caldwell sat down on the overstuffed, plush couch that was situated perfectly to catch both the view and the fireplace in the center of the wall opposite. There was no television in this room. There was, however, an antique console stereo system with a precision turntable. The stereo was part cabinet, part stereo, and part center speaker. It was a piece of furniture in and of itself. In racks to either side of the stereo were neatly ordered collections of vintage vinyl albums and more recent compact discs. This was a music lover's altar.

Emma observed all of this as she circled the room, holding an approach pattern as she prepared to make her landing on the couch next to the doctor. She didn't want to presume to know his feelings or his needs one way or the other. She could just float from point of interest to point of interest in the room, sharing the space without actually invading his. He could be alone, if he chose, without being isolated in his grief.

Finally, he said, "Do you wanna sit down?"

From in front of the window, Emma turned and admitted, "I don't know what I should be doing here. I didn't want you to be alone but then I didn't know what I should do and so I just..." She had to stop because her sobbing was making her speech unintelligible to even her. She took in a deep breath and finally said, "I should probably just go. I'm really screwing this up."

She started to leave the room, but Dr. Caldwell calmly patted the seat on the couch next to him. "Why don't you have a seat, Emma. You're probably exhausted."

Once she'd seated herself, Emma apparently lost all control of her emotions and erupted into a series of laughing sobs and gibberish. Dr. Caldwell guided her cheek to his shoulder and then placed his hand on her hair.

He looked around the room and really saw all that was there for the first time in an age. There was the artwork that Valerie and he had picked together. The beautiful forest hues of the oil paintings matched perfectly to the view out the window. He remembered the day they got each of the paintings, and spending the better part of an afternoon, while the kids napped, choosing just the right locations for each on the wall and then hanging and re-hanging each as Valerie considered variations and combinations. She wanted to open the room and make it seem like you were surrounded with windows; a goal she had admirably accomplished.

To add to the green, there were several large plants in the room. He noticed that the ficus trees to either side of the window, the larger than life lily plant on the top of the stereo, and the several hanging plants in the corners of the room and on the higher portions of the stone wall framing the fireplace all were dead and wilted as he observed the room, but when they were alive the room was damn near a jungle, making the living room a truly 'living' room.

Like a moth to a flame though, there was no denying his eyes being drawn to the photographs and keepsakes on the mantle above the fireplace. He didn't need to get up to see them or remember them. They were a lifetime of memories of much happier times.

He finally let his emotions take him. His tears were silent, but they were real. He could feel them working their way out of his stomach, up through his chest, and finally into his eyes. He always assumed that it would be reversed; that Val would be the one sitting on the couch needing consoling. He wished it were that way in fact.

In teams, the others checked the rest of the house, finding nothing alarming. In a laundry room downstairs, they found some more food and some beer but no water. There was also a locked cabinet that very much resembled a gun safe in a back bedroom converted into an office.

In the master bedroom, they found a suitcase on the bed. It was still open and only half full. Most of the drawers were either pulled out or actually on the floor. On top of the folded clothes in the suitcase was a framed portrait of four happy, smiling people. One of the faces was that of their good friend Dr. Caldwell. There was no arguing with the physical and very visible proof that the last few weeks had considerably aged him. Neil opened the back of the frame to remove the picture. Meghan shot him a questioning look.

He said, "The picture is important. The frame is impractical."

"That's his family."

"And this is our and his survival. The picture frame has glass that will only get broken and cut his hands or get into the plastic packaging of the food he's carrying. Then he'll be eating glass. I get that we need to be sensitive about this and I'm trying to be. But we have to approach everything pragmatically. We can't have extra weight or our limited backpack space being taken by non-essentials."

From the doorway, Dr. Caldwell's voice startled them both, "Neil's right." He extended his hand and took the frame, finishing the job of removing the picture. He added, "I think I'd like to put some of my own clothes on. Can I have a few minutes to change? Meghan, I bet you and Emma and Claire could all fit into some of Val's clothes if you'd like some fresh duds."

"I wouldn't want to..."

"Please. Val would have liked to know that she was helping in some way. That was always important to her."

"If you insist."

"We do."

# CHAPTER 64

The balance of the day they spent resting in front of the generous fire they built in the fireplace and enjoying some of their new provisions. They drained the hot water heater and the boiler into empty plastic bottles, pitchers, and any other containers that were available. Both appliances were still relatively new, so the water had neither odor nor color to it.

Danny and Jules drank Cokes they found in the garage while everyone else indulged themselves in the cool beers. The tantalizing flavors and textures scintillated their senses and helped them all settle in for some much needed rest.

Deciding that the day was spent, Neil and Jerry found a tarp in the garage and used it to cover the back door, using generous strips of duct tape to affix it to the frame. This effectively ended the draft, but a trickle of cold air still found its way through the less than perfect cover. The two men then moved the heavy, formal dining table, tilting it up against the open door to add some level of security. Luckily, the table was taller than the door, so they were able to drive a handful of carpentry nails through both the table and the doorframe. It wasn't perfect, but it would do, especially if it wasn't large crowds of ghouls pressing themselves against the barrier. They hadn't seen one since leaving the Fred Meyer several miles behind them. There was some comfort in that.

Given that the living room was the only one with any degree of heat in it, a pair of mattresses was brought into the large room, turning the floor into a large bed. The fire was kept at a new raging level to maintain the little bit of warmth that kept the room comfortable. They all hungered for real rest and each in his own time was able to partake of that morsel.

The next morning, everyone save Dr. Caldwell arose feeling refreshed. Dr. Caldwell's face looked as lifeless and ravaged as a zeke's. He tried to smile and join in conversations, but the effort needed for such gestures was evident in his expression. Upon waking, he opened another beer for breakfast. Before rising from his chair, he'd had another.

He found himself only wanting to leave his chair to relieve himself and to get another beer. He brought them upstairs from the laundry room one at a time, figuring that if he got to the point that he couldn't make it up or down the stairs then it was time to stop.

Dr. Caldwell joined Danny and Jules in a lively game of Aggravation, which most everyone else watched. The beer was helping, though he realized that all it was doing was pushing his grief to the side temporarily. Eventually he would be forced to deal with it. He was a doctor and had seen it all before. For the time, he was happy consorting with the likes of Amber...Alaskan Amber.

Curiously, Meghan and Emma noted to one another that the doctor was careful not to venture into the kitchen. He avoided that room like he was cursed and it was hallowed ground. He didn't seem to be evading the truth, but perhaps the kitchen with its grisly reminders was too much truth for him to want to embrace.

They kept a watchful eye on him for the balance of the day. His drinking was worrisome, especially if they were prompted to be on the move again, but who were they to advise him on dealing with his pain? He seemed to be a happy drunk so far, so they elected to smile a lot and always be on hand.

Jerry, Claire, and Neil meanwhile decided that it would be prudent to check out the houses in their immediate vicinity. With only a handful of houses to check, it just made good sense to know what was around. It was Jerry who offered the first objection. He suggested that if there was something in the other houses or the immediate adjoining land, it might be just as well to leave it alone, and that maybe they could avoid detection by just staying out of sight. If they got out there and had to use their guns, they might attract attention to them that wouldn't be there otherwise.

Neither Neil nor Claire disagreed that it was a possibility, but they both felt that it was worth doing a sweep. For simple peace of mind, they needed to know if there were any threats already around them. There was always the likelihood that something would come their way, but if it was already in their backyard, it might be worth knowing about it.

The three of them were armed with baseball bats, clawed crowbars, shotguns, rifles, and handguns. To Gerald, who closed the front door behind them, they looked like battle hardened warriors venturing back into the field and, on a certain level, they were.

The Caldwells' house was the second to last house, so they chose to go to the last house and then work their way back. The mailbox at the end of their driveway announced that the Higgins family resided there. The front door on this house was open, as were three of the four car doors. As they walked by the car, they saw that the window on the closed door was so caked with blood that they couldn't see through the glass.

Going around to the other side of the car, Jerry looked in but recoiled almost immediately. He'd once seen the picked clean carcass of a moose on the side of the road near Hatcher's Pass. He saw more or less the same thing sitting on a child booster seat where bits of red vinyl cloth, white faux down stuffing, and small shards of bone all commingled into a single, horrible vision.

Neil looked at him and asked, "Does it need to be dealt with?"

"Man, there isn't enough in there to have turned. They ate him down to the seat."

"How do you know it was a him?"

"Spiderman boots."

"Anything else?"

"Naw. Looks like maybe the kid was strapped in and waiting on the rest of the fam. Doesn't look like anyone else made it out...at least this direction."

Claire swallowed audibly and said with no humor whatsoever, "I really don't know how you guys do it."

Just as quickly, Jerry answered, "Not much of a choice really. Doesn't mean that it doesn't make me wanna retch when I see something like that."

The path leading to the small concrete porch sitting in front of the front door was strewn with clothes. They appeared to be a young girl's sized and styled clothes. They saw purple butterflies, rhinestone hearts, and Hello Kitty. On the porch sat on its side a purple suitcase, its hearts less than cheery.

Some have posited that events so utterly imbued with emotion or trauma can leave an inanimate object with the memory of that happening imbedded in the fabric of that object. Many paranormal psychologists had explained ghosts and poltergeists in such a manner. Looking at the suitcase and then remembering all the seemingly everyday items that were carried by their owners until that terrible day when all this started, Claire wondered what kind of memory each would impart.

Standing at the threshold, Claire asked, her eyes never stopping their desperate scan of the immediate interior of the house, "Why don't we just shut this house up and seal in whatever is inside?"

Jerry asked, "What about supplies? There might be something in there that we could use."

"If we've been able to get by this long without whatever that is, then I guess we don't really need it. Besides, we can always come back if we have to. In the meantime, if we can just close the houses and make getting out tough, then maybe we don't have to, you know, get Medieval on their asses."

Jerry chuckled. "Great Ving Rhames reference by the way, but it seems like we're all dressed up. Might as well go for a dance."

Claire leaned back and gave Jerry the "what did you just say?" look.

Neil compromised. "Why don't we check this place and decide after? No tellin' what we're gonna find in there. It's another big house, lotsa rooms. Claire, do you wanna stay here at the door?"

"You ain't leavin' me alone anywhere."

"I was just—"

"Yeah, well, whatever ideas you get better not have me alone."

"Okay, okay. Well then, I think we should shut the door behind us and then do the same with every door we pass."

Claire smiled and, gesturing with her hand, said, "After you."

They chose to check downstairs first, hoping that the scarce daylight from outside might help to illuminate the rooms. Luckily, the window shades on the large window in the recreation room were open, letting in a generous portion of the flat light of the sun. The bittersweet pungence of decay wafted up to them before they had made it down the stairs. They immediately knew that they weren't alone.

In the corner of the large room there stood a longhaired, languishing wraith. It had its back to them, but turned slowly as they entered the room. Its ragged clothing, looking more like a funeral shroud than garments, hung from its bone thin emaciated grey limbs and frame. Its skin, festering with rotting sores, was pulled tightly across protruding bones.

At first its eyes only seemed bewildered, like it was trying to remember something. Smelling the salty temptation of flesh that walked in with these pink skinned creatures, a deep, lurking hunger suddenly awoke, firing aggression into its congealed veins. The confusion washed from its eyes, replaced as it dissipated by a ravenous craving for raw flesh.

Claire was already heading back up the stairs when Jerry yelled, "Stop! Don't get separated!" She wasn't waiting though, her legs acting of their own accord.

Neil was already stepping forward with his bat. Putting the likes of Babe Ruth and Mickey Mantel to shame, Neil swung the bat with force and purpose. The metallic knell was still echoing as the beast hit the floor, a deep gash opened on its temple. The wound slowly filled with a dark fluid resembling black jelly. With a gurgling growl spilling from its mouth, it tried to rise back to its feet, but Neil was already bringing his second swing down onto the back of its head.

The only sound in the room afterward was Neil's breathing. From the top of the stairs, Claire called down, "I think I'm ready to go back now."

"We gotta finish first. Please come back down here. If we separate, we're easier to pick off," Jerry answered.

She came back down the stairs slowly, her eyes as wide as saucers as she tread. When she was back on the basement floor she snapped to Jerry, "Zealot!"

The next door in the basement was in the same room but over toward the back of the house. It was likely a bathroom and its door was locked from the inside. Listening to the door, Neil confirmed what he and Jerry both thought. There was something moving around on the other side and, judging by the sounds it was making, it didn't sound human...well, not anymore.

"Another one," Jerry said. "That's two for two."

Neil nodded. "Yeah, not a good start at all. What if all these houses have the same?"

Claire added, "Or worse?"

"What should we do?" Jerry asked.

Neil said, "Let's finish up here and then head back. I think we may have bitten off more than we can chew."

The rest of the house was largely empty. There were some bloodstains on the carpet upstairs and a broken window in a back bedroom through which it looked like someone had either jumped or been pushed. Aside from that, there wasn't much else of interest. There were some cans of food and some unopened bottles of juice, but most everything else had spoiled or rotted. They journeyed back to their own refuge to take stock of the situation with the rest of the group.

When all was said and done, they didn't really feel any safer. They were warm, however, and that was enough to have them take a day or two to reconsider their options. That they were going to be on the go again in just a handful of days was very clear to all of them, though. Was there anywhere left where they could go to be safe? Was there any haven left?

# CHAPTER 65

"I don't want to go back to Anchorage!" demanded Emma.

"Not *to* Anchorage, *through* Anchorage," corrected Jerry.

"You sound like Bill Clinton. To and through are the same damned thing. Either way, I'm not interested. Are you crazy? We just got outta there and now you wanna go back. Huh-uh. Count me out."

Neil intervened. "We need to discuss our options. Going through Anchorage is one. It may not be the best, but at the moment, it's the only option on the table. Emma, what do you suggest? Or anyone else for that matter?"

Emma asked, "Why can't we just stay here?"

Dr. Caldwell answered, "And live on what? There's not enough food in this house to feed us all for more than another day. And if we dare forage for anything from the Pendergrass' or the...from all the neighboring houses, how much could we possibly get? Not enough to keep us going for long. The more time that passes, the harder it's going to be for us to get away. It's going to get really cold, really fast and moving in that is not going to be fun for any of us. We've got to use the time while we have it."

Emma looked at Dr. Caldwell, who was still disheveled and appeared possibly hung over, and smiled as she said, "Glad to have you back. You doin' okay?"

"As compared to what?"

"Okay. Do you really think it's a good idea to leave? This is your house. This is home for you. Don't you think we can make it here?"

Dr. Caldwell didn't hesitate before saying, "We'd probably starve or freeze to death here."

Emma asked, "But south? Why south?"

Claire surprised everyone when she decided to weigh in. "Because we've already seen what the north has to offer and goin' south can't be any worse."

Besides, Denali Park might already be snowed in. It's cold here. There's no tellin' what's up north."

Emma retorted, "You sound like Jerry and Neil. They've brainwashed you, sister. You need to hang with me and Meghan more. We'll help you resist their voodoo charms."

They all smiled at Emma's comments as well as her flamboyant body language as she said it. Dr. Caldwell even went so far as to wrap an arm around her shoulder and hug her to his side.

Emma remarked, "South, huh?"

Neil asked, "What do you think? Do you want to try heading north and risk running headlong into winter?"

"No, but...damn. Every time we get somewhere that starts to feel comfortable, we just gotta pack up and move out again. I'd just like to find a little place to put my feet up for an extended time. This house just seems like it could be that place."

She knew that she was continuing to fight a battle that had already been conceded and decided, but she couldn't help herself. She had an uncle who used to call people who blindly consented to any new perceived government intrusion into personal liberties "sheeple". He used the word very liberally despite his being a very conservative person. She was pretty certain he burned a candle every year on the anniversary of William F. Buckley's death. She hoped that their group wasn't becoming a herd of "sheeple" being led by the whims of Neil. She didn't think that was the case, but whenever there was no dissenting opinion it kind of felt like that. Maybe her final gasp of protest was in deference to her uncle and his ideals.

Neil said hopefully, "Maybe we could skirt the far eastern side of the city. We wouldn't even necessarily have to follow the highway and Muldoon Road. We could move along the undeveloped spaces between the mountains and the city."

"That place is full of moose and moose-hunting bears. Seems like we're just trading one problem for another with that option," answered Meghan. "Isn't there a better alternative?"

Dr. Caldwell hadn't really been paying close attention to the discussion, but something just hit him with Meghan's remark. His smile at everyone brought the debate to a halt. He said, still wearing the same smile, "There is an alternative. The Crow Pass Trail. It heads all the way down to Girdwood. Actually, it's supposed to be walked from Girdwood to Eagle River, but I think we will be permitted to take it the opposite direction this time. We could totally avoid Anchorage and it shouldn't take us more than a couple of days; three tops."

Claire asked, "How tough of a hike is it?"

Dr. Caldwell smiled with a little teasing menace. "You afraid you're not up to the challenge?"

Claire smiled right back and said, "No. I'm in. How about the kids?"

"Val and I always wanted to take Jacob and Laura on the trail but we never got around to it. There's some serious hiking and maybe some climbing." He looked at Jules and Danny and asked them, "We could be climbing up pretty high and walking lots. You guys up for that?"

Danny knew the only answer he could give was yes, so he did so with an enthusiastic nod. The hike did interest him and the climbing excited him. Climbing trees was so much fun and the heights, though sometimes seemingly significant, were not in the least bit intimidating. He couldn't think of anything that would possibly make him not want to take this adventure. There was no denying or ignoring the caution in Dr. Caldwell's voice, however. He smiled and added a thumbs up to cement his position. He nudged Jules, who followed suit.

"Good. I think we've got some work to do. We should have everything we'll need for the hike here; thermal underwear, extra gloves, and good socks. You can't put too high a premium on good socks for hiking. We've got some rope in the garage too and some bungees. I guess we can get into the gun safe too. Jerry I think there might be an item or two in there that might interest you. Unfortunately, most of what's in there isn't going to do us much good."

Neil looked at him for clarification. Dr. Caldwell explained further. "I've got mostly black powder guns and rifles. Kind of a hobby really, but not a whole lot of good to us. There are a couple of nice old hunting rifles with very nice scopes and an old service revolver my dad carried with him in Korea and Vietnam. There are a few boxes of shells too but not much else."

"What kind of a hobby was it?"

"My father's. We used to build them—sorry, smith them—together in his shop when I was younger. I learned all the steps in assembling a black powder firearm. It was quite an art. They're fun to shoot but I was never much of a hunter."

Jerry said, "Let's go check it out."

As a group, they had gotten very adept at preparing themselves to be on the move. Being on the go had just become a simple fact of life, and a proficiency for readying oneself and knowing what was both essential as well as feasible to carry was of the utmost importance to their survival. It probably helped in that regard that the more they traveled, the less there was to carry.

They were going through supplies at an alarming rate and they weren't even eating that much per person. The doctor was right in his observation about their prospects if they chose to stay. They'd likely starve to death if they remained at his house. However, simply being on the road didn't necessarily solve the problem of supply. In fact, their being on the run could exacerbate that particular issue just as much as it could be solved. There was no telling what awaited them around the next bend in the road.

# CHAPTER 66

Most of the daylight of the next day was spent on the journey to the trailhead. It sat at the Eagle River Nature Center on the farthest reaches of Eagle River Road. Getting to the hike was proving to be a hike in and of itself.

Much of the first leg to the Nature Center was spent at a trot. They were passing through a largely residential area with rows and rows of homogeneous houses, lawns, and streets, an entire neighborhood propagating a sense of deja vu to the hapless passerby. Each of the streets was luckily devoid of movement or threat.

The pavement under their feet was dark and damp but virtually colorless, as were the houses on either side of the road. Like looking at an aged color photograph reproduced in a book, the color that stubbornly persisted was dulled and muted, its vitality having been sapped by the heavy grey sky. No one spoke; no one dared. The only sound any of them heard was the rhythmic staccato beat of their footsteps and the gasping struggle of their collective breathing.

Danny's voice gave them all a start. "Jerry? Can you—"

"Hear that?" finished Jerry, interrupting him.

"Yes."

Jerry admitted, "Yeah. I was getting ready to mention—"

Neil said soberly, "Don't bother. I can see them. Everyone keep running."

Emma protested, "But we're running right at them?"

Neil answered, "There's only a handful. We can take 'em. Just keep running. We're faster than they are now. We gotta use that." He was out of breath and couldn't continue.

He slung his shotgun on his back and pulled his bat from its sleeve on his backpack, wielding it like a two-handed sword. Jerry did likewise. Dr. Caldwell was well ahead of both of them. In point of fact, he was sprinting ahead of them. He was at full gallop when he passed between the four ghouls. He swung the bat hard and fast, hitting each of them as he passed.

The beasts struck with his first and third swings were down and didn't show any sign of rising again. The other two, though toppled from their feet, were back up in an instant and starting towards him. Dr. Caldwell, unfortunately, had spent all his momentum in his first swings, and was now facing the wrong direction to fend off their attacks. He tried his best to turn, but he was utterly defenseless for a second or so.

That certainly would have been the good doctor's end had it not been for the very timely intervention of Neil's and Jerry's bats. The undead were now facing away from the two men, so pummeling them with impunity suddenly presented itself just as they arrived. They took full advantage and dispatched the devils. They hit the beasts so hard that the now lifeless carcasses hit the pavement and slid several feet forward, passing Dr. Caldwell as they went.

At first the doctor smiled at his two friends but almost at once he broke down. His grief hit him so forcefully that he fell to his knees, gripping his stomach as he did. "I'm so sorry, Val," he moaned. "I should have been there. I might have been able..."

Quietly, Neil finished for him, "Died with her? That's all that would have happened. As it is, you've got a chance to get to your kids and protect them with the knowledge that you've got now. But that means we have to keep moving, Doc. You've got people here that are counting on you, now more than ever. You know where we're going and how to get us all there. I need your help. Please."

The doctor swallowed one final sob and felt the dull pain that squeezed his chest and punched his gut. He stood up and turned away from Neil. At the moment, he was near to hating the man and he knew, in some rational part of his brain that was on momentary hiatus, that Neil didn't deserve such enmity and that it wasn't real anyway. He paced a few moments, trying to corral the pain and control his breathing.

Jerry cautioned them both as the others started to gather around, "I can still hear them and it's getting stronger. I don't think we should have this conversation here."

Emma asked, "What conversation?"

Dr. Caldwell looked over with his swollen, red eyes. "Just boy talk. You know, hunting, football, chicks."

Jerry had to press, "I really don't think we have time for this."

Claire said, "It's starting to make me feel ill."

"Look!" Gerald said, pointing down the road from where they had come.

Coming down the road were hundreds of the things. Some were struggling to walk, despite past injuries or desiccation, and still others were getting the pace up faster and faster as they neared. They were emerging from the streets and neighborhoods they had passed only moments earlier. Many of those houses must not have been as empty as they appeared. A singular, collective moan emanated from the mob like a beacon leading them to their prey.

Already running, Jerry said, "I think we should haul ass!"

They all followed his lead. Neil was holding Danny's hand and Meghan was holding Jules'. They pulled the children along to help them keep pace with the others. They took full advantage of the fact that their legs could produce much more speed than those of the zombies. Of course, the undead never grew tired which helped close that difference if one wasn't careful.

Dr. Caldwell, gasping, said, "We can't keep this up indefinitely."

Meghan said, "Find a place to stop and let'em pass?"

Emma agreed. "Yeah, I don't think I can keep running like this."

Neil panted, "Doc, where to?"

"The greenhouse is up here on the right. We can probably find some pretty good places to hide and the smells from the plants will give us good cover."

They ran into the main greenhouse building, breaking a small window in the process. They got in and moved to the far side of the building, making their way between the wilting and dying plants. The warmth in the structure had helped to keep the air damp, providing the slightest moisture to sustain the plants but even that moisture was rapidly fading. Only the hardiest of flora was still persisting.

There was another exit at the back of the building. It was around that door where they gathered to collect themselves and catch their breath.

Emma asked them all, "We still sure that leaving the Doc's house was the best idea? We're not too far off to be able to turn around and head back."

Dr. Caldwell said, "Emma, if I can let go of my own house then it should be a snap for you. Let it go sweetheart. I'm never going back there again. It's just an empty building now. There's nothing back there for any of us."

Starting to cry despite her best efforts, Emma forced out, "But is this all there is now? Run, hide, survive, and repeat? There has to be more to make me want to keep on living."

Dr. Caldwell hugged her to his chest and pulled her in tight. He whispered into her ear so that no one else could hear. Her tears increased for a moment but they quickly changed to tears of release and acceptance. Dr. Caldwell kissed her cheek gently and then hugged her tightly again.

Over her shoulder, he said to Neil and the others, "I think we should keep moving."

Meghan asked, "But if those things just passed us by, then how are we supposed to keep moving in that direction? Won't that just put us on a collision course with them?"

"When they realize they've lost the scent," Jerry said, "they'll stop. They're not very bright. They'll completely forget about us because their minds won't likely be able to keep hold of a single thought. If the Doc knows some way around the main road, we can probably bypass them and then get back on our way without them even remembering we were ever around."

And that was exactly what they did. They waited for roughly an hour until everyone was sufficiently rested and then resumed their trek. They found side streets to skirt the main road until they felt comfortable enough to get back onto Eagle River Road, arriving at the Eagle River Nature Center by the late afternoon.

There were cars in the parking lot as if this was just a normal day. The front doors of the main building were off their hinges and collapsed inward. The windows too had been shattered from every frame facing out into the parking lot.

Dr. Caldwell said as they passed the ruined building, "I think there might be better options up the trail a bit. I seem to remember there being yurts and cabins further along. Maybe we'll have better luck there."

"And maybe we'll just see more of the same or worse," Emma complained forlornly.

Dr. Caldwell pleaded, "We have to believe."

And Emma answered, "I'm trying. I really am. But when we just keep seeing the same thing over and over again, well, it's gettin' tough is all I have to say. Can you really fault me for being the slightest bit pessimistic?"

They smiled at one another, which definitely made her feel better.

As they passed the main building, the true destruction became much more apparent. A fire had claimed most of the back of the structure, leaving only partial walls to contain the destruction within.

Emma asked, "We still thinkin' that we might have better luck up ahead?"

"Yeah. Just your average layperson would have never gotten past this building and the experienced hiker would leave the yurts still intact. Let's keep moving."

# CHAPTER 67

"Hate to admit my ignorance, but Doc, what's a yurt?" asked Meghan.

Dr. Caldwell smiled. "Unless you were a Mongolian nomad or an avid hiker, you probably wouldn't have much of a reason to know. You've probably seen them before and wondered what kind of a tent it was. A yurt is a little more than a tent but not as much as a cabin in terms of structure."

"So like a party tent from an outdoor reception or something?"

"Not exactly. It usually sits on a wood or concrete platform, and has a wood or sometimes fiberglass frame that is covered over with canvas or some other more waterproof material."

A few steps later and they were looking at a yurt, which was fairly aptly represented by the doctor to Meghan. She wasn't the only one who didn't know, but she was the only one curious enough to actually ask.

The interior was surprisingly clean, warm, and inviting. A couple of glass windows allowed in some light. They were all very excited to see the wood burning stove and a small pile of wood next to it. Danny was the first to notice the board nailed to the wood lattice frame. His intent reading drew others' attention. Neil walked over, asking as he did, "What'd ya find there?"

"Names, dates, and..."

"What?"

He pointed and said, "I think it's from others who came here before us. Look."

Neil read, "September. Lauren Miller, Rose Custer, J. Williamson, Ty Herron. Heading south on the Crow Pass. Hoping to find others."

"Late Sept. 2 weeks after event. Dr. Connor Wolverton, Maxine Parker, Tuck Pleasant, Chris Simpson, Doug Warring. Supplies gone. Fire at Fred's. No more food. Everyone else is dead. We all hope Whittier is still safe."

"There's more. Lots more. And it looks like they're all heading to Whittier."

Jerry said with a slap to his forehead, "Of course! The tunnel."

The realization not hitting him as fast as it did Jerry, Dr. Caldwell asked, "The tunnel?"

"Yeah, they can close the tunnel. If they got it closed before it was too late, then they could still be good there."

Emma, always the skeptic, asked, "What are the chances really?"

"Think about it. There are really only very limited options for access to the town other than through that tunnel. If they were able to shut it and then wait, there's a good chance that Whittier could be the one place left that is still holding on. I think it's worth the look and we've already decided that we're heading in that direction anyway."

Emma said, "Which I haven't necessarily agreed with from the beginning."

Neil said, "Read some of these notes. They all say the same thing. There's not enough food left in Eagle River. We're running out of options and it sounds like Whittier is our best one right now."

Quietly and directly to her, Neil pleaded, "Please. We need some goal, some purpose. A focus that will help to drive us, or we're just running for the sake of running and that's infinitely harder to do. Whittier can be that purpose."

"Have you ever been there?" Emma asked. "If Whittier is at the end of our rainbow then things are worse than I originally thought."

Neil smiled back at her and thus ended the debate. For the rest of the afternoon they rested and ate and prepared their packs once again for the coming challenge. The cold temperatures were held at bay by the yurt's sturdy walls and the radiating warmth of the stove. They ate heartily and even managed to find the few laughs that were still hanging around. It was a good evening and a restful night.

In the morning, Neil went to the board with his knife and carved their names, his best guess at a date in October and the following: "Don't forsake hope. There are others. Don't stop believing. We can make it. Heading to Whittier. Good luck to you and us."

# CHAPTER 68

The hike on the next day started out very pleasantly. Neil was starting to wonder if perhaps Dr. Caldwell's admonitions were merely for show. Most of the trees had put on their austere winter coats, shedding their more delicate summer apparel. So thick was the carpet of leaves under their feet that on more than one occasion they were in danger of veering off the path and losing their way.

The path's grade grew somewhat, and then some more and then some more. They were all but climbing and then they were on fairly level ground again. At this elevation, though, there was snow in patches here and there. Snow! New snow! Fresh, white, and looked-like-it-just-fell-that-morning snow! The air was cool but not completely unpleasant. They knew to expect the air to chill a bit but none of their lungs were prepared for the change. They all felt as if they'd just jumped into water that was a little colder than they expected. Speaking of water, the Eagle River was making its way next to them, its current healthy but not fast. As they walked and watched the water cutting its course, each in his or her own way imagined the chill that lurked below the water's surface. As close as they were to the glacier that fed this river, the temperature in its flow couldn't have been much above freezing.

With each step, they were huffing and puffing a small white cloud all around them. Down to the two kids, they all seemed to be handling the rigors thus far; no one needing extra encouragement or motivation to keep pace with the others, their moods surprisingly positive. They were able to follow handily placed trail markers to verify their route and their pace. Their progress could be charted, gains could be cataloged, and goals could be achieved. It was amazing how merely being able to claim that one had just walked a mile or half a mile or whatever could boost morale. Having a sense of accomplishment about what one was doing, especially if it included saving oneself, was a tonic for the soul, so to speak.

He couldn't ask for things to be going any better. Neil was feeling like maybe they'd turned a corner. He matched his pace to Dr. Caldwell's and pulled alongside the man. "Hey, Doc. What about the river?"

"What do you mean 'what about the river'?"

"Do we ever have to cross it?"

"I'm sure if we do, there will be a foot bridge or something else for us to use. I can't imagine the trail would involve fording a river."

"Good. You're probably right."

They marched along at a fairly healthy pace until a little after midday. They came to a small trail marker with words like "Crow Pass Trail" and "Eagle River" and "recommended fording locations."

All the good feelings and positive possibilities suddenly frosted over with the prospect of wading through possibly waist deep, frigid water. And it didn't appear as if it was merely a prospect. The trail markers definitely led them to that spot.

Dr. Caldwell addressed all of them. "Here's what we should do, and we've got to do it fast before we start second guessing ourselves. Take off your shoes and your socks. If you can, I'd recommend taking off your pants as well."

Emma gasped, "What?!"

"Emma! We've got to stay dry. If we get wet and can't dry ourselves properly, we could all die of hypothermia."

Meghan asked, "Bare feet though, Doc. What about the riverbed? You know, rocks and such?"

"As fast as the water is moving, it seems like the rocks should be worn pretty flat. You can wear your shoes, but I'm telling you that I think this is a better option. Like I said, let's do this fast."

Neil said as he pulled off first his shoes and then his socks, "Good idea, Doc. Now get to it yourself."

Dr. Caldwell had Jules secured to his chest with the help of bungee cords and carabiners and Neil had Danny similarly strapped. All of the adults grabbed hold of a rope they'd found at Dr. Caldwell's house and then one by one they stepped into the cold, grey water. And cold it was. Dr. Caldwell was correct about the rocks. Much of the bed was soft glacial silt but the few stones were smooth.

Gerald was the last man into the river and right away he was having problems. Whereas everyone else was facing into the current, Gerald was facing down river. He seemed to be having difficulty finding his footing. His arms lurched skyward twice as he struggled and then he was down. He splashed and fought to get his feet under him so he could stand, but he couldn't seem to find his balance. Immediately in front of Gerald were Jerry and then Claire and then Emma.

With Gerald, still tied into the rope line, pulling and tugging as he tried to get back to his feet, he eventually pulled over Jerry who then pulled down

Claire. Emma screamed and tried to stay up but those smooth rocks were also fairly slippery rocks, so she went down too.

The water was cold as it surged around all of their legs, but the icy chill that overwhelmed the senses as each one was submerged in the flood was completely unexpected. The cold was absolute, stealing away sensation and thought. All that every one of them could think to do was get up and out of the water. There was nothing else. There wasn't room for anything else in their thoughts.

Meghan was lucky enough to have grabbed a pair of rubber galoshes. The water had flooded the boots, but the tread on the bottoms helped her to stay upright and steady the line enough to allow Emma to pop back up fairly quickly. Jerry too was up to stay in a flash. And soon they were all back on their feet. Gerald corrected his mistake and faced up river instead of down. Shivering and miserable, they one by one emerged onto the opposite bank.

Dr. Caldwell said as he pulled on his boots, "We need a fire and fast. We've got to get you folks dry. Get out of your packs and your clothes. If you have anything in your packs that's still dry, I recommend throwing it on, no matter what it is. Neil, Meghan, kids, we've got to move fast. Grab anything that looks dry enough to burn. We need fire and we need it now."

They scurried around within earshot of one another and did as they were told. Meanwhile, as the others stripped down and put on anything they could find, Gerald kept chastising himself for endangering everyone else due to his clumsiness. Despite the objections and reassurances of the others, he just wouldn't show himself any mercy.

The small pile of twigs, branches, brown reeds, discarded paper, and whatever else that seemed flammable that they came upon didn't look like it would make much of a fire. Dr. Caldwell wasn't to be deterred though.

"I brought something with me that should help."

Neil asked, "Butane? Gasoline?"

"Kind of," and he produced an instant fire brick used by many a household to help start that occasional fire in the family fireplace. He quickly lit both ends and set it on a pair of rocks. The bits of kindling were then piled onto the brick and soon they had a much-appreciated fire that was growing as larger and larger pieces of timber were added.

Dr. Caldwell said to Neil, "I guess we'll just have to call it a day. We can't have them hiking in these temps with wet gear. It'll likely take most of the night to dry them. This is probably a good place to stop anyway."

"What else do we have ahead of us, Doc? How bad does this trail get?"

"Like I said before, Val and I always wanted to take the kids but we never did. I've never been out on this particular trail."

"And why didn't you? Ever get around to it, I mean?"

"I think we always thought that the kids weren't either ready or interested."

"Are we gonna be able to get everyone through this Doc?"

"If anyone can, Neil, I think you can."

# CHAPTER 69

Though dry and relatively warm, the clothes from the previous day were stiff and reeked of the river the next morning. Regardless, they were adorned once again by their thankful owners.

Her eyes still half closed, Emma moaned playfully, "Mom, was it too much to expect a little fabric softener?" That was as far as anyone went in discussing or complaining about the river crossing. They all knew that things could have gone much worse. The current could have been the slightest bit stronger and the water just a fraction deeper, and they all could have gone in. Someone could just as easily have drowned. Any number of combinations of variables could very well have taken them from inconvenience to tragedy. That fact was not lost on any of them.

The morning was crisp and damp, but brighter than those of recent memory. Fully dressed again, Claire asked, "Is it later than normal? Why is it so...? My god, is that snow? How could I have missed that it snowed last night?"

Surveying the area, Jerry shrugged and nodded alternately as he surrendered himself to a powerful yawn and stretch. Jerry was feeling pretty good this morning and something as trivial as an inch or so of new snow was not going to ruin his mood. The previous night he and Claire decided to zip their sleeping bags together.

Borne of practical intent, the warm coziness and the scintillating sensation of flesh against flesh had Jerry in near bliss all night. He'd never really had a girlfriend outside of middle school, so he'd never experienced such intimacy. For a variety of reasons, Jerry and Claire steered clear of actual intercourse. They did, however, enjoy one another's company just short of that. Jerry, though clumsy, enjoyed exploring Claire's body with hands and lips, feeling and tasting her soft skin with each new discovery. There weren't many words exchanged but they spoke to one another with fingers all night long. And despite having gotten no sleep, Jerry felt reinvigorated and restored.

Sitting next to the young man on a log as the two laced their boots, Neil said, "That's quite a smile you've got today."

"It is, isn't it?"

"It's good to see. Kinda makes me want to smile too. D'you mind me asking if it was your first time?"

"It was a night of a lot of firsts but it stopped short of being a first for everything."

"It doesn't seem to matter too much."

"No, it certainly doesn't."

Claire walked up, kissed Jerry on the cheek and shot Neil a playful look. She asked, "You ready old man?"

Holding his chest in protest, Neil said, "Old man? Old man? You must have me confused with..."

Claire leaned over and kissed Neil on the cheek too, saying as she did, "Just kidding. It's about time to be going though, isn't it?"

Neil said, "I think I've just got about enough time to put in my dentures and take my pills." As he walked away, his voice trailed off, "Young whippersnappers, telling me when it's time to go..."

Claire kissed Jerry on the mouth as soon as they were alone. "Thank you for last night. You were great and just what I needed. Maybe next time we can...you know, finish the show."

Jerry kissed her back. "All in good time. Last night was the best night of my life and I couldn't think of anyone better to spend it with than you. Was it okay?"

Claire jumped to her feet from his lap and whispered, "It was okay several times, if you know what I mean."

Jerry's grin grew to an ear-to-ear beaming smile with Claire' comment. He watched her walk away, forgetting what he'd been doing only seconds before. His head feeling very light as he looked around, he caught sight of Neil who was smiling back at him. Jerry suddenly felt like he was finally being considered for membership in an exclusive club and he wanted in, figuratively and literally.

# CHAPTER 70

The hike was starting to more closely resemble Dr. Caldwell's description. The going was getting much tougher. The trail, though groomed, seemed to increase its incline with every step. They were being required to use their hands much more to pull themselves up especially steep stretches of the trail. Regardless of Jerry's earlier mood and enthusiasm, he too was feeling the rigors of the day's journey.

They passed a beautiful waterfall and a fantastic view of a glacier; both points of interest still awing them. It was moments like that in which their feet felt a little lighter and the way seemed a little less grueling. They were just fleeting moments, however, and didn't lend themselves to savoring or to holding for any length of time.

When the trail pulled alongside more water, they all became agitated, anticipating the worst. The thought of crossing another river did not interest any of them in the slightest. This was starting to seem like a bad idea. They still weren't that far into the trail, a few miles at most. They could turn around and head back to the…and that was where everyone's thought ended. At different moments, most of them fought back the urge to argue for a different plan. In the end though, there weren't many options to consider.

The group was increasingly apprehensive, and were extremely anxious by the time they spied the sturdy wooden footbridge. The sense of relief they all felt was overwhelming and immediate. At that precise moment, nothing else much mattered. No one spoke; there really was no need. The feeling they all shared was quite clear. Meghan and Emma, arm in arm, actually skipped a bit. Dr. Caldwell thought he might have even heard Neil humming tunes to himself. Trying desperately to witness this rare moment of levity, the sun, though still obscured by the grey blanket hanging heavily overhead, tried its best to participate as well.

A small, flat piece of moss-carpeted land next to the bridge seemed as good a place as any to eat lunch. The wisdom of stopping was questioned but Dr. Caldwell pointed out that they should eat or risk coming upon trouble without the energy to fight or run. Besides, the location was absolutely striking, and the air smelled green and fresh. It was a postcard photo waiting to be taken. They ate dry cereal, cold canned chili, and the last of the juice. It was a delicious, if eclectic, feast.

The rest did them good and was well timed, because the road before them did its level best to challenge them. The dirt beneath their feet became mud; slippery, sticky, bad smelling mud. They found the angles at which they had to walk had sharpened as well. On more than one occasion, one of them would lose his or her footing and slide back down the hill, sometimes catching another of their number as they went. They pushed and pulled one another to help the forward momentum continue, but the demands of the trail were slowing them.

And then the weather also decided to play more of a part in the happenings of the day. A distant fog was suddenly not so distant, and with it came a damp bite in the air. In little time, the dampness evolved into a hanging mist that formed little beads on all of their parkas. The beads formed themselves into pools, which then ran down the coat surfaces, dripping onto pants and shoes and those around them. The breeze gained strength and the mist became a steady drizzle.

The inclined trail, its mud running with water, became harder and harder to traverse. Thankfully, it wasn't raining very hard or the trail would be mostly impassable.

With that thought in his mind, Neil caught up to Dr. Caldwell. "How concerned should we be about the weather?"

"Very. In fact, I'm surprised there isn't more snow up here. I'd say we're pretty lucky right now if this is as bad as it gets. Even if it gets worse, I think we've gotten through most of the harder sections of the Pass. I'm guessing that we might have just a bit longer before we're heading back down."

"I thought you said that you'd never been on this trail before?"

"I haven't, but we've been going up since we crossed the river. We're hiking a trail, not climbing a mountain. It just stands to reason. Besides, I'm starting to see a gap between where we are and the next peak over. I think we're coming to the end."

Despite the doctor's seemingly informed prediction, they did continue to climb. They were using their hands as much or more than their feet. At least, that's how it felt. Neil was reminded of his friend's stories about his Outward Bound experiences in rural Colorado and Wyoming. He hoped that he would find more than just a sense of accomplishment at the end of his journey, though.

Having to use them to steady themselves against muddy rock outcrops and wet tree branches, everyone's hands were cold and wet. Their gloves helped somewhat, but only until they too were soaked and cold. Their leg and back muscles, deprived of calories, began to protest with each demanding step. They forced their feet forward all throughout the day, electing not to take any more breaks; not that there were reasonable places in which to take them anyway.

They eventually came to a crest of sorts. The odd rock configurations gave the impression that someone or something had created this rock pile in a different time and then got distracted, forgetting about the pile and leaving it there for them. The large slabs of grey rock protruded out in any number of angles. There was a particularly large rock that sat over a nice flat area. The rock overhead kept much of the space underneath dry and shielded from the elements. They all thought the exact same thing that hundreds, likely thousands, of those who had preceded them had thought: this was an excellent spot to pitch camp. And so they did.

It had been a long, arduous day but they'd made it. Tomorrow would be literally all down hill.

# CHAPTER 71

The morning was dark and cold, and there was snow again. More this time. It hung in the trees and covered the ground. The trail and all of its perils was likewise concealed. Neil hurried from the relative warmth of the tent over to the fire Gerald tended.

"Mornin'."

"Mornin'. You plannin' to catch some more zzz's before we head out?" asked Neil.

"No, I think I'm up to stay."

Gerald wasn't much of a talker and this morning proved to be no different. He looked off toward the east, hoping to catch the slightest hint of the rising sun. Hoping some friendly interaction might help to stave off the chill, Neil asked, "Gerald, what did you do before all this?"

At first there wasn't a reply. Thinking that perhaps Gerald had dozed and didn't hear his question, Neil was about to ask again when Gerald said, "I've been lots of things in my days. Student. Teacher. Soldier. Husband. Father. Widower. Lately, I've been taking classes at the university."

"What kind of classes?"

"Dance."

"Dance?"

Gerald looked over at Neil with a playful protest and continued, "Yeah, dance. What's wrong with dance?"

"I don't know. Nothin' I guess. It's just that...well, what's the attraction?"

"What do you think the pretty girl ratio is in a dance class as opposed to, let's say, a political science class? It's a chance for me to get out, get some exercise, and remember what it was to be a man."

"What kind of dance?"

Gerald smiled. "All kinds."

"Like what? Ballet?"

"No. Things like ballroom, tango, and the like. We've been doing a lot of the cultural dances of Western European countries. We even learned some interesting gypsy dances."

"Please don't take this as an insult. All I have to say is wow. That's pretty cool. So are you retired?"

"Yeah. I worked for the Post Office and the retirement is pretty good."

"I've heard."

Jerry woke next, like clockwork. He huddled around the fire but didn't say anything, trying to warm himself as he pulled on the shirt he was carrying.

Neil winked at Gerald and then turned to Jerry. "You know, Jerry, if you kept your stuff on at night like the rest of us you would probably stay warmer and then not have to dress by firelight in the morning."

Shivering, Jerry was unable to give a response other than lifting his middle finger as he rubbed his hands together for warmth. Instead, he observed, "Looks like it's goin' to be a clear day. Probably colder though, too."

"Yeah. Maybe the sun will melt some of the snow from the trail before we hit it. We'll have more mud but at least we'll be able to see where we're steppin'."

That day's journey consisted not of climbing, but of sliding. For much of the trail, they leaned back and, rather than fighting and losing, allowed the path to lead them down. There were some tumbles and still some significant hiking to be done, but the going seemed to be much easier.

And then there was another river, full of angry energy, coursing near them. Its voice was loud and intimidating, which produced a flurry of questions. "Another crossing?" "Are we going into the water again?" "What if…?"

All of the questions and the dread came to an abrupt end when the first Tram Car sign came into sight. They stopped and considered the sign, smiling at one another. None of them were experienced enough hikers to have used a tram car in the past, however, the prospect of using one now was very appealing and exciting.

When they spied the heavily constructed tram car platform and the sturdy metal cage hanging, they stopped in their tracks.

"So that's a tram car, huh?" Gerald asked.

Neil nodded. "Yeah, I guess that's your run of the mill tram car."

They hurried onto the platform and a couple of people at a time piled in and pulled themselves across. The effort was much more toil than it was fun. The rope was heavy and the car was heavier. Their muscles moaned and their hands screamed, but they pulled themselves and each other across the river.

When the last two to cross, Claire and Jerry, finally pulled up to the opposite side and climbed out of the still swinging car, there was a collective pause. It felt like they had somehow arrived. The water raging one hundred or more feet below them still taunted and teased but it sounded more like empty threats thrown in desperation after the fact. Neil looked down at the dark frothy current and thought about all that was behind them. He thought about the opportunities lost, the lives lost, the world lost. All the loss, but the river had been overcome, so maybe they could make it after all.

They soon found themselves on largely flat ground. The trees began to get bigger and thicker, as did the trail on which they were walking. It didn't appear as if the snow had made its way to this elevation yet. The air, however, smelled, tasted, and felt like it was already inviting winter in for the season. The cool moisture was just this side of snowing. It felt like they were walking through the world's largest refrigerator that had been set a notch too cold.

Neil looked back over his shoulder at the enormous mountain they had just overcome. The small bump on the topography was barely swollen enough to be a bruise. Then he looked at the mountains around them and wondered what it was like to climb one of them. His interest was fleeting and his attention returned to the muddy trail ahead and the tired ache in his muscles.

By and by, there appeared along the trail evidence of man. There were discarded backpacks filled with absolutely ridiculous items: laptops, DVDs, iPod docking stations, compact disc players, and portable DVD players. There were family scrapbooks and sports trophies. There were precious few supplies worth carrying in any of the many backpacks they examined. They all knew they were getting closer to the end of their trail and the beginning for a lot of others in the past.

Jerry said, "These were probably from people who were just starting out and probably got caught up in the mess. Probably trying to shed weight so they could outpace their pursuers. I wonder if any of them got away?"

"How do you know they were just starting out?" asked Meghan.

"Why would they carry all that junk all the way across the Pass only to drop it when they got to one potential destination? They were headed the other way. Had to have been."

Emma said, looking back at the path behind them, "Kinda begs the question then: what are we heading into that they were trying to get away from?"

Neil agreed, "It does beg that question. Doesn't it?"

From behind them, Gerald said, "Found one."

All of the others spun. "One what?" Neil asked.

"One of the folks you've all been talkin' 'bout. Didn't get too far. I'm guessing not many of them did. Probably wandered off the trail with those things hot on their tails. The foliage and undergrowth would have slowed them just enough to make them easy catches."

Sure enough. Just off the main path was a broken skeleton picked clean of flesh and sinew. All four of its limbs had been separated from the main set of bones. One of the arm bones was still missing, perhaps carried off by one of them as a trophy or, more likely, a snack for the road. The man's shoes had been peeled from his feet like a fruit's skin, allowing access for gnashing teeth to the sweet flesh inside.

Meghan turned away. "I just saw another one," she said. "Over that way. Just a pair of legs sticking out from behind a tree."

Jerry said, "Well when those people were coming through here, there were a lot of them and they were being chased...the other direction...toward the trail. There's no sign of either people or those things, so I'd say that we're probably safe...for the moment at least."

Emerging onto the trailhead and its remote parking lot, it felt as if they had found a long lost civilization hidden by an all but impassable forest. The handful of designated parking spots was not enough to accommodate the more than a handful of vehicles abandoned all around. There were Fords and Chevys, Subarus and Hondas, cars and trucks, and SUVs and campers. Most were simply left where they had come to rest without any care given to propriety. Disaster and the apocalypse, after all, do not lend themselves to good parking etiquette.

Emma and Meghan saw the little outhouse building amid the car chaos and started to run toward it. Their enthusiasm melted away abruptly when they caught sight of the brown-tinted handprints splayed across the light-colored doors. They knew all too well that there was likely more than just water-filled toilet bowls awaiting them inside. Almost as an answer to their thoughts and suspicions, something on the opposite side of the door stirred and began to pound itself against its confining walls and door. The two women stopped dead in their tracks and backed themselves away slowly, their disappointment pale in comparison to the rising alarm in their chests.

They picked their way cautiously through the vehicle graveyard, careful not to move too close to open windows or doors left ajar. At times, Neil and Dr. Caldwell considered foraging for supplies from the automobiles, but both decided to just leave well enough alone.

Shortly after leaving the parking lot, the vehicles began to thin until the survivors found themselves once again marching along an empty road leading to the unknown. The trees to either side of them, though largely missing their full summer foliage, reached themselves overhead and formed a dense ceiling. The dulled light of the sun found it exceedingly difficult to weave its way through the seemingly interlaced fingers of the trees' outstretched hands...organic claustrophobia at its best.

They moved along the road quietly, their crunchy footsteps upon the gravel the only noise around them. It was as if the world was holding its breath and awaiting the next act to play itself out.

Upon reaching the seam where the gravel gave way to pavement, they knew they were nearing whatever awaited them at the end of their journey. It was a short walk to the famous Double Musky Restaurant, which was only a few hundred yards from the main drag into and out of Girdwood.

The town was actually a part of Anchorage though, like its bigger sibling Eagle River, its residents generally tended to consider themselves anything but Anchorage citizens. The residents themselves were an eclectic mix of retirees, business people with a penchant for eco-enterprises or marketable experiences, many of the service workers for the Alyeska Resort at the end of the road, and young adults in their early twenties who were living out of parents' bank accounts and typically referred to by most as Trustafarians. In addition to the world class Alyeska, there were some fantastic bed and breakfast establishments that always drew in affluent guests. And, of course, there was the Double Musky, one of Alaska's greatest restaurants. The strong, rustic looking restaurant was sitting dormant and gutted. Without wasting their time, they already knew not to expect anything to remain in the building. With the numbers of people who had filed by it, there was no way that the Musky would have escaped pillaging.

Like a displaced tour guide, Neil announced, "Welcome to Girdwood."

# CHAPTER 72

They stepped onto the open highway, looking both left and right. They didn't see anything in either direction. Actually, they saw quite a bit, but most of it no longer even registered. There was an overturned school bus, which had been heading away from the town center toward the left. There were three other cars sitting off the road near where the bus had come to rest. Across the street and down a bit on the left were the charred remains of a business that had burned to the ground, leaving nothing but a blackened skeleton atop a scorched foundation.

A volunteer fire department vehicle was a short distance down the highway on their right, sitting on its side in a ditch. The door facing away from the pavement was still open.

Jerry said, "There's probably no reason to go to the resort. I can't imagine there's anyone down that way."

"What about that restaurant on the top," Meghan said. "What's it called again? It's got glaciers in the name."

Dr. Caldwell answered, "The Seven Glaciers. There could be people up there, but getting there would be a bit of a chore because it is on the top and I bet the tram isn't running these days."

Emma asked, "So we go out to the Seward Highway and head south then?"

"Yeah," Neil confirmed. "I think that makes the most sense. Any other ideas?"

With a serious face, Emma suggested, "There's always goin' back to the doctor's house." She almost started laughing before she got it out. She couldn't help it. She just loved to laugh; whether it was appropriate or not really didn't matter to her.

Danny shushed them all with his hand and cupped the other over one of his ears. He'd heard something.

Neil asked, "What is it Danny? Is it them?"

"Unless they're comin' in on a different frequency," Jerry said, "or he's more sensitive than I am, then I don't think so."

"I can hear something," Danny insisted. "It sounds like growling maybe."

Jerry shook his head but peered through his scope in the same direction Danny was facing. "I'm not seeing anything. Oh wait. There they are."

"Undead?"

"No. Dogs. And they're heading this way."

Meghan started to wring her hands. "What do we do?"

Dr. Caldwell said, "We can't rely on bats. I don't think we have any choice." Out of habit, he checked the load on the M4's magazine and then readied the firearm for action.

Jerry, using his scope, sighted the first animal as it ran at them. He took a deep breath and as he exhaled he squeezed the trigger. The little black Labrador mix tumbled forward and then did several cartwheels until it came to rest, dead. He found his next target and brought that one down as well. He said to the others, "I don't know that I can get all of them before they get too close, so get ready."

Danny crouched next to Jerry and fired his rifle. The bullet skipped off the pavement, falling a few yards short of its target. Jerry fired again, missing this time. He quickly operated the bolt action, chambering another long bullet. Danny fired again as Jerry readied his rifle. He had more luck this time. He hit the dog, slowing but not killing it.

Jerry fired again and again, but by then the dogs were within distance of the other weapons in the group. A wall of fire erupted as they all began pulling their triggers. A grey-white cloud, filled with choking animosity and death, stormed and raged in front of the firing line. And from the opposite side of the hellish fog, the entire pack of dogs uttered a single, collective, pained yelp and was no more. The bullets shredded both air and dog flesh with equal ease.

An avid video game player, Jerry took the immediate moment to reload his rifle, advising the others to do the same. Neil was smiling and Dr. Caldwell was actually starting to laugh. "I think we're getting good at this," he said.

They had neither heard nor seen the three undead creatures that had wandered out from behind the restaurant up the road. The ghouls had silently followed them down the road, stalking their prey in their own awkward and clumsy way. The dogs provided just the unforeseen opportunity they needed to get in close to their quarry.

The first one grabbed hold of Gerald, who was once again at the tail of the line. The thing bit the older man on the back of his neck, just below his ears. Its brown teeth dug themselves into the soft warm flesh and tore away a mouthful before he could scream. He did, however, pull the trigger on his shotgun.

A second ghoul grabbed hold of his now extended arm and bit the soft inside of his elbow joint. Gerald fell over backward, with both of them falling onto him as he did. Claire screamed and skittered away with both of her hands to the sides of her head. Neil shouted to Emma, *"Shoot!"*

She couldn't get a clear target without possibly hitting Gerald as well. Dr. Caldwell spun around and squeezed off a shot that scalped one of the beasts. Without a single word, the thing just rolled off of the still struggling man. One final scream from poor Gerald and then his arms and legs went limp, the other creature still chewing on his neck.

Dr. Caldwell was aiming the assault rifle just as the third beast got to him. He raised the barrel so as to be high enough to catch it in the head, but the grey, pock-skinned beast had other intentions. Its jagged, broken teeth found purchase on Dr. Caldwell's left hand. Not a second later the doctor's rifle barked, removing the top third of its head. Neil dispatched the one that was still gnawing on poor Gerald's bleeding neck.

The bite to Dr. Caldwell's hand had gone unnoticed. The tension was still such that they all kept their firearms at the ready. Those three had come out of nowhere. There could be more of them anywhere.

For the briefest of moments, they all realized that none of them really knew Gerald. He had come and gone so quickly and amidst so much chaos and loss, that his passing was only registered as another loss from their herd. It was becoming almost mechanical for them…the perpetual presence of death so much a part of their every day lives. That sense was to change in the immediate future.

Jerry said, "If we're going to get, then I think we should do that now. Those shots are going to attract everything that might still be down at the resort. We could have company very quickly."

"What about Gerald?" Neil asked.

Without a comment, Dr. Caldwell drew his revolver and shot Gerald's seemingly dead body in the head. The surprise of all of them kept pace with their relief that none of the rest of them had to pull the trigger on one of their own.

Meghan asked, "Are we okay? Can we get going now?"

Dr. Caldwell said as he raised his bleeding left hand, "Well part of that anyway."

Emma screamed and ran over to the man. "Noooooooooo! Nooooooooo! Godddddd nooooooooo!"

Dr. Caldwell looked at all of them, his eyes finally coming to rest on Neil. "I guess you guys should just move on. I can find something to do with myself until…" His eyes betrayed no emotion.

Emma pleaded, "No, you're gonna be okay. We can get to Whittier. Maybe they've got all this figured out. Maybe they can…" She realized how she sounded but she couldn't help it. She just couldn't accept it. The wound looked so insignificant. Maybe it wasn't a bite at all. When she looked in his eyes though, she knew the truth.

Dr. Caldwell placed his good right hand against her cheek. He leaned down and whispered in her ear, "It's all going to be okay. I promise. You're going to be alright."

"It's not fair. We're so close! We're almost there. And we need you. *I* need you. I don't think I can...are you sure it was a bite? It couldn't have been from something else. Maybe you just cut yourself or maybe...."

"Emma, it's a bite."

"But I just can't..."

"Yes you can. You just keep moving forward until you find somewhere safe to rest your feet. I'll be with you. I promise. Here." He took off the dog tags from around his neck and put them around hers, careful not to drip blood on her anywhere.

She whispered, "That's just not the same. That only works in the movies."

"Val said that to me years ago when I went off to Kuwait for the first time. And I'll tell you the same thing I told her. I know it's not the same but it's better than nothing. Besides, you'll be somewhere a helluva lot better than me."

Emma smiled and managed a tear choked laugh. She asked Neil, "Can he come along with us at least to the gas station out on the Seward?"

Neil, who was fighting back his own tears, said, "Of course. Doc, Emma may be right. I think maybe you should come along with us. There's still that off chance that maybe someone might have...there's still gotta be hope that this doesn't have to be..."

Jerry, still watching down the road said excitedly, "We're gonna have to have this conversation somewhere else. We've gotta go! Now!"

From down the road, scores of undead began to file onto the main drag from side streets. "Our shots are attracting everything around. We gotta go before we get boxed in. Doc, can you run?"

"Yes, but I don't know for how long."

Neil said, "We'll deal with that later. C'mon, let's go!"

They gathered themselves quickly and ran hard and fast for the Seward Highway. They wanted to put some distance between themselves and the horde behind...again.

As they hit the final bend in the road before arriving at the gas station, Dr. Caldwell began to stumble. He fell forward onto his hands and knees and vomited a bile and foam filled soup onto the street. The wound in his hand, like a furnace, began to radiate pain throughout his entire body. His vision wavered between clear and blurry, bringing on waves of nausea and a general loss of equilibrium.

Neil and Emma each hooked a hand under the doctor's arms to help steady their friend. They hoisted him back to his feet, which weren't doing much more than dangling under him as he set most of his weight onto their shoulders. Neil forced out between huffs, "Sorry about this, but we gotta keep going. Hang in there."

Dr. Caldwell looked over at the voice, thinking to himself that he recognized it but the pain was corralling all thought. His eyes, though open, were clouded, allowing in only dull outlines and the color red. Everything seemed to be draped in sheer red. The foul contents of his stomach threatened once again to come churning to the back of his throat. He forced his fingers, which seemed so distant and so foreign, to ball themselves into Emma's and Neil's shoulders.

They stopped and immediately looked at him. His chin was resting against his chest, concealing his tortured expression. He shook his head and nodded. "I'm okay to run. Let's keep going."

He seemed to emerge from a fog, getting some control of his faculties. His pace quickened, helping all of them to gain a much more comfortable lead on the ghouls following them.

The short distance to the convenience store and strip mall of shops along the Seward Highway was thankfully incident free. Many of the small cottages and smaller businesses along the highway were in ruins. Personal affects and commercial wares were strewn across yards, driveways, and the road. There weren't many other places that the creatures would likely congregate, but second guessing their assumptions was what was keeping them alive. It appeared as if all of the undead in the area were attracted to the resort and the residential center of the town. They were all still down the road and, with any luck, losing the scent and the will to pursue them.

The gas station, like most other businesses they'd encountered, was in utter ruins. The ground was crunchy with splintered glass from the empty window frames. There was nothing of value in or near the multiple shops. Like discarded rubbish piled haphazardly about the parking lot, the requisite and anticipated corpses of days gone by were there too. The doorways and window frames of the businesses along the strip were also adorned with bodies left to decay in horribly grotesque positions; some appearing to be trying to get out while others were trying to get in during their final moments. The slight breeze coming from the Cook Inlet lifted shredded bits of clothing, hair, and plastic shopping bags and carried them across the barren lot, like twisted tumbleweeds of the apocalypse.

Getting nearly to the gas pumps in the middle of the station lot, Dr. Caldwell collapsed. His mouth opened and out spilled more foamy white foulness. He spat several times and then motioned with his hands that he needed help getting back to his feet.

"Geez, do I ever have a hang over. Did I do anything that I'd regret last night? Do I owe anyone an apology?"

Emma said, "I'm supposed to be the joker here. We need to keep moving."

Dr. Caldwell shook his head. "I don't think I can anymore."

"Yes you can," Emma pleaded. "C'mon, we'll help you."

"Emma, I can't. I don't want to. I think I need to...to rest." He turned to Neil. "Neil, it may be asking a bit but may I ask—?"

"I'm not gonna shoot you, Doc. That's just out of the question."

"I was going to ask for some water before you guys leave. You should probably take everything that's left in my pack though. I can't imagine that I'll be needing any of that anymore."

"How about a gun?"

"No."

"How about a gun and a single bullet?"

"No. I don't know that I'd have the courage to do something like that. I may regret it later, but take everything. You're going to need it more than I will."

From a small open air picnic area next to the main station building, Jerry found an overturned plastic chair and a table that was still fairly intact. He brought both over to the doctor, who sat heavily in the middle of the parking lot. Dr. Caldwell wrapped a shirt around his hand, trying to apply pressure to the wound but having no success whatsoever in stemming the flow of blood. He was reminded of the little boy that had been brought to Providence with a similar wound all those weeks ago. He looked at Danny and Jules.

"You kids listen to Neil here. He'll get you home safe or at least keep you safe. That goes for the rest of you too. Stick together. Watch out for one another and you'll be okay."

Neil struggled to control his emotions. "We can wait a bit with you, Doc. You don't have to be alone. I mean, I just..." He was sniffling too much to speak, but his male pride largely stifled his tears.

"No. I think you all should get going. There's no point in hanging out around here. I think I'm just going to sit here and drink my water. See what happens."

Meghan leaned down and kissed Dr. Caldwell on the cheek. She hugged him tightly and, without saying a word, was back up and heading toward the exit to the station's parking lot. With tears in her eyes, Claire waved to the doctor but could not force the words out past the lump in her throat. She joined Meghan, taking Danny and Jules with her.

Jerry said, "Doc, you were always one of the coolest doctors at Providence. All the interns and the nursing staff thought you were one of the good ones. If it matters, all of the young ladies on staff thought you were a hottie." He shook the doctor's hand firmly and looked him in the eye. "Good luck, Doc."

"You too, Jerry. When you get out of this, I think you should go to med school. I think you're one of the smartest kids I've ever known. And thanks for keeping those two kids safe. That meant a lot to me." To this Jerry nodded and walked away.

Dr. Caldwell said softly, "Neil, can you give Emma and me just a moment?"

"Sure."

Once they were alone, Dr. Caldwell said, "Emma, you're a fine lady and if I had time, I wanted to see about starting a new life with you. But don't dwell on that. You can't. What's done is done, and there's no taking it back. You have to be strong. Be my voice for Neil. He's smart, but sometimes he needs someone to help him not doubt his every decision. I can't do it anymore. Please. If not for me, then do it for those kids and for yourself. Regardless of how things are to end, at least I'll know that you'll be safe."

Emma finally asked, "Can I say something now?"

"Yes."

"I love you. I can't imagine leaving you behind here to...please don't make me go away. I can stay here with you for a little longer and..."

"Emma, I love you too and that's why I can't allow that. You need to get moving now. There's no telling what might be coming up the road as we speak. Please. I need for you to go." He looked over at Neil who stepped up and physically had to move Emma. Jerry and Claire took over for Neil who walked over to Dr. Caldwell.

"You sure about this, Doc?"

"No, but I don't see any other options."

"Emma may be right. There may be something in Whittier."

"And all those cancer patients chasing after the magical cure might actually find it, but we both know the truth. Those are just dreams to help us to avoid the inevitable. Neil, you keep them safe and trust your judgment. Whittier isn't that far down the highway. You might be able to get there before dark. Just don't give up."

"Doc, I've got one last question for you."

"No, I don't want the gun. No, I don't want any food. No, I don't want to go with you."

"I just wanted to know your first name."

Dr. Caldwell smiled. "After all this time, you don't know my first name?"

"Never really came up in conversation. You were Doc or Dr. Caldwell or something else. I don't think we ever got around to that."

"Jonathon."

Neil took Dr. Jonathon Caldwell's hand for the last time and said, "It's been a pleasure, Jonathon. I'll never forget you."

"Likewise."

Their handshake lasted longer than did their words. They looked at one another without speaking for several seconds, both then nodded, and Neil turned away. Slowly, Neil made his way back toward the others who were nearing the exit and the highway beyond. He moved slowly, reluctantly, wishing that the bad dream would end before he got too far. With each loathsome step, however, he took himself further and further from that possibility. If Dr. Caldwell were to call out to him before he'd reached the end of the parking lot, Neil decided that he'd figure out a way to carry him along with them for as long as they were able. As Neil took his last step on the pavement of the parking lot, he looked over his shoulder at his friend Jonathon, but the other man had turned his back to them and was facing back toward the north.

Emma was crying and struggling to free herself from Jerry and Claire. She alone was still looking toward Dr. Caldwell. Neil approached her and wrapped his arms around her. He hugged her tightly and she melted, but still fought to see over his shoulder. Neil whispered, "He wants us to leave. He doesn't want us to watch him die."

Hearing those words didn't suppress the pain tearing at her chest; but they did get her attention. She looked at Neil with a thousand questions in her eyes but no will to ask them. She shook her head weakly and fell against him, burying her face into his chest. She wanted to tear herself away from him and run back to her love, but the fight had gone out of her. Her struggling gone, her legs felt weak and rubbery. She leaned into Neil for support, allowing herself to be led away, her legs unwilling participants in the exodus.

They walked steadily for some time, following the damp, dark road as it led them south. The green borders on either side of the meandering highway were in fast retreat from the pressing browns of autumn. The small trees here and there were only trunks and branches, their leaves having been shed for the coming season. It was as if the land and the season themselves were mourning. The sky too refused to be anything other than somber and morose in its own grey way, the sun deemed too cheery to be allowed an entrance. And the damp, chill air seemed to revel in its shivering embrace.

They walked largely silently, their quiet footfalls only occasionally interrupted by an isolated sob or sudden sniffle. When Neil braved a glance behind them, the gas station and its lone guest were well out of sight.

Other than the waning light of the fading afternoon, there was no measure of time. They progressed down the road with as much enthusiasm as bait onto a hook. Exhausted and emotionally spent, they had nothing left to give; their collective well was as dry as their eyes were wet. The path ahead of them was as bleak and uninviting as any they had traveled.

With the day coming to a close and Whittier still twenty or so miles south of them, Neil asked them, "What should we do?"

Their legs were as heavy as their thoughts. None of them were immune from their collective agony; even the children's footsteps were steeped in sorrow. This loss, the loss of Dr. Caldwell from their makeshift family, was somehow more painful than anything any of them had felt since that first day when the catastrophe was still new. For a time, it seemed like maybe they had gotten clear of the worst of the tragedy. They were smarter and more careful. It felt like they had perhaps learned to adapt and hold off the lurking specter of death. How wrong they all were. Even out of sight, terror could never be out of mind. It was all too real and always too close.

Their bodies, from head to toe, sagged pitifully with remorse. They were in no shape to continue their trek; at least not today. It was evident to all of them, even if no one had acknowledged it aloud yet.

Over the growing sniffles and sobs, Emma answered, "It's been a long day. Maybe this is a good time for us to call it quits until tomorrow."

"Until tomorrow then."

# EPILOGUE

The future...their future was never in more doubt or more peril since the first day the Alaskan undead tragedy began to unfold. The tight family formed as a result of those horrific events was struggling through yet another loss...another death...another nail in the proverbial coffin of their survival.

It was becoming ever more difficult to find those elusive reasons to continue. Mere survival did not seem to be enough for all of them to persist.

And yet, they did. Finding some untapped reserves of will, Neil, Jerry, Meghan, and Emma kept them on their path. Where that path ultimately led was still a mystery. There was no knowing what was still ahead of them. All that any of them knew was that they had to continue their journey.

And so they did...

The *Alaskan Undead Apocalypse* continues with *Mitigation*. Coming in 2013 from Permuted Press.

 READERS, PERMUTED PRESS NEEDS YOUR HELP TO...

# SPREAD THE INFECTION

☢ **Follow us on Facebook (facebook.com/PermutedPress) and Twitter (twitter.com/PermutedPress).**

☢ **Post a book review on Amazon.com, BarnesAndNoble.com, GoodReads.com, and your blog.**

☢ **Let your friends—online and offline—know about our books!**

☢ **Sign up for our mailing list at PermutedPress.com.**

# MORE TITLES FROM PERMUTED PRESS

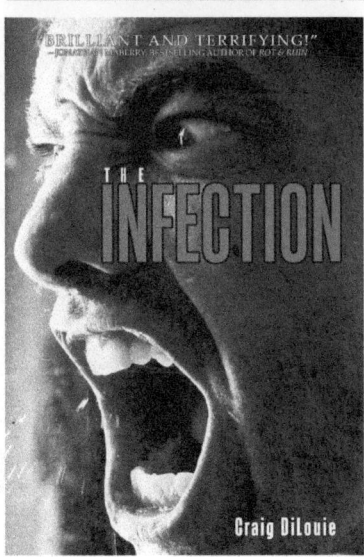
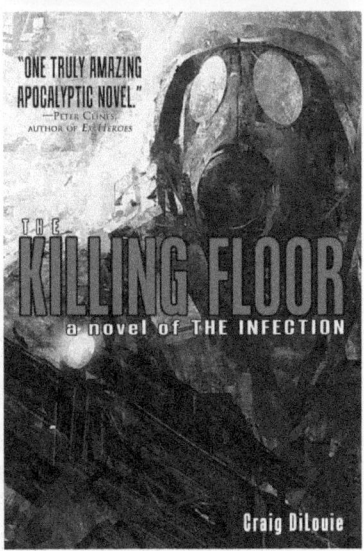

MORE DETAILS, EXCERPTS, AND PURCHASE INFORMATION AT
## www.permutedpress.com

# MORE TITLES FROM PERMUTED PRESS

MORE DETAILS, EXCERPTS, AND PURCHASE INFORMATION AT
# www.permutedpress.com

# MORE TITLES FROM PERMUTED PRESS

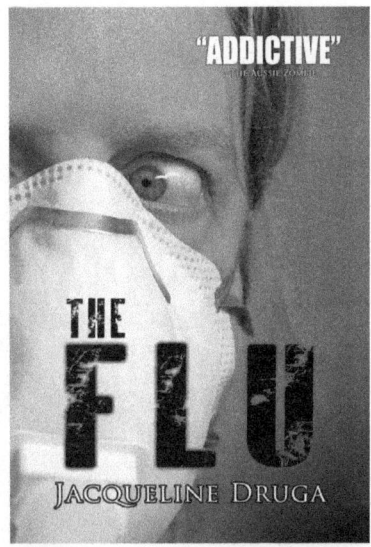

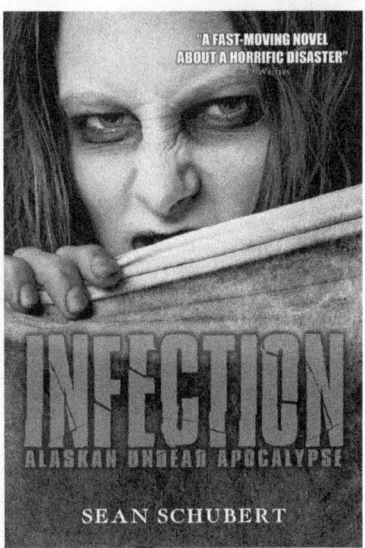

More details, excerpts, and purchase information at
# www.permutedpress.com

# MORE TITLES FROM PERMUTED PRESS

MORE DETAILS, EXCERPTS, AND PURCHASE INFORMATION AT
# www.permutedpress.com

# MORE TITLES FROM PERMUTED PRESS

MORE DETAILS, EXCERPTS, AND PURCHASE INFORMATION AT
## www.permutedpress.com

# MORE TITLES FROM PERMUTED PRESS

MORE DETAILS, EXCERPTS, AND PURCHASE INFORMATION AT
**www.permutedpress.com**

# MORE TITLES FROM PERMUTED PRESS

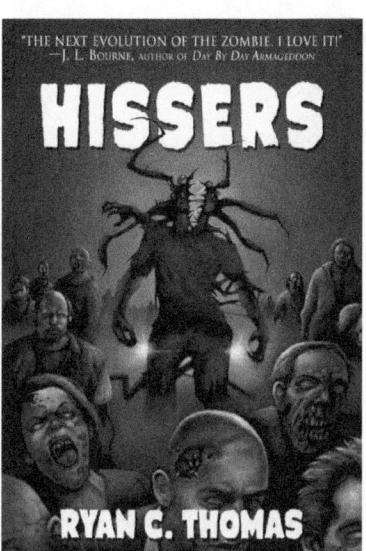

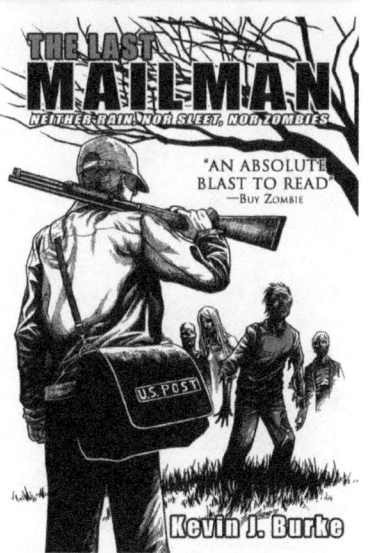

MORE DETAILS, EXCERPTS, AND PURCHASE INFORMATION AT
## www.permutedpress.com

# MORE TITLES FROM PERMUTED PRESS

More details, excerpts, and purchase information at
## www.permutedpress.com